JETHRO TULL

LEND ME YOUR EARS

THIS DAY BOOKS
IN MUSIC
www.thisdayinmusicbooks.com

JETHRO TULL

ISBN: 978-1919616582

The author and publisher gratefully acknowledge the permission granted to reproduce the copyright material in this book. Every effort has been made to trace the copyright holders of the photographs in this book but one or two were unreachable. We would be grateful if the photographers concerned would contact us.

Production Liz Sánchez and Neil Cossar
Design and layout by Gary Bishop
Thanks to Dave Evely and all at Sound Performance
Project Coordinator James Anderson

This Day In Music Books Bishopswood Road, Prestatyn, LL199PL

www.thisdayinmusicbooks.com

Email: editor@thisdayinmusic.com

Exclusive Distributors: Music Sales Limited 14/15 Berners St London W1T 3JL

Tull fans from top left: Brad Bishop, Bruce Hawkins, David Flintham, Paul Hurst, Arne Rasmussen, Ion Riley, Teresa Barnes, Lou Coruzzolo, Gustau Solé Diaz, Ross Payne and James Branagan

FOREWORD

Photo by Will Ireland

It must have been well into the third year of Jethro Tull's career before I began to fully recognise the loyalty and staying power of the fans and record buyers. Prior to that, a gig was just a gig and it was tempting to think of each audience as a one-off collection of ticket-buyers who you would never see again.

Suddenly, we started to notice some of the same faces in the crowd from tour to tour – even from night to night. The idea that these people would dig into their hard-earned wages to come repeatedly to concerts was hard to grasp in our heady upward climb from obscurity to being recognised in many countries of the world.

The loyalty and enthusiasm of these fans became a firm part of our success, continuing even to this day. It took me a long while to realise that a visit to a concert was more than just a night out for many of them. What was easy for us musicians to think of as just 'another day in the office' was, for many, an important memory which defined a pivotal period of their growing up, capturing the mood of the times and culture.

From the industrial towns of the UK in 1968/69 to the western states of the USA in the early Seventies, we built upon our growing following wherever we went. Well, almost wherever, since some countries stayed resolutely unimpressed with the musical style and occasionally theatrical performance. Japan was a tough nut to crack and the audiences - bemused as they were - displayed a hushed respect but mostly moved on to the next big thing when we didn't return to build on our initial early promise.

The core of the loyal fan base, apart from the obvious UK, was first Germany and then Italy. That spread to the other European countries over time with North America really kicking in from 1972 onwards. Australia and New Zealand were soon to follow. Then, at the end of the Eighties the Eastern European countries (newly liberated from the yoke of the USSR) and Latin America showed interest as we ventured further afield to less likely parts. Even in Russia itself, there was a growing underground scene of western rock music aficionados who managed to lay their hands on pirate cassette tapes and further copy them for friends.

Raisa Gorbachev, I was to learn much more recently, was the likely architect of allowing the first officially-sanctioned western acts to be released on the Russian state record label, Melodiya. Paul McCartney and Tull were those first two such releases in 1988. When I thanked hubby Mikhail Gorbachev for this act of wisdom and cultural bravery many years later, he looked at me as if I was from Mars! Clearly, his wife was the one who pulled the strings. So, when we were eventually allowed to perform in Russia, we found a ready and waiting audience who were largely familiar with the main songs from our works.

I have often heard from fans in Russia, Chile, Argentina and other places how possessing the forbidden fruits of western rock music were punishable by incarceration and worse. The gentle relaxing of tensions through the growing access to the arts and culture were a major factor in bringing nations and their peoples together.

We in the band and crew, over the years, have our own special inside recollections of the times and places which fill our memories. But we often forget the special viewpoints of the fans who attended shows and recall with varying degrees of accuracy, the detail and personal experiences which have remained with them for so long. Rather like a first date with a new romantic object of the heart's desire, with whom you have perhaps largely parted company but remember fondly for the rest of your life.

I can still vividly remember seeing JB Lenoir at the Free Trade Hall in Manchester on a blues tour in 1965. I can remember watching The Graham Bond Organisation at Nottingham Boat Club in 1966. Even Cliff Richard and The Shadows at the ABC theatre in Blackpool in or around 1963. But do I recall that same objective thrill about performing myself at the Isle of Wight Festival in 1970? Not really. The Festhalle in Frankfurt in 1972? Or Shea Stadium in 1976?

Robert Palmer of *The New York Times* certainly did and recalls of that concert:

Mr. Anderson mugged obsessively, but his repertory of grimaces was soon exhausted and the unending eye-rolling and head-shaking captured by the camera tiresome. The group's music wore thin almost as rapidly. The rest of the musicians are capable but anonymous – sounding like back-up players, foils, really, for Mr Anderson's peculiarly flat theatricality.

Ah well - you can't please 'em all....

Ian Anderson, March 2022

HOLY FAMILY CHURCH HALL

1964, BLACKPOOL, UK

IAN ANDERSON

The first attempts to actually perform followed on from getting together with two friends in the sixth form at Blackpool Grammar School. One was a known music student by the name of John Evans who we knew played piano, which was relatively unusual, and who did a music lesson as part of his school curriculum. The other was Jeffrey Hammond, who was a friend of mine in the first year of sixth form. He had no musical experience whatsoever but he liked music so I declared that he should be the bass player. Although John was a piano player as a student and his mother a piano teacher, she had bought him a drum kit because John wanted to be like Ringo.

So John was going to play drums, Jeffrey was going to play bass and I was going to play guitar. Then we found someone who was going to be our singer, but he only lasted one audition and it became quite clear that while he had an okay voice he didn't really fit the spirit of it. That left us without a singer and so I took on the role of singing and playing the guitar in that three-piece band, which we vaguely named The Blades after the fictitious night club to which James Bond belonged in the Ian Fleming novels.

Subsequently, that three-piece band played a couple of little shows to a bunch of little Roman Catholic schoolgirls on a Friday night youth club dance in the Holy Family youth club in a church just up the road from where John Evans lived. We were hearing things by the Rolling Stones or The Animals or other bands that had appropriated some of black American folk music and we tended to go back and listen to the originals. The music we played was based on blues and the pop music of the day that emulated the blues and our versions of the songs that were quite often being played around the amateur music scene were a little different, because we were making our arrangements of the original versions rather than copying the Stones or whoever. It didn't really work in the context of a youth club dance. As soon as we started playing, all the little girls went and sat down and then drifted off into the other room since we weren't playing danceable pop music stuff.

We then got a drummer in the band because John decided to switch to playing organ, so we became The John Evan Blues the year after. That band then morphed into The John Evan Band, which grew to incorporate a sax player and another guitar player. I was released to be the singer, having decided to part with my electric guitar since there were too many other great guitar players around playing sessions in London particularly – people like Ritchie Blackmore, Jeff Beck and Jimmy Page. It seemed pointless trying to catch up with those guys, so I traded in my guitar for a microphone, which was appropriate to a singer. And for no particular reason, the last £30 of my part exchange was spent on a student model flute. It was just a whimsical moment of seeing it hanging on the wall and thinking, 'Yeah, perhaps that would be fun. And Eric Clapton doesn't play the flute so I might be in with a chance.'

LONDON

MAY 1967

CHRIS WRIGHT, CO-FOUNDER OF CHRYSALIS RECORDS

I was a booking agent in Manchester when I started managing groups. One of the guys in my office, Don Read, was looking after a group from Blackpool called the John Evan Band. Don was a really nice guy and he came to see me and said, 'I want you to take this group over. You're doing a great job with Ten Years After. I think you can do a better job than I can do for the John Evan Band.' He managed them and also a group called Family, who did very well and who were quite successful. And he also managed a group called The Warriors who had a lead singer called Jon Anderson, who went on to be the Jon Anderson of Yes.

Don said, 'I want nothing out of it but the lead singer, Ian Anderson, is going to be a really great songwriter and what I want you to do is give me the publishing and let me be the publisher for every other song that he writes.' We said, 'Sure, no problem.' Because we didn't know what the fuck he was talking about. We didn't know anything about publishing at the time, so we just agreed to it and then nothing happened. But that was incredibly perceptive of Don to spot that this lead singer in the John Evan Band had the potential to be a really great songwriter.

We renamed them the John Evan Smash because we thought it sounded a bit more contemporary. They were a seven-piece - Hammond organ, guitar, bass, drums and two saxes. Ian was the lead singer. He played the harmonica a bit. He didn't play the flute. A lot of seven-piece groups in those days were soul bands, but they were like a blues group. There wasn't anything quite like them in England.

Although it was called the John Evan Band, I think we did all our talking to Ian rather than John Evans. Ian was almost like the band leader, even though it wasn't named after him. He was very young at the time. He wasn't 18. When we signed him, he had to get his father to sign the contract, because he was underage.

MARQUEE CLUB

19 JUNE 1967, LONDON, UK

JEFFREY HAMMOND

When Ian wanted to move into London from Luton, I found him a room in another house owned by my landlord. In Blackpool during the days of the John Evan Band we had speculated about living in London, even down to deciding which road would be appropriate for us to live in. When John began making bass speaker cabinets for me, I thought Glebe would be a good name for them and we decided that Glebe Road would be our London address, not having any idea whether such a road existed or – if it did – where in London it might be. So it was that I moved to Tremlett Grove, equally impressive I thought, but (more importantly for an impoverished art student) affordable.

Only a 15-minute walk away, Ian would come round with an array of luncheon ingredients to cook on my tiny Belling cooker. These usually included a tinned Fray Bentos steak pie, tinned sausages and beans, etc., all to be heated up in a frying pan in a glorious mish-mash. Needless to say, I ensured I had already eaten before he arrived. Afterwards we would pass the time by listening to albums on my record player (Ian didn't own one at the time), musing about performing on stage and all things musical. Of course, one of those albums was Roland Kirk's *Talk with the Spirits*, whose first track was 'Serenade to a Cuckoo'. Ian was much taken with this and included his version of it in their set list and later their first album, *This Was*. His flute solo in the middle of it quickly became the highlight of the evening and always 'brought the house down'.

We are all standing on the shoulders of giants, and I know Ian has acknowledged his admiration for Roland Kirk. (Indeed, we all went to see him perform at a small jazz club in Boston in the early Seventies).

Our rooms were pretty basic and heated only by a small electric two bar fire, fed by sixpences into the meter. Like me, during the winter Ian probably slept in his overcoat, which he wore during the day and then on stage, enhancing his somewhat

dishevelled appearance with the long hair and beard. Whilst in Blackpool I had known Jeff 'The Cake', a former air traffic controller who had been obliged to retire from his job following a nervous breakdown. I think in his early 40s, he now looked like what at the time was known as a beatnik, and used to hang out in the Railway Station Bar. He always had with him a paper carrier bag with string handles, the type sold at greengrocers for fruit and vegetables. As an art student, I adopted this habit for carrying various artsy accoutrements to and from college. Ian too saw the merits of incorporating this into his stage performance, where in his bag he would keep his harmonicas, but took it a little further by including a pre-set clockwork alarm clock and a hot water bottle, etc. - these fruits, I think, of our after-lunch chats.

I had the great good fortune to see and hear Tull's first performances at the Marquee. The first time, as virtually unknowns, they attracted perhaps only a few dozen more than the proverbial one man and his dog. By word of mouth the audience grew, in today's jargon, exponentially and within a few weeks the Marquee was packed out and they had a residency there.

Whilst there were many good and many not so good blues bands at the time, they nearly all featured a guitar virtuoso. Of course, the burgeoning Tull had theirs in Mick, but what set them apart at the outset was a flute playing virtuoso frontman who performed and engaged with the audience in a way few others had done before, combining humour with Ian's seriously well-written songs. It was just the right blend of Mick's powerful guitar, Glenn's lyrical bass lines and Clive's driving drumming topped off by Ian's vocals, guitar, harmonica and flute. Different and highly idiosyncratic, but accessible and very much of the moment. I was privileged at weekends to often travel in the transit to gigs in and around London as their support. Popularity grew further, and I basked in the pleasure and enjoyment of seeing their well-earned success, though one could sense this was only the beginning of what turned out to be a remarkable journey.

Tull supported The Herd at this show and were billed as 'John Evan Smash'. Their first appearance at the Marquee as Jethro Tull was on 2 February 1968, supporting the Savoy Brown Blues Band.

NOVEMBER 1967

CHRIS WRIGHT

I thought they could be Britain's answer to the Paul Butterfield Blues Band, but I didn't think the guitarist was strong enough. In those days it was all about the guitar. The guitar was king, and the focus was always on the guitarist more than on the singer. I told them I thought I could find a guitarist for them. They were going to move down south anyway, and there was another group I knew from Manchester called the Toggery Five from Luton, whose guitarist was Mick Abrahams. So I got the John Evan Band to get rid of their guitarist and moved the remaining six of them to Luton to work with Mick. And that's what they did. I never went to see their rehearsals. They told me it was all going well. They told me when they'd be ready to take gigs and we booked some college dates for them, because a lot of the gigs we were booking were in colleges.

Neither Terry Ellis or anyone else from the office went to the first gig or two, which may have been on a Friday and Saturday night. But we spoke to the social secretaries at the colleges on the Monday to see how they'd gone down. The first one said they were really great and went down really well and we thought that was great. Except they said, 'They were really great for a four-piece.'

We said, 'No, you're talking about the wrong group. This is a seven-piece.'

But the social secretary insisted. 'No, no, it's only four.'

Both colleges said exactly the same, so I got hold of Ian and said, 'What the fuck's going on?'

And he said, 'What did the social secretaries say about how we went down?'

I said, 'I don't give a shit about that. I want to know what's going on.'

He said, 'What did the social secretaries say?'

I said, 'They said you went down well, but that's not the point.'

He said, 'As long as we went down well. The point is that we are only a four-piece. The Hammond organ player and the two sax players and drummer all got homesick and went home to Blackpool. There's just me and Glenn Cornick the bass player, and this guy Mick Abrahams who've you've got to be the guitarist, and he's got his mate Clive Bunker playing drums with us.'

They were called Bag of Blues. A typical fee for playing a college at the weekend when they were the Bag of Blues was maybe 25 quid. Ian then picked up the flute and started playing it. In those days the guitar solo would take five minutes. The singer could look a bit stupid standing there doing nothing whilst the guitarist is doing a five-minute guitar solo, so Ian could play with his flute and not just play it. He could twiddle it around with his fingers and that kind of thing. He almost became a flute player almost by accident.

IAN ANDERSON

Around November of 1967 some of us briefly relocated to Luton to hook up with Mick Abrahams as a guitar player and his friend, Clive Bunker, as a drummer. Since only two of us finally remained from the Blackpool days, that became the immediate precursor to Jethro Tull, which we became at the end of 1967.

We knew Chris Wright from when he had been the social secretary at Manchester University, and his counterpart at Newcastle was Terry Ellis. Chris at that point had taken Ten Years After under his wing and, as students, they both had some practical experience of booking concert shows and dealing with agents and artists, and they got together to form the Ellis-Wright agency in London. Chris had spent a brief period of time working in Manchester for one of the established agents, and we did play some shows for the Ian Hamilton Agency.

When Chris went down to London to form the agency with Terry Ellis, we kind of followed him in the sense that he was our contact to try and perhaps get some work. And we did get a few shows, ostensibly as the seven-piece John Evan Band. But Chris kept getting phone calls from club owners saying, 'We were told it was a seven-piece, but only four people turned up. They were pretty good, and we liked them so we'd like to book them again.' When Chris found out there were no longer seven of us, he was a little perturbed. But he saw that the band had some potential because Mick Abrahams was a loud and gregarious character, whereas I was a little more withdrawn.

CLIVE BUNKER

There was a club between Luton and Dunstable, and Mick Abrahams said to me, 'There's a band on that you should come and see. They're really, really good.' It was Ian's original band – John Evan, Barrie Barlow – all of them were in that band. Then we saw them again and they said, 'Oh, we're thinking of moving to London because we've got this agent called Chrysalis.' And Mick said to them, 'Why don't you move to Luton? Because the rents are cheaper and it's only 20 minutes up the 'new' motorway.'

They moved to Luton, but the brass section moved back to Blackpool because they weren't making enough money and then Barrie, the last one, said he was going to move back. That was the end of the band. And so Mick said to Glenn and Ian, 'Why don't you form a band with me and Clive?'

IAN ANDERSON

Mick as a singer was a shouter in the Rory Gallagher style and played very much blues and rock 'n' roll guitar solos, so Chris saw him as the focal point of the band and Chris suggested to me that I should learn to play a few chords on keyboards and stand at the back of the stage and 'keep quiet and don't sing and let Mick be the front man'.

That didn't really hinder me in continuing to try and push forward, particularly playing the flute, which was our point of difference. I mean, who wanted to be in another band that was just playing the blues? There were plenty of those around London and some of them were better than us, so I didn't really see the point in carrying on just being a third-rate blues band. It seemed to me we should try to push forward for something different.

The flute was the obvious point of difference in the early Jethro Tull. It got people's attention, so I continued to try and keep the flute as an equal to the electric guitar as a strong front-line instrument and ultimately that paid off. Not without a certain part of criticism and reticence on the part of venue managers and on the part of record companies, who were pretty much disinterested in Jethro Tull, because they didn't see how a flute fitted into that world.

MICK ABRAHAMS

When I was a kid, I wanted to be Elvis. Didn't everybody? I was a big Shadows fan too. My uncle got my skiffle band its first gig, at the Royal Antediluvian Order of Buffaloes in Luton. I played four numbers, got paid one and sixpence, was given two pints of orange squash, and politely told to piss off.

I was in a band called McGregor's Engine, which supported the John Evan Band at the Beachcomber in Luton in autumn 1967, when their bass guitarist said, 'I'm quitting.' Five minutes later, Ian Anderson and Glenn Cornick came up and said, 'We've heard you playing. We like the way you play. Would you like to join our band?' That was the beginnings of Jethro Tull. Originally it was going to be me joining Ian's band, but that all fell apart when the others went back to Blackpool.

The Sunbury Festival was a big surprise to everyone, including us. It was what got us on the map. Before that we were playing little clubs and typically getting audiences of between 50 and 100 people.

Terry Ellis borrowed some money from his mum and dad to pay for the first album. We went down to a studio in Chelsea. The engineer was a nice guy called Victor Gamm, and we had a lot of fun doing the album. It was basically our live set.

Chris Wright wanted me to be the focal point of the band. He was into guitar heroes, but I wasn't a hero for any fucker and wasn't bothered about the spotlight being on me. I was more into blues and jazz, whereas Ian had more folky leanings and saw Tull as his band. We had different approaches to songwriting too. It wasn't one particular thing that made me think, 'Sod it, I'm going to leave.' It was lots of little things. I said I'd stay on until they found a replacement, because I didn't want to leave them in the shit. Then I was called to a meeting with Terry Ellis, the band's manager, to be told I was being fired.

After Blodwyn Pig, I gave up the music business for a while. But if music is in your heart, it will stay there, and as much as you try and quit it, it won't let you. I was at a music conference at the Russell Hotel a few years ago where I was demonstrating guitars for Yamaha. I bumped into this bloke who said, 'Hi, you're Mick, aren't you? I like all your work.' It was Hank Marvin. How fantastic is that, that my childhood hero knew who I was?

I've played on stage with Ian in the years since I left Jethro Tull. If he asked me to get up and play on stage with him again tomorrow, I'd do it.

JANUARY 1968

CHRIS WRIGHT

Ian grew his hair long and started looking very dishevelled and wore a really long overcoat. The guy that worked for us in the office thought he looked like pictures we'd seen of the agricultural pioneer, Jethro Tull, so we decided to call them Jethro Tull.

CLIVE BUNKER

We began playing and took on anything at the time. We didn't tell anybody. We used different names. Then Terry, the manager, came along to a gig and saw us and thought, 'Oops, it's better than I expected.' Then we did a single and Terry said, 'Right you've got to have a name now.' One of the guys in the office, who had studied history, said, 'Why don't you call it Jethro Tull? Because Ian looks like this guy that invented the seed drill.'

JETHRO TULL: "Sunshine Day" (MGM). Jethro was originally the man who invented the seed drill.
This Mr Tull, misnamed on the label as Jethro Toe, is going down a storm with his group in London clubs with an unusual sound and approach.
While not a hit, this West Coast flavoured tune will break the recording ice.

Sunshine Day was recorded on 6–7 January 1968 at CBS Studios in London and was produced by Derek Lawrence, who is credited with purposely designating the band as Jethro Toe. Apparently, he did not like the name Jethro Tull

CHRIS WRIGHT

Ten Years After were my primary act at that point. They hadn't gone to America yet – they went in June '68 – and it was in early '68, the spring, that we started really working with Jethro Tull.

We inherited the old manager and got them a record deal with MGM Records, which was a very small record company in England and an offshoot of the big American company, MGM, run by a guy called Rex Oldfield. Terry and I went round to see this chap and said, 'They haven't signed the contract. They will do, but we need an advance.' We asked for an advance of £1,000 for them to sign a long-term deal with MGM Records, and he wouldn't agree to that. So we said '£500 then', but he wouldn't agree to that.

We said '£50. It's the principle.' He wouldn't agree to that either. In the end he wouldn't agree to anything.

JETHRO TULL

NEW British Blues group, Jethro Tull, have signed a £50,000 contract with the Ellis-Wright Agency, and have also negotiated a five year recording deal with MGM Records.

Their first record, an original composition called "Sunshine Day", is to be released on February 16, on MGM in Britain, and on the Music Factory label in America. They also have an L.P. for release in the U.S. in March.

The group is at the Marquee on February 2 and 9, and at the Speakeasy on February 5.

But they'd already made a single, which was ready to be released. I don't know how many copies they'd pressed, perhaps not much more than 1,500, but the labels were printed and they'd got the name wrong on the label. They'd put them down as 'Jethro Toe'. Because we couldn't get an advance, we wouldn't let the group sign the contract, so the record had to be withdrawn. There are copies somewhere of this single by Jethro Toe which was never released.

What happened next was that they started developing a following and beginning to do really well. So we thought we would sign them to Decca and let them be produced by Mike Vernon, who was producing all the blues records at the time and who had produced the Ten Years After record. He was the producer, Gus Dudgeon was the engineer - who went on to work with Elton John - and Roy Thomas Baker - who was called Roy Baker at the time and who went on to work with Queen and God knows who else - was the tape operator. But Mike, being a blues-orientated producer, basically said to us, 'I'll sign them, but I'm really only interested in the guitarist, and maybe you should drop the singer. Certainly don't let him play the flute!' So that didn't go anywhere.

MARQUEE CLUB

2 FEBRUARY 1968, LONDON, UK

GRAHAM BONNET, MUSICIAN

I've always loved their music. My cousin Trevor Gordon and I were in The Marbles back in 1968. The bands that played at the Marquee were always great. Tull were number one on our list. That year we would always go to see Jethro Tull whenever they played at the Marquee. They played there constantly. It was always an entertaining night. The Marquee was a shithole. It needed redecorating. It smelled of piss, beer and cigarettes, and there wasn't much room. It was sweaty as well. Every time Tull played there it was absolutely packed. But it was always good for a night out. We'd go there in the hope of picking up girls, but usually the audience for Jethro Tull was mainly guys. I didn't use to drink back then either. It was incredible that I went to a club where I didn't drink. Sober nights and really, really great nights, because the music was so good.

The Jethro Tull songs were always interesting because they were so different, and my cousin and I tried to get elements of their music into our music. When I was in Rainbow, I found out that Ritchie (Blackmore) was a huge fan of Ian and he wanted to do something Jethro Tull-like. I'd hear a lot of that stuff when Ritchie played music at his house in Long Island years ago. He had a big white cello at home, and said to me, 'Can you play guitar? I'd like to do something sort of like Ian Anderson.' He wanted to turn the band around to do more weird and wonderful Tull-like music. He wanted to get away from just 'Smoke on the Water' and 'Since You've Been Gone'. I said 'okay', but it never came to anything.

I didn't know the guys but felt like I knew them, because of the circle of people I was around. Ian Anderson wasn't one of those guys that went to the clubs on his night off. I think he was very anti-that. I think he's very anti-pop music too. But that's what made them interesting in 1968. There was a lot of guitar shit going on. But a guy with a flute? Come on, what is that? And that band was so good.

OWENS UNION BUILDING, UNIVERSITY OF MANCHESTER

10 FEBRUARY 1968, MANCHESTER, UK

KEITH MULLARD

I saw Cream at Manchester University with Jethro Tull in support in 1967 or 1968.
I had seen Hendrix at Sheffield City Hall a couple of weeks earlier, so it was a good
comparison. Admission was six shillings (30p). When I came into the hall, Tull were
already playing. But then I turned around and saw everyone was looking at the other
end of the hall where the main stage was. Cream had Triumph PA speakers that were
never that good. But Cream came on and it was good. Great bass playing, great vocals
and the guitar playing was perhaps not Jimi, but it was tight and worked well with
the band. Ginger was Ginger and played a great solo. All in all, it was a great show and
well worth the six shillings!

STAR HOTEL

18 MARCH 1968, CROYDON, UK

GRAHAM MAISEY

I first saw Jethro Tull at the Star Club in Croydon
in early 1968. Most of my collection of magazine
and record covers were obtained at the time of their
publication. It's been a long trip from '68 to the
present day and I wouldn't have missed it for the
world.

*Ian Anderson and Graham Maisey, Exeter 2011.
Photo: Graham Maisey*

RAMBLING JACK'S BLUES CLUB, RAILWAY HOTEL

18 APRIL 1968, BISHOPS STORTFORD, UK

BARRY EARTHEY

It was an amazing time back then. A friend had seen Tull and said, 'You must see
this band – they are so different.' Rambling Jack's was upstairs in this pub called
the Railway Hotel. It only held about 200 or so people. As was the case back then, it
was very smoky and most of us there didn't know what to expect. They came on and
performed numbers from the album, *This Was*, highlights being 'Bouree' and 'Cat's
Squirrel'. In hindsight it was a privilege to see Mick Abrahams play an extended

version of it live. At the end of the gig the place was in uproar in excitement.

I also saw them in a blues club at Finsbury Park, at around the same time, a club that featured bands that went on to become famous later, like Rambling Jack's. Since moving to Australia in 1973 I've seen Tull twice more.

IAN ANDERSON

It gradually built momentum on the strength of performances at the Marquee Club and the first Hyde Park concert and the Sunbury Jazz and Blues Festival. That all cemented the direction of that early Jethro Tull as being the one that should be followed. Chris Blackwell at Island Records was supportive and gave us a record deal and then extended that when Chris and Terry formed Chrysalis Records, a label with marketing and promotion and distribution by Island Records in Europe and Reprise Records, a Warner's division, in the USA. So we were rolling along by the summer of '68.

SOUND TECHNIQUES STUDIO

13 JUNE – 28 JULY 1968, CHELSEA, LONDON, UK

CHRIS WRIGHT

Chris Wright used his travel insurance money to pay for a US tour

The only way I could get Ten Years After to America was by getting them to sign a publishing deal. By now we knew what publishing was. I got £2,000, which was enough to get the air fares for me and Ten Years After to get to America to do a two-month tour. But Terry Ellis went and spent the £2,000 we owed the travel agent for the air fares on putting Jethro Tull in the studio and making an album - and they hadn't got a record deal!

By the time the album *This Was* was made, there was enough interest in them that we could have made a record deal with almost anyone, because by then they were really developing and were becoming great. But not at that point.

We couldn't pay the travel agent for the air fares because we hadn't got the money. But when I got to America, I got very severe appendicitis and had to go into hospital in San Francisco and have my appendix out, so I claimed on my travel insurance for the appendicitis operation. We used that money to pay the travel agent instead of paying the hospital. Eventually, in October, we managed to get a record deal for

Jethro Tull with Warner Brothers in America, and that was when we eventually had enough money to settle the travel agent's bill. The travel agent was five minutes away from bankrupting the company.

Because we were essentially booking bands into colleges and a lot of that payment came in by cheque, when the college season was running, we could cashflow ourselves by getting the money from the colleges and holding it for a couple of weeks before we paid the agent for the band we'd booked in there. That was fine until you got to June 1st and then you had three months or more of no college gigs and no cashflow. All of this was going on during that time when we had no other cash flow at all.

HYDE PARK

29 JUNE 1968, LONDON, UK

STUART LANGFORD

My wife and I have seen Jethro Tull with brilliant sound and we've seen Jethro Tull with terrible sound. When I was at college in Leicester, people used to hang round a little theatre in Leicester called the Phoenix. It was a very small experimental flexible space theatre that had lunchtime shows and gigs and put on films and short plays. Because I was at college just round the corner, we used to go in all the time and help with lunchtime shows and do bits of guitaring for them. The house electrician, Alan, used to teach me about lighting. The manager of the Phoenix was a guy called Robin Anderson, Ian Anderson's brother. If you went into the Phoenix during the day, Robin Anderson would almost invariably be playing pre-release Jethro Tull albums through the theatre's enormous JBL sound system.

You know how fantastic an empty theatre is? The black, the seats, the screen, the lights hanging there, the dust, the cobwebs. And belting out would be 'Song for Jeffrey' or something from *Stand Up* or *Benefit*. It was just wonderful.

The first time I saw Jethro Tull was at their first Hyde Park free festival. I was there with friends from Leicester. They were on with Roy Harper, Pink Floyd, Third Ear Band and Edgar Broughton. What a day. Pink Floyd did *Atom Heart Mother*. Jethro Tull were explosive and so energised. I rushed back to Leicester and bought the first album, *This Was*, which is still one of the best albums ever.

We've seen them loads of times. I've seen them with Glenn Cornick on bass and with Clive Bunker on drums a couple of times. We saw them in Nottingham, playing support to Ten Years After. We saw them at the Rink in Sunderland – the Top Rank – and we were right at the front. John Evans was with them by then with his ice cream seller's linen suit. We were right up against the speakers at the very, very front and it was incredibly loud. But it was about the best sound I've ever heard. Our ears didn't ring at all. It was like wearing amazing giant headphones. The balance was beautiful, and they were brilliant.

BLUESVILLE 68, HORNSEY WOOD TAVERN

2 AUGUST 1968, MANOR HOUSE, LONDON, UK

BILL GREEN

I was living in Crouch Hill at the time and my friend Mike lived at Finsbury Park, so we could both walk to the Bluesville at Manor House. It was our usual Friday night at Bluesville (we always went together to Bluesville and The Marquee) and we were queuing on the stairs to get in when Ian Anderson walked by, looking very dishevelled, with his long army greatcoat, extremely long and unkempt hair and his flute in a brown paper bag. Nanda Lesley was at the top of the stairs taking the money and we heard a bit of a commotion. When we got to the top of the stairs to pay Nanda our entrance fee, she had a bit of a grin on her face and told us she thought Ian Anderson was a tramp off the street and wanted to turn him away, but he said to her, 'I'm in the band', so she let him in. It's a story that makes me chuckle every time I think of it.

Nanda Lesley was a beautiful soul and her and Ron Lesley seemed to us young 17-year-olds a very incongruous couple to be running a blues club. They seemed very 'straight' and, of course, they were a lot older. Nanda was always smiling and used to welcome everyone to the club. I can still see her now, standing at the top of the stairs.

EIGHTH NATIONAL JAZZ & BLUES FESTIVAL

KEMPTON PARK RACECOURSE, 11 AUGUST 1968, SUNBURY-ON-THAMES, UK

DEE PALMER, COMPOSER, ARRANGER & MUSICIAN

By the summer of 1968 and two years after completing my studies at the Royal Academy of Music I had, as a newbie entrant into the sharp end of the music business, not only survived the vagaries of that life but had met with unqualified success and attendant praise in fulfilling those music writing commissions and piano- playing gigs which (via word of mouth recommendations) had come my way, and, at no less than a meteoric rate, had risen to that much vaunted but elusive realm of life associated, hitherto, with the 'fast gun for hire'-type or, perhaps more indelicately, 'an expensive tart' - namely, that of a session musician!

On the evening of Sunday 11th August 1968, following a pleasantly warm summer day and with my wife and children away at the seaside, I found myself with the rare luxury of time on my hands. At the time, alongside the regular flow of TV and recording commissions which were now coming my way, I had become ghost writer to a well-known English film music composer and was waiting to start work on a new

film. I chose to make my way to Kempton Racecourse, a mere couple of miles from where we then lived, where I purchased a ticket and joined the crowd for the final session of The National Jazz and Blues Festival.

I had no idea what I was hoping to get from the experience. I was a devotee of the Miles Davis and Bill Evans school of modern jazz and there wasn't much (if any) of that fare on offer. Having listened to a couple of groups, I decided to avoid the end of evening crush and had started to make my way to the car park when my ears were alerted to a burst of applause followed by musical sounds, the likes of which I'd not heard before. Just like Dick Whittington, I turned and sought the source of the sounds that were summoning me.

The stage was now surrounded by a packed, enthusiastic audience who clearly were fans of the group producing this singularly original combination of musical sounds. The name of the group was written in black on the bass drum: Jethro Tull.

On the drive home and with their unique sounds still fresh in my mind I concluded that this was a group who, with luck, might add a very interesting dimension to the shape of English music.

Early in the week following the Sunbury Festival, I received a call from a man called Terry Ellis. He told me that I'd been highly recommended to him as an arranger and could I work with a group he managed who didn't read music; also, could I write and add music to a track that was already recorded, and could I engage the musicians to play it? Answer affirmative. Furthermore, could he send to me a tape of the material they'd like me to work on and could we meet asap? Again, affirmative. I asked him the name of the group. Answer: Jethro Tull!

The tape arrived, I transcribed the song and we arranged to meet the next day, close to my home at The Mitre Hotel, Hampton Court. Ian and Terry arrived in Terry's Triumph Spitfire which, at the time, was a pay grade below the level of my gleaming, recently totally refurbished 1948 Triumph Roadster, the car favoured by Bergerac in the TV series of the same name. The next time I saw Terry in a car it was a Rolls-Royce with the registration number TCE 1. I've since heard Ian say to journalists who'd asked how we came to meet that, on the drive down to meet me at Hampton Court, Terry Ellis had asked how they would recognise me. Ian claims to have replied, 'He'll be fat, 40 and Jewish,' and David was all of those - not! (Ian's humour, you know.)

On arrival at my home, I asked Ian what instruments or sounds he had in mind for me to add to the track. He replied 'horns.' I played him recorded examples of French horns, hunting horns and the cor anglais (English horn), but none of these cut the mustard. I then asked Ian if he might be using 'horn' in the generic form, i.e. the one adopted in the USA to describe trumpets, trombones and saxophones, and played him a track written for the Count Basie Band by Quincey Jones. Immediate approval from Ian. 'How much will this cost?' asked Terry Ellis. Suits! What? I'd finished the score to 'Move on Alone' long before Ian and Terry got back to London.

SOUND TECHNIQUES

23 AUGUST 1968, FULHAM, LONDON, UK

DEE PALMER

The recording of 'Move on Alone' was at Sound Techniques, Fulham, from noon to 2pm on Saturday 23rd August. I booked the musicians for a 'half session', i.e. two hours. There were five of them and they were paid £6 each. My invoice for consultation, the score and conducting was £15.

My real reward, of course, was the forming of a lifelong friendship with Ian Anderson.

GRAND HOTEL

6 SEPTEMBER 1968, FELIXSTOWE, UK
GRAHAM DAY, AGE 18

My friend Rob and I would spend time going to local dances, and occasionally later frequented the Bluesville Club in Ipswich. Blues music was in the ascendancy, and we heard of a band strangely called Jethro Tull. I was intrigued as I thought that the real Jethro Tull had lived a long while before, and had been something to do with the agricultural revolution. For many years, as a family we had taken the *New Musical Express*, and in it there was a report of the 1968 National Jazz and Blues Festival at Sunbury-on-Thames, where Tull had put in a superb performance on 9th August.

On a sunny Sunday we made a trip to Felixstowe. At the Grand Hotel on the seafront was a poster advertising a gig there by Jethro Tull on Friday 6th September 1968. We thought it would be good to go. Like me, Rob was a civil servant, in his case at the Ministry of Agriculture in Ipswich, and he had an older colleague who was keen to go, and who drove us there.

On the day of the gig we arrived and went to a rear first-floor room of the hotel which was used for musical events. It was small, hot and quite crowded, with a stage at the far end and on which had been set out the band's instruments. Not long afterwards there were resounding cheers as Jethro Tull walked on stage. In those days the lineup was Ian Anderson (vocals), Mick Abrahams (guitar), Glenn Cornick (bass) and Clive Bunker (drums).

Ian Anderson was the most impressive figure on stage, reminding one of an Elizabethan court jester with his long hair, beard and strange clothes, including a long overcoat. A real original, he was also very proficient on the flute, which seemed to only graze his lips, and gave the impression of almost being able to stand on one leg whilst he was playing it. Mick Abrahams was a very accomplished blues guitarist, and the rhythm section of Glenn Cornick and Clive Bunker laid down a solid beat.

They played many memorable songs, including the blues standard 'Stormy Monday', which I later found out was a T-Bone Walker classic, and 'Love Story', which featured Ian Anderson's proficiency on the flute and which was then eclipsed by 'Dharma for One', which really displayed Ian's virtuosity as well as a stunning drum solo from Clive Bunker. Mick Abrahams played the blues standard 'Cat's Squirrel', which showcased his huge ability. My interest in the blues was aroused by this and the blues would form my musical tapestry from early 1969 until the present day. It was not long afterwards that, as they say, there was 'a difference in musical policy' as Ian Anderson wanted the band to become more of a rock band, whereas Mick Abrahams wished to continue to plough the blues furrow and went off eventually to form his own band, Blodwyn Pig.

As always with enjoyable gigs, the performance and the encore went by in a flash and we emerged into the early autumn air, hot, tired and happy but also hungry. We found a burger van on the seafront and soon bought hot dogs to satisfy our hunger.

Sadly, this was the only time I saw Jethro Tull live. The following year, they were rumoured to have been booked to appear at Ipswich Corn Exchange. But unbeknown to them the gig had been cancelled. They turned up, the venue was closed, and they ended up in the Swan pub opposite.

THIS WAS

RELEASED 4 October 1968 (UK)/
3 February 1969 (US)

UK CHART POSITION 10

US CHART POSITION 62

CHRIS WRIGHT

We created Chrysalis initially just as a production company. We owned the rights to the Tull album, having paid the costs of making the record, but we weren't planning on having a label. We then sold the rights to Island Records for Europe and did a separate deal with a company in Scandinavia. We kept back the American rights, which we sold later to Warner Brothers.

When we did the deal with Island we said to them, 'We might have other groups we want to sign so we don't want this just to be a deal for Jethro Tull.' And they were fine with that. And we said, 'By the way, if we have seven top-10 singles or albums then in future everything in England will go on the Chrysalis label.' Island agreed to that, thinking it was very unlikely to happen. But between Jethro Tull and Blodwyn Pig it happened within a year. The first Jethro Tull record came out in October '68 and by the time we got to October '69 we'd actually had seven top-10 records and in future everything would indeed come out on the Chrysalis label. So we created Chrysalis by accident really.

During that time, we were hands-on management for Jethro Tull, Ten Years After, Blodwyn Pig and a couple of other groups. Plus, we had the booking agency – we booked the first Led Zeppelin dates – and a music production company and publishing company. We were pretty busy.

CALIFORNIA BALLROOM

1 NOVEMBER 1968, DUNSTABLE, UK

MICK CLARKE

My band Killing Floor supported Jethro Tull at the California Ballroom in Dunstable. California Ballroom was a very large room with stages at each end - we of course were on the small one at the back. We played there several times with bands such as Ten Years After, Chicken Shack and others, including some pop groups, and also Georgie Fame one time and - my favourite night - Junior Walker and the All Stars.

I'd seen Jethro Tull a few times at the Marquee and always enjoyed the band - I really liked Mick Abrahams' playing. I enjoyed them on the Dunstable gig as well. It was always a good sound there. What I particularly remember was that Ian Anderson came down to our end and watched some of our set, standing quite near the stage. As it happened, we had learned a new song with quite a complicated arrangement. When we started it, I started off in the wrong key, so we had to stop and start again. At that point Ian turned and walked off! I don't blame him.

IAN ANDERSON

Things were happening and I was writing the next batch of songs for the second album, which were clearly no longer Jethro Tull, the little blues band. It was Jethro Tull as in what became known as progressive rock in 1969. That's how that developed into a world beyond the four-piece blues band. Mick Abrahams didn't take to the songs that I was writing, because they weren't straight-ahead 12-bar blues and he felt it was not really his thing. We clearly were on a musical collision, which for a number of reasons resulted in Mick departing from the rest of the band in November of '68 and ultimately being replaced.

CHRIS WRIGHT

Ian was very young. He got rid of Mick Abrahams from the group, and Mick was a very good guitarist. There was obviously a clash there as to who was the most important. Ian wasn't taking any chances that he wasn't going to be seen as the person in charge. He was obviously writing songs then. He had this image, because of his appearance, of being really weird, but he wasn't really weird at all. One of the attractive parts of the group was his image, but he wasn't really the person in the image. He performed the role really well, but it wasn't the person that he really was.

BLUE BOAR SERVICE STATION

24 NOVEMBER 1968, LEICESTERSHIRE, UK

CLIVE BUNKER

We were playing blues to start with and then we got more progressive with it, which is not what Mick Abrahams wanted. Mick is an old blues guy and never will play anything else. That's why in the end it was good news for Mick and everybody that he left, because we were trying to get more progressive, and it was working a treat, but Mick used to stand in the corner in the studio to make a point that he wasn't enjoying it.

  He didn't want to play what we were playing, and he made it awkward for everybody. I didn't know it but the other two had been talking about it between themselves. One night we stopped at the Blue Boar motorway service station on the M1 on the way back from a gig. I was the driver, so I was having a little kip while they were in there, and Ian and Glenn came out and said, 'Look, we know you're mates with Mick, but we feel he needs to go,' and I said, 'Yeah, he's obviously not enjoying himself.' So we said to Mick, 'If you're not enjoying it, why don't you form a little blues band on your own again?'

We had played a gig at the Van Dike Club in Plymouth some weeks before and Martin Barre was in the support band. He played some flute on one or two of the songs. When Mick was going to leave, we said, 'Right, who do we get?' and I suggested we try to get in touch with Martin, 'because you don't want two flute players!' We had some auditions which he didn't come to until the last day, so we just got him in time.

We were at Blue Boar Services with Fairport Convention another time. They were in two vans, and left before us. We were driving back down to London, and where the last services now are on the motorway before you get to London, there's a bend in the road. There were police and fire brigade and everything there. The Fairport van had crashed, and Fairport's drummer Martin Lamble and Richard Thompson's girlfriend at the time had died.

ROLLING STONES ROCK AND ROLL CIRCUS, REDIFFUSION STUDIOS, WEMBLEY

12 DECEMBER 1968, LONDON, UK

CHRIS WRIGHT

Tony Iommi from Black Sabbath briefly took over as guitarist after Ian got rid of Mick Abrahams. I can't remember why that didn't work out. He did do one or two gigs with them, including the *Rolling Stones Rock and Roll Circus.*

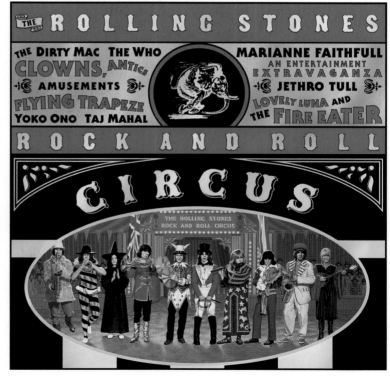

IAN ANDERSON

At one of our final concerts with Mick Abrahams, the opening act was a band called Earth from Birmingham. What struck me about them was Tony Iommi's guitar playing. It was very forceful, it was simple, it was direct, it didn't have complicated chords. It was just open fifths and very simple direct music, and he had a good strong tone. And it wasn't a blues band, it was something else. It was a precursor of course to their later name change to Black Sabbath. It was the same guys.

I somehow got in touch with Tony and asked if he'd like to come down to London and have a play about with us in rehearsal. You couldn't call it an audition because it wasn't as cold-hearted and functional as that. It was just a get-together to try a few things out. I ran a few songs by Tony, which he didn't find that easy to cope with. I didn't realise until later that the reason was that he'd lost the tips off a couple of fingers of his hand and so certain chord shapes were very difficult or impossible for him to play, which is why he developed the style that he did, which of course is what made Tony unique and Black Sabbath a huge hit. So Tony's limitations turned into

Everett Collection Inc / Alamy Stock Photo

Tony's strengths, much as they did in a way for Django Reinhardt, who was similarly afflicted by a lack of digital possibilities due to finger damage.

Tony was a nice guy. We got on well, but it clearly wasn't right for him to join Jethro Tull and he went back to his pals in Black Sabbath. But we called him back to do the *Rolling Stones Rock and Roll Circus* with us because he was the only guy that we knew really. We said, 'Would you mind coming down to do the Rolling Stones TV show?' We weren't playing live. We were just miming to a backing track. There was no time to learn and I don't think Tony played bottleneck guitar anyway. It was a particular piece of music that required a different guitar approach, so Tony mimed to the backing track. I sang and played live, and the others were Memorex. They were battery-powered!

I asked Charlie Watts and Bill Wyman how it was that we were invited to take part in the *Rock and Roll Circus* and, according to them, they were the architects of our appearance at short notice on that show. They had seen us play somewhere, perhaps at the Marquee Club, and recommended us as a potential guest act to Mick Jagger and the show's producer, Michael Lindsay Hogg. The Stones were trying to get a very broad mixture of musical talent, from a classical violinist to the screeching Yoko Ono, to appearances by John Lennon and The Who, who were the major draw after the Rolling Stones, and a few other folks. Jethro Tull were the rookies, the new kids on the block that no one had heard of, that rounded out the broad balance of musical talent.

We went along and felt a bit awkward and out of place, but we did what was asked of us. Then the show was shelved for many years because of the death of Brian Jones and, so rumour has it, because the Stones – or at least Mick Jagger – were not very happy with their performance. The Stones perhaps ended up looking a little ragged compared to the full-on performance of The Who, who were combat-ready. The Who had been on tour and were fighting fit, whereas the Stones had been off the road for a long time and had muddled through an album called *Beggar's Banquet*, actually a very good album. The TV show was a promotional vehicle for that album release.

But Brian Jones by then was somewhat marginalised from the band and not really a full participant. I remember he sat down to begin the rehearsals and was fumbling in his pocket, then he came over to me and said, 'I don't suppose you've got a plectrum I could borrow? I mean, a guitar pick.' I thought that was interesting. I'm not playing the guitar. I'm the flute player. But I just happened to have a plectrum with me, so I gave it to him. He then attempted to join in, playing whatever they were rehearsing.

CLIVE BUNKER

Tony Iommi came to the auditions we held. We had to do the Rolling Stones' *Rock and Roll Circus* and, because we didn't have a guitar player at the time, we said to Tony, 'If you're good enough at miming, you can get the gig!'

WINTER GARDENS

30 DECEMBER 1968, PENZANCE, UK

Martin Barre makes his debut with Jethro Tull.

INDUSTRIAL CLUB

11 JANUARY 1969, NORWICH, UK

I WAS THERE: MARTIN BOOTH

I saw Jethro Tull at the Industrial Club. The ticket cost two and sixpence or twelve and a half pence. During their set, when the band was playing 'Cat's Squirrel', Ian Anderson got into the cage with one of the go-go girls.

This performance is unverified. Jethro Tull did play the Gala Ballroom in Norwich twice in 1969.

REDCAR JAZZ CLUB

12 JANUARY 1969, REDCAR, UK

BRIAN SMITH

Jethro Tull were first scheduled to appear at the Jazz Club on 12 January 1969, but the band was going through changes, with Mick Abrahams leaving the group to form Blodwyn Pig. Replacements were being recruited (Tony Iommi - later of Black Sabbath – briefly filled the slot before Martin Barre replaced Abrahams). As a result, their appearance at the Jazz Club was cancelled at the last minute.

Jethro Tull were initially billed to play Redcar Jazz Club in January 1969 - photo Brian Smith

Pre-ticket sales had resulted in a sell-out full house. We had to call on one of our club members, Paul Rodgers, a member of the group Free, and he got the group together to replace Jethro Tull for that night's performance. With it being a full house, with just short of 1,000 paying customers, it turned out to be a very beneficial night for Free. The group performed well and got their name established on Teeside and surrounding areas with those present on the night.

In January 1969, Jethro Tull embarked upon their first North American tour.

IAN ANDERSON

The first tour was following on from the year before, when Ten Years After had been to the USA and done pretty well. Chris Wright got them hooked up with an American manager by the name of Dee Anthony and an American agent by the name of Frank Barsalona, and Barbara Skydel at Premier Talent. So Jethro Tull were similarly signed up ,rather on the coat-tails of Ten Years After. We weren't Ten Years After. We were not so formed at that point. It was pretty early on in our days. Martin Barre had only been in the band for three months or something.

We were there for 13 weeks on that first tour and played maybe a couple of shows a week, usually in some club we were told we should play because industry people went there. But we did get a couple of proper gigs, one at the famous Boston Tea Party, a big club run by a local promoter by the name of Don Law, while in New York City we performed at the Fillmore East for Bill Graham. Both of those were really important to us, because we did okay, Bill took to Jethro Tull, and Don Law saw the potential, so we were booked again. And that gradually began the break-out from the north east of the USA via radio play in New York, spilling over into neighbouring states. It all spread from that fortuitous support from Don Law and Bill Graham.

People tended to follow what was happening in New York or in Boston because so many bands began there, particularly the British bands, because it was the point of arrival – the nearest bit! Not many people went to the USA and began their careers in San Francisco or LA. We tended to get off the plane as soon as possible and start in the thick of the action.

FILLMORE EAST

24 & 25 JANUARY 1969, NEW YORK, NEW YORK

CLIVE BUNKER

When we first went to America, we did a month of just playing clubs. It was what all the new English bands did. Nobody played English bands in the middle of America. We stayed in the same hotel in New York and would just drive to different places. Because we were staying in the same hotel, I would go for walks and wander around Central Park and explore New York. I even walked into Harlem. People thought I was mad, but I didn't know anything about it. The doorman at the hotel when I went back said, 'Where have you been today?', I told him and he said, 'What?' What he meant was, 'We never go there!' But when you don't know, it's great.

Then we flew straight over to Los Angeles, people met us at the airport, and it was like we were stars overnight. It was incredible. Everybody from the East Coast had been phoning their friends. Overnight, we were stars, and we were playing bigger and bigger theatres. It was just unbelievable. By the time we finished that tour, which was four to six months in total, we were rock stars. It was amazing.

The last time we played the Fillmore East, before we went over to the West Coast, we went on and played, but then the top-billed band – Blood, Sweat & Tears - went on and they were unbelievable. You'd do two sets a night there, so when they finished their set, I went up to the drummer and said, 'Do you know anybody that can get me a flight home tonight?' He said, 'What?' I said, 'I've never played with bands as good as you lot,' and he said, 'Oh, we were just saying the same thing.'

I said, 'Oh come on, you're just trying to be nice,' and he said, 'No, I've phoned a friend of mine and told him to come and see the band on the second set. And here's my mate now.'

It was Buddy Rich. He'd phoned Buddy Rich to come and see us. Buddy was great. He said, 'I've got to get to my seat because I want to catch the show.' I said, 'Don't worry about it. Go to the pub or something.'

But after we finished, he came back and said, 'Thanks for that. I really enjoyed it. And if you're in Los Angeles in the next couple of weeks, we're playing there. Come and see my band.' And we were, so when we went to Los Angeles, I went to see Buddy's band, and he was wonderful, a real gentleman.

We thought all these people we shared a bill with were stars. Some of these bands don't think of themselves as stars. And we never thought of ourselves as stars until it happens where you have to go to gigs early because of fans waiting outside and stuff like that. We were lucky boys, that was what we thought.

There was no rivalry between the acts. We did thousands of festivals where there were maybe two or three English bands and lots of American bands and bands from elsewhere, and everybody seemed to get on with everybody else. In those days there was none of that jealousy thing that started to happen later. We'd share each other's equipment. Sometimes at festivals they would book too many people, so doing the changeover would take a while. Quite often we would say, 'We'll check the kit earlier and if you want you can play it,' or, 'The next one can play it as well,' and we'd leave the amps or whatever.

DOANE PERRY

I grew up in New York City. In ninth grade I was in a not-very-good power trio that was ill-advised named Nirvana. After the first gig I nixed that choice of names. We were obviously never going to get anywhere with a name like *that*. I was at the apartment of one of the band members after a band practice when 'Cat's Squirrel' came on the radio. They were using it to advertise an upcoming gig at the Fillmore East for this new band just coming over to the US to promote their first album, *This Was*. I heard some very interesting and original music going on behind the radio announcer which immediately caught my attention and wondered, 'Who is that?' This was Jethro Tull.

I went out and bought the album. It was very new sounding, and nobody really knew who they were. I was about 13 or 14 years old and bought tickets to see them at the upcoming Fillmore appearance, where they were opening for Blood, Sweat and Tears. Tull's equipment didn't make it from Boston because of bad weather, so Blood, Sweat and Tears kindly lent them their backline. Despite not having their own equipment, they sounded fantastic.

One of the things I loved about most British bands was that they sounded quite different from one another, yet geographically it's not a big country. Many of them had an exotic sounding quality, but of course we often didn't realize they were reimporting some of our own music back to us, albeit slightly reimagined.

I wrote Clive Bunker a letter after *Benefit* and just before *Aqualung*, and he wrote back to me. It's funny, I recall he had excellent penmanship. It was a very articulate and encouraging letter. Really not expecting a response, I was surprised to receive such a generous letter from this extraordinary drummer. Without question, Clive was one of the biggest influences on me stylistically during that period. I felt he was the musical bridge between the styles of Ginger Baker and Billy Cobham. He had a natural gift and a unique, theatrical but musically advanced way of playing that was like watching an amazing dancer. He was graceful yet he played with tremendous power, authority and subtlety. I talked to

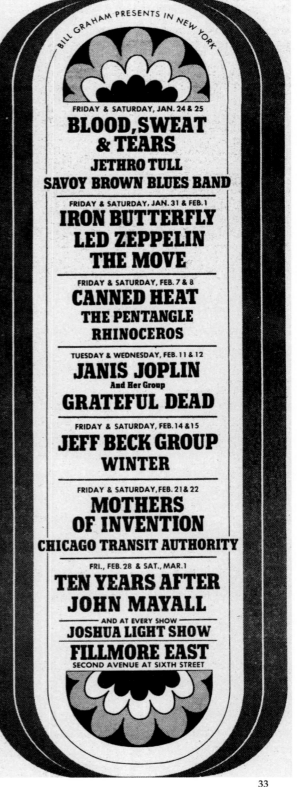

BILL GRAHAM PRESENTS IN NEW YORK

FRIDAY & SATURDAY, JAN. 24 & 25

BLOOD, SWEAT & TEARS
JETHRO TULL
SAVOY BROWN BLUES BAND

FRIDAY & SATURDAY, JAN. 31 & FEB. 1

IRON BUTTERFLY
LED ZEPPELIN
THE MOVE

FRIDAY & SATURDAY, FEB. 7 & 8

CANNED HEAT
THE PENTANGLE
RHINOCEROS

TUESDAY & WEDNESDAY, FEB. 11 & 12

JANIS JOPLIN
And Her Group
GRATEFUL DEAD

FRIDAY & SATURDAY, FEB. 14 & 15

JEFF BECK GROUP
WINTER

FRIDAY & SATURDAY, FEB. 21 & 22

MOTHERS OF INVENTION
CHICAGO TRANSIT AUTHORITY

FRI., FEB. 28 & SAT., MAR. 1

TEN YEARS AFTER
JOHN MAYALL

AND AT EVERY SHOW

JOSHUA LIGHT SHOW

FILLMORE EAST
SECOND AVENUE AT SIXTH STREET

somebody from the band Chicago, who shared a bill with Tull at the Boston Tea Party, and when Clive Bunker did his solo, *everybody* was paying attention.

BRADLEY CONVISER

In 1968 I went to the Fillmore East to see Blood, Sweat and Tears. The backup band was Jethro Tull, who had just got off the plane, so this was the first time they performed in America. Blood, Sweat and Tears performed, then the audience called back Jethro Tull, who tore the house down. The second show was so late, people were banging on the doors and protesting on the streets, and the police came to break up a riot for the second performance because it was two hours late.

GRANDE BALLROOM

1 FEBRUARY 1969, DETROIT, MICHIGAN

ROBERT BURWELL

I saw Jethro Tull at the Grande Ballroom the first time they appeared in the US. They were second-billed, but I knew within a heartbeat they would be the 'next big thing'. I think the top-billed act that night was Spirit. I saw them later at Olympia Stadium, where I saw The Beatles years earlier. By that time, they were top of the bill and Jeffrey Hammond had rejoined. He was quite animated. Ian Anderson made a point of introducing Jeffrey to the audience.

BOSTON TEA PARTY

13 FEBRUARY 1969, BOSTON, MASSACHUSETTS

LOYD GROSSMAN, AUTHOR & BROADCASTER

Growing up in coastal New England in the Sixties, our counter-cultural lifeline to the larger world was provided by a couple of Boston-based radio stations. First and foremost, WILD, the radio station of Boston's black community. I owe my enduring love of James Brown, Dyke and the Blazers, Rufus Thomas et al to hours spent in the virtual company of their great DJ, Wild Man Steve. But my principal game-changer was another DJ, the smoothly cosmopolitan Dick Summer of WBZ. Of the two mainstream Boston radio stations, WMEX was much the most progressive, but every Sunday night, boring old WBZ presented *Dick Summer's Subway.*

Dick had two obsessions. First, he was an enthusiastic promoter of a musical dead-end known as the Boston Sound, meant to rival the music coming out of San Francisco. Sadly, The Ultimate Spinach, Boston's greatest local band at the time, were never going to dethrone the Jefferson Airplane. Summer's other obsession was British rock. And it was on his show that I first heard Led Zeppelin, The Nice and, crucially, Jethro Tull when the station broadcast on successive Sundays, 'Living in the Past' and 'Dharma for One'.

As someone who had only ever heard 5/4 time played by Dave Brubeck, I was instantly hooked by the Tull's audacity. Of course, the flute was cool too, at a time when some bands were seeking to get away from the tyranny of lead guitar. Remember David Laflamme's violin and his band, It's a Beautiful Day?

But back to Tull. Some weeks later, an expensively airmailed copy of *This Was* arrived from Harrod's Phonographic Department (where I had a standing order for Who records). Most exciting of all was Tull's gig at the Boston Tea Party in 1969. The Tea Party was a frequent first stop for British bands breaking in the States. I saw Fleetwood Mac, Led Zeppelin, Brian Auger and many others there. At that stage I was a Tea Party regular and writing for *Fusion*, Boston's 'underground' music magazine. I first saw Tull there on 13th February 1969, and also on the 14th and the 15th. I've been devoted ever since.

Fast forward 46 years and I stepped on stage with Jethro Tull to play guitar at one of Ian Anderson's annual series of Christmas concerts to benefit English cathedrals. As the Grateful Dead said, 'What a long, strange trip it's been.' Six years of concerts later – we skipped 2020 thanks to the pandemic – I'm still part of the lineup.

IAN ANDERSON

That first American tour was not an entirely agreeable experience. Coming back from the USA in the summer of '69 and beginning to write the songs for the *Benefit* album, I was a bit jaded. I felt alienated from American society, having travelled right across America to different states. I didn't find culturally that it was an experience I really enjoyed. I wanted to get home.

And at that point we were also building a bit of a reputation in other European countries, which I find much more interesting. The culture and language and historical significance of the countries we were playing in in Europe were for me an easier mix. I guess I just felt more European and did not fall under the spell of Americana, which clearly attracted many British bands even before they went. To be big in America was the absolute pinnacle of everybody's dreams, including Cliff Richard – who never was.

The interesting reality is that the bands who made it big in America back then didn't give a shit. First of all, Cream. They barnstormed across the USA. They didn't give a shit whether the Americans liked or loathed them. They went on stage and did their show, and didn't seek approval. Same thing with Zeppelin. They were a bunch of Viking raiders, pillaging and plundering. They didn't care what people thought. They just went on and did their show as if they were doing it for them.

And Jethro Tull probably gave the appearance of not being there to please the audience and ingratiate ourselves, but there were other acts that did that. Maybe it was just too obvious to an American audience that this was bringing coals to Newcastle, in the sense of copying American music and trying to be successful within the American musical and cultural range.

Yes did very well. They supported Jethro Tull in 1970 or '71. They had a hit single and were becoming very popular in the USA. They gave us a run for our money in terms of being a powerful opening act, and it was another example of British music that didn't really owe very much to what was happening in America at the time.

FREE TRADE HALL

6 MAY 1969, MANCHESTER, UK

TONY MICHAELIDES

The band had in 1968 released *This Was*, which I totally loved, so when it was announced they would be playing in Manchester around the release of *Stand Up* the following year there was no way I was going to miss that. My friend Ken and I turned up at the concert hall before the place even opened and to say we were excited would be an understatement. It was my first 'proper' gig, as before then I'd only seen a few smaller acts playing in clubs. There were supposed to be two other acts that night, Ten Years After and Clouds, although Ten Years After cancelled at the last minute. I think you always fondly remember your first show for all the sentimental reasons ... it's your first show! But I do remember this was something extra special because it wasn't just a progressive rock band, as they called them back in the day, shaking their heads and rocking out.

Ian Anderson was almost demonic, a front man in every sense of the word. He stood at the front of the stage, perched like a flamingo on one leg, gently stroking his beard. At the same time he was peering out at the crowd, almost leering at us. We were seated right at the front so could see it all. As well as being the lead vocalist, he also played the flute and it's important to add his flamingo stance was whilst he was playing the flute and not when he was singing.

Tony 'The Greek' Michaelides, DJ, PR exec and podcaster, in more hirsute days, around the time he first saw Jethro Tull

ROYAL ALBERT HALL

8 MAY 1969, LONDON, UK

STEVE ELPHICK

A little under three weeks before my 15th birthday, I went to my very first gig - not in a local pub or club as you might expect, but the grandiose setting of the Royal Albert Hall in London. Clearly my parents had no qualms about their 14-year-old son travelling, with a mate or two, up to 'the big Smoke' from deepest south London. This was probably because I'd previously done this on an almost daily basis, as I'd been going to school near Tower Bridge for a few years beforehand.

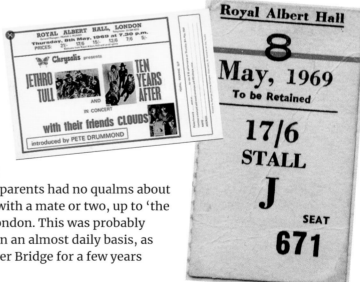

My ticket, at the princely sum of 17/6, got me a seat in row J of the stalls with, as most seats at the venue have, a great view of the stage. Using my hard-earned wages from a Saturday job, I'd previously bought Tull's first LP, *This Was*, which I really liked, and had heard great reports of how exciting and different their stage performances were, so I was very keen to catch them in concert.

They'd recently returned from a fairly extensive tour of the States (from January to April) so they were well honed at giving a great live presentation - which they did. There had been one personnel change since the *This Was* album came out, with Martin Barre coming in to replace Mick Abrahams, which, for me, gave the band a far more 'rocky' feel. They premiered many tracks from their yet-to-be-released next LP, *Stand Up*.

As a first concert it was pretty mind-blowing, particularly as we also had Ten Years After joint-headlining. This was just a few months before TYA's famous Woodstock appearance and consequently their setlist here was virtually the same. I still have the programme that night, plus the one when I saw Tull again at the Royal Albert Hall that October, supported by Savoy Brown and Terry Reid.

I also caught them at the Empire Pool, Wembley, when they were supported by Robin Trower in June 1973, rescheduled from a postponed gig on 29th April that year, and finally at the BBC Hippodrome studios in Golders Green, London in February 1977 for the recording of the *Sight & Sound - In Concert* TV show, broadcast on the 19th of that month.

REDCAR JAZZ CLUB

11 MAY 1969, REDCAR, UK

BRIAN SMITH

Jethro Tull were rebooked to appear on 11 May 1969 and again it was a sell-out on pre-ticket sales. Before taking the stage, the group arrived at the club via an open-topped vehicle, doing a performance for the watching crowd along the seafront during the evening sunset. Because it was a sell-out concert the crowd waiting for admission circled the perimeter of the club, all facing the seafront.

The stage performance was something very special. Ian Anderson produced stage eccentricities, comprising of different postures and poses which looked like those of a demented tramp. The group produced a combination of riffy little songs, strong on melody and heavy on wit, a move away from their earlier blues renderings. During the performance, Ian declared that the name Jethro Tull was taken from the 18th century English agriculturalist.

They performed their hot single, 'Living in the Past', which was actually at No.3 in the charts at the time, combined with numbers from the top albums, *This Was* and *Stand Up*. We tried to rebook the group later, but they were keen to exploit their popularity in the USA. It was ironic that the following club session was to front Blodwyn Pig and Free.

NATIONAL STADIUM

28 MAY 1969, DUBLIN, IRELAND

LEO O'KELLY, TÍR NA NÓG

I first saw Jethro Tull in the National Stadium, Dublin, in May 1969, shortly after I moved there. I little knew that the following year, Tír na nÓg, which hadn't even yet been conceived, would be on tour with them on the first of three UK and European tours - *Benefit*, *Aqualung* and *Thick as a Brick*. The Dublin show is still memorable for me. I especially remember 'Bouree' for the flute and the bass, and 'Fat Man' with Ian sitting and playing mandolin. Clouds played support, and their version of 'Big Noise from Winnetka' was remarkable for the drummer playing a solo with his sticks on the bass guitar.

So I have many 'first' memories. *Thick as a Brick* was particularly memorable, as they created new realms of theatricality and brought the concept album to levels previously unheard of. Even Sonny's brother, John, was recruited, dressed as a jockey, to 'remove his horse from the foyer'! The memories are all fond ones, musically and personally, and I never missed watching them any of the 50 shows we played with them. A real privilege to have experienced it all, first-hand.

ULSTER HALL

29 MAY 1969, BELFAST, UK

JACKIE BOYCE

I first saw the group in the Ulster Hall in Belfast. As the group appeared on stage, someone fired a catapult at Ian, hitting him. He rightly stood firm and demanded the person be removed or the performance would not continue. The friends of the guy who fired the shot gave him up to the bouncers, who not only removed him but gave him 'a sore head' (and other sore parts of the body) before kicking him out onto the street.

Years later, I was working for the Prudential Assurance Company and called on a customer on the outskirts of Ballygowan, Co. Down, Northern Ireland. As I drove in the gates of the drive of the house, a jeep was driving out. I stopped and reversed, only to find the jeep had done the same thing. Moving forward to enter the drive, the jeep moved forward also. This happened a couple of times. The jeep then reversed and parked. A man jumped out of the passenger side of the jeep and ran back into the house. He had forgotten a briefcase. I got out of the car and went to thank the driver. I recognised him from somewhere in the past. I got talking to him and said I knew him from somewhere. I asked if it was through music, and did he play folk or traditional music? He said, 'Well, sort of, I suppose.' The passenger returned and I said I knew him from somewhere also. They had a bit of a laugh at it but didn't say who they were.

As they drove off, the customer I had called to see said, 'Well, did you recognise them?' His daughter was standing beside him on crutches. I told him I knew them from way back but couldn't think where from. He said, 'Try *Top of the Pops*.' I immediately said 'Jethro Tull.'

His daughter got on the phone and asked whether, if they were not in a hurry, could they return? It turned out that the daughter ran Ian's fish farm, and organised dates or tours. She had slipped and broken her leg and they brought her over from Scotland and back to her father's house. She asked Ian to send a signed photo to me for my niece, who was a dedicated fan. A week later the photo duly arrived, signed and with a lovely note attached. One month later, Jethro Tull were back playing the Ulster Hall and my niece and I went to hear them. That made it all special. The thing that struck me was that they didn't have airs and graces or act like pop stars. They were down-to-earth guys, polite and with a devilish sense of humour.

BAY HOTEL

13 JUNE 1969, SUNDERLAND, UK

DAVID SNAITH

Tull and the Sunderland football team have been the story of my life. They have been a thread throughout my life. I've seen virtually all the concerts they have played in the north-east since '69. And I've travelled around Edinburgh, Manchester and Hull and various other places watching the band.

I was introduced to Tull in the lower sixth in 1968. I was in my late teens, at the age when people become more interested in serious music. I went there from *Sgt. Pepper's*. There was more than a minority interest in bands such as Cream, Family, Jethro Tull and Free. This was the beginning of progressive rock and blues rock, with bands such as Led Zeppelin. Anyone who had money in the sixth form would buy LPs and would share them around. Those of us that didn't have any money - such as myself - borrowed other people's albums. Tull were massive in the sixth form.

The Tull album which changed my view on music was *This Was*. I'd never come across anything like this before. I borrowed it and played it non-stop, and I managed to record it reel-to-reel. Tull vied for top-notch amongst the sixth formers with Free, who became massive in the north-east way before they became massive in the rest of the country. It was like Beatlemania with Free. They just absolutely took off for some reason. They even recorded their live album in Sunderland.

My first viewing of Tull was in June 1969. There was a venue called the Bay Hotel, the equivalent of the Marquee for the north-east. The bands that played there would be playing arenas these days. Jeff Doherty talks about the Tull concert that I saw in his book, *A Promoter's Tale*. About 75% of his recollection is correct. The place held about 800 people. We've been to see Family, Pink Floyd and Free there. When we arrived on the Friday night to see Tull, there was a queue which snaked around the whole building. We thought we'd never get in. There were about 1,500 people there that night. We got in and I remember standing there and being unable to move.

The way the building worked, the band's dressing rooms were the other side of the room to the stage. Normally bands would just walk through the dancefloor to get to the stage, but Tull couldn't do that. They had to walk through the car park. It was a fireman's nightmare. The glass double-doors were boarded and they had chains around them. If anything had happened that night, there would have been carnage. But they eventually got to the stage and the atmosphere was absolutely fantastic.

It was in the old days when bands used to tune up on stage. We were perhaps 10 yards off the front of the stage. I remember the band were tuning up and Anderson had his back to the crowd. There was chatter amongst the crowd and Anderson turned around and went 'shush!' The crowd went silent, and you could hear a pin drop. I just thought 'this man's got something.' He wasn't being bad mannered because people were making too much noise. It was, 'Shush, we're about to start now.'

It was fantastic when they were on. The upside was the sound, the occasion and the atmosphere. The downside was they only did about 40 minutes. Some of that included a drum solo on 'Dhama for One' and a bass solo on 'A New Day'. I remember five of the six songs they played. The idea was that they would come back for an encore, but they couldn't get back on because of the crowd.

The band were staying in a hotel a couple of miles further along called the Seaburn Hotel, and Anderson apparently asked if he could have his meals in his room because the residents of the hotel were frightened by the look of him.

What's the attraction for me? It's got to be the quality and the variety of the music and the intelligence of the lyrics. I like Anderson's observations of life. His songs aren't just love songs. There are certain themes which strike a chord. A critical point in my life was in my late teens when *Aqualung* came out. You start to question things in your teens. I couldn't understand what relevance organised religion had, when I saw people going to church on a Sunday and praying and then leading the same kind of lifestyle they always led for the rest of the week. They go to church and get forgiveness and then carry on as normal, doing what they were doing.

'Wind Up' is an example of Anderson's ability with a catchphrase. Or 'The Dog-Ear Years', which sums up exactly the feeling of getting old. Throughout his whole career you've got songs and phrases which make you think about issues in life. He is not necessarily preaching, but he's making observations. It might be something I was already thinking about, but I wasn't able to articulate it in exactly the same way as he does. It's a combination of brilliant music, great melodies, thoughtful lyrics and fantastic live performances.

STAND UP

RELEASED 25 JULY 1969 (EUROPE)/29 SEPTEMBER 1969 (Rest of World)

UK CHART POSITION 1

US CHART POSITION 20

ALEX VUICH

Alex Vuich and friend

I was learning how to play the harmonica in my youth. My dad was very encouraging. One day he gave me a CD of *Stand Up* by Jethro Tull so I could learn 'A New Day Yesterday', but little did he know that he would be kickstarting my longstanding love for Jethro Tull. For that, I am forever grateful. If I had to name a favourite Tull album, it would likely be a tie between *Benefit* and *Stand Up*. Both albums resonate with me personally, and I just think it's the band on top form. Ian's writing has always been influential to me as a person and a musician, and those albums are a few of my desert island favourites. I want to say thank you to Jethro Tull for the wide variety of music they have produced throughout their career. Everything from *This Was* to their *Christmas Album* is a gem.

BOB FENHAGEN

Tull were the epitome of what a band should be, an energetic, flamboyant yet gently human frontman backed by skilled, dedicated craftsmen on their musical instruments, enhancing and complementing excellent music, playing loudly but softly when needed.

ERLING PEDERSEN

Erling Pedersen's band was inspired by the album Stand Up

I have been a great fan since the album *Stand Up*, and have loved to see how the musical style of the band has developed during the last 30 to 40 years. My band at that time made an album called *Tales from a Misty Forest* that was greatly influenced by Tull.

STEVEN SHEPARD

In 1974 I was living in San Antonio, Texas and had no idea where or what kind of music to buy. I ordered a dual record album set from Warner Brothers Records that contained demo collections of songs recorded and offered by Warner Brothers' recording artists. One of the songs on that set was Jethro Tull's 'Nothing is Easy'. I heard the tune once and was hooked. I eventually bought the album *Stand Up* and have owned that album in three different mediums (vinyl, cassette and CD). At one time I could play every flute solo from the album. My last copy was a Costco purchase with extra songs on the CD. I enjoyed and loved that CD very much until some clod stepped on it and ruined it. I have been without my own copy of Jethro Tull anything since then. I've been enjoying them on YouTube, but it's not the same.

KEITH GALL

As a 13-year-old kid with a love for music and aspirations to become a rocker, I walked into high school for the first time in 1977. Music Appreciation was a class we all took at our small conservative Catholic school, and I didn't have much enthusiasm for the class. Then I met Mrs. Hull. This wasn't some young teacher who could relate to a group of zit-faced kids. Mrs Hull was a grandmother, and you can imagine the eye-rolling of a group of uniform-wearing punks, forced to listen to her 'granny tunes' for 40 minutes several times a week. She broke out the portable record player and began telling us of the array of music she planned to expose us to.

She rattled off some names I couldn't possibly remember, but then said, 'And my personal favourite, Jethro Tull,' before dropping the needle on my first conscious listen to a Tull tune, 'Bourée'. She won the class over that day, and every day thereafter. Although she was old, her spirit was young.

Some 45 years later I've had a lifetime of Jethro Tull, with me and many of my friends becoming hardcore fans, seeing concerts and even having our own band, where we did decent (in my opinion) renditions of 'Aqualung' and 'Locomotive Breath'.

Jethro Tull returned to North America for their second tour in June 1969.

IAN ANDERSON

During our second North American tour in the summer of '69, we supported Led Zeppelin on some shows, and during the next couple of years we again appeared as an opening act with Led Zeppelin. It was a good opportunity to see a band that was a year ahead of us in terms of building a reputation in the USA. You couldn't watch Led Zeppelin and not pick up some useful tips. The most useful tip I picked up was don't try to be Robert Plant. I didn't look like him, I didn't do that kind of strutting cock-rock vocalist thing and there's no way I could have sung anything remotely within his range. Robert Plant was in a very unique stratosphere of his own when it came to his vocals.

Led Zeppelin really knew how to create excitement with a dynamic range and the impetus they got from quiet passages suddenly becoming symphonic loud. I watched them a few times, not from the wings but from somewhere in the venue, and it was always an illustrative experience to see how they worked. It didn't always go well. Zeppelin had bad nights, the same as Jimi Hendrix had terrible nights. They weren't all great shows. And you learn what it is that went wrong and how it affected the band and how they responded to the difficulties, whether they were technical or being upset with something musically, or the audience or whatever. It was interesting and educational to see how things could go wrong even for great talents. You would expect every night would be a winner, but it wasn't always like that.

We didn't have so many bad nights. Our nights were more even in terms of performance and what happened. Perhaps that's because we were dull and not so interesting. I just tried to create a standard that was achievable and to then replicate that from night to night at different venues in different parts of the USA.

SCHAEFER MUSIC FESTIVAL CENTRAL PARK

28 JULY 1969 NEW YORK, NEW YORK

RON DELSENER, PROMOTER

Back in the mid-Sixties and early-Seventies, Ian Anderson and Jethro Tull played a concert in Central Park in the middle of Manhattan, at an outdoor ice skating rink which I converted into an 8,000-seat capacity summertime venue. Ian dressed like someone out of a medieval forest, standing on one foot with his flute, his long hair flowing, seemingly menacing the crowd to challenge him. He would prance around the stage, stopping occasionally to pose on one leg. He was (and is) a truly unique performer.

Jethro Tull were so popular that they performed at Shea Stadium, a baseball stadium used by the New York Mets, and sold it out. Howard Stein was the promoter, Frank Barsalona the agent and Dee Anthony the manager. It was rumoured that some other gentlemen had a big piece of the show as these men were friends of Howard Stein and his dad, Ruby.

Later on, when I got to know Ian, and I was able to approach him without him 'putting a spell on me', I found him to be a gentle person with a lovely wife. He became a cultivator of salmon as a sideline, which became a huge project for him. I enjoyed working with him, year after year, in such venues as the Jones Beach Amphitheater on Long Island, New York, the Beacon Theater in Manhattan, and of course in Central Park. He is a classy Renaissance gentleman with a medieval flair, and one of the greatest unique talents that ever existed.

ANAHEIM CONVENTION CENTER

9 AUGUST 1969, LOS ANGELES, CALIFORNIA

KEN KNOTTS

I loved going to Jethro Tull concerts. I saw them four times. The first time was in 1969, when Led Zeppelin played with them at the Anaheim Convention Center. I walked to that show because I was too young to have a driver's license, and I lived just two blocks away from the arena. I got my first Jethro Tull album as a birthday gift. At the time, I thought it quite odd that a flute was being used in a rock band.

WOODSTOCK MUSIC AND ART FAIR

15 – 18 AUGUST 1969, WOODSTOCK, NEW YORK

CHRIS WRIGHT

It took them a while in America. They weren't like an overnight sensation there. A lot of hard graft went into making them big in America, and a lot of good records as well. They didn't perform at Woodstock, which was a defining moment for a lot of people that did perform there. It was a bit too early for them, but soon after that, in '70 and '71, they began to establish themselves. I was pretty pre-occupied with Ten Years After, and Terry was the one that had organised taking them into the studio. He was much more hands-on, and it was he who basically developed their career.

TOWN HALL

7 OCTOBER 1969, LEEDS, UK

TIM SULLIVAN

The support acts were Terry Reid and Savoy Brown, who both played good but not exceptional sets. I have two memories of Jethro Tull. At that time, I thought the only people who actually enjoyed a drum solo were the band themselves; the drummer as it put him in the spotlight - and the rest of the band as they could go off and have a drink. However, at this concert the crowd were really into the drum solo. I believe it was called 'Dharma for One', and people enjoyed it. And Ian Anderson, who used to make quips about the band, said to Martin Barre, 'What have you done with your hair?'

GUILDHALL

20 OCTOBER 1969, SOUTHAMPTON, UK

MARTIN WEBB

'So when did you first see Jethro Tull?' is a question I have been asked many times in the last 50-plus years. Well, it depends what you mean by 'see'. Pedantically speaking, the first time I ever clapped eyes on them was looking at the cover of *This Was*, which I borrowed from a school friend's sister in early 1969. I was intrigued by this strange hybrid of blues–jazz–rock, although after the first few plays, I still wasn't quite

GUILDHALL — SOUTHAMPTON
Monday, 20th October, 1969, at 7.30

Chrysalis Presents

JETHRO TULL in CONCERT

The Concert is timed to finish at **10.30**

STALLS 7/6

ROW **EE** SEAT N°. 29

South Coast Printers Ltd., Totton, Hants

Martin Webb first saw Jethro Tull perform live in 1969

sure what to make of it, flute'n'all. John Mayall, it wasn't. Nevertheless, I returned her LP and bought my own copy, and after persevering - because its uniqueness seemed to demand such effort - the penny dropped, and I was duly smitten.

I next saw a couple of small photos of Tull in music papers such as *Melody Maker* and *New Musical Express*, which indicated that they weren't actually old men, but were a bunch of hairy oddballs, with a new guitarist. And the first time I saw them perform was in June 1969, in the comfort of my own home in front of a small black and white TV, as they mimed to 'Living in the Past' on Britain's premier chart show, the BBC's *Top of the Pops.*

Little could I have imagined that 18 years later I would be writing the foreword to the 1987 *Crest of a Knave* tour programme. Here's how I described my life-changing reaction:

'Our fledgling fan waited anxiously in front of the TV for *Top of the Pops* to see what this group Jethro Tull actually looked like. The shock was nearly as great as hearing the music for the first time. Filling the screen was this scruffy, bug-eyed, grimacing and above all hairy creature who was the very antithesis of what a pop star should look like. To the adolescent inmate of an old-fashioned grammar school where short hair, smartness and uniformity were the law, the revulsion expressed by his mother was confirmation that this was what he had been seeking. Not only was the music stunningly original and invigorating, but the weirdo playing it was a dangerous threat to the nation's morals. The picture was complete — the image matched the music, and one impressionable teenager was mightily impressed.'

My Jethro Tull initiation was complete when I saw them in concert for the first time on 20 October 1969 at Southampton Guildhall, on what was effectively the *Stand Up* tour. I was 15 and totally entranced by every aspect of them – the music, the image, the frenetic performances, the whole package. So began a journey which has taken in between 300 and 400 live shows (I lost count long ago) in 25 different countries so far, and which continues today. Not so much living in the past, as loving the present and looking forward to the future.

MIKE ROBERTS

We didn't have tickets but me, my older brother Geoff and his friend Ian drove from Portsmouth in appalling weather – a real peasouper – to Southampton with the hope of buying some at the venue. When we got to the ticket box office, we were told it was sold out, but being determined to see if we could get in, we hovered around the doors to the auditorium and sneaked in to stand at the back. We tried to merge in with the audience and not look out of place, but it didn't work and an official came up and asked what we were doing. We explained that we didn't have tickets but had driven a long way to get there and asked if we could please just stand at the back and watch the gig? He was a great chap, said 'OK' and walked off.

Just before the concert was due to start, we were accosted by a different official. 'You can't stand there,' he said. 'Fire hazard. Look, there are empty seats down there,' he said, pointing at the seats, 'go and sit there.' We thanked him and did as we were told. A marvellous evening was had by all three of us, but I must admit I felt sad for those three people who had seats but obviously couldn't make the concert due to the bad weather. This concert is still very fresh in my mind, especially Clive Bunker's drum solo on 'Dharma for One', which I believe he did later at the Isle of Wight Festival, and of course Ian's 'Fat Man'. Geoff is sadly no longer with us. It is he who brought home the album *This Was*, which started us off as lifelong fans.

FILLMORE EAST

5 & 6 DECEMBER 1969, NEW YORK, NEW YORK

JESSE SWEETMAN

I grew up listening to Jimi Hendrix, The Moody Blues, the Rolling Stones and other assorted rock bands, but I always had a special place in my LP collection for Jethro Tull. Ian Anderson, in particular, fascinated me. It was like watching a crane standing on one leg, playing the flute. In 1969 I attended Jethro Tull, Fat Mattress and Grand Funk Railroad at the Fillmore East. I hadn't heard the Grand Funk Railroad album until that very day, and their opening act blew me away.

There are so many incredible Jethro Tull songs, but the one I love more than any other is 'Look into the Sun'. I've tried to play and sing it for years, and will always cherish the beautiful music of Jethro Tull.

ANDY SZEGO

It's late February or early March 1969 and I'm in the record section of Alexander's department store in Queens, New York when I hear this great music playing, which is unlike anything I'm used to. After hearing nearly the whole album, I ask the guy, 'Who is this?', and he says, 'Jethro Tull, a new group from England.'

I bought the album on the spot and listened daily for months until *Stand Up* came out and then – repeat. Fast forward to December and I got tickets for Tull at the Fillmore East. Opening was Fat Mattress, with Noel Redding, and then Grand Funk Railroad, another new group that formed earlier that year. It was a great show so far and then out came Jethro Tull, playing the best concert I'd seen up until then - and possibly ever. It was an exciting show with an excellent sound, and they were playing *This Was* and *Stand Up* in equal parts. I was a big fan, from then to now.

ROBERT URBAN

I was a huge Ian Anderson and Tull fan from the beginning. I can recall as an adolescent teen hearing songs from *This Was* and even the single 'Love Story' on NEW-FM radio in the late Sixties. For both the *Stand Up* tour in late 1969 and the *Benefit* tour in the spring of 1970, my friends and I took the train in from Connecticut to New York City to see Tull live at the Fillmore East. I consider it one of the great formative experiences of my life.

In 1970, we performed 'My Sunday Feeling' in the sophomore year talent show at Central Catholic High School in Norwalk, Connecticut and won first prize. At other talent shows in high school, I also performed 'Fat Man' and 'Bouree'. And in my very first rock band later in 1970, we covered 'Nothing is Easy', which helped us become a winner in the 1970 Jaycee Connecticut Statewide Battle of the Bands.

Thanks to Ian, when I went on to college I became a music major, with flute as my primary instrument. In the mid-Seventies, I won the University Concerto Competition, and as a result performed the Quantz Flute Concerto in G with the Bridgeport Symphony. Eventually, guitar became my main instrument, but I still love the flute, and continue to perform with it.

I never got to meet Ian Anderson - but this at least gives me a chance to say thank you.

Robert Urban went on to study flute thanks to Ian

Jake Quinn was 17 years old and ecstatic at seeing Jethro Tull

UNIVERSITY OF MASSACHUSETTS

7 DECEMBER 1969, AMHERST, MASSACHUSETTS

JAKE QUINN

My friend John Porter returned to school in September 1969 with some albums he'd got when he was in England that summer, including Jethro Tull's *Stand Up* and The Who's *Tommy*. I loved those records and listened to them so much that I had them memorized. Then on December 7 that year I got to see my first honest-to-God rock concert at The Cage at UMass, the show that made me a concert fan for life.

I had been to parties and dances with live bands, and there were bands that performed on stage at the high school, but this was a real rock concert. I didn't know anything about the two opening acts, Spooky Tooth and Johnny Winter, but I was dying to see the headliner, Jethro Tull. Porter and I were way off to the side during Spooky Tooth, but started inching our way toward a better vantage point, and when the set ended we got in better position for Johnny Winter. Winter was wild, and I liked him better than Spooky Tooth, but neither was close to what I wanted to hear and had come for. After Winter's set, we saw an opportunity to move again and ended up dead-centre on the risers in front of the stage, with an unobstructed view. Just what we wanted. And Tull did not disappoint, with spectacular performances of most everything from *Stand Up* and more that filled me with an ecstasy my 17-year-old self hadn't experienced before.

I thought I knew every song on *Stand Up* inside and out, but their live performance was a wonderful revelation. I was so elated that I thought my face might break from smiling so hard. It was simply incredible. I have seen hundreds of live music performances since, chasing that ecstasy and treasuring it every time I feel its glow. But Jethro Tull was my first and they got me hooked for life. To Glenn, Clive, Martin and Ian, my deepest thanks.

MEMORIAL HALL

10 DECEMBER 1969, KANSAS CITY, KANSAS
DANIEL EDWARD SMITH

This is one of my all-time favourite concerts. Jethro Tull were virtually unknown then, but they walked away with a rabid fan base in Kansas City. Joe Cocker and Fleetwood Mac were also on the bill, proof that, post-British Invasion, England was still delivering iconic acts to America.

It was a dark and stormy night (well, there was drizzle). The weather was bad enough to affect ticket sales. In fact, concert promoter Michael Waggoner later said, 'It was an amazing evening, even though it lost money.' I remember an announcement from the stage inviting everyone in the cheap seats to come on down and fill the main floor, making the event more intimate.

Daniel Edward Smith was in KC for a British triple header. Poster: Greg Leech

Woodstock was just a few months before this concert and years before the movie that showed Joe Cocker's famous performance there, so his gyrations on stage were a new experience. Fleetwood Mac, long before the pop supergroup lineup known to most people since the mid-1970s, was still an all-male and purely British rock/blues band with serious chops.

After a solid set by Fleetwood Mac, and before Joe Cocker delivered a rousing performance, the MC introduced Jethro Tull, and everyone was mesmerised by Ian Anderson spending half of the band's set on one foot. Who knew that a flute could rock the house? It was one for the books.

BENEFIT

RELEASED 20 APRIL 1970

UK CHART POSITION 3

US CHART POSITION 11

GORDON STEADWOOD

My first encounter was when I got stuck in Glasgow due to lots of snow in 1987. I crashed at a friend's flat, with his extensive record collection. The first album he played me was *Benefit*. I was hooked. My favourite track was (and is) 'Sossity; You're A Woman'. As an encore he put *Thick as a Brick* on and gave me the sleeve, complete with newspaper to read. They've produced such a variety of incredible music over all the years, in different styles.

SANTA BARBARA BOWL

22 APRIL 1970, SANTA BARBARA, CALIFORNIA

CLIVE BUNKER

I think it was on the third tour that we did a theatre where we were top of the bill and Led Zeppelin were billed as support. They had taken off really, really fast, so I went into their dressing room and said to John Bonham, 'Look, we're top of the bill, but why don't you go on last, because you're more popular than us now.' Bonham went and had a chat with the others and I could hear them laughing, so I thought, 'Here we go.' They were really good fun, that mob. But Bonzo came back and said, 'Nah, let's leave it as it is,' laughing his head off. I thought, 'Oops.'

I went back to Ian and everyone and said, 'They want to leave it where we're top of the bill.' And we said, 'Okay we'll just be stupid about it all. We'll go for it.' The Zeps went on and went down unbelievably well. Then we went on, and it was amazing. The audience went berserk. When we finished the gig, I went into their dressing room and said to John Bonham, 'Thanks for warming them up for us.'

FILLMORE WEST

30 APRIL – 2 MAY 1970, SAN FRANCISCO, CALIFORNIA

DAVE PEGG, MUSICIAN

I'd only seen Jethro Tull three times before I was in the band. In 1970 Fairport supported them for three nights at the Fillmore West in San Francisco. I remember all the bands on the bill - Jethro Tull, Fairport Convention, Salt 'n Pepper, and Clouds - because I've got the poster framed and hanging up in my house in Brittany. The poster's worth about 1500 quid.

They only did three of the four nights they were supposed to be headlining, because they had a bigger gig somewhere else on the last of the four nights. The lineup was Glenn and Clive as the rhythm section and Martin, Ian, and John Evans.

It was Fairport's first American tour, and I was the new boy, having only joined the band that year. I can't remember any of the songs Tull played, but I do remember the first day. We got to the Fillmore West, a big ballroom or theatre where they'd taken all the seats out. It was a flat floor and during our soundcheck the Jethro Tull boys and their crew were playing football, kicking the ball around in the venue. Some of them had shorts on, with all the outfit and everything. I don't think I got to meet any of the guys. The Fillmore would have four acts on, so you didn't get much time to socialise, but I remember thinking how professional they were compared to the Fairports. Our approach was fairly shambolic.

DAVID SANFILIPPO

I was in college in San Jose, California in 1969, listening to KSAN out of San Francisco while doing homework. KSAN was known for playing progressive rock and deep cuts from albums. It was probably October or November when I first heard them play 'Look into the Sun'. I felt like the music was pulling me up from my chair and I just stood in front of the speakers. I bought *Stand Up* and fell in love with the guitar work on 'Back to the Family', and have been a Martin Barre fan from that day. I still play 'We Used to Know' as part of my very personal performance setlist.

In April 1970, a friend came over with his new copy of *Benefit*. While it was playing, he kept talking, but I was only able to concentrate on the songs that were playing. Halfway through 'Play in Time', the second to the last song on the American album, I stopped the music and told my friend I had to go right then and get my own copy. No music had hit me like that since *Revolver* and *Sgt Pepper*.

In May 1970 at the Fillmore West, I was there when Fairport Convention did a set and then Jethro Tull opened with 'Nothing is Easy'. In the Bay area, we were lucky to be able to see all sorts of live groups from San Francisco, Los Angeles and England, so we considered ourselves pretty sophisticated music lovers of the time. However, this concert blew us the hell away. After 'Nothing is Easy', I turned to my friend and just said 'whoa', with my eyes as wide as they could go. The second song was 'My God', which no one had heard before, of course, so I was not expecting Martin Barre to come in on the second verse with those two perfect notes and then the rest of the hook. His guitar was loud and crystal clear. I swear to you that I can still hear him playing it in my head when I think about that concert. 'With You There to Help Me' was in the set and has always been a personal favourite, so I was surprised when Ian introduced 'Sossity' as 'probably the best' song on the album.

Over the years I've seen Jethro Tull a couple of times in the Bay area, and a couple of times in Atlanta after moving here. The last time I saw them was at The Tabernacle in Atlanta, a church now converted into a great music venue, with my two grown sons (both Tull fans, of course). While talking to them in the lobby before the show, I noticed a guy 'wearing shabby clothes', sprawled on the steps at the entrance. I turned to say something to my sons and then immediately turned back, wondering if Ian was playing a prank and scoping out the audience. He was nowhere to be found, so I don't know if it was Ian or some crazed fan who was dressed as Aqualung, but it doesn't matter. It's a great memory of another concert where Martin played so expertly, he could bring tears to your eyes.

TUCSON SPORTS CENTER

7 MAY 1970, TUCSON , ARIZONA

MARK LOPEZ, AGE 14

I was excited about seeing one of my favourite up-and-coming bands, Jethro Tull. I had somehow acquired their latest album, *Benefit*, and was digging it. I knew they were coming to Tucson and was really stoked about seeing them live. It was one of the best shows I've ever seen, next to Led Zeppelin. It was a great time that I will take to my grave.

SELBY STADIUM

28 MAY 1970, OHIO WESLEYAN UNIVERSITY, DELAWARE, OHIO

PHROGGE KOEHLER

I studied at Ohio State University, which I called the School of Revolution. I saw Jethro Tull not long after the Kent State Massacre. There were 3,000 national guardsmen and 1,500 spectators. For the first song, as they were getting settled in, Ian Anderson walked to the microphone and politely said, "Something I'm working on," and on one leg began to play 'Bouree'. Wow!

ARAGON BALLROOM

5 JUNE 1970, CHICAGO, ILLINOIS

LINCOLN ZIMMANCK

I had a sound company, Euphoria Blimpworks, in Chicago and we were providing the sound system at the Aragon Ballroom when Jethro Tull was on the bill. A mutual friend came to the show with her friend, Sandra. I was mixing sound, so couldn't talk to her much, but we eventually met, fell in love, and moved to California. We married, are still happily together, and thank our friend and Jethro Tull for our happiness. We also visited Chicago in 2015 and stopped by the Aragon Ballroom, and the manager was kind enough to let us in before the show. It was very emotional; we told the manager our story, and he wanted a photo of us to put on his office wall.

Lincoln and Sandra Zimmanck first met at a Tull show and have been together ever since

I also later got to know, and work with, the bass player Glenn Cornick with his later band, Paris. Fond memories.

ST STEPHEN'S GREEN

SUMMER 1970, DUBLIN, IRELAND

KAREN MULLEN

I was 16 and visiting my cousin in Dublin. She was hosting two Italian exchange students, as were many of her neighbours. They called me 'American Woman' and the eight of them escorted me around the city in the evenings. One day they said, 'American Woman, we go to park, listen to music'. I said that if bagpipes were involved, I was outta there. But after the sound that would curdle stone, out walked a wild red-haired man with a flute. He wore a long coat made of lumberjack red plaid and danced while he played. At one point he took the flute apart and played both pieces. I didn't know who he was, but I fell in love with his style. Years later, he did the same trick in Dallas. I screamed, 'I told you so!' to my friends, who'd doubted my claim. I passionately love Ian Anderson and have been a huge fan of Jethro Tull ever since that summer day at St Stephen's Green.

I've instructed my family to play Tull at my celebration of life.

BOSTON TEA PARTY

10 JULY 1970, BOSTON, MASSACHUSETTS

BABO GRUNDITZ

I heard the band on underground radio before catching them play the Boston Tea Party theatre in Boston. The orange lighting was great as I watched ringside. They were a spectacular band.

SUMMER CAMP

JULY 1970, UNITED STATES

ODIE RON

I have a distinct memory of the first time I heard Jethro Tull. It was July 1970. It was the first day of camp and I was walking down the hall and heard this strange music coming from one of the rooms. I walked in and listened and asked, 'Who the hell is this?' It was the opening flute and strings of 'With You There to Help Me' from the album *Benefit*. I will never forget that moment and the transcendent feeling it gave me. I have been a fan ever since. The first concert I took my sons to was Jethro Tull in the Nineties, and they're devotees too.

Odie Ron remembers hearing Benefit, and his kids are now fans

RANDALL'S ISLAND FESTIVAL, DOWNING STADIUM

17 JULY 1970, RANDALL'S ISLAND, NEW YORK

BILL SCARNATI

Bill Scarnati (right) has seen Tull over 20 times going back to 1970

I've seen Tull over 20 times, the first being with Jimi Hendrix, Grand Funk Railroad, Steppenwolf and John Sebastian at Randall's Island in New York. My dad had a record store all through the Sixties and Seventies, and the kid that worked with us got me into Tull. He was a regular at the Fillmore East. Being my first concert ever in 1970, I went to that show to see Tull because I was a huge fan. Ian stole the show, as usual. They were awesome in those days. My buddy and I got on a bus to Manhattan from Queens to see the show. John Sebastian opened at around 9pm, followed by Steppenwolf and Grand Funk. Then Tull came on, and I was mesmerised. I remember Ian wore that tattered coat at the show, and they did a fabulous 'My God'.

For 10 years I saw pretty much every MSG show they played through to 1980, and a few Nassau Coliseum shows too. Because he ran a record store, my dad had advanced knowledge of when tickets for the Garden would go on sale. I was online numerous times at the box office the night before they went on sale and, consequently, I got front-row centre for a number of shows. I remember a show in the mid-Seventies where some jerk threw a bottle on stage and Ian threatened to end the show. He was really pissed (off). I also remember the *Thick as a Brick* tour, where they would come on stage in trenchcoats before starting playing, and the movie of the ballerina starting the *A Passion Play* show, with that heartbeat sound.

PACIFIC COLISEUM

11 AUGUST 1970, VANCOUVER, CANADA

DON MERCER

The first time I saw Jethro Tull live was in Vancouver, British Columbia in, I believe, 1968. They were the opening act and touring *This Was*. They were so good, and different from anything I had seen to date. I don't remember the headline act. That happened a lot back in the Sixties, with so many new unknown bands that were better than the headliners (the first time I saw Led Zeppelin they were the opening act for Vanilla Fudge – two months later Zeppelin were the biggest act in world).

This Was is still a favourite, and they have made lots of great albums; *Stand Up*, *Aqualung* (released while I was in Vietnam after being drafted) and *Thick as a Brick*. *This Was* was very live - jazzy and bluesy. The original guitar player, Mick Abrahams, was my favourite. Ian Anderson was amazing. He never stopped moving, and dancing on one leg. I have attended three or four Tull concerts over the years in Seattle and Vancouver, with various different band members and always Martin Barre on lead guitar, with the exception of seeing them with Abrahams.

Many years ago, I was at a smaller venue than the ones they played in their heyday, and they had put a couple of couches on stage and decorated it like a living room. Ian Anderson would go out in the audience and collect people, bring them onstage and set them down. He would serve them all drinks and they would sit and watch up close and personal for a couple of songs. Then he would replace them with others. It was very cool.

Although Don recalls a 1968 show, 1970 is the first officially recorded performance of Tull in Vancouver. A billed appearance at Capilano Indian Reserve in September 1969 remains unconfirmed.

ISLE OF WIGHT FESTIVAL, EAST AFTON FARM

30 AUGUST 1970, ISLE OF WIGHT, UK

GERALD CLEAVER

I saw the classic lineup of Jethro Tull twice within a month: at the Isle of Wight Festival in 1970 and, on the back of that performance, on their UK tour on 25 September at Birmingham Town Hall. The lineup consisted of Ian Anderson (flute), Martin Barre (guitar), Clive Bunker (drums), Glenn Cornick (bass), and John Evan (keyboards), who was making his UK live debut with the band. I believe it was their first time using keyboards on stage in the UK.

Tull appeared on Sunday evening at the festival, following The Moody Blues and preceding Jimi Hendrix. I remember their iconic performance to this day for a number of reasons. I watched all the acts who appeared prior to The Moody Blues from Devastation Hill, which overlooked the festival site. However, on Sunday afternoon the promoters declared the festival a free festival from then on, and opened the gates. From my perch on the hill, I could see an entrance just below us, so we packed up and moved on down. We entered the site right in front of the stage, so watched the Moodies, Tull, Hendrix, Joan Baez, Leonard Cohen and Richie Havens from close range.

Tull had a soundcheck written into their contract and had insisted on it. They woke up the sleeping throng with an early morning sound rehearsal (for which they later apologised), and it paid off. They sounded superb. I don't think any other act on the bill, except possibly The Who, sounded half as good. Consequently, they went down very well, in fact much better than most other acts on the exhaustive bill. Given the audience were all pretty exhausted after five full-on days and nights of music, it says a lot for Tull's performance that they managed to engage the audience.

They, at least Ian Anderson, also looked great. Ian was wearing what I took to be a torn dressing gown, a yellow combination, a sort of cod-piece contraption, long wavy hair and a manic beard. And calf-length boots. It was the late Sixties, after all. He also had by now perfected his flute playing while standing on one leg, along with his lunges across the stage and frantic and amusing facial expressions. They played a nine-song set, most of which were familiar to their fans, and were simply brilliant.

So brilliant in fact that I went to see them again four weeks later. I wasn't quick enough purchasing tickets after their Isle of Wight triumph, however, as the concert at Birmingham Town Hall had already sold out. But they played a second show at midnight, which was also a sell-out, and this time I managed to get tickets.

Despite the smaller venue and an audience of just 2,000 fans, I was about the same distance from the stage as I had been at the festival.

This tour had a super lineup: the first act on were Procol Harum, fresh from their 'A Whiter Shade of Pale' success and with their best album, *A Salty Dog*, on release. Apparently, they also played at the Isle of Wight festival a few weeks before, but I have no memory of seeing them. They too had their classic lineup, including Robin Trower on guitar, and were certainly one of the best support acts I have ever seen. Next up were an Irish acoustic duo, Tír na nÓg, who were very popular at the time, and also went down well. Jethro Tull, playing their second show of the night, were better than their Isle of Wight performance, if only because they played a longer set. They were at the top of their game, thoroughly professional and thoroughly entertaining. It was to be at least 50 years before I saw Jethro Tull again, but that's another story.

DE MONTFORT HALL

28 SEPTEMBER 1970, LEICESTER, UK
RUPERT BOBROWICZ

Rupert Bobrowicz first saw Tull at Leicester's De Montfort Hall

My Tull interest stems from 1969, my first concert being when I saw them at Leicester's De Montfort Hall. As a young teenager I was delighted to attend, this being only 20 miles from where I lived. How excited was I? On the night Tull brought two support groups – a duo called Tír na nÓg and Procol Harum, who played some *Salty Dog* and 'Homburg' before ending with 'A Whiter Shade of Pale'. But it was Tull I had come see, and it wasn't too long before my expectations were met, then exceeded beyond measure.

I was in Seventh Heaven and more, because Tull were on stage before my very eyes: Ian Anderson complete with flute and chequered coat; Glenn Cornick with hair and bass; Clive Bunker with Tull drum kit; Martin Barre on lead guitar; and introducing 'Mr Ice Cream Man', John Evan, with Cheshire Cat smile and keyboards.

What a fabulous set they played. Tull were on a high, Ian retorted, after their Isle of Wight concert. They were all buzzing. Songs from *This Was* and *Stand Up* greeted us, along with some bluesy numbers. Then came newer material, including 'With You There to Help Me', along with a long John Evan keyboard solo. Clive, Ian and John were all on form for the revised 'Dharma for One', which was akin to the live version on *Living in the Past*. 'My God' included a long-ish, exaggerated flute solo. 'For a Thousand Mothers' was well received, especially with its false ending, as was 'Nothing is Easy', while Glenn exceeded his bass solo on 'Bouree'.

Guess what? I was surely hooked by Tull, making every effort to see them whenever I was able to after that. I went on to see them on the following tours: *Thick as a Brick* (De Montfort Hall); *A Passion Play* (Wembley, front row); *War Child* (the Rainbow); and later in Nottingham and Peterborough, where I also saw Ian Anderson solo.

ROYAL ALBERT HALL

13 OCTOBER 1970, LONDON, UK

ADRIAN HARRISON, AGE 16

Back in 1969, aged a mere 15, a keen drummer and Beatles fan in addition to other popular bands, as usual on a Thursday night I watched *Top of the Pops.* My music taste changed forever that night, as appearing were Jethro Tull. I was transfixed. The music, the hair, the flute and – what nailed it – my mum calling them 'ugly, unwashed and totally undesirable.' What more could a rebel teenager want? I remember going out to the local record store that Saturday with pocket money, buying *Living in the Past.*

I joined the Jethro Tull fan club and still have my membership card, a folder to keep info in, and the only ever issue of *Jeffrey's Journal*, dated 15th February 1970. There was no further contact until 9 September 1970 (the day before my birthday), saying the fan club was ending. As a thank you, rather than returning the five shillings (25p in new money),

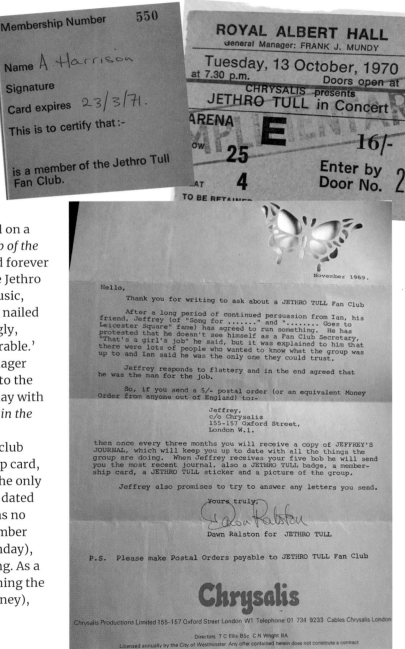

they sent me a complimentary ticket for a concert happening in September or October. Living in Chelmsford, Essex at the time I requested the Royal Albert Hall gig on 13 October.

Just turned 16, I took the train into Liverpool Street, then the Tube to Kensington. My mum, meanwhile, was having kittens at home, this being the first time I had ventured into London by myself – and in the evening too This was my first ever gig, and what an occasion. When I arrived, I purchased a programme and took my seat – Arena E, Row 25 Seat 4, stamped 'complimentary', the cost of which would have been 16 shillings (80p).

I can't remember anything about Tír na nÓg or Procol Harum apart from 'A Whiter Shade of Pale' (which I can't stand), but then Tull came on. My overriding memory is of Ian Anderson moving all over the stage like a madman, a long drum solo which I loved, and lots of head banging around me. I don't remember it being excessively loud, but as it was my first gig I had nothing to compare it to.

So there we are. My first ever gig, courtesy of Tull, who have remained my favourite band to this very day.

UNION COLLEGE FIELDHOUSE

13 NOVEMBER 1970, SCHENECTADY, NEW YORK
JAMES W MANNING, AGE 15

Jim Manning saw Tull at the Union College Fieldhouse

I was 15 at the time my sister Jill parted for Union College to become a member of the first class of women admitted, in the fall of 1970. It was a sad affair, actually, as my dad was leaving my mom at the same time.

In November, as a ninth-grader from Westport, Connecticut, I went by myself to visit my sister and her freshman friends at an all-girls dorm at Union College. I spent the whole weekend trying to impress the 'chicks' and 'babes' (those were terms of endearment at the time), and found one of whom was apparently interested in talking to me … I guess for being a coolish dude. I played in a rock band covering mostly Beatles; I was soccer captain at Long Lots; a dancer in *The Music Man*. Her name was Kate White, and she went on to be one of *Glamour*'s 'Top Ten College Women'. Yup, she was cool from the beginning.

Hopefully you now understand what was happening for me at the time of the Tull gig. This was my first major concert experience. Jethro Tull's 'Nothing is Easy' was an impressive and creative rock song, fucking unique in an era when rock 'n' roll was happening anew everywhere. I always remind myself how fucking fortunate I am to have lived at this time in my teens.

The Fieldhouse had a freakin' dirt floor. The place smelled like pot, something I had yet to want to experience (I was a jock who dug liquor, but weed was too out there for me). I was psyched and, as the place filled up, I thought, 'Hey, now is a good time to go shoot close-ups of the rock band!'

My personal experience, however, was that of a member of a ninth-grade rock band, where we all carried and set up our own equipment. I took the whole roll of 36 photos of the guys setting up the equipment, went back to my seat, sat on a blanket and waited for the show to start. The house lights went down, the stage lights came on and the band came on, with people cheering and all. At that moment I realised I had used my one and only roll of film to photograph the roadies.

It was just the wildest presentation. Ian mostly maintained his balance on one leg, looking every bit like one of the biggest rock stars of the time. Amazing music, amazing experience.

TEATRO SMERALDO

1 FEBRUARY 1971, MILAN, ITALY

FRANZ DI CIOCCIO, PFM

In the early Seventies I listened to many records and had my own band. In the UK there was a great ferment and many artists had begun to create more sophisticated compositions, if compared to usual songs. Not just blues or rock, but songs full of improvisations and new sounds, which characterised the new genre called progressive rock. This evolution excited me a lot, so I thought of an ensemble different from the usual quartet of guitar-bass-drums and Hammond organ. We became a quintet, adding a musician who played the violin and the flute. PFM was born.

I was struck by several bands of the English scene, Jethro Tull in particular. Ian Anderson, with his magic flute, was leading an extraordinary band. His peculiar type of voice and histrionic stage presence amazed everyone, both on records and live.

PFM did not follow a single genre. We played our own compositions and covers of particular songs, carefully chosen. The track-list included 'Bourée', 'Nothing is Easy' and 'My God', along with improvisations that captured the audience of progressive music.

February 1st, 1971 was an important date: Jethro Tull played in Italy for the first time, at the Smeraldo Theatre in Milan, my town. I couldn't miss the premiere. The concert began with 'My God'. Ian entered the scene alone, illuminated by a spotlight, while the whole stage was in semi-darkness. Leaning against a chair, he began to play the theme of 'My God' with his acoustic guitar, singing the verses with a portamento that had captured the entire audience. He was punctuating the lyrics with pathos in a superb interpretation, until he came to the line, 'And don't call on Him to save'. At that precise moment, Ian left his guitar and kicked the chair out of the way. At the same time, all the lights on the stage went on. The band went into sync with his flute and, together, they started the musical riff. It was an unforgettable moment, which thrilled the audience. It was just the beginning of the show, but that fantastic performance had already conquered Milan.

Meanwhile, PFM's five-musician line-up had grown. In 1972 we made our first album of unreleased tracks and, right away, began our adventure in the UK with Manticore.

Years later, fate gave us a surprise. In 2010, PFM took part in the Prog Exhibition event in Rome, a festival of Italian bands who would share the stage with an English artist from the progressive area. I proposed to have Ian Anderson as PFM's guest. We met, at last. We played 'Bourée' together, with an intro specially arranged by us for the performance with Ian. At the end of the song there was a long-standing ovation. Unforgettable! Then it was the turn of 'My God' and, in the end, Ian took part in a PFM song, 'La Carrozza di Hans', where the flute is the main instrument. It was another standing ovation for a memorable concert. It was exhilarating and we hugged each other... although only with the elbows, according to Ian's style.

The passage of time does not cancel friendships. In 2021 PFM was working on a new album and, in particular, on a song entitled 'Kindred Souls'. The music and lyrics flowed well, but I was feeling something was missing. The title of the song inspired me, and I thought about Ian and his flute. We got in touch via email and, after a few days, he sent me a few tracks with his inimitable sound. They were perfect for the song, whose title speaks about the affinity between people. Music is magic, it can do this too.

AQUALUNG

RELEASED 19 MARCH 1971

UK CHART POSITION 4

US CHART POSITION 7

CLIVE HARRISON

Barely entering my teenage years, I began to get into rock music, aided by my elder sister's boyfriend. I then discovered prog rock. Listening to bands such as Genesis, Yes and Pink Floyd, I was vaguely aware of a band named Jethro Tull that was of a similar genre, so headed off to the local record shop to purchase an album by the band. Or was Jethro Tull a solo artist?

Flicking through all the albums, I had no idea which one to buy, so decided on *Aqualung* purely because I liked the image on the cover, which reminded me of Fagin from *Oliver!*, and the writing style of text on the back. I got it home, put it straight on the turntable and was blown away. I have never looked back since. Ihave been a fan of Tull music for the last 45 years.

Clive Harrison was drawn in by the cover of Aqualung

DEAN PLATT

I was a senior in high school in 1975. I had to have a coat just like the poor old sod on the cover of *Aqualung*. I found an old gambler's jacket at my grandmother's. Everyone said, 'You cannot wear that ratty old thing…' but, oh boy, I could, and did proudly. One morning, I was standing in front of the school building having a quick pre-class cigarette. When the principal walked towards me, I cupped the lit smoke in my hand and hid the hand and the smoke in my jacket pocket. I was so clever.

About an hour later I heard 'fire!', but it was no big deal, and everyone was laughing. It was then that a voice came over the school PA system that said, 'Mr Dean Platt, your coat is on fire, hanging on your locker!' That's the day I heard 1,200 students laughing in unison.

MICHAEL HASS

My story is about an American interpreting British slang. 'Aqualung' was so out of it. 'He's picking dried faeces off a dog's behind?'. It was only years after first hearing the lyrics that I found out a 'dog end' is a cigarette butt.

JIM KAUFMAN

It would take hours to tell my stories over 50 years, but I have some Tull memorabilia I bought at an auction, raising money for an AIDS charity.

JOHN DEGENNARO

When my wife sometimes went out and left me in charge of our infant daughter, I would feed her, then pull out *Aqualung* or another Tull album and crank up the stereo. I'd hold her horizontal in my arms, she'd find a soft spot on my inner arm to suck on, and within a short period of time she'd be asleep – after giving me a sizeable hickey. She is now 40, and still appreciates Tull.

GUILLERMO DE CARLI

Jethro Tull arrived in Argentina in the shape of a single, 'It's Breaking Me Up', backed with 'Jeffrey Goes to Leicester Square' and, immediately, *Stand Up.* It was 1969 or 1970.

Argentinian high school students usually go on a graduation trip together; they must

Guillermo De Carli remembers Aqualung fondly

obtain the funds for that trip by themselves, with parties, dances, shows, etc. We had to name the dancing parties in order to legally sell tickets and drinks. I read in the Argentinian music magazine *Pelo* that, 'Jethro Tull is preparing a new album. All very secret, we only know the name: *Aqualung*. Ugh! Horrible!' No one understood it, but we called our dancing party Aqualung a year and a half before we got the album and raised the funds for a trip to the mountains a year and a half before the album was released. We stole Tull's name. So, thank you, the trip to the mountains was a pleasure. Shortly thereafter, my Aunt Bocha travelled to London. 'Please!' I begged, 'Bring me anything from Jethro Tull!' My aunt went to a record shop in Piccadilly and, a bit embarrassed, said, 'Do you have anything by Jethro Tull? It's for my nephew.' 'Your nephew has excellent taste, ma'am,' said the salesman, and handed her *This Was.*

ED DUBE

It's 1975. I'm in high school. I've heard 'Fat Man', 'Bouree' and 'Living in the Past'; all the radio hits. But then a buddy of mine dies in a car crash. High speed driving, drunk, high, a road with too many potholes, too many curves and one big ass tree that stopped my buddy's life forever.

After the cops, the funeral and the tears, some of the guys went to the yard to clean out his car of 'stuff' that maybe he wouldn't want the world to know about. In the cassette deck was *Aqualung*. The song that was playing when Jimmy hit the tree was 'My God'. I had never heard it, or the rest of the album, before then. I became an instant fan. I have seen numerous concerts. I've never been able to get enough Tull music. But whenever I hear 'My God', I think of Jim.

GINGER AKERS

My eldest sister used to shop yard sales a lot. Linda is 16 years older than me. I was in high school in the Eighties. One night she brought me an album she'd found. 'I used to listen to them when I was in high school,' she said. I put it on and heard 'sitting on a park bench...'. I thought, 'OMG, what?' '... eyeing little girls with bad intent'. I listened to *Aqualung* three times through that night. Then I started buying used old albums as well as the newer ones.

Ginger Akers was hooked on hearing Aqualung

DOMINIC GRIEK

When I was in college in the Seventies my girlfriend at the time, Diane, painted a wonderful watercolour of the cover of *Aqualung*. It still hangs in a place of honour in my man cave.

BECKY HALL

When my kids were little, they took turns riding in the front seat, picking the cassette that we would listen to whilst driving. My daughter, who was only four or five years old, wanted to hear 'Aqualung'. She called it 'The Snot Song'. She said, 'Play the first of the very Snot Song.'

Dominic Griek's girlfriend painted a picture he still has

TIMOTHY MAZE

It was April 2019, and I was travelling into the Upper Peninsula of Michigan to visit the faculty of a graduate school I was considering attending. I was listening to Neil Young on Spotify as I traversed the snowy, early spring landscape. At the end of your selection, Spotify will play a 'radio station' playlist of similar (or not so similar) artists. After a few other artists, I heard for the first time a disgustingly heavy guitar riff. 'Dun dun dun dundun dun.' 'Aqualung' kicked in, blowing me away. I listened to the song over and over before eventually putting on the record and being swept away by the riffs, the lyrics and the flute.

Timothy Maze was introduced to Jethro Tull by Spotify

71

I called my dad. I had a grievance to air. 'Why is this the first time I have heard *Aqualung*?' I demanded. He chuckled. Just too proggy for my simple tastes. He told me to listen to 'My God', 'Locomotive Breath' and *Thick as a Brick*. I was not yet done with *Aqualung*. I would often return to one short, simple song, 'Wond'ring Aloud'. The guitar, the lyrics. It had a warmth to it that I just could not get enough of. This particular version of *Aqualung* I was listening to was an extended version, with demos of this song or that, but it was not until 'Wond'ring Aloud, Again' that I realised the

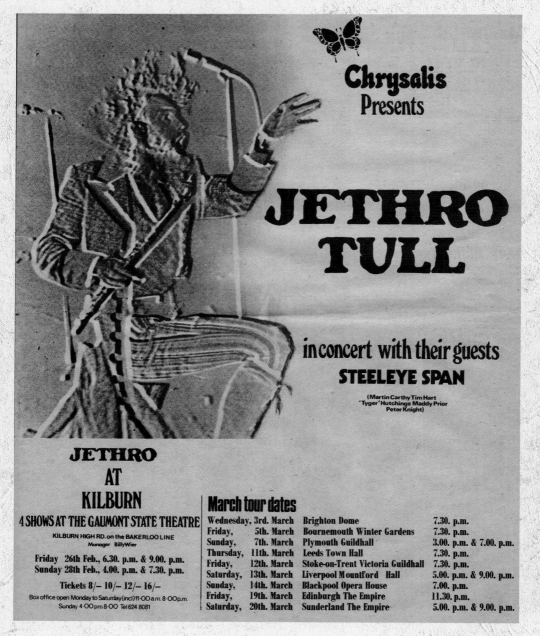

Chrysalis Presents

JETHRO TULL

in concert with their guests
STEELEYE SPAN

(Martin Carthy Tim Hart
'Tyger' Hutchings Maddy Prior
Peter Knight)

JETHRO AT KILBURN

4 SHOWS AT THE GAUMONT STATE THEATRE

KILBURN HIGH RD. on the BAKERLOO LINE
Manager Billy Wier

Friday 26th Feb., 6.30. p.m. & 9.00. p.m.
Sunday 28th Feb., 4.00. p.m. & 7.30. p.m.

Tickets 8/– 10/– 12/– 16/–

Box office open Monday to Saturday (incl) 11·00 a.m. 8·00 p.m.
Sunday 4·00 pm 8·00 Tel 624 8081

March tour dates

Wednesday, 3rd. March	Brighton Dome	7.30. p.m.	
Friday, 5th. March	Bournemouth Winter Gardens	7.30. p.m.	
Sunday, 7th. March	Plymouth Guildhall	3.00. p.m. & 7.00. p.m.	
Thursday, 11th. March	Leeds Town Hall	7.30. p.m.	
Friday, 12th. March	Stoke-on-Trent Victoria Guildhall	7.30. p.m.	
Saturday, 13th. March	Liverpool Mountford Hall	5.00. p.m. & 9.00. p.m.	
Sunday, 14th. March	Blackpool Opera House	7.00. p.m.	
Friday, 19th. March	Edinburgh The Empire	11.30. p.m.	
Saturday, 20th. March	Sunderland The Empire	5.00. p.m. & 9.00. p.m.	

true genius of Jethro Tull, with a special emphasis on Ian Anderson.

Not long after, I dove into *Thick as a Brick*, *Minstrel in the Gallery* and *Songs from the Wood*. I was taken away by all of it. I decided to attend that faraway graduate school. And often, as I drive around the Keweenaw Peninsula, observing the post-industrial ruin that has made itself home in the trees, I let myself imagine that the magical motor car world had long ceased to be and realise, truly, that it is only the giving that makes us what we are.

NARENDRA KUSNUR

On first hearing, the lyrics made no sense. 'Backward on my bench,' Ian Anderson seemed to sing on *Bursting Out*. Only after a friend insisted did I realise he was singing 'Aqualung, my friend', not that I understood that term either. This was in 1982 when, as a college-goer in New Delhi, I was being exposed to music that would later be called 'classic rock'. Yes, it was fashionable those days to drop names like Traffic, Santana, The Doors, and Cream. With Tull, knowing the 'poet and the painter' lines of *Thick as a Brick* or singing 'backward on my bench' was good enough to prove your elite snobbery. The intellectually-deprived danced to 'Funky Town'.

It took me a few months to borrow assorted and unpaid-for cassettes of *Aqualung*, *Songs from the Wood*, *Heavy Horses* and *Stormwatch*. At that point, little did I knew that I would eventually interview Anderson six times - twice in person, thrice on the phone and once over mail, besides being in regular correspondence with him three times a year. The gentleman that he is, he responds to each mail, often with a slice of his famous wit, a description of his cats and a mention of Indian curry dishes.

All this comes to mind with the album *Aqualung* celebrating its 50th birthday. Having heard it for close to 38 years, the songs still sound fresh. The only time I skip forward is on my once favourite 'Locomotive Breath'. I blame myself for overhearing it, yet it's a song I have frequently hummed in the shuffling madness of Mumbai rail journeys, imagining the guy next to me with steam breaking down his brow is playing a flute solo.

Over the years, different lines have had different meanings to me. 'When I was young and they packed me off to school' from 'Wind Up' reminded me of childhood. 'Wond'ring aloud how we feel today' from 'Wond'ring Aloud' was meant for a bright sunny day, a damp gloomy night and anything in between. 'Snot is running down his nose' from 'Aqualung' and 'Your nose feels like an icicle' from 'Up to Me' were for a bad cold, or maybe just bad grooming.

I remember clearing an exam when I went unprepared but kept singing, 'Do you still remember December's foggy freeze?' from *Aqualung* on a cold winter morning in the dim-m-m and distant past. The line 'brush away the cigarette ash that's falling down your pants' from 'Cheap Day Return' was for the nicotine breaks. Maybe I'll find new meaning when I'll be an 'old man wandering lonely, taking time the only way he knows.'

And Martin Barre's guitar parts made me flash my air guitar, feeling like a dead duck, spitting out pieces of my broken luck, wond'ring aloud why I could never tune my guitar and play barre chords like him. The flute solo of 'My God' made me try standing on one leg like Anderson, often tripping and almost breaking my jaw, till my neighbours sang, 'People, what have you done?', flashing their half-assed smiles and the book of rules.

KONRAD HANSON

I was about 15, sitting in the passenger seat while my mum, Marilyn, was driving. 'Locomotive Breath' came on the radio, and my mum pulled up to the red light. She started talking about the song, and how it has a great bit at the start. The piano intro built up, in came Martin on guitar, then finally when 'that moment' arrived, she took off, not realising the light was still red. She was so busy waiting for that moment in the song, she forgot she was waiting for a green light.

Konrad Hanson became a Jethro Tull fan after his mum ran a red light listening to 'Locomotive Breath'

STEVE RYDING

I discovered Jethro Tull by accident. I asked a friend to record some Beatles for me. He had some space left on the cassette so added 'Aqualung' and 'Thick as a Brick' at the end. I said to him that the last two Beatles songs were good and I had not heard them before. It was then that he told me they were Jethro Tull.

BRETT TURNER

My old man was an avid fan. Every few months he would buy *Aqualung* and every

Brett Turner's old man loved Aqualung

few months Mum would throw it out. I grew up listening to *Aqualung* and always wondered who was actually sat on the park bench eyeing little girls with bad intent.

WENDY WIGGINS

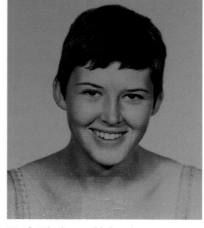

I was in Hong Kong, attending the Army School (St George's), and taking A-levels in the early Seventies. We used to go to various discos, the smallest one of all called Thingummy's. We entered via a spiral staircase, and the dancefloor was tiny. We'd go there after hockey matches and drink freshly squeezed orange juice. There was no alcohol – from choice, not because they didn't sell it. The abiding musical memory is 'Aqualung', and we knew all the words, singing them with relish.

Wendy Wiggins would sing along to Aqualung

An American lad approached us. 'What are you on?' 'Fresh air and orange juice!'

'Oh, wow, man it must be good. Seriously, what are you on?' 'No, seriously, fresh air and orange juice.'

Moving on, my absolute favourite has to be *Heavy Horses*. Oh, and when I came back to the UK, I went to a catering exhibition and who should be there, but the one and only Ian Anderson. Salmon!

ETHAN CALK

The first time I ever heard a Jethro Tull song was at a high school dance in my sophomore year. The band, comprised of friends and classmates, played 'Cross-Eyed Mary'. I immediately went out and bought *Aqualung* and have been a fan ever since.

PAULO ARAÚJO

I first encountered Jethro Tull when I was 13, through my brother's record collection. I had a local artist paint the *Aqualung* cover for me back in 1999 and it still hangs in my living room.

Paulo Araújo has a passion for Aqualung

NOEL KENNY

In 1980, I travelled from Dundalk to Dublin, along with a buddy named Brendan to see Thin Lizzy. We were only 13. It wasn't that there was an open-door policy at home. It was just that people were more trusting. So, the idea of two 13-year-olds boarding a train, walking around Dublin for hours, going to the show then eventually bunking in with Brendan's student older brother in his digs was perfectly acceptable. And sure enough, we were fine.

Along with Brendan's older brother, there was a hippy-trippy-looking student, who was commanding the record player in the corner, playing various records and smoking wacky backy. After a while, rock 'n' roll's equivalent of Beethoven's Fifth began belting out and I became transfixed. After a while, I timidly asked what he was playing. He told me the album was called *Aqualung* and the band was Jethro Tull. He then kindly handed me the cover. We listened to the whole album. Thin Lizzy were a good band, and I really enjoyed the night, but my standout musical memory from that evening took place in those run-down digs. Stupidly, I put this memory to one side and reverted to the music I was accustomed to at home.

Two years ago, I took a day off work and travelled to Belfast and Richer Sounds. I walked out with top-class gear and have been enjoying the listening experience ever since. On the way back from Belfast, I stopped into Tower Records in Dublin. It seemed apt to buy an LP on the back of my Belfast purchase. After a few minutes leafing through the racks, everything seemed to turn full circle and suddenly made sense. There he was, the dishevelled beggar. The LP had been lovingly restored by Steve Wilson.

To say that, on first listen, my 13-year-old self's view of the world had been validated is an exercise in understatement. I was shocked (and still am) at how good this album is. If there was a downside, it was that I began to think there was no point in buying any more Jethro Tull. Surely *Aqualung* could not be topped? Masterpieces are, by definition, rare. Jethro Tull on the other hand have, in my view, eight, and the following are my favourite albums in wafer thin order of preference:

A Passion Play
Thick as a Brick
Minstrel in the Gallery
Aqualung
Benefit
Songs from the Wood
Heavy Horses
Too Old to Rock 'n' Roll

Is there anything I don't like? I am not a fan of 'Kissing Willie' – we'll say no more about that – while it's almost impossible to split between 'Baker Street Muse' and 'Jack-in-the-Green' as my favourite song.

40 years ago, I arrived on a winter's night at a house in Dublin, for some kip after a Thin Lizzy concert, before starting for home the following day. Then I heard those immortal notes, '*Dah, dah, dah, dah, dah, dah!*', followed by that immortal line, 'Sitting on a park bench ...', and everything changed.

CLIVE BUNKER

Recording *Aqualung* was hard work. I played my drum part and then Ian was playing it in the studio and saying, 'I'm not sure that this works, can we record it again?' I said, 'Is it the drum part, or what?' and he said, 'It just doesn't feel right.' He did that about four times, so I played the same thing about four times, and he still wasn't happy with it at all. But the rest of the band? We loved it, and were proved right in the end. It's the biggest album Tull ever had. I asked him why then, and I still sometimes ask him now when I meet him, 'What was it?' And he says, 'It just didn't feel right to me' Fairly recently I said, 'It's still the biggest album you ever had, so why don't you do another one that doesn't feel quite right?'

EMPIRE THEATRE

20 MARCH 1971, SUNDERLAND, UK

PETER SMITH

Jethro Tull are one of those bands I grew up with. I was heavily into them in the early Seventies, as were my mates – Norman Jones, Bill Gillum and Doug Walker – and *Stand Up* was an album that we listened to again and again. I remember marvelling at Ian Anderson on *Top of the Pops*, his mad crazy eyes staring at me through the TV, and his eccentric garb shocking my parents. Their early singles were classics. My favourites were 'The Witch's Promise', 'Teacher', and 'Sweet Dream'. I first saw Jethro Tull in concert at Sunderland Empire the day after the classic album *Aqualung* was released. I was 14 years old.

Early gigs are very important in shaping musical tastes for the rest of your life, and this one certainly did that for me. Tull played two shows at the Empire that evening, and I decided to go along to the late show with a few mates. We felt very grown up, being allowed to go to the late show, and felt sure the band would play better at the second concert. We had good seats in the 'slipper', to the left of the stage.

Support for the gig was Steeleye Span, a newly formed folk-rock band, who delivered a pretty good set. But we were there to see our heroes, Jethro Tull. By this relatively early point in their career, their line-up had already changed several times, and was Ian Anderson on flute and vocals, Martin Barre on guitar, Clive Bunker on drums, John Evan on keyboards, and Jeffrey Hammond-Hammond on bass. I recall they started with 'Nothing is Easy', and the set featured a number of Tull favourites, and some tracks from the *Aqualung* album.

We were just blown away by Jethro Tull that night, and by Ian Anderson in particular, one of the most charismatic performers, at the height of his craziness in those days. And so started a lifelong obsession with this band. I have seen them quite a few times since and watched their line-up and musical style change over the years. But for me and a group of mates, in the early Seventies Jethro Tull were legends and one of the bands we returned to again and again.

RICHARD VALANGA

When you get to my age, a memory from 1971 can be an elusive beast. You have to try and conjure it up best you can and simply hope it is close to being accurate. But these days there is the web-checking facility of the all-knowing, mighty Google to help you out, and that is a godsend.

I was at the Sunderland Empire on 20 March 1971 as a star-struck teenager, aged 15. My 2021 memory tried to fool me though; it was not the Amazing Blondel that were supporting Jethro Tull, but the electric folk-rock band Steeleye Span. I now realise I saw Amazing Blondel with Free.

Richard Valanga was at the Sunderland Empire

Blondel and Tull had merged together in my mind, maybe because they were similar musically and visually. But Amazing Blondel were not as electric and as powerful as Jethro Tull.

Tull played two concerts at the Empire that day. Considering my age, I think I attended the early show. I do not recall owning a Jethro Tull album at that time, as my vinyl collection was in its infancy, but I was aware of the unique brilliance of the singles and of the TV performances, featuring the visually striking and energetic Ian Anderson.

My vivid memory of the concert is of the singer in his iconic stance of playing the flute, standing on one leg, the half-ragged brown-check antique-looking jacket and the amazing frizzed-out flowing hair that sometimes looked like it had a life of its own. Then Ian strutting across the stage; waving his flute about like the wand of some wild manic magician from the medieval ages, trying to draw us all into his spell.

The rest of the band were Martin Barre on guitar, Clive Bunker on drums, John Evan on keyboards, and Jeffrey Hammond-Hammond on bass. They were not quite as visual as their curious enigmatic front-man, but they were brilliant musicians at the top of their game. The album *Aqualung* was only one day old, and confirmed this. The setlist was probably 'Nothing is Easy', 'Aqualung', 'Hymn 43', 'My God', 'Cross-Eyed Mary', 'With You There to Help Me', 'By Kind Permission Of', 'Sossity; You're a Woman', 'Reasons for Waiting', 'Wind Up', 'Locomotive Breath', 'Hard-Headed English General', and 'Wind Up' (reprise). I remember leaving the Empire thinking, 'Wow, I've just seen one of the world's greatest rock bands!' I know for a fact that the next day I bought *Aqualung*, and I have a vivid memory of playing the record in my bedroom, the windows wide open just to give the neighbours a slice of brilliant rock. The next album for me would be the excellent *Stand Up*. From that moment on I was an avid fan and have remained so to this day. I now have a large collection of all things Jethro Tull, CDs and DVDs, in my music library. Those now distant, sometimes hazy faraway days were Tulltastic (I wonder if Alan 'Fluff' Freeman ever said that?) and I am so glad I was there when The Golden Age of Rock Music was just beginning.

JOHN PARTRIDGE

I got into Tull in the latter years of my schooldays, 1969/70, and by the time the '71 tour came to the Empire I was probably as big a fan as they had at that time. I recall during the long slow intro to 'Locomotive Breath', as Jon Evan soloed at the piano, there was disruption in the stalls. Restless rockers, presumably. Ian Anderson burst onto the stage, flute in hand, and took the front stage mic to absolutely berate the 'fucking louts', as he put it. He said his piece and ended with a self-effacing joke, which restored the ambience, and left the stage to reappear with the band as the song began. The concert was memorable as my first time at a Tull gig. I didn't miss many for several years after that and have at least their first nine albums, including a shocking-pink vinyl bootleg called *My God*.

PAINTERS MILL

4 APRIL 1971, OWINGS MILL, MARYLAND

ELLEN PEPPLER

I was 15 years old. I have numerous friends who attended this show. My girlfriend Bobby thinks it was rescheduled because Ian Anderson had laryngitis. Either way it was an awesome show. My favourite LP is *Stand Up*, and Jethro Tull remains in my top-10 favourite bands of all time.

MUNICIPAL AUDITORIUM

13 APRIL 1971, ATLANTA, GEORGIA

MICHAEL DAVID MARTIN, AGE 16

Michael David Martin (right) saw Tull the first time they played Atlanta, Georgia

I was a high school kid who spent many hours a week listening to this new thing called 'Album-Oriented-Rock' (AOR) FM radio on the station WKLS ('96 Rock') in Atlanta, Georgia. This was a very different sort of radio station from the top-40 format AM stations that only played the current pop hits amid a relentless spate of DJ chatter and commercial jingles. AOR featured lots of really interesting tracks from rock bands I already loved, but also tracks from bands I had never heard of. One band that really intrigued me was Jethro Tull. The music was something completely new to me. I wasn't knowledgeable enough about music to recognise it was a synthesis of blues, jazz and English folk; I just loved the astounding energy and unique flavour of the sound, which was unlike anything else on the radio. As a beginner on guitar, I appreciated how many of the tracks seemed to be built from something started on acoustic guitar then richly embellished with other instruments, including, of all things, a flute! My new girlfriend Jackie loved music as much as I did, and when we saw Jethro Tull were coming to play a show at the Municipal Auditorium in downtown Atlanta, we decided to go. We had no idea what to expect in terms of the performance; we didn't know anything about the band members. 'Who is this Jethro Tull guy, anyway... maybe he's the flute player?'

In those days, there was really no way to see a band perform unless you went to a show. We could only afford the cheap seats, located high up in the balcony level, looking down at the stage and all those lucky people sitting at the main floor level. I think there was an opening act, but can't remember anything about the performance. But I will never forget what happened after the lights went down, just before the main event. In the darkness, the MC announced, 'Ladies and gentlemen, please welcome JETHRO TULL!' and the crowd applauded. The stage lights came on simultaneously with the very dramatic flute intro to the song 'Nothing is Easy', a track we had been hearing on the radio. The flautist was front and centre, dressed in some sort of medieval thrift-shop garb, standing on one foot and then, as the pace of the intro revved up and the flautist started singing, everything on stage exploded. Throughout the song, the entire auditorium was just gobsmacked, watching this fantastically tight band play this incredibly great song with this unbelievably frantic character in the middle, prancing and singing and playing all these wild flourishes on his flute, which he waved around like a baton between riffs. The song ended, and from our elevated perspective we witnessed something utterly spontaneous. Literally every one of the hundreds of people seated on the floor rushed the stage, packing themselves tightly together, cheering and waving their arms at the crazy flute-man above them. It was pandemonium. Jackie and I were so envious of the fans down below, stuck as we were high above the joyful madness. This went on for what seemed like a long time; finally, after the MC implored people to return to their seats, the outmanned security men were able to direct the crowd to back away from the stage.

Once everyone settled down, the band began their next song. I don't recall which song they played next, but when it ended the exact same thing happened - fans rushed the stage, the MC implored them to go back and sit down, the overwhelmed security guys struggled with crowd control and eventually everyone moved back. When the third song started and then ended, it all happened yet again. At this point, the beleaguered security guys gave up, and for the rest of the show the fans on the floor were packed tightly in front of the stage, jammed together in order to be as close as possible to the extraordinary action onstage. We wanted so badly to be down there with them. This was my first big time concert. I have been to a great many other concerts during the ensuing 50 years, but this one was the absolutely the best. Who knew that such intriguing music could be presented so forcefully, and that the performance could so electrify everyone present, even those of us stuck up in the cheap seats?

STATE FAIRGROUNDS COLISEUM

20 APRIL 1971, DETROIT, MICHIGAN

KEN MCNEILL

The first time I heard Jethro Tull was on an FM station called WABX in Detroit, Michigan. This was in the early underground radio days where album cuts were the norm and singles were rarely if ever played. The song was 'A New Day Yesterday'. I thought, 'Wow, what a great blues rock tune.' However, it was when

Ken McNeill (left) was in Detroit in 1971

a friend of mine lent me his copy of *Stand Up* and I heard 'Look into the Sun' that I realised this group was much more than just another Hendrix/Cream hard rock outfit. I was mesmerised by that tune and the whole album.

Benefit followed and again I was blown away at the songwriting and musicianship. I played those two albums over and over during 1969 and 1970. We knew Tull had played at the Grande Ballroom in Detroit before. However, being only 15, our parents had forbidden us to go to that venue as we were underage. In 1971 we heard they were playing the Michigan State Fairgrounds that May. By then some of my friends had vehicles and we bought tickets and attended the show. It was general admission and completely sold out.

Edgar Winter opened up and, though very good, it was Tull we were there to see. Though none of us had purchased *Aqualung* it had been getting airplay on WABX and we were somewhat familiar with the new material. Edgar Winter finished and right on cue came Tull. I had only seen pictures of Ian and the band and had no idea as to his stage presence. Needless to say, when his maniacal, flute twirling, Faginesque coat and incredibly smooth moves with his legs and arms began, I knew this was the greatest audio and visual concert experience I'd ever seen. The rest of the crowd knew it too. The response to the band was unlike anything I'd ever seen, and I saw Jimi Hendrix!

It wasn't just Ian, but Jeffrey Hammond-Hammond and his storming around the stage, and John Evan and his white coat arms flailing, legs stomping the ground as he played. Martin Barre would move back and forth with Ian, and Clive Bunker was, well, Clive Bunker. Amazing musicians all. Clearly this band was much more than a rock band. Ian's demeanour and general good nature and humour were totally foreign to most rock bands and concerts.

KUTZTOWN UNIVERSITY

2 MAY 1971, KUTZTOWN, PENNSYLVANIA

DON BALOGH

I had been selling the supremacy of the band to anyone who would listen since witnessing a Fillmore East performance in August 1970 when Bill Graham announced, 'Invading our stage once again, Jethro Tull.' Martin began the 'To Cry You a Song' riff with ever-increasing amplification, and they were off. And so was I.

In May 1971 a car-load of Moravian College students parked near the gymnasium at Kutztown College for a performance by Jethro Tull, with the added attraction of opening act Mott the Hoople. I had in my possession the UK release of the *Aqualung* album. As far as I knew, it hadn't yet been released in the US. I actually thought I might be able to get it signed by the man himself.

Don Balogh has framed his signed gatefold copy of Aqualung

Yet another great Jethro Tull performance later, I devised my plan. It took no Einstein to figure out the band equipment had to load out, most likely at the rear of the gymnasium. Sure enough, as the equipment rolled out, I made my move in, to find our star mid-court, engaged in conversation about charity concerts. I stood there, album in hand, and offered small talk about a benefit concert Creedence Clearwater Revival had just done. Ian, still in his stage robe, Tareyton cigarette in one hand and coffee cup in the other, looked my way. Believing the US release had not yet occurred, I asked, 'Have you ever seen this?' whilst proudly holding my trophy album, and asked him to sign the image that most suited him. He chose the inside of the gatefold and scribbled something under his name that I haven't been able to decipher for 50 years. A secret message for the Tull faithful, no doubt.

Postscript: On the UK album release, Martin plays the opening *Aqualung* riff twice, whereas it is only heard once on the US version. Who knew?

FILLMORE EAST

4 & 5 MAY 1971, NEW YORK, NEW YORK

JOHN IULO

I really, really liked the early LPs with the original line-up, and caught them a few times at the Fillmore East in NYC. One show was to be the debut of *Aqualung*, but it was cancelled due to illness, which turned out to be fine as Steve Marriott's new band, Humble Pie, with a young Peter Frampton, filled the slot. Tull debuted *Aqualung* a month later. Ian opened the show, sitting centre-stage under a single spotlight playing the 'My God' intro on acoustic guitar, until the stage flooded with light and the full band kicked in.

ROBERT GOLTZ

I've seen Jethro Tull 50 times. First time was in 1969 at the Filmore East, NYC. The next time was in 1971, again at the Fillmore, A band called Cowboy opened. I started a huge outpouring of noise because, quite frankly, they were not that good (it really wasn't too nice of me). Bill Graham came on stage, yelled at me and told me to go home and listen to my 45s … which was a big insult in '71.

Robert Goltz got yelled at by Bill Graham

CLIVE BUNKER

I'm not the sort of person that likes being a rock star, if you want to call it that. It got to where we'd have to leave the hotel at a ridiculous time to get to the gig before the fans started turning up outside. Then after the gig we'd have to stay at the venue until whatever time in the morning, or work out ways of getting into cars where the fans wouldn't know it was us. And we'd book six or seven hotels so nobody knew where we were staying.

It happened overnight almost, where we just had such a fanbase, and I'm not that sort of person. Somebody like John Bonham loved all that but I'm more of the Charlie Watts way of thinking. Me and Charlie got on so well because of that. If ever we were around somewhere together, we would slope off and have a couple of beers together. It was great.

I said to them, 'I'm not enjoying myself. Why don't you get another drummer? Why don't you just get Barrie (the old drummer) in?' And they said, 'Oh, all right,' and phoned Barrie, and he said he'd love to do it. So, I said, 'Right, I'm off'

I left and started some businesses – an engineering factory, a bus company and then I bought a farm and we started some boarding kennels, which was wonderful. Being a rock star wasn't my life. It still isn't. I'm playing with Martin Barre later this year. I still feel a bit weird when there's a bunch of people waiting outside for autographs.

RED ROCKS AMPHITHEATER

10 JUNE 1971, MORRISON, COLORADO
BOB BUNTING, AGE 20

Bob Bunting was at the infamous Red Rocks show

My friends and I had tickets, though thousands without tickets tried to crash the concert by climbing over the rock formations in the back of the facility. The cops were having none of it and let loose with barrages of tear gas. However, the wind was blowing from the west and the gas drifted down through the crowd. We pulled our t-shirts up over our mouths and noses and periodically had to close our eyes. I understand that the band almost did not perform, but play they did, and it was one of the greatest shows I ever attended. I will never forget that show. Ian Anderson said, 'Good evening and welcome to World War Three.'

IAN ANDERSON

We were due to play the performance at Red Rocks. We set off to go from our hotel in downtown Denver on the 40-minute drive up to Red Rocks Amphitheatre, in the foothills of the Rockies. We were met with a police road block and they refused to let us up. They said, 'No, there's a riot going on and you can't go up there. You'd be arrested if you tried to go and … blah, blah, blah.' And we said, 'But we're the band. If you don't let us go up there, it's going to get worse.' And as soon as they heard we were the band we were even less welcome. So we retreated a little and decided to run the road block.

It was reminiscent of the final stanza of *Convoy*. 'Just let those truckers roll, ten-four!' We ran the roadblock and shot off up the mountain road pursued by police cars. We jumped out at the venue and ran into the backstage area, which by then was awash with tear gas.

Punters had gone to the venue, it was sold out and they couldn't get in, so they were turning over police cars. It was complete mayhem and madness. The police sent in a helicopter, which was dropping tear gas not only outside but inside the venue. It was a really over-the-top response so I went on stage and pleaded for calm – 'don't react against the police' - and we attempted to play our show. We had to come off stage because no one could breathe, and they were passing children and babies down through the audience, who were choking with tear gas. It was pretty awful. I was saying, 'Stay calm. Keep quiet. We'll try to keep on playing. Don't do anything to make the situation worse.' It's not the only time that I've been tear-gassed. There were a few more. But this was potentially one of the most dangerous ones, that could have really gone wrong.

We got through the show and the police were waiting for us, because they saw us as the architects of the downfall of American civilisation and were out to get us. We had to be smuggled back down the mountain road in the back of an unmarked station wagon, hidden under blankets. It was one of Barrie Barlow's first gigs as our drummer. He was under the blanket next to me, hiding as police were shining their torches into vehicles looking for the band, and said, 'Is it going to be like this every night?' I said, 'Yeah, well probably.'

Rock music was banned from Red Rocks Arena for a period of eight years following that, before they let any rock music back in. I think they let John Denver in strumming a guitar, and the Denver Symphony Orchestra were allowed to play, but there were no rock bands for a long time. When we eventually came back it was with some trepidation, because of course the papers were full of the fact that we were coming back to play again, reminding everybody of the brief carnage of some years before. But by then the mood had changed. The police had relaxed a lot. There was no big drama. And I've played at Red Rocks several times since.

LA FORUM

18 JUNE 1971, LOS ANGELES, CALIFORNIA

JOEL MORSE

The first time I saw Tull was right after *Aqualung* came out. It was a fantastic concert. Ian came out alone at the beginning and started the acoustic part of 'My God'. The weirdest part was the opening act was Livingston Taylor - a quiet acoustic guitar player. We weren't sure what to think.

SCOTT PASSEROFF

My 17-year-old cousin and I had first row seats. As I first approached my seat, two football player-sized attendants asked to see my ticket. I wanted to hang on to it, but showed it to them. The next thing I knew, I was on my back and one guy ripped my ticket out of my hand. They looked at it, then returned it to me.

My cousin was wearing a top hat and flung it to Ian, who tossed it back like a frisbee. My cousin, who has now seen them scores of times, still has the top hat.

EDMONTON GARDEN

24 JUNE 1971,
EDMONTON, CANADA

SHAWN ROSVOLD

I saw Jethro Tull just once, on June 24, 1971 at Edmonton Garden in Edmonton, Alberta. They were on the same bill as Yes. It was an amazing show, and cemented my love of both bands. Fast

Shawn Rosvold saw Tull in 1971 and caught up with Ian again around 25 years later

forward about 25 years and I was working on the morning radio show at Q104.3, the New York City classic rock station. Ian Anderson was our guest, promoting a new album. We were not told that he wanted to perform live on the show. He arrived with instrumental music tracks on a portable music player which he wanted us to play on the air and he would sing to them live. Of course, our station engineer was not at work at 6am, and we had never done what Ian wanted us to do before. Ian was not amused, and I could tell he was quickly losing patience. I grabbed a bunch of cables and crawled beneath the sound board. We managed to jury-rig a cable set-up that would work after a few unsuccessful tries, and it sounded like all of Jethro Tull was in our studio.

PACIFIC NATIONAL EXHIBITION COLISEUM

25 JUNE 1971, VANCOUVER, CANADA

MEERA KAMRA-KELSEY

I was 16 years old, travelling across Canada with my parents and younger brother in a tent trailer from Ontario to British Columbia. It was a memorable trip with many interesting sights and highlights, but as a slightly surly teen I occasionally wanted to get away from my family. When we stopped to camp in Vancouver, I saw a flyer for a Yes and Jethro Tull concert at the Pacific Coliseum. I talked my parents into letting me go and we went and bought a ticket. That evening, my father dropped me off to go to this concert alone and we arranged a later pick-up at the same spot. I believe this was the first Canadian concert Yes ever played. They were a bang-up warm-up band. I have remained a big fan of both Yes and Jethro Tull ever since – that's over 50 years.

Meera Kamra-Kelsey saw Tull supported by Yes

LIFE IS A LONG SONG EP

RELEASED 3 SEPTEMBER 1971

UK CHART POSITION 11

CIVIC ARENA

21 OCTOBER 1971, PITTSBURGH, PENNSYLVANIA

GARY MEILAHN

It was the *Aqualung* tour. I went with a group of friends from the Carnegie Mellon campus. We had tickets on the floor. The first song was 'Jesus Saves' ('Hymn 43'). The arena was pitch black when a lone spotlight shone down through the thick clouds of (mostly) marijuana onto a lone figure holding an acoustic guitar, a shadowy figure in the dimness. As the word 'save' trailed off in the second verse, the bass guitar hit the entire arena with decibels matching a comet-like flash of brilliant light, bringing the entire stage into view, the band rocking and in full regalia – leopard-skin suit included. The audience gasped for five seconds and inhaled loudly for five more in an almost stunned silence. Then all hell broke loose. It was the greatest live play I have ever seen.

SANDY MUZOPAPPA

The first time I saw Jethro Tull was in 1971. It was a trip planned from PSU campus in Beaver, Pennsylvania. A friend and I were so excited to see the band live. We talked another girl into going with us, telling her how wonderful they were. She had never been to a concert, and rock music was like a foreign language to her. We assured her she'd love it. She didn't! She said she just didn't 'get it.' We didn't understand what there was to get.

Sandy Muzopappa was at the Civic Arena in 1971

I went to another concert some years later and my husband went close to the stage and took a number of pictures. One of them is a picture of Ian Anderson that has hung on our wall for the last 30-odd years. I never thought to tell my kids who it was. For years my daughter thought it was some relative she'd never met.

INTERNATIONAL AMPHITHEATRE

26 OCTOBER 1971, CHICAGO, ILLINOIS

PETER RUDOFSKY

The Chicago Amphitheatre had the worst acoustics of any concert venue in the city. As a 14-year-old, it was the height of my drinking and drug use, so everything's a little fuzzy. But I am a big Jethro Tull fan and had really fallen in love with *Stand Up* and *Benefit*. 'Nothing is Easy' is a great song, as is 'Living in the Past', which in the winter of 1972 became something of a soundtrack to my life and always brings me to a special place when I hear it. A good Jethro Tull memory for me is when I would hitchhike to rock festivals in the mid-1970s and carry a portable cassette recorder the size of a hardcover book with me. 'Reasons for Waiting' was on one of my cassettes and I would listen to it in the forest at night. When Ian Anderson's flute took off was a very 'in that moment' experience that later in life becomes one of those experiences you don't forget.

WAR MEMORIAL

30 OCTOBER 1971, ROCHESTER, NEW YORK

MICHELLE PATTERSON

My dad Doug Patterson introduced me to Tull as a young kid and I have been a fan ever since. He loves to tell the story of when he saw Tull 'before Tull was Tull'. He was a freshman at Rochester Institute of Technology and he and some buddies bought the cheap seats ($5) all the way in the back. When the concert started all of the expensive seats ($25) were open and they were able to move all the way to the front, ending up about five rows from the stage. He said it was an amazing concert. The following year they bought the cheap seats again. However, that time they couldn't get down front as the concert was sold out.

Doug Patterson bought tickets for the cheap seats but ended up five rows from the front

MEMORIAL AUDITORIUM

1 NOVEMBER 1971, BUFFALO, NEW YORK

DENNIS THOMANN

I remember, when I was 15 and first heard Jethro Tull on the radio, how I immediately loved this band. I went to the record store in Buffalo and bought *This Was*. Soon after I bought *Stand Up* and loved how the band popped up when you opened the album up. *Benefit*, *Aqualung* and later *Thick as a Brick* became staples on our record player. When we heard Tull were performing a concert in Buffalo in November 1971, we immediately bought tickets, and my brothers and I were in the centre of the front row. We arrived early and waited in anticipation. I think the opening act was Freedom. They were just okay.

When Tull came on stage, the crowd erupted and nobody on the ground floor remained in their seats. We ended up with our hands on the stage, right at the feet of Ian Anderson. Wow!

The first song I remember was 'My God'. Ian's flute solo and Martin Barre's guitar playing were awesome. They performed all our favourites from their albums, including '*Aqualung*', 'This Was', 'Locomotive Breath' and 'Nothing is Easy'. I remember being blown away by Martin's amazing guitar solo towards the end. I can still see his face, like it was yesterday. The encore was a long version of 'Wind Up'. It was an absolutely fantastic concert.

NJÅRDHALLEN

10 JANUARY 1972, OSLO, NORWAY

ARNE RASMUSSEN SANDMOEN

As a young musician, my first encounter with the band and their fantastic music was in Oslo in 1972, with Ian Anderson's charismatic performances on flute central to the performance. They completely blew me and the rest of the audience away. This was something totally different from what we had experienced with other groups. The concert was completely sold out, but many still wanted to attend and quite a few managed to break windows and enter the building that way. Everyone wanted to see the Jethro Tull phenomenon. My only memento from this performance is the ticket to the concert, because things like t-shirts and other merchandise for sale did not exist at that time.

Many years and many record purchases later, there was to be a new concert in Oslo, on 4 October 1995. Tickets were bought and we lined up at the concert venue, Sentrum Scene. But there was no Ian Anderson. He had fallen ill in Copenhagen and had to drop the concert in Oslo. This time I was able to buy a t-shirt as a memento, which softened the blow a little.

Many more years passed, and even more record purchases, until 2016 and a concert at the Oslo Opera House. Not by the band itself, but with Ian Anderson and the music from his entire career, set up with a great background of photos and film.

To make the occasion extra special, I had a t-shirt made with a picture of the ticket from 1972. This t-shirt is unique, except that I had two of them made and would have loved to have given one of these to Ian, but I understand this is almost impossible. My last encounter with Ian Anderson and Jethro Tull's music was on the 50th Anniversary tour at the Royal Albert Hall in April 2018. There, I posed wearing a suit and the aforementioned t-shirt. Anderson was just as vital and active on stage as before, and his music just as amazing.

Arne Rasmussen Sandmoen was in Oslo in 1972

CITY HALL

5 FEBRUARY 1972, NEWCASTLE, UK

PETER SMITH

When Black Sabbath played Newcastle City Hall, support came from Wild Turkey, featuring Glenn Cornick, who had recently left Jethro Tull. I recall Glenn displaying some pretty frantic bass-playing, his long hair waving about. He was wearing a tassled waistcoat and his trademark headband. Although I don't recall the music too much, I remember it was great to see one of Tull in action. Wild Turkey were short-lived, releasing a couple of albums, and were not particularly successful. Glenn Cornick sadly passed away in 2014.

ALAN RAMSEY

Ian went off to the left of the stage. The stage went dark and then a beam shot out from the lighting crew, illuminating the blue star label of a bottle of Newcastle Brown Ale that he was taking a gigantic swig from. The whole place erupted.

TOP RANK

21 FEBRUARY 1972, SUNDERLAND, UK

PETER SMITH

There is a story surrounding this gig. You won't find it listed in any of the Tull gig histories on the internet, but it definitely took place, and I remember it well.

I first heard of this gig directly from local promoter Geoff Docherty. I was in the Rink (Sunderland Top Rank, to give it its formal name) buying tickets for another event, and Geoff was in there at the same time.

'I've got Jethro Tull coming in a few weeks' time,' he said. Now I already had a ticket to see Tull play the City Hall in Newcastle in early 1972, as part of the tour they were doing to promote their new LP, *Thick as a Brick*. The tour was already advertised, and the only North East date was the City Hall concert, so an extra Sunderland date prior to the tour didn't seem very likely. But sure enough, posters advertising the gig with support Tír na nÓg soon appeared outside the Rink, and I bought tickets with a group of mates.

Gigs at the Rink at that time tended to be on a Sunday night, and I think that was the case for this concert. The gig was obviously a warm-up for the *TAAB* tour. I returned my ticket for the City Hall (they would let you do that in those days, as long as they could sell it on), as I didn't fancy seeing the band twice within a few days. A big mistake, as it turned out.

The night of the Sunderland gig came, and it was excellent. It was great to see Tull play a relatively small ballroom venue, and I was right down the front, straight in front of Ian Anderson. The place was full but not too packed. But the gig wasn't quite what I had expected. First, Tír na nÓg didn't play. They were support for the main *TAAB* tour but weren't at this gig. The other surprise was the set itself. I was expecting an early run through of the *Thick as a Brick* album, but what we got that night was a Jethro Tull favourites set, which was great, but also meant I never got to see *TAAB* played live in its entirety until many years later.

The band had the stage set up ready for the *TAAB* show, with the telephone there ready to ring, but they didn't perform any of the album. Anyway, it was a great gig. Looking back, I should have made the effort to go along to the City Hall as well. I'm not sure why I didn't. The line-up of the band had changed since the last time I saw them, with Barriemore Barlow replacing Clive Bunker on drums.

JOHN PARTRIDGE

I was present at the Rink for a gig which, as I vaguely recall, was arranged to precede the start of the official tour, which commenced at Newcastle a few days later. The 'Rink', as it was known, was a dance hall with no seating at gigs. I originally stood

John Partridge was at the Top Rank in Sunderland in 1972

directly behind a young couple who were effectively in the front row. The young girl became so disturbed by Ian's antics on stage that every time he came near or looked in her direction, she screamed as though she felt in genuine peril. By the end of the second song, even Ian was becoming noticeably concerned with this, so I offered to change places with her. She reacted as though rescued from a potential fate worse than death, and that was how I came to be in the front row at the centre of the stage for the remainder of the concert. Ian was commenting on the low height of the stage area. The height of the rigging above the stage prevented his throwing his flute in the air and catching it; the flautist's equivalent of R. Daltrey's microphone sling, I guess.

He suggested he could throw his flute sideways and, if attached to a cord, he could retrieve it by winding it back. I suggested, jokingly but unhelpfully, that he could bounce it and catch it on the way up. He cocked his head on one side, leered at me and said, 'Yeah, do that 'n' all...'

I have a poster from this gig, removed from the back wall of the Rink and autographed by Ian, Barrie Barlow and the great Martin Barre. The ticket stub still exists somewhere in my loft and the support band were advertised as Tír na nÓg, a whimsical Irish folk duo who did not appear at the Rink but accompanied Tull at the later Newcastle gig.

The conversation with band members took place outside a room at the back of the auditorium from which all the band emerged sometime after the gig had ended. My mate Bill Ferguson and I hung around as I tried to persuade the Rink staff member to remove the poster from the notice board, which he eventually did.

During the course of our encounter with Ian and Martin, my mate (part jokingly) broached the subject of whether Martin had 'a spare Les Paul' he could let him have. There was a genuine delay as Martin looked at us, at the Les Paul at his feet, at Ian and then back to us before, reluctantly it seemed, saying something like, 'Nnnooo, I think I'm gonna need them, sorry.' We both remained convinced that, had this been the end of the tour rather than the start, he would have handed it over. There was a feeling around that time that if you caught these guys at the right moment, they would hand stuff over. A friend of mine swore that he knew someone who had acquired a guitar from Pete Townshend, and there were similar (but unconfirmed) reports of similar giftings.

This is probably something only a Tull fan would know, but the album *A Passion Play* appeared in an episode of *Coronation Street* in around 1973/4. Joanna Lumley was playing the posh, sophisticated girlfriend of Ken Barlow. A scene began with the two of them on a sofa as a piece of music came to an end on Ken's turntable. I instantly recognised it as the 'heartbeat' fade to a side of the album. The album cover, of course, featured on one side an elegant ballerina against a pink background while on the other side was a stark picture of the body of a ballerina in an empty theatre. Ken took the vinyl off the turntable and replaced it in the cover with the elegant ballerina to the camera and said how much he had always admired that piece of music, the inference being that they were listening to a piece of classical ballet. I was extremely amused but was largely unable to share the joke as not many of my mates' mums were as avid a *Street* watcher as mine. I supposed someone in the cast or crew was a closet Tull fan and wanted to win a bet.

I was never disappointed at a Tull gig and was at Newcastle City Hall a couple of years ago to see their 50th anniversary gig, which I enjoyed very much, but I felt Ian's voice had lost its edge, which surprised me as he was never a screamer or strainer, albeit approaching his 70s.

The Rink is long gone but during its demise a cousin of mine retrieved a quantity of boards from the dancefloor, refurbished them and relaid them as parquet flooring in his living room. They remain there to this day.

THICK AS A BRICK

RELEASED 2 MARCH 1972

UK CHART POSITION 5

US CHART POSITION 1

IAN ANDERSON

The *Aqualung* album had been a slow burn. It wasn't a huge hit out of the box in any country. It probably scraped into the bottom of the top 20 or something. But it then continued by word of mouth reputation and radio play to steadily sell and so after a year it had clocked up a lot of sales and many people were describing *Aqualung* as a concept album, which really had more to do with my dressing up of the album cover to give the notion of there being two distinct sides to the album that gave people the excuse to call it a concept album.

It was really just drawing certain things together. There were a few songs that did have something in common but when I say 'a few' it was three, maybe four at the most, that had something more spiritual or connotations to do with religious perception or criticism on my part. To this day I maintain that it was not written as a concept album.

I tried to drag it together by the scruff of the neck to give it some uniformity in the final text that I wrote for the album cover, because the visuals were nothing to do with me at all. I then thought, 'Well, they thought *Aqualung* was a concept album. Let's show them what a concept album really is about, and so *Thick as a Brick* was born. First of all, it was the notion of doing something extravagant and crazy to out-Yes Yes in terms of up-yer-arse concept prog rock, so I started off by writing the words, 'I really don't mind if you sit this one out,' which was a perfect way to turn people off. Right from the word go, it was a 'take it or leave it' proximation, a laying down of a gauntlet. 'You're not necessarily going to like this so why don't you leave the room now?' It was a brave thing to do.

So I would write three minutes of music every morning, go and meet the guys in the afternoon and we would learn it and rehearse it, and the next day we would replicate that and add what we did that day to what we'd done the previous day. So over a 10-day period we had the album pretty much rehearsed as we would play it live. We then went in to record it, which probably took about seven days, and mixed and mastered. The artwork actually took longer than recording the album, because it was quite a complex album cover.

It was all designed to be a little bit of a spoof, a little bit of a parody of the notion of concept albums. It was mocking in a light-hearted way the likes of Yes and Emerson, Lake and Palmer and the early Genesis and the other proggy bands coming to fruition as prog became known as 'prog', as opposed to the more dignified previous title of progressive rock.

Monty Python of course reigned supreme on our television screens in the early Seventies and we all watched it, and I think people pretty much thought the same thing, that half of it was incredibly funny and half of it was embarrassingly awful. The Americans certainly didn't find Python funny. I remember going to see the final cut of *Monty Python and the Holy Grail* with the band on a night off in New York. It's a film that I, along with many other people, helped finance. The theatre was not even a quarter full. We sat together and at every gag, every funny bit, we roared with laughter ,and the rest of the audience were totally silent. They didn't get it. And then at some of the more slapstick moments, the silly things that we thought, 'Yeah, bit crap that,' the American audience roared with laughter.

It was a very illustrative example of how American and British humour at that point were really not allied at all. Python probably found that things that worked in the UK did not necessarily work in the USA, while some things crossed over pretty well. But gradually Python did penetrate the USA, to the point where they were a huge hit.

It was the surrealism of their approach that was the attraction, the unlikely scenarios that were a bit schoolboy-ish, a bit university Footlights Revue kind of silliness, a bit naïve, a bit silly, but nonetheless it was captivating because the relatively young Monty Python team carried it off with aplomb and conviction, so it was an approach to performance I felt could be employed a little in our performance of *Thick as a Brick,* without overdoing it.

We just did a little bit to fool around, and the audience were amused by it, utterly confused by it in Japan, and bemused by it in America. I always figured if half the people found it entertaining and amusing and the other half were left scratching their heads thinking, 'What the hell was that about?', that was probably a pretty good balance and a good thing to aim for. The half that don't become painfully aware that they're missing out on something. You want to get the joke too. You don't want to be left out in the cold, so it makes it a bit more important to try and understand it and try and get to grips with it.

That worked in our favour not only in live performance but also in terms of radio play for *Thick as a Brick.* It was about exploiting the cultural differences between British humour, which was well established since the post-war years and was much more of a surreal affair, and the rather slapstick or one-liner kind of humour of well-known American comedians.

From '72 onwards we employed a certain amount of theatricality, but not to any great extent. The only other band in the early Seventies that was developing that same approach was Alice Cooper. Alice Cooper and Jethro Tull were the bands that pioneered theatricality in rock music. Eventually other people cottoned on to that, and it was aptly parodied later in the *Spinal Tap* movie.

SARA MARTINEZ

In 2002 I did a thesis to obtain a degree in sociology. My research was into progressive rock, and it took me five years because in Mexico there was no internet and no information on progressive rock. I had to send for the books I wanted to read from the University of Birmingham. One of the reasons why I did this research was because of my great passion for progressive rock and especially the music of Jethro Tull. The question I always asked myself when I was 12 years old and first heard *Thick as a Brick* was, 'Why do they play it like that?' Being such young musicians, their virtuosity made their music spectacular, and there was something magical that was fascinating to me. My research discovered that the band

Sara Martínez wrote a thesis on progressive rock, majoring on Jethro Tull

used a technique called tonal harmony, little used in the world and even less so by young people at that time. I got a distinction for my degree.

GARY LUCERO

I was 11 or 12 and my stereo system was an AM/FM cassette player, one of those you carry around. I belonged to the Columbia House Music Club. I decided to get *Thick as a Brick* and I loved it. I think my older brothers were fans but I was into Cat Stevens and Elton John at the time, so Jethro Tull was new to me. I've been a huge fan ever since.

LISA MARTINEZ

I don't remember how, but I first fell in love with Tull's music when I was 12. The first album I had was *Thick as a Brick*. My mom would pay us for ironing, so I would listen to it while ironing. I learned all the words and would sing along with the album. Then we moved to a new state, and the kids at school were very unfriendly and I had no friends. In music class we had to do these oral reports in front of class where we picked a song and broke it down into the instruments used, and explain the different parts of the lyrics. Chorus, bridge, verse. I chose *Thick as a Brick*, knowing I would never be called on to give my report since the song was longer than the class.

Lisa Martinez loves Thick as a Brick

I also don't remember what my first Tull concert was, but in high school I went to a lot. Once, I went to a concert that was four hours' drive from my house. On the way home, something went wrong with the car, and I could not go more than 30mph. It took all night to get home, but it was still worth it. I loved Jethro Tull concerts, for the music and also the entertainment. The way Ian Anderson plays the flute is so unique, and I love the sound. Thank you for all the years of music.

GUILDHALL

2 MARCH 1972, PORTSMOUTH, UK

MARK THUNDERCLIFFE, AGE 15

Mark Thundercliffe with his copies of the single credited to 'Jethro Toe'

My love of Jethro Tull started with the brilliant 'Sweet Dream' single of October 1969. I was 13, but as my parents never had a record player there was no point in buying it, and that brilliant song would only be in my head until … for Christmas 1971 they bought me a mono record player and, never forgetting 'Sweet Dream', I asked my older sister for the *Stand Up* LP, which she bought. I'd also found the 'Life's a Long Song' EP as an ex-jukebox single, and so it started to come together.

By chance Tull premiered *Thick as a Brick* at Portsmouth Guildhall, my home city. My mother miraculously found me a ticket and I went as a 15-year-old Johnny Nomates on his own. Purchase of the *Thick as a Brick* LP obviously soon followed, although unfortunately it was released a week or two after that concert, which was a lot of music to take in cold.

From that point I had to catch up on the previous four years of music and *Aqualung*, *Benefit* and *This Was* LPs were quickly added. The release of the *Living in the Past* double-album that summer filled most of the singles' holes, but I soon discovered there was this phantom, impossible to find but must-have single, 'Sunshine Day'/ 'Aeroplane' by Jethro Toe.

Now in Fratton, Portsmouth was a massive Co-operative department store which had a unique record department, in that it retained everything they never sold. I enquired about the possibility of them having a copy of this 1968 oddball, but after disappearing in the back for five minutes, the shop assistant came back with the expected ''Fraid not.'

Later in 1972 I turned 16, left school and started my engineering apprenticeship. My pay was £10.20 a week gross (about £8.50 take home, minus three quid keep to Mum). I had started to buy *Sounds* weekly music paper and they had a free small ads column, so I thought, 'Try it, why not...?'

'WANTED – AEROPLANE / SUNSHINE DAY – JETHRO TOE SINGLE'

Sure enough, the advert appeared. I thought I had no chance but in a few days I had a letter from someone who said they had a copy and I could have it for £2.50. That was almost half my weekly earnings after paying my keep, but I had to go for it. I could have been easily scammed, but I sent the postal order and the seller was as good as his word. The (well-packed) single fell through the letter box the following week and I became the smug owner of that impossible rare gem.

About two months later the Co-op had a change of policy and announced their massive singles backlog was to be sold off. I went to see what obscure Sixties and early Seventies gems I could find. I was flicking through countless rows of singles no one has ever heard of when – bang! – I found myself looking down at a brand-new copy of 'Sunshine Day' by Jethro Toe. I couldn't believe it. After gathering myself, and without looking desperate, I asked, 'How much is this one please?' 'Um, er, er ... 10p.'

ABC CINEMA

3 MARCH 1972, EXETER, UK

REVEREND GEORGE PITCHER

On 3rd March 1972, about 6.30pm, I was 16 going on 17, in a hired minibus with half a dozen friends, travelling 15 miles from our boarding school in Tiverton to Exeter in the west of England. It was a bit, I imagine, what being in an open prison was like – confined to a few rural acres with occasional, closely-controlled trips into the community. We'd persuaded a new, trendy young drama teacher to take us to a Tull gig. One of us had been given *Aqualung* by his sister for his birthday and we'd played it loudly in a study to annoy our housemaster. But any band would have done – we just wanted to get out.

Tír na nÓg were supporting. It was at the ABC cinema and I remember them noticing a harmonic resonance and striking a note while chanting, 'The ABC resonates in D....' Then it was Tull. I remember the caretakers' caps and coats that the roadies wore and which the band donned to steal on stage without us noticing. We got *Thick as a Brick* for the best part of an hour – the album had been delayed in the shops (remember them?) - and we had no idea what was coming. 'Just a little jamming to warm up,' said Ian. God, was it loud.

During the more familiar back catalogue that followed, I saw one of my friends sitting in the aisle, eyes closed and doing that sent-hippy head movement meant to show how deeply he appreciated the bassline. Even then, I remember thinking he had the whole damn thing all wrong. What was appealing about Tull was that, when prog rock was in its pomp, it was all about self-deprecation rather than self-reverence; the idea that 'heavy' could be witty and thoughtful too; Ian's cut-glass, Anglo-Scottish vowels undermining the glottal-stopping Mockney of rock stars from Surrey suburbia.

And the theology wasn't bad either. I won't say that night in Exeter started me on the road to ordination as a vicar in the Church of England. But, half a century later and on the road as the band's 'Field Chaplain' for the Christmas cathedral shows, I notice there's not much separates my faith and Ian's. Maybe one of us has the zealot gene. Maybe neither of us does. But me a man of God and Ian an atheist? You have the whole damn thing all wrong ...

COLSTON HALL

5 MARCH 1972, BRISTOL, UK
BILL JOHN, AGE 16

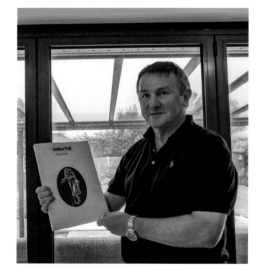

I first saw Tull at the Colston Hall in 1972 on the *Brick* tour and became an avid fan from then on. As part of my apprenticeship with the Post Office Telephones, I went to a local college where the curriculum requested a non-technical study, and I chose to do something on Tull. The intention was to produce an audio tape to accompany a booklet, but sadly the college recording equipment failed me and I had to submit just a script and the booklet I compiled, using many clippings from *NME*, *Melody Maker* and *Sounds*, and for which I received an 'A' ... probably because the lecturers hadn't seen anything quite like it.

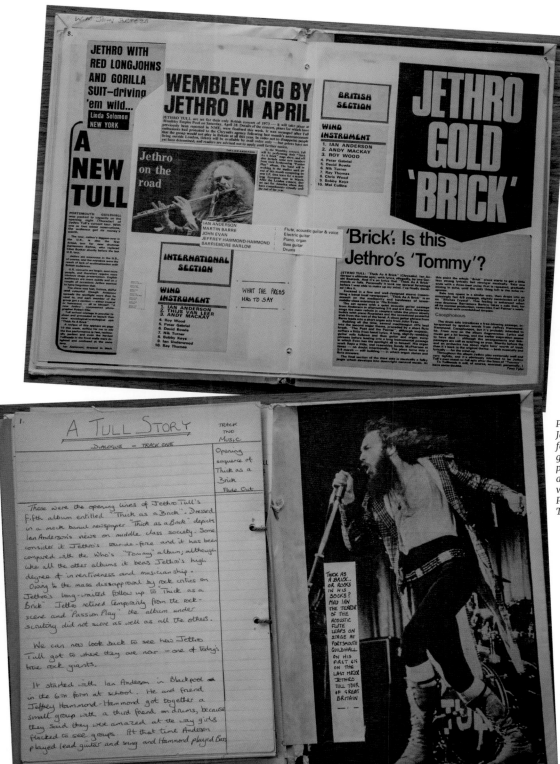

Pages from Bill John's booklet, for which he got an A as part of his apprenticeship with the Post Office Telephones

JOHN BENNETT

I first saw the band on *Top of the Pops* in 1971 playing 'Life's a Long Song'. I was 13 and really liked the music and the way-out look of Ian Anderson, so I bought my first ever record and was pleased it was on an EP with four other songs. I learned that the band had an album and I asked for *Aqualung* for Christmas. I wasn't prepared for the heavier sound of some of the tracks but quickly knew every word of all the songs. The other LP I had that Christmas was *Jesus Christ Superstar*, which complemented the second side of *Aqualung* in a way that encouraged me to think a great deal about what I believed about Jesus and God.

Lines from 'Wind Up' resonated with me. I had been sent to Sunday school. I attended a boy's grammar school where the headmaster was a strict disciplinarian but where school assemblies with hymns and prayers were a daily feature. 'He's not the kind you have to wind up on Sundays,' challenged me

John Bennett saw the Thick as a Brick tour

to be serious about my Christian faith and is one of the reasons I am doing what I am now (I was ordained in 1982).

I saw the band in concert for the first time in March 1972 at the Colston Hall in Bristol, shortly after the release of *Thick as a Brick*. I paid for four tickets and persuaded a friend and two girls we knew to come with me. I was so shy I hardly spoke to the girls and never saw either of them again afterwards. Still, it was a great concert.

RICHARD KENNEDY

Richard Kennedy has quite the collection of Tull memorabilia

I had my back turned to the television back in 1969 when I heard the opening flute lines of 'Living in the Past' on *Top of the Pops*. I'd heard of Jethro Tull by that time, along with Pink Floyd, Led Zeppelin, Free and others. This guy stood on one leg too - what a wheeze! That was it for me and I have been a devoted Tull fan ever since. The pleasure that this band have given me over so many years is really beyond measure. I will never tire ....

I especially remember having two front-row seats for the *Thick as a Brick* tour at the Colston Hall in 1972. I was at boarding school in Cheltenham and, without permission, we got down there, had a great time and got back into our dormitories around midnight. We made the mistake of asking permission for a Pink Floyd gig at the same venue a bit later, and were refused. It was all seminal Tull, of course, that night, and everyone seemingly 'went bananas'. Naturally, I came away with a sweaty catalogue.

JONATHAN ROBERTS

In 1972 I was 14 and like many teenage boys had a crush on my best friend's elder sister, a petite blonde of 16 impossibly sophisticated years. She played the piano, had an acoustic guitar (an instrument I had recently taken up, with so far distinctly mixed results) and most significantly played the flute to grade eight. One day I went to visit and as usual she was playing in the lounge, but unusually she was blowing along with the record player. 'Life's a long song...' came the lyric, and she would unleash a flute line along with the music, a flurry of perfectly articulated notes which hung in the air like diamonds.

Jonathan Roberts' teenage crush's flute-playing proved to be his way into loving Jethro Tull

I didn't know the song, but to my Brit blues attuned ears it was very strange. Sort of folky, but with none of the finger in the ear earnestness you'd hear at the folk club. Also, the singer's voice was at once tender and gentle, edgy and almost angry sounding, with uneven phrasing where words would arrive a beat later than they should have done, which gave an unsettling feel to what could have been just a pretty acoustic ditty.

'Who is this?' I asked, uncool and gormless. 'Jethro Tull,' came the reply, before the chorus demanded another trill of glittering flute. I was smitten.

After earnest promises to treat it with the greatest care, I borrowed what I then learned was an EP, with 'Life is a Long Song' accompanied by four other acoustic based songs, all of which had the same unsettling mix of appealingly accessible acoustic guitar and tasteful instrumentation coupled with that voice, which seemed to be at once to be sharing seductive and intimate moments ('Nursie'), horsing about (exaggerated Northern accents and semi-drunken singalongs with seemingly off-mic side-comments on 'Up the 'Pool') and deep disillusioned anome ('Dr. Bogenbroom'). My ears picked up on 'For Laters', with its sinuous electric guitar playing in unison with the flute or knocking off tasty little licks and riffs on the side.

I loved Peter Green, Eric Clapton and Paul Kossoff, but I could tell immediately that this bloke was something completely different. Martin Barre hopped straight into my top five guitarists and has stayed there ever since. And, of course, the title song, which still sounds just about perfect, even at a distance of 50 years.

I was intrigued, too, by the acoustic guitar, which I knew was played by Ian Anderson but which defied comparison with anyone else – sounding at once quite simple, with precise strumming which even I could imagine doing, but held together with unintuitive fills and runs which were unheard of then when acoustic guitars were either robustly thrashed or delicately finger-picked. This hybrid style was quite unique to my ears.

'They don't always sound like that,' my friend told me, handing me his sister's LP, *Aqualung*. 'Much rockier.' Looking at the cover, with its painting of a leering tramp cringing in an urban street, an individual both scary and also an object of pity, things started to fall into place as side one played. The tenderness, the anger, the irreverent sneering, the detached observation. One minute into the title track I was completely hooked. The combination of muscular riffing, lyrics from who knows where, acoustic guitar interludes (no flute, oddly) and that voice told me everything I needed to know. This was very different.

The lyrics were thrillingly decadent – a population of whores, underaged girls, beggars, drug addicts and high church notables wandered between songs of domestic bliss with butter melting on hot toast and spinning helplessly in the slipstream. Wailing about lemons this was not.

More of the band now, too – stately piano, drums which syncopated rather than holding down the backbeat, the build-up to one of the greatest guitar solos of all time - played, I learned many years later, under the beady eye of Jimmy Page watching from the control room. No pressure, Martin.

The thrill of that early exposure to the Tull has never left me. They have hit other highs, the odd clunker, the lineup has changed, Ian's voice has understandably suffered after decades of touring and recording, they've been rock, prog, folk (frequently all at the same time) but they remain an endlessly fascinating listen which moves the feet, the heart and the brain all at once. What more can we ask of a band?

'THE WITCH'S PROMISE'

JOHN TAYLOR

Like many, I first encountered Tull when they appeared on *Top of the Pops* performing 'The Witch's Promise'. As an impressionable 11-year-old, I was most taken by the bug eyes of the crazy singe, and I persuaded my dad to buy the single. After that, I have to admit I sort of forgot them pretty quickly. So, we roll on to 1972. I was in the basement of Guy Norris's record shop in Barking, probably intent only on buying 'Virginia Plain' or similar. However, Norris's had those old listening booths, where people could ask to hear stuff, and they had gone all upmarket and installed headphones too. In one of the booths there

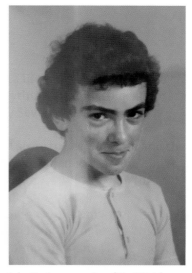

John Taylor remembers 'The Witch's Promise' on Top of the Pops

was a guy, with admirably long hair, pretty much freaking out. He pulled one earpiece to one side and yelled to his mate, 'This is brilliant, it's even better than the last one,' then proceeded to get back into the groove.

For some very odd reason, his body language and words so impressed me that I asked the guy behind the counter (yes, me, a 13-year-old who would blush if relatives spoke to him) what the lad was listening to. He held up the album - the divine newspaper of *Thick as a Brick*. Even then I did not make the connection between this and 'Witch's Promise'.

Within a week, I was back there, handing over my pocket money for this mysterious album. I still hadn't heard any of it. After all, it was unlikely to be a staple of Radio 1 - so effectively I bought it blind on the basis of the reactions of one teenage local. And then to find it was all one track too? Man, this was something else. Suffice to say it was full steam ahead after that. I'm now 62 years old and still buying *A New Day* magazine. And despite everything that has come since, and all those 'animal deals', I still maintain *Thick as a Brick* is the greatest record I have ever heard.

Funnily enough a few years later I did the same with *A Farewell to Kings* by Rush. I'd never even heard of them but bought the album on the basis of the intriguing album cover. And as above, I've never looked back.

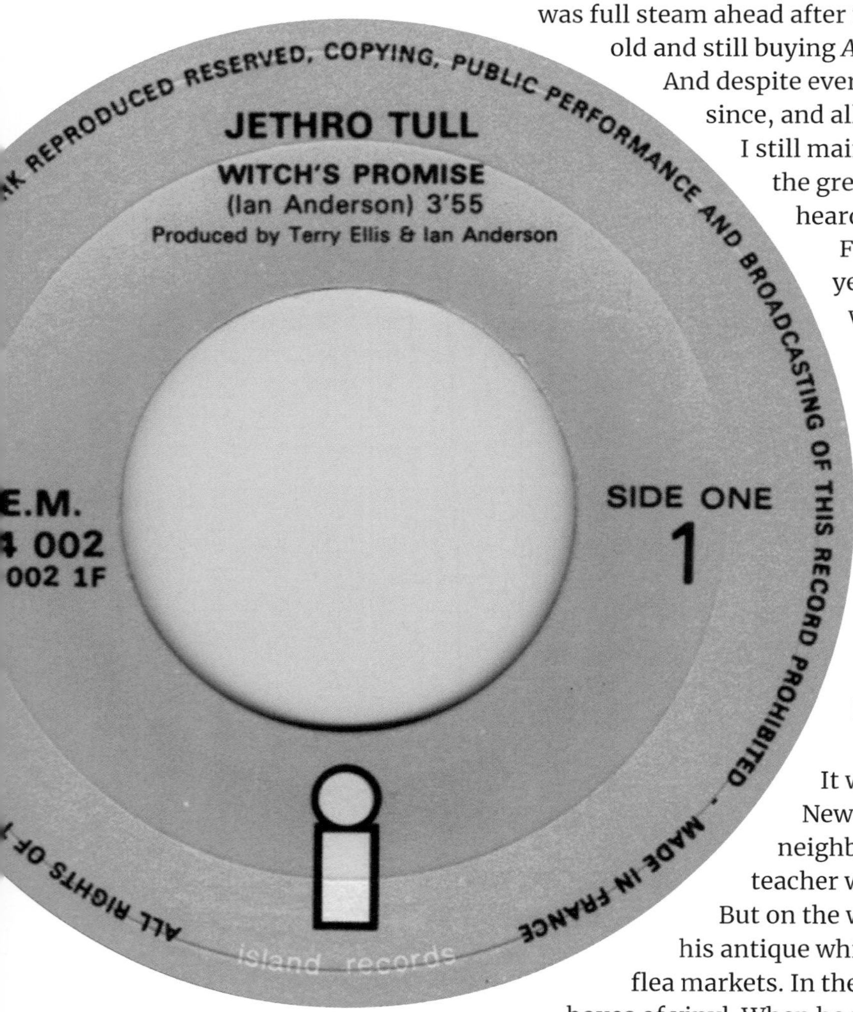

JETHRO TULL
WITCH'S PROMISE
(Ian Anderson) 3'55
Produced by Terry Ellis & Ian Anderson

SIDE ONE
1

RICH GILSON

It was the late 1970s in New Jersey. My next-door neighbour was a NYC school teacher who commuted by train. But on the weekends, he drove his antique white VW bus to local flea markets. In the back were boxes and boxes of vinyl. When he returned home, and in sympathetic support of my home life living with an alcoholic, he would let me go through the boxes and pick out anything I wanted to give a listen to. The day my creative and musical heart beheld and held the double LP of *Thick as a Brick* landed me in awe, and with the opening notes I instantly became a Tull fan. By the end of my first full listen, Ian began being my lifeline musical hero and influence.

Rev Rich Gelson became an instant fan on hearing Thick as a Brick

BARRY ROSEN

In 1970 I was 16 and a camper-waiter at a camp in Colchester, Connecticut. A fellow bunk-mate had a reel-to-reel tape deck (remember those?) on which he would play music for the bunk while we were chilling. There was one album he would play that fascinated me because the group's sound was so unique, so different. I had to ask him who it was. *Benefit* was the album that was in constant rotation all summer long.

When summer was over, I educated myself on Tull and found out *Benefit* was the third of three albums, so I went to the record store in search of *This Was* and *Stand Up* and was knocked out when I finally saw the group on the cover. That incredible sounding music was emanating from those seedy looking chaps? No way!

Aqualung knocked my socks off, and when I heard they had recorded a new album, *Thick as a Brick*, I rushed to a record store in the Bronx, New York to score the Chrysalis pressing as the Warner Brothers version wasn't set to be released for a while. I went home, slipped the platter on my record player, donned my Koss Pro4AA headphones and lay down in my bed to listen. I was 18 at the time and had a rough relationship with my dad, so the themes of the record dealing with authority hit home. When the crescendo near the end happened, the music takes you skyward and tears began streaming down my cheeks as Ian sang, 'Where the hell was Biggles when you needed him last Saturday?'

Now, 49 years later, *Thick as a Brick* is still my all-time favourite piece of music. I have of course bought everything Ian has recorded and am happy to have shared planet Earth with him at the same time, as he has brought untold joy to my life with his music, as he has for millions of others.

JORDI ACETA

I'm from Barcelona. I was born in March 1972, right after the release of *Thick as a Brick*. My older brother bought that record and I grew up listening to it but not really being aware of what it was. I was aged 12 when I started to take over our home stereo, play my brother's records and re-discovered this jewel. I created my own visual movie around it, shaped by its wonderful and epic music. I read parts of the newspaper too. The first minutes of each side were screwed

Jordi Aceta loves Thick as a Brick

because a former girlfriend of my brother broke it. It looked like a bite on the vinyl (you can guess why that relationship ended) and the central pages of the newspaper were missing.

I soon started to hit record shops and grow my own record collection. I found a complete copy of *Thick as a Brick* and bought it for a reasonable collector's price. This album goes with me wherever I go, even if I have no turntable (I have it on CD too, both the original and remastered versions).

Jethro Tull are one of the greatest and most genuine bands, but *Thick as a Brick* is their greatest album. I grew up thinking it was a serious concept album until one day I read a magazine article explaining that it was a parody of concept albums. You know those moments in which life is laughing hard at you and you … join in the laughing?

Recently I was asked by the company I work for (related to technology services) to create a space for employees where I would recommend music albums and films. Guess what my first article was about.

ST GEORGE'S HALL

15 MARCH 1972, BRADFORD, UK

STEVEN LANGFIELD

When I learned Jethro Tull were to play in nearby Bradford, I had to go. My ticket for the dress circle cost £1.50, at that time the same price as an album. Buying early meant I had a seat on the front row overlooking the band, my favourite spot, and I

Steven Langfield recalls Thick as a Brick being the 45-minute opener

went on my own as none of my mates shared my taste in music. The capacity of the hall was 3,500, so quite a large venue, and it was pretty near full on the day. Irish folk duo Tír na nÓg played a short set in support. I'd not heard of them previously. Or since, to be honest.

I was reasonably familiar with Tull's new album, *Thick as a Brick*, though it had only been released the previous week, and the band played it, note-perfect, in full as a 45-minute opener. What a great way to kick off. The rest of their almost two-hour set came mainly from *Aqualung*. I have seen many bands over the years but still class this gig as the best I've ever seen. Great songs, great musicians, great light show, and then there was the wild onstage antics of Ian Anderson. As it happened this was the only time I saw the band.

VICTORIA HALL

16 MARCH 1972, HANLEY, STOKE-ON-TRENT, UK

DAVID BAGGALEY

I saw Jethro Tull at the Victoria Hall on the *Thick as a Brick* tour. About five minutes into the 'Thick as a Brick' suite, the band were in full swing when the music stopped and a telephone placed on the piano began ringing. Ian 'listened' to the caller and then made this announcement: 'Will the gentleman who has left the thoroughbred horse parked outside the theatre please remove it, because it's now got in and it's fouling the foyer.' The band then continued to play and a minute or so later a jockey was leading a racehorse down the aisle towards the stage and then to the right front row to exit the theatre. The band carried on playing whilst the jockey and horse came in, and no other comment was made.

ABC CINEMA

17 MARCH 1972, STOCKON-ON-TEES, UK

LAURIE WITHERS

I first saw Tull as an 'innocent' 16-year-old and still at grammar school, having worked the previous autumn half term potato picking for a farmer in Northallerton. For two weeks of backbreaking work, I earned £90, an absolute fortune in 1971. I bought a corduroy jacket and a ticket to see Tull at the ABC Cinema, Stockton-on-Tees. This was my first rock concert and *Thick as a Brick* got me hooked for the rest of my life.

I have bought every album the band ever produced, I have probably seen them 30 to 40 times over the years and will continue to do so until the end. I have been to many Christmas concerts over the last few years and hope they continue, but the choice of venues must be starting to run thin. I have my *Ballad of Jethro Tull*, am eagerly awaiting my *Silent Singing Ultimate Edition*, have bought all the anniversary re-mixes, and will buy any more that get released.

Ian Anderson is a rock genius and at the age of 75 shows no sign of slowing down. I last saw them on *The Prog Years* tour at the Brighton Dome in September 2021. I was very impressed with both Joe Parrish-James and the quality of Ian's voice, which seems to have benefited from the break due to Covid.

I wish I had kept all my ticket stubs from over the years. It would have made a great piece for my lounge wall. No-one will ever replace Martin Barre, who I believe is probably the most underrated guitarist in the world. I have seen his band twice since he left, and will continue to see him whenever I can. Long may Ian, Jethro Tull and Martin Barre continue to tour and entertain.

Laurie Withers saw Ian most recently in 2021 at the Brighton Dome, almost 50 years after the first time

GREEN'S PLAYHOUSE CINEMA

26 MARCH 1972, GLASGOW, UK

ARCHIE PEEKY SCOTT

I met Ian Anderson and his lady in Union Street outside Glasgow Central not long after the release of *Thick as a Brick*. We spoke for about 15 minutes, and he was a gentleman.

WIGAN GRAMMAR SCHOOL

1972, WIGAN, UK

PHIL GORNER

It was de rigueur for young music fans in the early Seventies to walk around secondary school with an album tucked under the arm or plonked beside the desk, with the cover there for all to see. You showed off your music 'tribe', for all to honour. Heavy rock and progressive were the two main camps at the top of the respect tree. *Led Zeppelin II*, *The Yes Album* and *Thick as a Brick* were the favourites.

Our particular form loved *Thick as a Brick* and, for five or six weeks, that particular album found itself borrowed by different classmates who, of course, strutted around school with it and placed it prominently on the floor ... which was rather disconcerting for our form teacher. Every morning registration for six weeks, he'd come in to see *Thick as a Brick* at a different desk, followed by a different desk in the afternoon registration. It became a game. Guess how long it would take him to spot it.

Drove him bonkers. To the end that, after the six weeks, he almost broke down and threatened the next time he saw the *Thick as a Brick* album front cover staring at him by a desk, the culprit would be given a detention. The next day, the *Thick as a Brick* album was there ... but with the back of the cover showing. I swear he sobbed quietly to himself ...

I'm still great pals with a number of my old schoolmates and, as students (and beyond), we used to make a point of having 'cultural' trips around the country every Easter and New Year. Well, drinking trips, really. One particular trip was to Harlech. On the Sunday evening, after a meal at a restaurant with copious drinkies (pubs were shut as it was a 'dry' county), we made our way down to the beach, already populated by families and others with small bonfires for cooking meals, etc. One of our mates started singing the opening lines to *Thick as a Brick*. We all decided to join in, and for the next 45 minutes, went through the entire album, musical sections, solos, sound effects, spoken bits, the lot. Seven or so 'merry' Wiganers ... Funny how the beach quickly emptied.

Tull kicked off their next North American tour in April 1972, taking in 60 dates across the US and Canada in support of *Thick as a Brick*.

MEL LINDSTROM

I was a 22-year-old rock fan. I worked for my father, who ran a sound company in central Illinois. One day around 1972 I overheard him in his office talking to a promoter about booking a midwest tour. When he got off the phone I asked, 'Who was that you were talking to?' He said, 'It was some band called Jethro Tool and they wanted a huge amount of power, so I turned it down.' I about died on the spot. My dad turned down Jethro Tull!

FORUM

14 APRIL 1972, MONTREAL, CANADA

NICOLA BRIZZI

I saw them in 1972 at the old Forum in Montreal. The aura that came out before, during and after the show was magical, especially being relaxed on hashish. The concentration of Ian's words and music were easily interpreted and understood. The frenzy of tickets going on sale, knowing all those beautiful teenage girls would be attending. It was mystical and magical, just like his music.

GEORGIA COLISEUM

28 APRIL 1972, ATHENS, GEORGIA

VAN EPPERSON

When Jethro Tull played the University of Georgia Coliseum on the *Thick as a Brick* tour, the album was not even in the local stores yet. They opened with *Thick as a Brick* and played an hour-long version of it, with a bunch of added 'performed' sections with various characters in costumes thrown in, as Jeffrey Hammond-Hammond read stories from the album cover newspaper. After that first hour and song ended, Ian said, 'For our second number...', and that got a big laugh.

It was also Greek Week at UGA, so the fraternity and sorority houses had voted for 'Miss Greek Week', a sort of Greek beauty pageant. During

Van Epperson was there for a great night at UGA

Tull's set, the show was briefly stopped to crown Miss Greek Week but, to the shock of all the 'Greeks', when she was announced and crowned, Tull sent a man in a gorilla suit on stage to grab her (she started kicking and screaming, dropped her flowers) and the big ape ran off stage with her in his arms. Tull stood off to the side laughing their asses off, and it was indeed funny as hell.

Captain Beefheart and His Magic Band opened – the *Trout Mask Replica* line-up when that album was brand new. It was a great night at UGA.

THE AUDITORIUM

29 APRIL 1972, WEST PALM BEACH, FLORIDA

DON BROWN

I was in tenth grade. I had gotten my driver's license in February and life was pretty good. I was ready for my first rock concert. My friends and I had started a band and 'Locomotive Breath' was on our setlist. The West Palm Beach Auditorium held around 6,000 people and we were up pretty close to the stage by today's standards. I was mesmerised by the vibe, the lights and how exciting the moments were leading up to the opening of the show. Joints were fired up and passed along the rows as soon as the lights went out and the band came on. It was my first toke.

I recall Ian Anderson wearing some strange clothes, tights and a cape. He played a small parlour guitar and I was impressed with his picking style. Later on, when he was dancing all over the stage with his flute, I was truly in awe. Near the end, a guy came out in a wetsuit with a scuba tank for 'Aqualung'. 'Locomotive Breath' had us all standing up and dancing.

During this same time period, the WPB Auditorium held shows for Yes, Emerson Lake and Palmer and *Jesus Christ Superstar*. It was an amazing venue where you could be so close to the action. Today, tickets for a show like that would be $500 to $1,000. I think we paid around $6. Looking back, the Jethro Tull show was the best ever. At the time I didn't realise how lucky I was.

ROSS PAYNE, AGE 15

It was the first rock concert I ever attended. My friend Dave, 17, had a car. We drove the 60 miles from our hometown of Miami to West Palm Beach, with my other friends Jeff and Rick. When we arrived, the marquee said 'JETHRO TULL SOLD OUT'. We were very disappointed. We parked the

Ross Payne jumped the gate in 1972

car and joined a crowd of people who were milling about outside the gate. At some point, there was a rush of people jumping over the gate, and we went with them, ending up with some seats high up and behind the stage. Captain Beefheart, the opening act, was playing at the time.

I had wanted to see Jethro Tull since first hearing the album *Benefit* in 1968. I know that it was wrong to see the concert without paying. Back then the tickets were probably $5 each. If you provide an address, I will happily send a check.

KIEL AUDITORIUM

5 MAY 1972, ST LOUIS, MISSOURI

TONY CZECH, AGE 17

Tony Czech first saw Tull in 1972

I had returned to Missouri in March 1972 after being in Corpus Christi, Texas for the past six months. I discovered that Jethro Tull were playing in St Louis on my best friend's birthday. We drove the three-hour trip there in my 1961 Chevy Biscayne, with only one issue – the thermostat got stuck and the water pressure went up. The general fix for that is to take out the thermostat (and remember to replace it by winter, so your heater will work).

The bassist for opening act Wild Turkey was Glenn Cornick, who had been Jethro Tull's original bass player. Tull's show featured the full *Thick as a Brick* album and, once over, Ian Anderson gave the best line of the show: 'And for our second number...' before they tore into 'Aqualung'. The next 30 to 45 minutes were other songs from *Aqualung* and older Tull albums. After the show, we had to drive back home to Camdenton, because the next night was junior and senior prom ... and I had a date to go with.

COBO HALL

8 MAY 1972, DETROIT, MICHIGAN

BOB BARBER

One or two memories of a love affair with a band over 50 years? It can't be done, so I'll touch on highlights and keep it as brief

Bob Barber is a big fan of Tull

as I can so as not to bore anyone. My first Tull concert was *Thick as a Brick* at Cobo Hall in Detroit, perhaps the most underrated venue for sound in the United States. I loved the album, as I had the previous Tull releases, but this show made them my band. The encore remains the best I've seen from any band and is superbly captured on the second side of the bootleg LP, *Ticketro*. Martin is extraordinaire! The one thing I missed was that Ian dropped the entire acoustic section from side two of the album, substituting a flute instrumental and a Barrie drum solo, which worked great. But I loved the acoustic portion, especially the 'Do You Believe in the Day' reprieve, and missed it being played. Ian dropped most acoustic numbers for a period as he tired of fans being disruptive during the acoustic numbers.

Fortunately, Ian did play the entire second side for his *Thick as a Brick* 2 tour, which makes that concert one of my all-time favourites. Having *Thick as a Brick* 2 played with the entire *Thick as a Brick,* including the 'Do You Believe in the Day' reprieve, was a dream come true. I was fortunate to see the show approximately a dozen times in the United States and England.

HERSHEY SPORTS CENTER

10 MAY 1972, HERSHEY, PENNSYLVANIA

JEFF

Jeff recalls Ian ad-libbing a line when an object was thrown on stage

I attended three concerts in the early Seventies. One was an open admittance concert in Hershey, Pennsylvania, one was in Baltimore, Maryland, and the third was in Philadelphia, Pennsylvania. I attended the one in Philly knowing I had a college exam at 8am the following morning. However, I needed to see Jethro Tull and wasn't going to forego that just for a college exam. At Hershey Park, someone threw something on the stage while Ian Anderson was singing '*Thick as a Brick*'. He was very angry and just at the right moment sang, 'Thick as a fucking brick like you'. He stopped the song and said he was going to stop playing if this continued.

SUSAN WALES

I first discovered Jethro Tull in 1971 with the release of *Aqualung* in the US. My taste in music, artists, bands, and genres was quite varied at that time, ranging from rock, pop, psychedelic, folk and the blues to classical and jazz. I was most drawn to bands who combined genres and wrote poetic lyrics. Obviously, I had been obsessed with The Beatles for these very reasons. When I first heard Jethro Tull's *Aqualung*, I became immediately obsessed. Their sound was genre-defying, with elements of rock and classical, sometimes tender, often driving, sometimes orchestral, often invoking a renaissance sound I'd never heard before. I liken my first hearing of *Aqualung* to hearing The Beatles' 'A Day in the Life' for the first time ... mind-blowing. There was no other sound, no other music you could compare them to at the time. *Aqualung* with Ian Anderson's flute was a sound that excited me musically and poetically, and as I did with the Beatles' *Sgt. Pepper*, I played their album over and over. A year later, *Thick as a Brick* was released, my appreciation of the band cemented, and I became an ardent fan.

In the fall of '72, I learned Jethro Tull were coming to a town approximately an hour from where I lived and knew I had to see them. I had graduated high school the year before and was working at my first real job as an illustrator for a national retail store. A girlfriend of mine and I decided we needed tickets, along with two guy friends of hers who I didn't know, and get ourselves there. It was of no consequence to me that I didn't know the boys. I was laser-focused on getting to that concert. On our way, one of the guys handed each of us a little white tab and without thought, we all took them. It was the early Seventies and my friend and I were 19, so need I say more? This was only my second concert. The Animals had been my first and only live performance experience several years earlier. You must remember that in 1972, there was no YouTube or digital media. Exposure to artists was either from the radio, TV, albums or live performances. By this time, I was familiar with Jethro Tull's music but had not seen them perform.

Our seats were up in the nosebleed section, but the venue was fairly small and the acoustics were good. Jethro Tull came on stage and opened with 'Thick as a Brick'. 'Cross-Eyed Mary' followed, the excitement was building, the effect of that little white tab was kicking in, and inhibitions were loosening. Aside from the music itself, Ian Anderson's performance was unlike anything I had ever seen, heightening the experience with each song. He was absolutely electric. Late into the performance, they finally built the momentum to 'Locomotive Breath' ... and that's when it happened. I was completely taken over by the music. I was living it, breathing it, I had melded into the experience (heightened by the hallucinogen, I'm sure), and had become one with the music, with Jethro Tull, and with Ian Anderson. I do remember what I did but have no recollection of any responses from anyone around me. I was insular in my experience.

I've only told this story to two people, my husband and daughter, mostly because few people who know me now would believe it - though I fully embrace and treasure the memory. In this state, consumed by the music of Jethro Tull, I stood on my chair and began to dance. I danced and danced and then I was overcome with the need for even more freedom. And off came my sweater. And yet this was not enough, and I was overcome with the need for ... well, let's say I had a need for absolute freedom of expression and ... need I paint this picture more clearly? But I will say that I had never been so moved before and have never been so moved since my complete immersion in the music of Jethro Tull.

I have thought about this experience throughout my life and finally, at the age of 68 years old, have perhaps come upon an explanation. When I was quite young, an aunt took me to a Pentecostal church service. I remember sitting there, as a child, being completely bewildered by these otherwise normal adults jumping and leaping and speaking 'in tongues'. My aunt explained to me that they were filled with the spirit of God, and this was how that fulfilment manifested itself. The spirit of the Lord had to be released and set free. So this is what I think happened to me. I danced at the altar of Jethro Tull, in their presence, and was filled with the spirit of their music. And it just had to be set free and, in that moment, it was the natural thing to do.

SPECTRUM

11 MAY 1972, PHILADELPHIA, PENNSYLVANIA

FRED BORDEIANU

My brother and I travelled by bus to Philly and arrived about noon. Since I was a great fan, especially of Ian, thanks to whom I acquired a flute and taught myself to play, I was wearing the traditional knee-high brown leather boots with laces and a black ankle-length trench coat. My brother was wearing a white ankle-length trench coat. The concert was due to begin at 7pm, so we had a long walk to the venue. We arrived fairly early and were able to get right to the front of the stage. As the crew was setting up the stage, I noticed they all were wearing long white trench coats. So I switched coats with my brother and went backstage, with nobody stopping me. I got to the stairs leading to the stage, and just then Ian came up to go on stage. He looked somewhat surprised. Obviously, he must have wondered who I was. He just said, 'Hello, lad,' and got on stage. I, too excited and happy, ran quickly back to my place in front of the stage and enjoyed the wonderful and unforgettable show.

BOSTON GARDEN

12 MAY 1972, BOSTON, MASSACHUSETTS

JACK CORCORAN

My Tull journey began in 1971 in my friend Bill Cavanagh's basement. We had always listened to music of all genres. He said, 'Jack, listen to this - *Aqualung* from Jethro Tull.' I never heard anything like it, and could not get over the lyrics and blend of hard rock and acoustic folk-rock. I played it over and over.

The following year we saw the *Thick as a Brick* show in Boston Garden, and never missed a show in and around Boston for the next 50 years. I always rented a bus and bought tickets for all my friends. We would go to dinner, hit the show and (depending on our behaviour) head home for the night. Through the years a new generation of Tull fan joined us - our children! My girls always loved our annual Tull concert. We met the guys many nights, including backstage, and were always met with grace, laughter and wonderful musical insight.

I remember one night in Providence my daughter Mary, aged just 10, was overwhelmed when Ian played her favourite song, 'Wond'ring Aloud'. Ironically, Ian asked her backstage what her favourite song was, Mary recounted her story and Ian said, 'Did your father make you say that?' Ian told her the song was easy on him because there was no flute. Mary said, 'There's no flute on 'Aqualung' either.' He laughed and said, 'Well spotted!'

Another fond memory was a show in Austin with my daughter Kathleen. I went to buy a t-shirt and asked the adorable little girl behind the counter how she got the job. She whispered, 'Ian is my grandfather.' I said, 'Be kind to him. God made him special.' I went on to tell her mother I think I bought Ian his house with all the shows I've been to.

Fast forward to many shows home and abroad and planning vacations around Tull shows. Last year I got sickened by cancer and was sidelined, but I ordered an Ian replica parlour guitar from Brook Guitars and Ian's head joint from All Flutes as heirlooms for my girls. I have been trying to learn some Tull pieces during my ordeal, and have been working very hard with some wonderful and patient teachers. It has taught me to admire Ian's tenacity, but more importantly his gift of musicality and songwriting.

Ian's music provides my pals and family with common ground. Keep at it, Jethro Tull. My grandchildren are getting ready to get on the bus.

MAPLE LEAF GARDENS

4 JUNE 1972, TORONTO, CANADA

GEDDY LEE, RUSH

I think it was on the *Thick as a Brick* tour. The show began with the house lights on and a bunch of people in overalls sweeping the stage. Gradually there were less people sweeping, and then, all of a sudden, one of them would pick up an instrument, and next thing you know, it's the guys from Tull launching into the show. For me that was the first band that combined incredible musicianship with complex songwriting, and they were funny. That influenced me a lot in the later years of Rush. That attitude of taking your music seriously but not taking yourself seriously.

(as told to *Classic Rock* magazine)

Thick As A Brick is my favourite Jethro Tull album. I know it is partly a send-up of the idea of 'concept', but it is delivered to perfection. I was a massive Tull fan from very young ... I was mesmerised by Ian Anderson. His presentation was simply magical, and he delivered it with such a sense of humour and great style. There really wasn't anyone else who looked or sounded quite like them, and that holds true to this day. We saw it as a huge challenge to try and create something that can seem so dynamic onstage. They are probably best regarded as a live band, although their series of albums around that period were exceptional.

(as told to *The Quietus*)

SEATTLE CENTER COLISEUM

11 JUNE 1972, SEATTLE, WASHINGTON

BARB RUDEN

Growing up in Seattle, Washington, I had a brother seven years older than me. He had a huge musical influence on me – I know just about every word to every single Beatles song and have never purchased an album. One day when I was around 13, I was at my brother's house and he played *Aqualung*. I was hooked. Since then, I have purchased many albums, including a couple of bootlegs I still have. I have seen JT in concert several times, including the June 1972 concert at the Seattle Coliseum. I remember a huge balloon or rubber ball being tossed around the crowd and also recall the opening band getting booed off the stage; we were there to see Jethro Tull.

Jethro Tull have been the biggest musical influence in my life. I wanted to name one of my sons Ian (I ended up naming him John, which is close). I've had a huge musical influence on my own children and brought my 25-year-old son with me to see Ian Anderson at Seattle's Moore Theatre in October 2016. When I listen to Tull now, it takes me right back to the Seventies, some of the happiest times of my life.

Barb Ruden with her brother Doug

OAKLAND COLISEUM

16 JUNE 1972, OAKLAND, CALIFORNIA

LINDA MARTIN

I'll remember this show forever, because we had to wait for the parking lot to clear before we could find our car.

MEMORIAL COLISEUM

18 JUNE 1972, DALLAS, TEXAS

DEBORAH GRIFFIN FERRETTI

We had a second or third row ticket by the amplifiers. My right ear rang for two days after the concert. Fast forward 49 years later, and I suffer from hearing loss. But I loved every minute of that concert, and it was worth the loss in my old age.

LIVING IN THE PAST

RELEASED 23 JUNE 1972

UK CHART POSITION 8

US CHART POSITION 3

ALISTAIR MUTCH

Alistair Mutch discovered Tull via 'Living in the Past'

I was 14 years old and at school in the UK when I saw Ian and the band playing 'Living in the Past' on the TV. I liked the music but, to be honest, it was the crazy image Ian projected that really grabbed my attention. The adverse reactions from the older generation were just what was needed to cement the attraction. The first single I ever bought was 'Sweet Dream', bought in Leicester.

I think it was Ian Macdonald in his great book on The Beatles who describes the popular culture of the period as the revolt of the sons against the fathers, and that's a fair description for me. Like Ian, my father was a fairly strict Scot, so I warmed to the songs on that theme on *Benefit*. But there was also the exposure to 'Mother Goose' via a sampler LP, which gave another dimension. So it was that when I could afford it - music was very expensive then for a schoolboy - I bought *Thick as a Brick*.

In common with many of the boys at my school, I was a music snob so the more pretentious the better. It was a stereotype, but it was rock for the boys, Tamla for the girls. There was something about the whole package that reinforced the liking for the music. I have to admit, though, I parted company with the band over *A Passion Play*. Not only did I find it over-pretentious and musically a little incoherent but I was also at university by that time and, I'm ashamed to say, fell under peer pressure where the approved music was from the US West Coast (although always with a sub-note of British folk). It was through the latter that I re-encountered Tull much later through CDs that came through a circuitous route from Dave Pegg. I gradually realised what I had missed and what a tremendous body of work there was, such that the band re-established themselves at the top of my favourites pile.

I've written about Tull in a couple of academic journals: 'Following better things: Grammar schools, religion and English rock music in the early 1970s' (*Popular Music History*, 11(3), 2018, 228-251); and 'National identity and popular music: questioning the 'Celtic'' (*Scottish Studies Review* 8(1), 2007, 116-129).

I was at a grammar school, and Ian's critique of organised religion chimed with me, hence the first piece. Is there something about Tull that appeals to academics?

LA FORUM

23 JUNE 1972, INGLEWOOD, CALIFORNIA

STEVE LUKATHER, TOTO

I discovered Tull when *Stand Up* came out and have been a lifelong fan since. I wore out the records. When *Aqualung* came out, I learned everything off it in a blacklight room whilst partaking of some Mexican herb in the early Seventies. LOL. No one sounds like Tull.

When *Thick as a Brick* came out, we all ran to the record store to see what Ian and the boys had up their sleeves and, man, it was an epic album. We listened to it four times in a row that first day. Then we heard the tour was coming to LA. We lined up for tickets at our record store (remember those days?) and all got seats.

The show was life-changing. Theatre rock was not a thing at that time, not that I was aware of anyway. Ian and the boys took it to a new level, and I would say *Thick as a Brick* at the LA Forum changed my life. It was the most amazing show I have seen, with flawless sound, lights and staging ... it was jaw-dropping. I am a Martin Barre fan too, and he was great. They played the whole new album and left the stage to an over-the-top roar of the crowd, and after a long cheer the boys finally came back out and gave us some older 'hits', where they raised the roof. It is a show that me and my friends still talk about.

SPORTS ARENA

25 JUNE 1972, SAN DIEGO, CALIFORNIA
MARTHA STODDARD

Life-long Jethro Tull fan Martha Stoddard

I am a life-long Jethro Tull fan. I love the intricacy of the pieces, the melodic richness and the rhythmic innovations, especially in *Songs from the Wood*. As a high school student, I played flute and guitar, and my best friend introduced me to Tull via *Benefit* and *Aqualung*. We listened to them every day. He also introduced me to Bach and Stravinsky, so Tull were in good company. I particularly loved 'With You There to Help Me'. I was really drawn to the acoustic guitar playing and of course the flute solos, which completely changed my thinking about rock music.

My first Tull concert was at the San Diego Sports Arena in 1972. Ian Anderson blew me away. I set about learning the acoustic guitar and flute parts to every song and played them non-stop, including *Thick as a Brick*. Figuring that out by ear was an obsession. For a Hallowe'en party I dressed up as Ian, with flute in tow. Being somewhat shy, it was very liberating to pretend to be a rock star. I've gone on to a career in (mostly) classical music, but still listen to Jethro Tull frequently, and marvel at the intricacy of the compositions.

James Pickard was at the Vets Coliseum

VETERANS COLISEUM

27 JUNE 1972, PHOENIX, ARIZONA
JAMES PICKARD

I heard *Benefit* in my college dorm. When they

came to town, I was at the ticket counter the first day. I had front-row seats, just left of centre. The opening act couldn't appear, so after finishing the *Thick as a Brick* performance, Tull took a short break and came back to play some of their older tunes. The concert ended with 'Locomotive Breath', with strobe lights flashing as the keyboardist danced his way across the stage from the piano to the organ. I will never forget that experience.

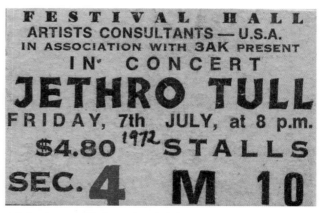

Rob Hastie saw Tull in '72 and again in '74

FESTIVAL HALL

7 JULY 1972, *MELBOURNE, AUSTRALIA*
ROB HASTIE

I remember the first song was *Thick as a Brick*, and after a 40-plus minute performance, once the applause had died down, Ian sauntered up to the mic and said, 'Now for our second song.'

I also remember an article in the local music magazine entitled 'A case of the crabs down under' as Ian was constantly scratching and adjusting his junk (cock and balls), which prompts another memory – Ian taking great delight in introducing John Glascock as 'Old Brittle Dick'.

APOLLO STADIUM

8 JULY 1972, *ADELAIDE, AUSTRALIA*
PETER GREGORY

The Apollo Stadium was a basketball stadium that staged many concerts. I remember being really excited about Jethro Tull coming to Adelaide after discovering their music from a friend, loving the record *Stand Up*, so I bought tickets to see them as soon as I heard they were coming. I remember that just before the concert started there were blokes in long overcoats on stage. We didn't realise it was the band until they removed them and went straight into *Thick as a Brick*, which had just been released. The concert was the entire album, which blew everyone away. From that time, I was a Jethro Tull fan. I'm pleased to say I still am.

HORDERN PAVILION

11 – 13 JULY 1972, SYDNEY, AUSTRALIA

TIM MENDHAM

I've been a fan of Tull since the year dot, albeit from Australia, which hasn't always been easy. I relish my stand-up (gatefold) copy of *Stand Up*, which wasn't released here in that format, so I had to slip my mint copy of the vinyl album into the slightly tarnished copy of the cover (the record inside was in terrible condition, so it wasn't a difficult decision to make the change).

I saw *Thick as a Brick* at the Sydney Showground pavilion, seated on the side with an appalling view (ie. none), having to move down to the back for the second half to actually see the band.

I remember going to a concert in Sydney when Ian was a 'solo' act – the *Under Wraps* tour – and I still have a burst balloon that was sent out into the audience.

And in the early Seventies some friends had a fancy-

Tim Mendham (front) went to a fancy dress party as Ian Anderson, but didn't win

dress party and the theme was 'come as your favourite rock star'. Naturally I chose Ian. I frizzed my hair, put on some tight striped trousers and boots, borrowed a flute and ran around like a loon. Unfortunately, I didn't win the best-dressed competition, probably because I looked like that all the time. The winner was a friend who put on a pair of ladies' briefs and suspender belt and posed as Mick Jagger, based on one of Guy Peellaert's pictures of the Stones in *Rock Dreams*. Ian was featured in the same book, in a rather disconcerting image from *Aqualung*.

CIVIC CENTER

16 OCTOBER 1972, SPRINGFIELD, MASSACHUSETTS

PENN JILLETTE, MAGICIAN & ACTOR

Jethro Tull was one of the first stadium shows I ever saw. I'm from a dead factory town in Western Massachusetts, and it was a big deal to drive to Hartford, Connecticut for the Tull show. I announced over the school PA that I had an extra ticket, and a ride, but we'd probably have to skip school the next day because we'd be home too late. It was a long drive, and I was always the designated driver.

Everyone else from my school who saw the show was tripping on LSD, but I was drug-free even then. The others thought the show was great while tripping balls, but I think it might have been better stone cold sober. It was so smart, honest and theatrical. Inspiring. Tull has always had everything I want out of art - there is pure skill, they were good at what they do. They seemed to enjoy what they were doing and wanted us to enjoy it too. They were sincere, not ironic. But more important than all that, they weren't afraid to be very heavy and deal with real important stuff, and be silly at the same time.

Tull helped me see that the sombre and the surreal could live together very nicely in a stage show. We were in the world of *Aqualung* - life, death, paedophilia, suffering and God, taken there by a guy standing on one foot, grunting with a flute. Then at a seemingly random moment the silly spectacle of a guy struggling to walk on stage in full scuba gear for no reason except the album title.

I learned from Tull that artists could take themselves very seriously and not very seriously at the same time. I hope a little bit of that lesson shows up in our silly (and sometimes heavy) Las Vegas magic show. Those other children, who were tripping and seeing their own show ... they don't know what they missed.

CIVIC ARENA

17 OCTOBER 1972, PITTSBURGH, PHILADELPHIA

BOB WESSEL

A friend was trying to figure how to record music from his stereo all-in-one turntable to a simple mono cassette player/recorder, so he was playing the beginning of *Aqualung* over and over. The music was unfamiliar but quickly grew on me. My first Jethro Tull concert was at Pittsburgh's Civic Arena, and I have seen every Jethro

Bob Wessel got into Tull via Aqualung

Tull Pittsburgh concert from that point on at the Arena, Palumbo Center and the Starlake Amphitheater. I have every Jethro Tull recording on vinyl and CD, and several on eight-track. Some of the earlier albums I have two copies of, because the first was worn out. I also have the Ian Anderson recordings on CD. I can't explain the joy Jethro Tull's music has brought to me over the years. Thank you for the music and the memories.

BAYFRONT CENTER

3 NOVEMBER 1972, ST PETERSBURG, FLORIDA

WILLIAM BALDRIGE

In 1971, Jethro Tull were appearing at the Bayfront Center in St Petersburg, Florida on their *Aqualung* tour. My brother and good friend were going, and I was already a big fan as I had all their albums on eight-track and would listen to them in my car, so they were hearing me talk about Tull all the time. Unfortunately, I couldn't go to the concert, but when they came back the next year I wasn't going to miss it. My wife and four of my best friends all loaded up in my car for what was the *Thick as a Brick* tour. I remember it like it was yesterday.

    The Bayfront Center was full of illegal smoke and the opening band was Gentle Giant. When they finished, I said to my wife, 'If Jethro Tull are going to be better than these guys, they're going to have to be awful good.' As it turned out, they were incredible. My wife and I went to every concert by Jethro Tull from that point on, and when our son was 10, we took him along for *The Broadsword and the Beast* tour. It became a family tradition. At the last count I've seen Jethro Tull 44 times, and every show was fantastic. I hope they come back to Florida. Believe me, I won't miss it.

SPECTRUM

30 OCTOBER 1972, PHILADELPHIA, PENNSYLVANIA

JENNIFER KING MAGGIO

Jethro Tull was one of the first concerts I ever went to, at the Spectrum in Philadelphia when I was a young teenager. I was entranced by the passion of the music, the romance of the outfits ... so timeless! It spoke to the artist in me. A few years later, in college as an art major,

Jennifer King Maggio gave her husband Ed two drawings

I met the musician who would become my first husband, Ed. My guitar string had broken, and I'd heard him playing guitar next door. I bravely went over and asked if he had an extra string. I soon learned that he was also a huge Tull fan. Two years later we were married and expecting our son. We went back and forth over what to name him until almost simultaneously, with a Tull album playing in the background, we said, 'Ian!'

Ian was born in 1979, the light of our lives. He was a born musician too, brought up on Tull. I gave Ed two Tull-inspired artworks in those early years. Our paths diverged later down the road, but we always cherished our early life together, with *Songs from the Wood* as our soundtrack. Sadly, Ed passed away just a few months ago. But his music and legacy play on through his own songs and those of Jethro Tull and our Ian, all interwoven into a beautiful symphony.

'Life's a long song... but the tune ends too soon for us all.'

VETERANS MEMORIAL COLISEUM

5 NOVEMBER 1972, JACKSONVILLE, FLORIDA

JOHN KIRKPATRICK

This was my first time seeing the band. It was an awesome concert and we went to get a hamburger after it was over at the Krystal. At that time, they had kerb service. I could not believe my eyes when a limo pulled up to the parking spot where you ordered your food with the band in it, including Ian Anderson. We told them how much we enjoyed the concert. They were nice and we left so they could eat in peace.

COBO HALL

9 NOVEMBER 1972, DETROIT, MICHIGAN

KEN MCNEILL

The next live show I saw was at Cobo Arena in Detroit. Barriemore Barlow had joined the group. Though disappointed at first because I love continuity in bands, Barriemore didn't miss a step and fitted in perfectly. Bob Seger was the opening act. He was a local favourite and Cobo Hall was where he years later recorded his now legendary *Live Bullet* album. However, Mr Seger couldn't hold the crowd, as Tull was who they came to see.

Tull played an excerpt from *Thick as a Brick*. It was the infamous John Evan organ intro riff into 'I've come down from the upper class to mend your rotten ways' segment. Well, we'd certainly never heard or seen anything like that before. Though the album wasn't released yet, the crowd was stomping and clapping their hands to the riff like they'd heard it all their lives.

CHICAGO STADIUM

11 NOVEMBER 1972, CHICAGO, ILLINOIS

PAUL BOURJAILY

The first concert I ever attended was Jethro Tull at the Chicago Stadium during the *Thick as a Brick* tour in '72. They played the album for nearly two hours, with everyone getting a solo. Ian did his solo, about 15 minutes as I recall, on one foot. The band took a break and then Ian came on stage by himself, with a single spot on him. He perfectly deadpanned, 'And now for our second number.' The crowd went wild. The band played for at least another hour. An amazing show to be sure.

MADISON SQUARE GARDEN

13 NOVEMBER 1972, NEW YORK, NEW YORK

BRUCE MIRONOV, AGE 15

Live shots of Tull in 1977 and 1978. Photos: Bruce Mironov

When I was 11 years old in 1968 my brother, two years older than me and who played electric guitar, picked up the album *This Was*. It had a very weird cover with very weird looking people on it, but I heard the music so much I soon knew the album. I was aware of *Stand Up* and *Benefit*, but *Aqualung* was the album that got me really going. The first time I saw Tull, on the *Thick as a Brick* tour, I was just amazed. From then on there was no looking back. I saw them on every tour through to the 2000s.

I got my first SLR camera in time for the *Warchild* tour in March '75 and got to photograph Tull in concert. I brought my camera to many Tull shows over most of the tours in the Seventies and Eighties. Back in the day, we had a scalper in NYC named Lenny. He would get us tickets in the front 10 rows for around $40. Many times when everybody rushed the stage for the encore, 'Locomotive Breath', I would be at the very front of the stage with my camera. It was so intense.

Live shots of Tull in 1977 and 1978. Photos: Bruce Mironov

PALASPORT

17 MARCH 1973, BOLOGNA, ITALY

ALBERTO CADOPPI

I was playing basketball with my team. We were winning, perhaps. Who cares? Zelio, Luigi and I were thinking about something else. It was the great day when Jethro Tull were about to perform at the Palasport in Bologna. We were 15 years old. My parents didn't want me to go, but luckily Luigi had a bigger sister, and she and her fiancé would take care of us and take us there, so I was able to convince my parents. We arrived in Bologna with our regular ticket a few hours before the show. In Italy, those days, there were a lot of people who thought music should be for everybody, and free. That's why at the gate thousands of people without a ticket came and tried to get in. It was like an enormous riot.

The police came and used tear gas against the crowd. Luckily, we were not in the wrong place, probably because we had arrived early. We waited in the middle of the crowd for a long time, and at last we got in. We managed to sit somewhere and sat and enjoyed the concert. I had with me a small Phillips cassette recorder. Just before leaving home, I realised I had no blank C120 cassettes. The only one I could find had a Genesis concert on it, recorded a couple of months before, in Reggio Emilia. As a Tull fan, I decided to bring it with me and tape over the Genesis concert to record the Tull concert.

The recording is of course a disaster, but the concert was fantastic. Tull were at their best. Ian Anderson was running and jumping as a beast on stage. Everybody knows how Tull were in those years and we enjoyed watching Martin, Barrie, John and Jeffrey. They were absolutely part of the show, even if our idol was Ian. There was an intermission with the weather forecast: John, as Tony Tempesta, was forecasting the weather in Italian.

The music and the band were powerful. We had an hour of *Thick as a Brick* and other classics such as 'Aqualung' and 'My God', during which I remember we could hear loud noises and shouts, which was probably the police attacking the ticketless people outside.

In the end nine people were arrested, 26 were charged with criminal offences and some people were injured. Probably my parents were right. I shouldn't have gone. But I made it. The encore was unbelievable: 'Wind Up', 'Locomotive Breath', 'Hard-Headed English General' and 'Wind Up' again. It was the best way to finish such an unforgettable concert.

Back then I couldn't imagine that more than 20 years later I would become the co-founder of *Itullians*, the Italian Tull fan club, with my younger friend Aldo Tagliaferro, who missed that extraordinary tour simply because in March 1973 he was still a small boy.

EMPIRE POOL

28 & 29 APRIL 1973, WEMBLEY, LONDON, UK

RUPERT BOBROWICZ

I had just finished A-levels and left school, moving to London from England's smallest county. On arrival, I saw that Jethro Tull were performing their latest album, *A Passion Play*. London buses in Oxford Street were displaying the pink album ballerina cover advertising this. I hadn't got a ticket, but knew I had to attend. To resolve my dilemma, I went to the Chrysalis office just off Oxford Street and asked if tickets were available. After waiting a few moments, the guy at the enquiries desk came back with two tickets, for which I paid face value. Great. I knew I could get there and, in addition, take my older brother, who was already living in London.

On arrival at the stadium, we presented the tickets and my brother asked where we were sitting. To our amazement we had front-row tickets - a dream come true. The only downside was that the stage was so high we had to keep looking up, but we got a first-class view of the concert.

STUART CAROLAN

The first major band I saw live was this very gig. This was the first UK performance of *A Passion Play*. Through the mists of time, I remember it as a colourful, energetic and entertaining show. As part of the extravaganza, we also got to see the film of 'The Story of the Hare Who Lost his Spectacles'. How we laughed at a ridiculous Monty Python-esque moment.

I went to the gig with my friend Andy Gandolfi, a huge Jethro Tull fan at that time. I remember as well at the end when the band had left the stage a telephone rang on stage (with amplified sound through speakers) and was answered by someone on stage who informed us all, 'It's for you.'

JENISON FIELDHOUSE, MICHIGAN STATE UNIVERSITY

12 MAY 1973, EAST LANSING, MICHIGAN

BOB BARBER

In the early summer of 1973, I saw *A Passion Play* at Jenison Field House on the campus of Michigan State University in East Lansing before the release of the album.

We were blown away. Ian on the soprano sax was a fantastic addition to the sound and fitted with the material perfectly. That fall I saw four *A Passion Play* shows at Cobo Arena. The shows were paired, the first two on a Thursday and Friday followed by two more the following Thursday. An interesting tidbit is the Ministry of Information website, which catalogues all Tull shows, incorrectly lists a Buffalo date for the last Cobo show date.

This was the beginning of me seeing multiple shows across the Midwest every tour. I am approaching 500 Tull, Ian and Martin shows across four countries, two provinces and 37 states, plus Washington, DC.

Besides the shows I've mentioned, what others stand out? The *50th Anniversary Show* at Royal Albert Hall for certain. Jorge Tovar and I were granted passes to the after-show party, where we mingled with the band and many other individuals who had worked with Tull over the years. Other stand-outs are the last show in the United States where Ian, Martin and Doane shared the stage at the Rosemont Theater in Chicago in the fall of 2011, and two shows in Reykjavik in 2007 with Mr Boo. I could go on, but I won't ... so many shows, so many wonderful memories, so many friends made.

I have been fortunate to amass what I believe is one of the largest Tull memorabilia collections in the world. Highlights include the comedy mask which hung above the stage for the *A Passion Play* tour, signed by Ian and Martin and personalised to me, and the infamous *Crest of a Knave* banner, stolen after a show in New York and showing up on eBay in 2014. I purchased it with some reluctance after Ian expressed no interest in having it returned. I have numerous official record awards, including Ian's gold *Crest of a Knave* and triple-platinum *Aqualung* awards, John Evan's *War Child* white matte and *Minstrel in the Gallery* UK awards, and his *Festival Record* award to commemorate the band's second tour of Australia in July 1974. And I have Chris Wright's *Benefit* white matte, *A Passion Play* and *Songs from the Wood* awards. I also have hundreds of original posters, including the Isle of Wight, an entire set of Fillmores and a Fraternity of Man poster, where Tull appeared with Led Zeppelin, as well as tour posters and tons of rare promotional posters from both Reprise and Chrysalis. My lovely wife Maureen, who has tolerated my Tull shenanigans all these years, says, 'Just what are you going to do with all that crap?'

CAMBRIA COUNTY WAR MEMORIAL ARENA

16 MAY 1973, JOHNSTOWN, PENNSYLVANIA

BOB D'ARCANGELO

I've seen Tull so many times, but my brother saw them before me and turned me on to them. He saw them at the Cambria County War Memorial. The next morning, he played 'Locomotive Breath' and explained how the piano intro leading into the jam was unbelievable in terms of the energy and sound quality, and the best he ever saw. I agree.

MEMORIAL AUDITORIUM

29 MAY 1973, KITCHENER, CANADA

JANE MCGHEE SMITH

Jane Smith still has her 1973 concert poster

Kitchener, Ontario is located along the major highway in Southern Ontario, so bands would cross the American border at Detroit or Buffalo, play in Windsor, Ontario and then head to London, Ontario, Kitchener–Waterloo, Toronto and Ottawa, then off to Montreal. And in the 1970s there were so many bands that would pass our way. What a great time to be a young teenager! And because Buffalo and Detroit weren't far from us, it was easy to go over and see bands there.

My favourite band was always Jethro Tull. My first exposure to them was the album *Aqualung*. Then of course I had to get their previous albums - *This Was*, *Stand Up* and *Benefit* - and remained a huge fan. I saw the *A Passion Play* concert, which was incredible. When I found out they were coming to my town, I was so excited. My mum let me take the day off school so I could line up for Tull tickets – there was no Ticketmaster back then. Luckily, I got front-row centre. The concert was at our local auditorium. I've always been a huge Tull fan, and saw them quite a few times, including getting front-row seats and taking some amazing photos. I also did a copy of the *Aqualung* album for my art class, and received high grades.

EMPIRE POOL

22 & 23 JUNE 1973, WEMBLEY, LONDON, UK

NICK BAYLEY

The music of Jethro Tull has certainly been a prominent feature of my life since the age of 14 – I'm now 62 and a retired teacher after 40 years working in education, examining and

Nick Bayley was at the Empire Pool in '73

135

administration. My love of what was then described as progressive music began with the influence of my older sister, who was very much into all the enigmatic bands of the late Sixties and early Seventies. My father was an Army officer and while we were stationed in York, my sister would hang out with her great-coat-wearing hippie boyfriends and go and see bands like King Crimson, Gentle Giant, Genesis and Jethro Tull, who played at the York University Central Hall in 1969. She had a copy of *Stand Up* and I was fascinated as a 11-year-old not only by the sounds coming out of the hi-fi stereo unit that sat proudly in our dining room, but also with the fabulous album cover.

We moved to London in 1971, and a year later my sister had moved on to university in Brighton. In March 1972 she wanted to take me to see the *Thick as a Brick* shows at the Albert Hall, but my parents said no, I was too young. Thankfully in 1973, I and two schoolmates bought tickets to the now infamous Empire Pool shows, which were to be the only UK gigs from the band to promote the *A Passion Play* album. We paid 50p each for our tickets. We were more than a little disappointed to hear that the shows had been postponed from April until June, and by then I had purchased the album from Forest Gate market and played it almost continuously, much to my parents' horror.

Nick Bayley with his signed copy of Heavy Horses

Suffice to say that particular show will stay with me as long as I live. Robin Trower was the support band and for a good 45 minutes before Jethro Tull hit the stage, we were treated to the sound of the repetitive heartbeat and the white pin-spot on the cyclorama getting gradually bigger and bigger; culminating at the point when the house lights went down and the pin-spot morphed into the ballerina and the band kicked in with the opening of the album. It was an absolutely tremendous start. From then on, I was gripped.

I remember those moments in the show when the music suddenly stopped dead and the phone, neatly positioned downstage, would be ringing out over the PA. Ian would come across, followed by Jeffrey or Martin, to answer the phone and shout out some random names of audience members. They would then pick up from exactly the point where the music had stopped. Right at the end of the show, with Ian alone under a single spotlight singing the last lines of 'Wind Up', the phone rang again. This time he answered and shouted, 'It's for you', before exiting stage left.

EMPIRE POOL

22 & 23 JUNE 1973, WEMBLEY, LONDON, UK
MARK THUNDERCLIFFE, AGE 17

We travelled up by train from Portsmouth to Waterloo, then took the underground to Wembley Park for the Empire Pool and the first *A Passion Play* show. After the gig there was no chance of getting back for the last train home, so we stuck it out in Wembley. I walked around the stadium a few times until the small hours, dodging a patrolling panda car. We clearly looked dodgy. Eventually we found a programme-selling booth with the door open and managed to get a couple of hours' sleep. It was bloody freezing, even in June. We got the first tube to Waterloo at stupid o'clock in the morning to get the Portsmouth train home. I was knackered by the time I got home, but wouldn't have missed it for anything. I haven't missed a Tull or related tour since *TAAB* in March '72, when I was 15. But this was the most memorable.

UNIVERSITY ARENA

8 JULY 1973, ALBUQUERQUE, NEW MEXICO
STEVE BRITTENHAM

Steve Brittenham was grabbed by John Evans' Hammond sound

As best I recall, I was 'made aware' of Jethro Tull in 1973. I was born in 1956 and grew up with music. There were LPs and reel-to-reel tapes playing in the house. My dad played guitar, steel guitar, ukulele and organ. He had a Hawaiian band practising in the living room for a while, and they played the officers' clubs. He tried to teach me to play several times, but I wasn't interested. My older sister and younger brother listened to records and radio often. I heard music, and listened sometimes, but it was really peripheral to me. When I got to high school in 1970, I started to pay more attention because everyone else did, and in 1972 I finally started buying my own records. I probably heard Tull on the radio or at parties during this time, but it wasn't registering. A girl across the street went to see them in 1972, put a 'Biggles' license plate on the front of her car, and tried to tell me how great they were. I didn't get it.

One night, probably early summer 1973, I went to spend the night at a friend's house. His parents had a camper trailer on the side of the house. He brought his stereo out from his bedroom and invited four or five friends to spend the night in the camper, listen to music and have fun. Everyone brought some records to listen to, and that night, amongst other things, I heard Deep Purple's *Machine Head*, Yes' *Close to the Edge*, and Jethro Tull's *Thick as a Brick*, all for the very first time. The organ playing on these three LPs grabbed my attention that night and would not let go. Jon Lord's intro to 'Lazy' and Rick Wakeman's pipe organ in 'Close to the Edge' had the hair standing up on the back of my neck. How can music physically affect me like that? Then, John Evan's Hammond organ playing throughout *Thick as a Brick* ... what is going on here? This music, this arrangement, this sound .... This was the first time in my life that I recognised a deep physical and emotional response to music, inside me, that I didn't quite understand.

Several weeks later, Jethro Tull came to Albuquerque on the *A Passion Play* tour. Since that night in the camper, my friends and I had been talking about and listening to *Thick as a Brick* over and over again. Now I understood what Debbie across the street was trying to tell me. One of my friends turned me on to *Aqualung* too. I had never been to a concert, but we decided we should go see Jethro Tull. I had no idea what to expect, no real concept of what a concert was.

Our seats were several rows up, on the side of the stage, and luckily for me, right above John Evan's keyboard setup. The lights went down, and Steeleye Span opened the show, slowly walking on in hooded robes, singing 'Gaudete'. This was my introduction to a concert. Wow. They played their set, and I loved them. When they were done, the lights came back up and the arena was filled with smoke, very surreal. I was totally straight and sober – I hadn't experienced smoking pot yet. Wow.

The lights went back down, and an image of a ballerina was on a big screen behind the stage. Strange music, a heartbeat, tension builds, she rises, goes through a mirror and - BOOM! - Jethro Tull are suddenly onstage playing this incredible music. The crowd reaction is wild. I feel this same intense excitement too, an excitement I can't remember ever feeling before.

Our seats are above the side of the stage. I'm not seeing the front and centre concert view most people get. All night long, I watch from this vantage point as Jethro Tull perform their show. Ian Anderson is nothing less than jaw-dropping, amazing to watch and listen to. Jeffrey Hammond-Hammond, Barriemore Barlow and Martin Barre are absolutely fantastic. And John Evan ... it was the organ playing that first got my attention that night in the camper, and here I was right behind him, watching him do his thing. Wow again.

The music, performance and musicianship are incredibly amazing, but put that aside for a moment. What I'm really seeing from the side of the stage is Ian Anderson and company creating this ball of energy out of this music, tossing it back and forth between each other, then throwing it out to the audience. The audience grabs it and throws it back. This goes on all night long, the ball gets bigger and bigger, the energy more intense ... what is going on here? I'm just sat here, watching and listening, out of breath with excitement!

How do they do that? How does a musical performance by someone else produce this physical exhilaration in me? I have to learn how to do this. A year and 10 days later, I buy my first organ and begin teaching myself to play. Seeing Jethro Tull this night was, literally, a life-changing experience for me. I started going to other concerts after this, seriously got into music, and I'm still playing keyboards in a classic rock band today. That Jethro Tull show was the catalyst for all that.

A PASSION PLAY

RELEASED 13 JULY 1973

UK CHART POSITION 16

US CHART POSITION 1

MARINA MILDENSTEIN

Marina Mildenstein was first attracted to Tull by A Passion Play

I was given the album *A Passion Play* when I was about 14 and thought it was craziest thing I had ever heard. I loved it. I still quote from it. Then the summer I turned 16, a friend introduced me to the album *Aqualung*. I was fascinated by the old man on the cover and loved all the lyrics. The songs were kooky and so different from anything I had ever heard. I will always remember going to visit my friend, who lived in a flat above some shops, and out of his window, high above, would come the wonderful sounds of *Aqualung* for all the street to hear. That summer I listened to it just about every day, lying on my bed with my feet hanging out the window singing along, knowing every word, and dancing around my back garden with an extra-long straw, pretending I was playing Ian's flute. My Mum despaired of me. I still listen to it today with a sort of reverence. After *Aqualung* I was hooked and went to buy as many other Tull albums as I could (on vinyl, naturally). I think my other two favourites are *Stand Up* and *Broadsword*, as they remind me of a time and a place in my life. But truthfully? I love them all.

MICHAEL WOODY

It was 1977 in SoCal and within my high school there was an experimental 'open school' with four instructors and about 50 students. In a radical move for a public school, we were encouraged to participate in the development of the curriculum. For my English exam I chose the album *A Passion Play* and gave an interpretation of the lyrics illustrated with the programme that came with the record. The year before I started cutting classes so I could hang out in the school library (when not at the school theatre) and I became a voracious reader of Hesse, Vonnegut, philosophy and mysticism, which became the basis of my off-the-top-of-my-head interpretation. I got a passing grade and some praise for my choice of material and enthusiasm. How I wish I hadn't improvised it, because I'd love to read some notes to know what my 17-year-old self said about this most incredible record.

CHRIS AND GENESIS BOROS

My wife and I met because of Jethro Tull. She posted a picture of herself holding a vinyl copy of *Too Old to Rock 'n' Roll* on Facebook in a progressive rock group we are both members of. I commented on her picture, 'Who is this girl? Marry me?' and less than two years later, we were married. She is from Venezuela and I am from the United States. In order for her to come to the States, she had to get a finance visa, but the requirement is that the two people must meet each other. Going to Venezuela was not an option for me since getting a visa is quite difficult, and her coming to the States was also impossible. So we flew to Aruba and met there. I made sure to bring my iPod, with plenty of Tull songs, so we could listen while driving around the island. I knew she was the one when she told me her favourite Tull album was *A Passion Play.* Thank you, Jethro Tull and Ian Anderson, for bringing us together.

PROVIDENCE CIVIC CENTER

30 AUGUST 1973, PROVIDENCE, RHODE ISLAND

CINDY GORAI

My music and song appreciation began in the Seventies while growing up in Coventry, Rhode Island. As a teenager, aside from buying albums of my favourite artists, I attended concerts mostly in Providence, Rhode Island at the Providence Civic Center. Getting together with a school friend, having her parents drop us off at the door and then being there when the music stopped made for an exciting time, growing up and travelling to the 'big' city.

I remember the stage set-up where a section on the front stage jutted out into the audience. Tapping the shoulders of the young men in front of us, they would hold us on their shoulders and bring us to a higher level, where we were able to physically touch the brown suede-fringed boots of Ian Anderson. Those magical moments of the musical notes of the flute will forever be etched in my memory. In those days, there was more freedom, and we were most respectful of our idol. This was the best concert I ever attended in my almost 50 years of concert attendance. Thanks, Ian, for not objecting and for allowing us to fulfil our teenaged dream ... Rock on in the best of health, Mr Anderson.

Cindy Gorai remembers touching Ian's boots

COBO HALL

6 SEPTEMBER 1973, DETROIT, MICHIGAN

KATHRYN BLANCHARD, AGE 14

Me, my best friend Lisa, my brother Richard (formerly known as Dick) and his friend Lee all drove down to Detroit to see the *A Passion Play* tour. It was the first concert we had ever been to. Cobo Hall was massive and as I recall we were in the 'nosebleed section', but it didn't matter. The way the concert started with the film about the ballerina and the photographer is still so embedded in my memory, even 47 years later. The way the band appeared on the stage was the most brilliant thing I had ever witnessed, and to this day no concert has compared. That show was insane.

The film with 'The Hare Who Lost His Spectacles' ... what more can I say? Ian with his flute, John Evan on keyboards (my maiden name is Evans) ... just the whole thing. My mind was blown at the age of 14.

Since then, I've seen Tull in three different states over a 30-year period. The last time was in Reno, Nevada at an outdoor venue, the Grand Sierra. While I love Tull's 'radio songs' I am a true fan of the albums that have never seen radio play. I even have some my brother has never heard. Score one for little sis! My husband and I were sitting in the bleachers and the set was so amazing − 'One White Duck' (my favourite), 'Heavy Horses', 'Farm on the Freeway'. My husband was impressed that I knew the words to every song.

People were leaving and so we kept moving forward. Eventually the security just opened the floor section. A couple walked past complaining about the songs, saying 'When will he play 'Aqualung' or 'Locomotive Breath'?' I said, 'Stick around - they will for the encore.' Expletive deleted! I moved all the way to the front with the true fans and sang every song along with them.

Thank you to Tull for all the amazing music you have given us. I am so thrilled that Ian is still rocking. Keep on rocking, guys, and sharing with us dedicated and true fans some of the best and most outstanding music of my life.

KIRK KENNEY

We saw Jethro Tull perform in September 1973, just before my birthday. Cobo Hall was packed. Ian Anderson and the band put on a great show. The music was real loud and I loved it! We saw most of the great bands back in the day, and this was one of my favourite concerts. My favourite tune is 'Locomotive Breath'.

CIVIC ARENA

11 SEPTEMBER 1973, PITTSBURGH, PENNSYLVANIA

SHAWN MARGARET COHEN, AGE 17

The year was 1973 and I was with my best friend Roberta, her next-door neighbour and my friend, Stacy. We were 17 and Stacy 18. In those days everyone was smoking dope. Pot was everywhere. We had our tickets to see Jethro Tull in hand and off we went, climbing up to our seats, ending up in the first tier. We could see the stage perfectly and as soon as the lights went down, out hopped onto the stage the long-legged bearded wonder that was Ian Anderson, tooting his flute and dressed like a jester in an old English court.

The crowd roared as he began the intro to 'Aqualung'. As we settled in for what was going to be a brilliant concert, one of my illustrious girlfriends pulled out a joint. It was just like everyone else in the place, the smoke was in the air so even if you didn't partake you would get high anyway. Well, this was the hippie times and with our bell-bottom jeans, our platform shoes and Mary Quant eyeliner and lipstick, we did just like everyone else and toked on that joint. After a couple of puffs, somehow, the next thing we knew ... we woke up and the lights were up and the concert was over. Yes, it was completely over and most of the people in the huge Civic Arena were gone.

We were flummoxed. Whatever was in that joint completely put all three of us out for the entire concert. Think of the noise of a rock concert, yet we somehow slept through that. The message for one and all is – kids, don't do drugs or you may miss out on your favourite rock band. Luckily, we still had our handbags, and nothing was stolen so we got up, shook our heads and declared to each other, 'Wow, what a trip!', as was the terminology of the time.

COBO HALL

6, 13 & 14 SEPTEMBER 1973, DETROIT, MICHIGAN
KEN MCNEILL

My next live show was for the *A Passion Play* tour. James Taylor's younger brother Livingston Taylor opened as a solo. Talk about a tough gig. Nobody listened to him, although he was great. He was just a bit too light for what we were all anticipating. Needless to say, *A Passion Play* was jaw-dropping. Critics be damned. Of all the live shows I've seen of Tull, it is that one I would most like to see again. The band was as tight as a band could be and Ian was otherworldly from the moment he first ran onto the stage in the intro. Pure gold!

That year I attended college and the next year I saw the *War Child* tour, complete with the female string quartet, another incredibly professional, visual, musical extravaganza.

COLISEUM

21 SEPTEMBER 1973, JACKSONVILLE, FLORIDA
TERRY WEAVER

I remember seeing Jethro Tull in the early Seventies in Jacksonville, Florida for the *Thick as a Brick* and *A Passion Play* concerts. The crowd would wait for what seemed like an hour after the listed start time for the group to come out. The anxiety and tension would grow minute by minute, the packed Coliseum getting louder and louder. Then, in the dark arena – a small point of light was seen on the screen, pulsating with a sound like a heartbeat which grew

Terry Weaver was at the Coliseum

louder and louder. The image of a ballerina, laying backwards, arms spread out, not moving for a long while until we could see the arms moving slowly upwards ... until the group appeared, going right into the start of *A Passion Play*. The crowd roared with all we had. I always assumed the late start was planned to get this reaction, but I was never sure. I remember this from close to 50 years ago.

LARRY MANGUM

I saw Tull many times and they were the best live band I ever saw. The highlight was probably the *A Passion Play* tour. There was a large screen on stage and as we were milling around waiting for the band to come on, we heard a thumping sound and noticed a small red dot on the screen pulsing with the beat. The dot grew and the thumping sound got louder and became the heart of a ballerina. Then the band appeared on the screen, playing the song, and suddenly they jumped through the screen in the same costumes playing live. It blew our little stoned minds.

ROANOKE CIVIC CENTER

26 SEPTEMBER 1973, ROANOKE, VIRGINIA

EILEEN JOYCE

I was living in Arlington, Virginia. That summer I was staying with my sister Margaret at Virginia Tech in Blacksburg when I heard Jethro Tull was going to play at Roanoke Civic Center. I got tickets for my friend Dana, myself and another person.

Eileen Joyce and daughter Dana were at Roanoke Civic Center

When we went down for the concert, we stayed with my sister Patty and her family, who lived in Roanoke. We drove down in Dana's yellow Opel car. She called it Wolley Lepo. Patty was okay with us staying there, even though it would be a little disruptive, since we would be out late and she had a small child. But she didn't seem to mind being a free hotel for the night.

We went to the concert. Some of the roadies hit on us. They told us to meet them at the Holiday Inn across the interstate from the arena. They told us the band would be there to party with. We didn't go. We did go to a diner afterwards and ate. A guy tried to stick us with his bill. We stuck him with ours. Dana was pretty fast at leaving before the guy left.

When we were driving back to Patty's about two in the morning, Dana said we should go and see if the band was partying at the Holiday Inn, which looked kinda slimey. I told her the band wouldn't stay some place so yucky. The roadies yes, the band no. I told her they probably were staying at The Hotel Roanoke. We went there. Dana asked the night clerk if Jethro Tull was there. He said 'no.' Then she asked if Ian Anderson was there. He said 'yes' and Dana convinced him to call his room so she could speak to him. Ian Anderson answered the phone. She said, 'I just wanted to tell you that me and my friend travelled 240 miles to see your concert tonight. It was worth it.' He said something like, 'Thank you for coming.' Then he hung up. We went back to Patty's all psyched up from the phone call. It was an incredible adventure.

BOSTON GARDEN

29 SEPTEMBER 1973, BOSTON, MASSACHUSETTS

TIM FOREST

I was fortunate enough to get tickets to *A Passion Play* at the old Boston Garden, about four rows from the back door. The house lights went down, the crowd cheered but no band came on stage. There was just a heartbeat sound. I could see a small unfocused light on a screen, pulsating in time with the heartbeat. After a few moments, a ballerina appeared, lying upside down, blood running down her face, then slowly she started to get up and began dancing and twirling in a room with a mirror. She ran through the mirror and it shattered, leaving a dark stage and a spotlight on Ian singing, 'Do you still see me even here?' From that moment, I was hypnotised. Ian was jumping around, twirling his flute, standing on one leg. I'd never seen the like. Another great moment was during the film, 'The Hare That Lost His Spectacles.' Ian stuck his head in the frame and the crowd went nuts.

Press reports around this time suggested the Boston Garden show was going to be Tull's last ever concert. But the band were back performing in Australia in July 1974.

FESTIVAL HALL

28 & 29 JULY 1974, MELBOURNE, AUSTRALIA

ROB HASTIE

This show was a bit like a kids' pantomime, with band members dressed as rabbits and other cartoon characters for

a short time. John Evan had a piano on one side of the stage and his organ way over on the other side, and made great ceremony racing back and forth from one to the other. The *A Passion Play* tour was a very theatrical performance. At the end of the show, after the encore when the applause finally faded, there was an old black telephone on the stage, and it started to ring. Ian came back out to the stage, walked up to the phone and answered it. 'Hello,' he said, listened for a moment, then held the receiver out to the audience and said, 'it's for you'.

Following a series of Australasian and Japanese dates, Jethro Tull toured Britain and Europe in the autumn of 1974, promoting the release of *War Child*.

AHOY

12 OCTOBER 1974, ROTTERDAM, THE NETHERLANDS

KEES VAN DER WILK

We saw Tull play three times in Rotterdam in the Seventies.
    In my hometown of 25,000 inhabitants in the province of South Holland, there were quite a few Tull lovers, and we all went to their shows. There was a real Tull family.

WAR CHILD

RELEASED 14 OCTOBER 1974 (US)/26 OCTOBER 1974 (UK)

UK CHART POSITION 14

US CHART POSITION 2

RAINBOW THEATRE

4 – 6 NOVEMBER 1974, LONDON, UK

JAY SNYDER

I have lost count of the number of times I've seen Ian and/or Jethro Tull in concert over the years. I took some colour pictures at the Rainbow just as *Warchild* was released, but remember seeing the *Thick as a Brick* and *A Passion Play* shows in the Twin Cities prior to that.

AL NICHOLSON

We'd seen photos of the Australian tour in August '74 and the excitement level was growing. It was a new-look Tull, and the new album was to feature shorter songs for the first time since *Aqualung* in '71. The press reports were good, but by '74 we had become accustomed to their increasing indifference and annoyance at Anderson's confident, intelligent persona. But did we care? The band was so original, so different; what did they know anyway?

As a 16-year-old, having seen *A Passion Play* in '73 and followed them since late '69, I was totally hooked. It was November 1974, my hair was long, my greatcoat - with Tardis-like pockets - sheltering me from the London chill. With a group of fellow Tull fans I made my way to the Rainbow Theatre, a grand old cinema in Finsbury Park. I had heard great things about the venue. it was big enough to generate some atmosphere with an enthusiastic audience, yet intimate enough to feel that you were personally involved. The acoustics were also very good.

I can't remember whose idea it was, but we decided to see shows on consecutive evenings. Why not? It was something we did up until the *A* tour. I do remember that London was in the grip of live music fever. Pink Floyd were playing four shows in the capital at the same time. There was a definite feeling that you were about to witness something rather special. There were rumours that the gig would contain a few surprises. Nothing though, would prepare me for the opening.

The house lights dimmed and looking upwards to the ceiling, I remember seeing stars - literally tiny pinpricks of light creating an effect that the old cinema had no roof. The first surprise came in the form of Stirling Moss, who introduced proceedings. Quite what connection he had with the band was anybody's guess, but it set the tone marvellously for the rest of the evening. Suddenly music filled the air and Pan's People (an all-female British dance group that used to interpret hits on *Top of the Pops*) performed a beautifully choreographed piece dressed in spangly leotards with cutaway nylon-covered breasts, revealing nipples concealed by sequin-encrusted pasties. I think the audience, mainly shaggy looking neohippies, were spellbound, yet rather amused. The whole thing was, at that time, incongruous to say the least; the dance troupe were more at home dancing to Bony M or the like.

Out of the blue, Martin Barre came rushing onto the stage, blasting away with his new sounding cherry red Gibson SG guitar, dispersing the nymphs in all directions. Jeffrey Hammond joined the party dressed in a black and white striped outfit to accompany Barre. Having numerous vinyl bootlegs, I instantly recognised the passage as what was to become the intro to 'Minstrel in the Gallery'. The gigantic sound and spectacular visual treat of the two of them moving all over the stage was eclipsed by an explosion, lots of smoke and the appearance of Ian Anderson.

By this time, Barre had deftly announced the 'Wind Up' guitar break. Before you could catch your breath, the whole band was in full swing. Honestly, you didn't know where to look. Anderson, dressed in a brightly coloured long coat over an Elizabethan-looking jacket, codpiece and tights, swirling all over the place; Hammond literally bouncing backwards and forwards, making your eyes keep adjusting as the black and white striped effect was acting like a strobe; John Evan in an ice-cream salesman suit with a bright yellow shirt and massive red and white polka dotted tie, grinning and laughing manically whilst playing effortlessly; Barrie Barlow, looking like he had just come from a football training session, thundering away in his inimitable style; and Barre dressed in a highly-patterned floral suit, leaping all over the area to Anderson's left.

Just when you thought you needed to recover your senses, the band moved into a section of *A Passion Play* (my personal favourite). It was all too much. They really hit home. Having suffered the rather disappointing reviews of their last album from the music press (but not the fans), they appeared to be pressing a point. This was no half-hearted 'we'd better play some of it' appeasement. This was personal, and I loved it.

Next up was an imperious 16-odd minute section of *Thick as a Brick*. To me this eclipsed the 'Middle Bit' they played at Wembley. It was quite the best piece of music I have ever heard the band play. If my memory doesn't desert me, Anderson's future wife, Shona, dressed in top hat and ringmaster costume, ambled across the stage, and at a key moment gathered his acoustic guitar as he held it out. She surreptitiously walked off stage. It was only after the manoeuvre had been accomplished that you realised what had happened. That's what we loved about Jethro Tull - attention to detail and clever humour.

Ian Anderson was clearly having fun. The banter between songs was hilarious. There were many crowd interruptions, adding to the hilarity. Ian, of course, fuelled by the atmosphere, was not short of well-timed put-downs. Not only that, but the inclusion of the rather frivolous '(How Much is) That Doggie in the Window?' signalled that the show was all about the theatre rather than a tired run-through of the hits. This vaudeville ventriloquist act was performed by Jeffrey Hammond, Brian the dog and John Evan, and it was very funny. Maybe neutral concertgoers would have been slightly perplexed by the crazy humour, wondering where the rock 'n' roll was, but when you saw Tull you knew entertainment was high on the list. Especially if Hammond and Evan were in town.

The utterly sublime 'Wond'ring Aloud, Again' heralded the next surprise: the inclusion of the string quartet. Four beautiful and rather elegant ladies dressed in platinum blonde wigs. I have seen Tull play this song on numerous occasions since, but never like this. Ian Anderson's voice was, in my opinion, at its peak. The string accompaniment and piano work were deliciously deft. Once again it reaffirmed my belief that my favourite band was peerless. What other outfit could crash the house down with a song like 'Cross-Eyed Mary' then play something so touching as this? The quartet supported the band for the rest of the show. Their playing on 'Ladies' and 'Bungle in the Jungle' were particular highlights.

Noting that they had played 'Wind Up' at the beginning, I figured that the choice of encore opener could only be 'Back-Door Angels'. I was really hoping they'd play the song. It was one of my favourites on the new record. The encore gave Martin Barre the chance to stretch out a little, and for the band to include unreleased material, or, failing that, new arrangements. Sure enough, my hunch was correct, and we were in for a treat. The opening, heavily guitar-laden verses gave way to improvised music that Tull fans were used to. It all culminated in an amazing version of 'Locomotive Breath' and 'Hard-Headed English General'. As usual when his vocal duties were finished, Ian Anderson assumed Hammond organ duties, and John Evan strutted around at the front, having a lot of fun. The music reached its crescendo, and as band members gradually slid away, Anderson sang the last verse of 'Back Door Angels'. Once Anderson had left the stage a telephone started ringing, a now familiar feature. For the life of me, I can't remember whether IA came back on the stage and answered it.

The beauty of having a ticket for the following night was that you knew you were going to see the show all over again. I never liked *Dark Side of the Moon* much anyway. It really was quite the most amazing experience. For my money, they were never quite the same again.

APOLLO THEATRE

11 NOVEMBER 1974, GLASGOW, UK

RAB STRAITON

When I was a teenager there were some amazing bands hitting their peak. Fortunately, my mates liked a similar genre of music. Big Danny was into Deep Purple, Jimmy was into Wings and Blondie (to have a reason to stick a poster of Debbie Harry on his wall?), Colin was on the darker side and loved Black Sabbath, and my personal favourite was Led Zeppelin. Wee Rab was a fanatic of Jethro Tull. We'd

Rab Straiton, at the Apollo for the War Child tour and back for Heavy Horses

spend nights going to each other's houses listening to each other's albums. The first time I heard Jethro Tull was at Wee Rab's house, listening to the mindblowing *Aqualung* and *Thick as a Brick.*

The *Warchild* tour was announced in the *Sunday Mail* and, a year after my first gig (the Sensational Alex Harvey Band at Hamilton Town Hall) we toddled off to the Apollo in Glasgow to see Jethro Tull. As a 15-year-old I had already seen a few bands there. The support band was Fanny, a name obviously with a different meaning in the USA to over here. They were an all-girl band featuring Suzi Quatro's sister Patti, and a pretty decent band from what I remember.

The Tull gig started with a series of flash explosions. After each explosion a member of the band appeared on stage. The last flash/explosion was blinding, and Ian Anderson was centre-stage. He was mesmerising, with a wild look in his eyes as he blasted out tunes on his flute and belted out song after song. The band were superb. The albums, although amazing, couldn't do this live act justice.

After the gig we headed up to Buchanan Street bus station for the bus home.

An older guy who looked a tad like Aqualung was playing the gig back on a reel-to-reel tape, no doubt to make some tapes to sell at the Barras in the coming weeks.

APOLLO THEATRE

12 & 13 NOVEMBER 1974, GLASGOW, UK

STEPHEN FINDLAY

I went to see them for the first time at the Glasgow Apollo on the *War Child* tour in 1974. I became a fan for life. They were amazing! I'd only previously ever heard *Living in the Past.* Ian's voice was at its peak, and it was the classic line up, including Jeffrey Hammond-Hammond. They even had an all-female string quartet and a long-legged ring mistress. Since then, I have seen them several times in Glasgow and Edinburgh. I have every album, but my favourites are the ones from *Aqualung* to *Stormwatch.*

ODEON THEATRE

13 NOVEMBER 1974, NEWCASTLE, UK

PETER SMITH AND NORMAN JONES

Jethro Tull called at Newcastle in November 1974 to promote the *War Child* album. Support for the tour was all-girl band Fanny. We were, of course, quite intrigued by Fanny and also thought their name quite fun, a little naughty and inappropriate, even for those times.

This time Tull had graduated to playing the massive Odeon theatre, which hosted a number of gigs in the early Seventies and had a much larger capacity than the City Hall. It was a lovely old cinema with a massive balcony and if you were sat right up the back, as I was on this occasion, you could see very little of the stage below. Appearing at the Odeon signified the fact that Jethro Tull had joined the major-league of rock bands. Ian Anderson and co. were at their pomp best at the time, and this album and tour saw them returning to a simple straightforward collection of songs after the concept albums *Thick as a Brick* and *A Passion Play.* The single from the album was 'Bungle in the Jungle', which was quirky but also pretty catchy. Jeffrey Hammond-Hammond did a nifty version of '(How Much Is) That Doggie in the Window?' during the concert, and the band was accompanied by a string quartet. This was classic Tull at their best.

RAINBOW THEATRE

14 – 17 NOVEMBER 1974, LONDON, UK

NICK BAYLEY

A year after the *A Passion Play* show at Wembley, I went to the Rainbow to see the *War Child* shows. I went twice and both shows were incredible. The addition of a scantily-clad Pan's People as the pre-show starter was every teenage boy's wet dream come to life, and of course the string quartet all dressed in their resplendent black cocktail dresses and platinum wigs was a special treat. The set list, the quality of the playing and Ian's incredible showman skills were a treat. They all looked like rock stars should. It was a magic experience; no question.

AL NICHOLSON, LONDON, UK

I first became aware of Jethro Tull in 1969. I bought 'The Witch's Promise' single upon release and soon added *Benefit* and *Stand Up*. My first concert, at 15, was *A Passion Play* in 1973. By that time, I had amassed all their recordings (except 'Sunshine Day'), a collection of vinyl bootlegs, scrap albums full of press cuttings, guitar mags featuring the band and an almost complete crossword from *Thick as a Brick*. I saw them, usually two nights running, on all tours up until the late Nineties and have all the programmes and tickets. The *War Child* gigs at the Rainbow were a particular highlight. I have never seen another gig like it. Unfortunately, I found it increasingly difficult to witness the great Ian Anderson struggling with vocals and preferred to leave my memories intact.

I write music for Kaprekar's Constant, and we recently asked IA to read a poem in a long 20-minute track for our second album. Thinking this was an outside chance, we were amazed when he duly obliged and sent it over via a file on the net. He didn't want anything for it and wished us well. What a gent! Unsurprisingly, it's fabulous and just what we were after.

DAVID REES, EDITOR, *A NEW DAY* MAGAZINE

My introduction to Jethro Tull came in 1972, during the time when the world's attention was focused, bizarrely, on the World Chess Championship between Bobby Fischer and Boris Spassky. My friend and I were fairly keen chess players, and his parents were away for the week, so the two of us had our own chess competition, during which we not only had the freedom of the parents' drinks cabinet, but also the opportunity to explore his older brother's extensive record collection; previously unheard (by us) gems from Led Zeppelin, the Rolling Stones, and, notably, *Stand Up* by Jethro Tull. Up until that week I was a fan of Slade, T.Rex, Bowie ...

Front cover of the April 2002 edition of A New Day

the usual teen fare. What a revelation to hear this extraordinary music, featuring a flute in a heavy rock band.

Of course, I was late to the show, having somehow missed the first four years of Jethro Tull, but I quickly made up for it. I bought *Living in the Past, Aqualung, This Was* and then the astonishing *Thick as a Brick*. Wow! The first Tull album I bought on release was the (much-maligned) *A Passion Play*; I loved it from the very first play, and it remains, to this day, my favourite album of all time.

My first Tull gig was on the *Warchild* tour, at the Rainbow in Finsbury Park. I took the day off work to go to the box office in London, was first in the queue when the doors opened, and managed to secure only the fourth row. The first three rows had already been secured by the touts, as always. As the weeks passed, there were reports on Capital Radio that Tull tickets were changing hands for £35 and more – a month's wage for me in those days as an apprentice printer. But I hung onto mine.

STEVE HARRIS, IRON MAIDEN

I first got into Tull in 1971 when I heard the *Stand Up, Benefit* and *Aqualung* albums that I borrowed from a school friend. After buying those then the *Thick as a Brick* and *A Passion Play* albums, I was completely hooked! Although I have seen Tull many times over the years, one of the greatest early memories of seeing them was at the Rainbow Theatre in London on the *War Child* tour in 1974. I had seen them at other venues like Wembley, but this was different. I had second-row tickets and seeing them up close in a theatre was really something special.

They had all-girl American band Fanny supporting them, and then before they came on they had Pan's People dancing to 'The Witch's Promise' I remember they played five or six songs from the *War Child* album in the set and had a female ringmaster to assist Ian Anderson. Amazing memories of a show I remember clearly to this day. And showing such commitment in playing so many songs from a new album really resonated with me. It's something that helped influence me to do the same in Maiden.

COLSTON HALL

18 NOVEMBER 1974, BRISTOL, UK

KIM THONGER

Aqualung is one of my favourite LPs, and I still have it. Ian's a remarkable showman and unique. I saw them at the Colston Hall in late 1974, although I remember very little detail to be honest. I was there with three school friends, Ron, Andy and Tony, the last two identical twins. All three were subsequently in huge trouble at our sixth form for going to Uphill churchyard after a shift at the pub (at which we all illegally worked, underage) to smoke pot, where they were arrested and charged by the Old Bill. I didn't go that night, thankfully, as I had a long bike ride home from the pub. The three of them were in a prog rock band called Eustacia Vye, named after a Thomas Hardy character. Andy, one of the twins, played Anderson-esque flute. Then punk happened and Eustacia died, safety-pinned to death.

And he took unto him
Aqualung
the new album from Jethro Tull

released on March 19th

Chrysalis
records
ILPS 9145

CAPITOL THEATRE

25 NOVEMBER 1974, CARDIFF, UK
OWEN DAVIES, AGE 17

I have recently been listening again to a recording of the first of some 62 Tull gigs I have attended over the years, and this remains embedded in my memory. It was Cardiff in 1974. The recording is rough and ready, but a true account of what happened that evening. After queuing for hours to get tickets then some months of waiting, on the day of the gig I got to Cardiff in the afternoon, having truanted from school. I was in a group of six Tull fans from Swansea. We all had custom-made t-shirts with a banana on, in honour of Bungle. We must have looked shit, but we were only 17. We had a few too many drinks and visited a record shop. The owner saw we were Tull fans and were going to the gig and started chatting to us. I saw the *War Child* cardboard promo for the gig in the shop and asked if we could have it. To my surprise he said 'yes'.

   We took it to the show and made absolute arses of ourselves, waving it around and shouting. If you have heard the recording from the show, that's us shouting before 'Thick as a Brick' and Ian says, 'Which performance is it? And in an attempt to quieten us down, Ian then goes on to say, 'Cardiff Five, Jethro Tull Nil.' Later in the show you can hear me shout out and Ian says, 'Wrong again, old son.' You can also hear me shout out with youthful enthusiasm at the start of 'My God' and 'Back-Door Angels'. It's a bit embarrassing now, but I was just a kid.

After sleeping at the railway station that night, we got back to Swansea the next day. That cardboard display was in my bedroom from 1974 until 1979, and when I left home it was stored in my dad's garage. In 1996 I gave it to a Tull collector in exchange for some live recordings.

PAT BURNS

My favourite Tull concert was on the *War Child* tour. Martin's amp went down, the rest of the guys having to wing it for a few minutes while the amp was repaired. They continued playing and went seamlessly back into the song they'd been playing when the amp failed. It sounded like a very spontaneous jam. It was really cool seeing pros handle a difficult situation.

GAUMONT

26 NOVEMBER 1974, SOUTHAMPTON, UK

BEN LOVEGROVE

My earliest recollection of Tull's music is of borrowing some of my older sister's cassettes. She had taped *Thick as a Brick* onto one of them, so the quality wasn't that good, but 'once heard, never forgotten' and I resolved to find out more about this band. I began saving up pocket money and any other cash I could earn by doing odd jobs after school and on weekends. One Christmas in the early 1970s, my usual Airfix kit was replaced by *Benefit* and *Stand Up*. By the time *War Child* was released I was 14 years old and had already been to gigs to see bands like Curved Air, Focus, Status Quo, ELP and Hawkwind, so I was very keen to see Jethro Tull.   So it was that on 26 November 1974 I boarded a train at Winchester and alighted at Southampton station, just around the corner from the Gaumont (now The Mayflower). I distinctly remember Ian Anderson's on-stage presence. It was such a contrast to everything I'd seen before. His wild gyrations and the way he made eye contact with the audience was in stark contrast to the passive presence of other musicians or even the psychedelia of Hawkwind. He drew the audience into the performance and his enthusiasm was infectious. You felt as if you were watching a full-blown performance about life and joy, not just a band playing their songs.   Tull were already my favourite band by the time I first got to see them and that has remained the case to this day, nearly 50 years later. I bought every album and avidly read about them in the music press. *Songs from the Wood*, *Heavy Horses* and *Stormwatch* became a trilogy that echoed things that interested me then and still do; old Albion, history, megaliths, folklore, the old straight tracks and country ways. The lyrics resonated and were in sync with the books I was reading at the time. I didn't see them again until the *Broadsword* tour at the Nostell Priory gig in August 1982. I remember the way Ian Anderson walked on to the stage from the wings carrying an enormous broadsword and the strange creature with glowing eyes on his back during 'Beastie'. There followed another dry spell, but I have seen them at least three times since. Each time has been a joy, watching Ian doing what he loves the best. A poster of Ian had pride of place above the mantelpiece when I was younger. He inspired me to choose the flute at school and I got as far as grade five.

LA FORUM

4 & 5 FEBRUARY 1975, LOS ANGELES, CALIFORNIA

SCOTT FLETCHER

My first date with my wife was heading to see Jethro Tull at the Forum in Los Angeles in 1975. We were seniors in high school and 10 of us left the high desert of California in a van making the trip to Inglewood. The show was fantastic, and Tull has always been a favorite for both of us. When we returned and I was driving my date home, she informed me though we had a great time that she was already seeing someone, and we should go our separate ways. We have been married now for 46 years, and still are listening to Tull.

Scott Fletcher's first date with his wife was a Jethro Tull concert and 45 years later they are still together

GRAND HALL OF EL PASO CIVIC CENTER

6 FEBRUARY 1975, EL PASO, TEXAS

LINDA MARR

My big brother brought me to the show, and I remember sitting away from the stage. At the time, you were allowed to smoke inside, and the entire venue was filled with smoke.

THE FORUM, INGLEWOOD

10 FEBRUARY 1975, LOS ANGELES, CALIFORNIA

MILO PERICHITCH

My little league baseball coach was a huge rock music fan. From our conversations, he knew I was really curious about live music, yet hadn't experienced it yet. Coach became my rock 'n' roll mentor

Milo Perichitch saw Tull at the LA Forum

by taking me to my first concert. Our seats were on the floor in the 30th row; close enough to see the stage antics of Ian Anderson, the strangely attired singer. His outfit looked medieval, complete with codpiece. Ian performed outrageously and played his flute as a lead instrument rather than background. For reasons unknown to me then, and even now, he stood on one leg quite a bit. But regardless of his theatrics, the band behind him rocked hard.

Coach discretely smoked something, and it didn't smell like tobacco. In fact, it didn't smell like much at all. He didn't pass any my way, but I didn't mind. The whole sound and vision package was enough. This event blew my mind and left me completely enthralled by the sensory experience of live music. This show opened up a whole new world, one in which I wanted to play. Thanks, coach, I'm pleased to report that your generous ticket offer started me on my path to become a full-fledged rock concert junkie.

HERSHEY PARK ARENA

27 FEBRUARY 1975, HERSHEY, PENNSYLVANIA

ALTA DOG

The band released a dry ice smoke across the floor, where I was seated. It had a bit of an odour to it and being in an 'enhanced' state of mind, it appeared to me as if the act was a simulation of bring gassed during the war. If that was the intent, it surely got it across – I knew it was fake, but it was an intense feeling of what it must have been like in real life.

MADISON SQUARE GARDEN

7 MARCH 1975, NEW YORK, NEW YORK

MICHAEL RUGGIERI

Michael Ruggieri met the band when he was just 13

I was fortunate to see Jethro Tull in early 1975 (right around the time I saw Led Zeppelin for the first time) when I was just 13. My friend's father sent us down to Madison Square Garden in a black car with an adult cousin (being with an adult being the reason my mom let me go into the city). Did I mention my friend was wealthy? At the time, his father used to get the 10th row for every show at the Garden.

Anyways ... so we went to the show, and it was absolutely amazing. I know now that it was the *Minstrel in the Gallery* tour. When it came time for the encore, we were taken to the side of the stage and climbed a small set of stairs where we got to watch them play 'Locomotive Breath' while standing on the stage. This was mind-blowing for a 13-year-old who just months prior was listening to *The Partridge Family.*

Then, when the show ended, we were taken backstage to meet the band. I remember being enthralled with all the food and drinks that were in the room, all free for the taking. Beer, wine, booze, cake, sandwiches, chips, candy ...

I'll never forget meeting Ian Anderson. He was larger than life, like a big hairy beast, full of sweat. He had just finished a two-hour show. The look on his face when he was introduced to us was one of, 'What the fuck are these kids doing here?' He said hello and then was on his way to meet other people in the room. Being 13, we had some soda and snacks and soon were on our way home. How I wish I could see that show again today.

I've been listening to Jethro Tull a lot lately, even discovering some music that I missed (or at least was not familiar with) from all those years ago. They're a great, great band, and still one of my favourites. I would see Tull a few more times over the years, but nothing can compare to my first experience in 1975.

CIVIC CENTER

8 MARCH 1975, PROVIDENCE, RHODE ISLAND

RON THATCHER, AGE 15

This was my very first concert. I was totally blown away by the theatrics and the sound of the live performance. It was the *Bungle in the Jungle* tour. I was mesmerised! At one point, there was a phone ringing and this man in a big rabbit costume came out, pushing a big phone. Ian, acting like he was talking to him, said, 'This is not the story of the hare who lost his spectacles, it's the story of the hare who lost his underwater breathing apparatus.' Then they went right into 'Aqualung' and the crowd went wild.

CIVIC CENTER

9 MARCH 1975, BALTIMORE, MARYLAND

GEORGE MOORE

The *War Child* tour was a big production. Massive lights hung from the ceiling like giant flash-bulbs, and smoke machines made it like a war zone. Through the smoke came Ian with the mellow sax intro and the title cut.

BOSTON GARDEN

12 & 13 MARCH 1975, BOSTON, MASSACHUSETTS

DONALD PEARSON

Donald Pearson remembers security getting heavy over a piece of flying flute

Ian had a spike on the end of his flute that he was using to pop balloons floating around on stage. He twirled it, and the end flew off into the audience. The kid two rows in front of me caught it and turned around to us, jumping up and down all excited … then security yoked him by the neck over the chairs and beat the fuck out of him to take it back. They led him out like he had done something other than just catch that little piece of flute. Poor kid. I always felt bad for him.

The show was bomb. I really dug the zebra bass.

159

SEATTLE CENTER COLISEUM

24 JULY 1975, SEATTLE, WASHINGTON

BRIAN TVEDT

I saw Tull five times in Seattle and have great memories of all these shows. On Jeffrey Hammond-Hammond's last tour with Tull, some bonehead lit a string of firecrackers during Ian's flute solo. Man, Ian was pissed (off). He told the crowd to find the guilty person and bring them to the stage so he could kick their ass.

Brian Tvedt remembers Ian being annoyed at firecrackers being let off during his solo

SAM HOUSTON COLISEUM

2 AUGUST 1975, HOUSTON, TEXAS

ALBERTO CADOPPI

Jethro Tull didn't come back to Italy for a long time. It was understandable, after those riots and police charges. Italians had to go abroad to see Tull. Back in summer 1975, I was an exchange student (within a Lions Club programme) in Pasadena, Texas. I was staying with very nice people. My 'Texas parents', as I called them, did their best to help me enjoy my time there. There was no internet, of course. One morning I was reading the local newspaper and I looked up the list of concerts in the area. I noticed, to my big surprise, Jethro Tull were about to play at the Sam Houston Coliseum in Houston. I asked my Texas parents if they, or perhaps my Texas brother, were interested in going to the show. They weren't Tull fans really, but they phoned up some of the ticket outlets and found the very last ticket for the show, anywhere in the Houston area. The ticket counter was something like a one-hour drive from Pasadena, but my Texas parents drove there and bought it for me.

It was a fantastic show based on *War Child*, with a string quartet and a memorable Jeffrey Hammond, with his famous Zebra suit. What a night! I didn't enjoy too much my time after the show though. I had to wait near the Coliseum for at least half an hour, the longest half-hour of my whole life. That particular area of Houston was one of the worst in Texas in terms of criminality – or so someone told me then – and I was really frightened. But at last my Texas brother came and I was safe. And I became an even more convinced and enthusiastic Tull fan.

COLISEUM

9 AUGUST 1975, GREENSBORO, NORTH CAROLINA

GEORGE WHITE

Ian Anderson was wonderful and very active. I remember a really big balloon the crowd were pushing around over their heads. A special unexpected treat for me was seeing Jeffrey Hammond-Hammond wearing a zebra suit bouncing around back and forth on the stage as he was playing his bass guitar. It was quite impressive.

MINSTREL IN THE GALLERY

RELEASED 5 SEPTEMBER 1975 (UK)/8 SEPTEMBER 1975 (USA)

UK CHART POSITION 20

US CHART POSITION 7

JOHN BONE

As a callow 14-year-old I couldn't believe my luck when a seemingly incredibly old (in reality he was only about 25) and definitely incredibly cool (he was from rough and tumble Glasgow, me from suburban Kent) friend of the family took me under his wing in what was a very staid Britain of 1980. His treating my young self as his equal had several long-lasting effects. He offered me the occasional can of beer, thus introducing me to the delights of the ale in a responsible and controlled environment, and not the peer pressure, vomit-addled initiation to alcohol my contemporaries would encounter a couple of years later. He also lent me the LPs of a then lesser-known Scottish comedian called Billy Connolly, through whose ramblings I learned to laugh at absurdity and arrogance. But perhaps most influential of all, one day my friend handed me an album called *Minstrel in the Gallery* with the words, 'You might find something in this. Give it a listen.'

   I did indeed find something in that music, and it's something that's become an integral part of my life ever since. In Jethro Tull I found a band whose entire musical catalogue has resonated with me one way or another over the years. And although it sounds clichéd, Tull's music has been the underlying soundtrack to my life, just as beer has been a wonderful pastime and laugher in adversity my moral compass. So, thank you Ian Anderson, and every member of Jethro Tull past and present, without whom - musically speaking - my life would never have been as rich these last 40 odd years.

   And thank you, Arthur, wherever you are.

J ERIC SMITH

If really pressed to name a single band as my favourite artist throughout a lifetime of listening, I would pick Jethro Tull. The group first moved onto my most regular spins roster in the mid-1970s, and have never left it. I've seen them (or frontman Ian Anderson solo) in each of five decades and would eagerly add a sixth decade to that list if Anderson tours again. The amount of physical pleasure, intellectual stimulation and emotional joy they've given me over the years is unmatched by any other artist in my collection. The 1976 compilation *M.U. - The Best of Jethro Tull* was probably the first of their albums I purchased, but I heard their American AM radio hits ('Living in the Past' and 'Bungle in the Jungle') and free-form FM station favourites ('Aqualung', 'Locomotive Breath', 'Teacher', etc.) well before.

   Developing my top-10 favourite songs list for Jethro Tull was super hard. I consider Tull's last truly great album to be 1982's *The Broadsword and the Beast*, though I suspect many fans would consider their glory days ended after *Stormwatch*. That's when the classic era group fell apart following the death of bassist John Glascock, and a record label decision to issue what Anderson had intended to be his first solo album under the Jethro Tull banner instead followed, with long-time and much beloved members John Evan, Dee (then David) Palmer and Barriemore Barlow left on the sidelines for good.

There are some fine songs on various albums after *Broadsword* (Ian Anderson's solo album *Homo Erraticus* rises to classic era standards, with the same band line-up that also carried the Tull banner at the time), but I didn't see anything in there that would make a top 10 against the earlier works.

Thick As a Brick (my very favorite Tull album) and *A Passion Play* were both originally released as single, 45-minute long songs split over two sides of a vinyl platter. While subsequent compilations and reissues have broken those big song cycles down into smaller bits, the chunking and labelling has been inconsistent over the years - it's hard to meaningfully cull cuts from those two great discs. So it is that I am not then able to include arguably the most divisive moment in the entire Jethro Tull catalogue, 'The Story of the Hare Who Lost his Spectacles', from *A Passion Play*. Needless to say, I adore that little bit of atypical whimsy. When Tull originally toured *A Passion Play*, they created a short intermission film of 'The Hare' segment, and it's a weird gem featuring bassist Jeffrey Hammond-Hammond in fine narrative form.

As I culled my initial list down to just 10 cuts, I found myself keeping very few of the known hits and/or concert staples, while also preserving several borderline obscurities that some better-than-casual Tull fans may have never heard, or heard of. Indeed, my list contains just one overlap with the 15 career-spanning songs curated by Ian Anderson himself for 2018's *50th Anniversary Collection*, 1971's 'Life is a Long Song'. Oh well.

10. 'Glory Row'
9. 'Mother Goose'
8. 'Life is a Long Song'
7. 'For Michael Collins, Jeffrey and Me'
6. 'Summerday Sands'
5. 'One Brown Mouse'
4. 'Velvet Green'
3. 'No Lullaby'
2. 'Songs from the Wood'
1. 'Minstrel in the Gallery'

KONRAD HANSON

A few years after I had been listening to a lot of Tull, I stumbled upon 'Cold Wind to Valhalla'. I loved it the first time I heard it, so I decided to deliberately avoid listening to it until my exams had finished two weeks later. I went into my last exam, felt good about it, then walked out with my iPod preloaded with 'Cold Wind to Valhalla'. The combination of the end of exams, walking into town on a sunny day, and listening to the song I had been saving was the moment everything seemed right in the world.

NEW HAVEN VETERANS MEMORIAL COLISEUM

27 SEPTEMBER 1975, NEW HAVEN, CONNECTICUT

MARK THEODORE GANSER

I was invited by a friend to join him at a concert at Veteran's Memorial Coliseum. I said, "Sure, who's playing?". He said, "Jethro Tull" and I said, "Who the fuck is a Jethro Tull?". At that point in my life, I had been reared on the likes of Led Zeppelin, Deep Purple and Jimi Hendrix. But I went to the concert and it was all over at that point.

I've not missed a Tull or Ian Anderson concert in my area since, approaching 47 times the next time I see him. The music, the themes, the stories, and choreography all had a profound impact in terms of what I thought a concert should be, and I've come to a point where I can't miss seeing them if they come around.

Ian in action. Photo: Mark Theodore Ganser

RIVERFRONT COLISEUM

4 OCTOBER 1975, CINCINATTI, OHIO

GRETCHEN FORDE

When I was in high school, I got a tape cassette recorder for a Christmas gift. I started to buy pre-recorded tapes to play on it. One of them was *Thick as a Brick*. I knew about Jethro Tull from listening to a local FM radio station. Then when I was dating someone in college (now my husband) we listened to *Stand Up* and *Living in the Past* until we wore them out. In 1975, Cincinnati opened a new sports arena that could put on concerts, Riverfront Coliseum, and Jethro Tull was the second band to play there after Fleetwood Mac. It was a fabulous show.

TOO OLD TO ROCK 'N' ROLL: TOO YOUNG TO DIE

RELEASED 23 APRIL 1976 (UK), 17 MAY 1976 (US)

UK CHART POSITION 25

US CHART POSITION 14

FOREST NATIONAL

1 MAY 1976, BRUSSELS, BELGIUM

DEE PALMER

I joined Tull for the *Too Old to Rock 'n' Roll* tour in 1976. My first gig was at Forest National, Brussels. I bought my stage clothes from an ex-army store in Tottenham Court Road. I was impressed by the venue and the attitude of the crowd; I was much more accustomed to playing piano and conducting shows with Roy Orbison, The Walker Brothers, etc. in English cinemas adopted for the burgeoning pop industry and filled with screaming teenage (and younger) girls. It was difficult to hear the music.

CIVIC CENTER

15 JULY 1976, PROVIDENCE, RHODE ISLAND

DEE PALMER

My very first visit to the USA had been in 1964 with the Cambridge University Footlights Revue whilst I was still a student. Satire was the fashion then, though rock music (as per the Tullettes) was yet to arrive on the scene. My first American gig was in Providence, Rhode Island. Again, I was impressed by the venues there and by the manic crowd response when we played 'Thick as a Brick', 'Aqualung', 'Locomotive Breath' and other much favoured Tull flag-wavers. In fact, I think most of the songs were; the crowd certainly knew all the words.

COLT PARK

16 JULY 1976, HARTFORD, CONNECTICUT

BLAISE DONNELLY

I saw a relatively small impromptu event in the park in Hartford below the Capitol Building. If I am not mistaken, Ian was also playing a larger venue nearby and was all too ready to engage for his fans. What impressed me the most was the lack of potential drama because of fame and the energy he put forth in the show. He was an absolutely brilliant entertainer, dancing around the stage during the performance as though he was in another world. What I saw was a man playing an instrument with such passion and empathy that through the music we learned that music can give us things through sound that money can never buy and that no man can ever take.

SEEMA MUSTAFA

In the 1970s die-hard fans of Jethro Tull were pretty isolated. Technology had not come in to bring music lovers together, and Tull was still not palatable to Indian tastes. Those Tull fans who did exist were fiercely possessive of Jethro Tull and even more so of Ian Anderson. They did not tolerate any criticism and collected records and then later CDs with wild passion. A friend who went on to become a doctor painted the cover of *Aqualung* on a humungous canvas that all of us wanted but could not get. She hung it in a place of honour in her living room, possibly to have us visit more often than we might otherwise have done perhaps, as she certainly was not a Tull fan.

In 1976 I visited Hartford, Connecticut during the United States Bicentennial celebration. It was my first visit to anywhere outside of India and my excitement was thus touching new peaks. But nothing had prepared me for the gift I received from an indulgent older brother: tickets to Jethro Tull's Colt Park Concert. I could not believe it. I kept the tickets under my pillow.

On the day I reached the venue two hours before, only to find that I was at the end of the park, far away from the stage, as hundreds and thousands had made their way for the concert long before I. The cops were there in full strength and to an Indian looked pretty sinister, grabbing hold of young men, slamming them against trucks, frisking them thoroughly and throwing them into vans. It was continuous, and I don't know how many from the concert must have been put into the slammer for - I guess -drugs, but judging from the reaction of the others this was just par for the course.

This was before the big screens, so one heard more than one saw. I could hear Ian Anderson's magical flute, but just see his figure and not his face as he danced elf-like across the stage. Oh, but it was amazing - thrilling, so exciting - to hear what was just vinyl before come alive before one's eyes. Everyone present was on the same page, all Tull lovers together, lost in their music. This was so unlike India, where most did not know Tull at the time and could not understand the crazies who belted out 'Aqualung' and 'Locomotive Breath' in tuneless voices, trying unsuccessfully to learn the flute and strumming at guitars that were barely functional.

The passion remained. The world got closer. One heard and read more of Jethro Tull. And could soon – well, not that soon – watch their concerts across the world. I had thought that was it, that I was fortunate to have been at a Tull concert at least once in this lifetime.

And then came 2009 and an indulgent son, a music lover too, who got us tickets for a concert at the Piazzale del Castello in Udine, Italy. I had never heard of Udine, let alone been there, but I immediately prepared for a holiday in Rome and Florence.

We took the train to Udine. The excitement equalled that of the 1970s, with age being reduced to just a number. Udine was beautiful and nothing could have been more picturesque that the Piazzale del Castello. It was stunning. Open air, smallish, beautiful and, because it was a little higher than the rest of the town, it was as if the world ended there. Well, mine certainly did, as this time I found myself close to the stage, so close that every line on Ian Anderson's face was visible. There were young people of course, but there were those who were young in 1976 and had aged 30 plus years since and knew every song Tull belted out.

Everyone was singing along with the newer numbers – 'Nothing is Easy', 'Beggar's Farm', 'Serenade to a Cuckoo' – and they just had to sing 'Thick as a Brick', '*Aqualung*' and the rest. Anderson played the flute as beautifully as before and moved across the stage with the same grace and ease, though if I am required to be honest, he had adjusted both to the fact that he, like me, was three decades older since the time I had seen him last. But all that mattered was that one could see his eyes and his expressions, as he sang for us. For me. Time had stopped and so had the world, for the moments that make life so worth the living.

CAPITAL CENTRE

18 JULY 1976, LANDOVER, MARYLAND

FRED RIDLEY

In 1971 I was 16 years old and I bought the album *Aqualung* mostly because I liked the cover. I had never heard a note of their music before, and I had never heard anything like it before. The tone of Martin Barre's guitar and Ian Anderson's flute mixed with heavy music blew me away. From that day I became a huge Jethro Tull fan. My first Tull concert was in 1976 at the Capital Centre in Landover, Maryland. I would see Jethro Tull at this arena five years in a row and 11 times in total, as well

Fred Ridley's Tull tickets

as Ian Anderson's *Rubbing Elbows* tour in Wilmington, Delaware at the Grand Opera House, 2002. At the Trump Marina Hotel show in Atlantic City in 2001, I ran into Martin Barre at the elevator. We didn't talk long. I just told him he had played great that night and he said 'thanks' and shook my hand. What a thrill that was.

SHEA STADIUM

23 JULY 1976 QUEENS, NEW YORK
RICH NAMAGA

I've seen Tull many times. They are one of my favorite bands. My biggest memory was the *Tullavision* show they did at Shea Stadium. What a great show it was. Rory Gallagher opened, followed by the great Robin Trower Band, then Tull. It was a rocking show.

Rich Namaga saw Tullavision at Shea Stadium

PETER PECK

I saw Tull at Shea Stadium around 1976. Robin Trower played with them. It was a hot summer's night and they premiered *Tullavision*. Move the time clock many decades later, and I saw and spoke with Martin Barre in Pawling, New York. I told Martin I was at the Shea concert. He pointed to his wife next to us and told me he met her that night at Shea. A great guitarist and a gentleman.

KIEL AUDITORIUM

7 AUGUST 1976, ST LOUIS, MISSOURI
MICHAEL MARESCO

I had older brothers and first heard Tull from their room in the mid-Seventies. Through high school, Tull were always on the mix-tapes. At one point I had a Ford Bronco with large cabinet speakers rigged for keg parties and what-not. I can still remember the feeling of when a Tull song hit. Cruising along, cranking it absolutely up, living the dream. I ended up overseas for decades and pretty much got away from Western music, but a Tull song by chance has always raised a smile, and any mention always starts a song in my head. I love that about the band. It's kind of a blur, but I think I only got to see them once and I have the same kind of memory, a big fat smile. The seats were good, a bit back on the floor. They were so awesome, so unique. We knew that from the albums, and it carried right over to stage. I'm so blessed to have been born in that era.

ARROWHEAD STADIUM

8 AUGUST 1976, KANSAS CITY, MISSOURI

TONY CZECH

This show featured a powerhouse of guitarists, including Rory Gallagher, Robin Trower and, in his own right, Todd Rundgren. The seating was still festival seating for those who wished to get close to the stage, but we decided to enjoy the seats in Arrowhead Stadium. We were at one end of the field and the stage was directly in front of us at the other end.

MCNICHOLS SPORTS ARENA

12 AUGUST 1976, DENVER, COLORADO

GINGER GAINEY

Ginger Gainey caught the first of her 50 Tull shows at the McNichols Sports Arena in 1976

I had heard a little of *Aqualung* on the radio the previous year because I had my own radio and was discovering my own brand of rock music on the local AM radio station, but I was properly introduced to Jethro Tull at the age of 14 when my dad brought home *Thick as a Brick* in 1972 on the recommendation of one of his good buddies who had common musical interests. I was immediately obsessed with the album – every note, every difficult timing change, every orchestration. I loved the length of the performance and felt the difficulty of the composition was a language I understood.

I quickly went back to the beginning and started to collect the previous album releases, and they began a never-ending rotation on my turntable. I was too young to have witnessed some of the historic concerts, and had to wait until 1976 before I had to chance to finally see a live show, at the McNichols Arena in Denver, Colorado. I had learned about the infamous 1971 concert at Red Rocks Amphitheater and wished I could have been there, but I'm also a bit glad I wasn't.

Since 1976, I have been to over 50 Jethro Tull concerts, and my husband and I have had the opportunity to travel to a lot of cities to see both Jethro Tull and Ian with his solo band. I have collected every album I can find, and am always ready for the next one.

In the beginning of my concert experiences, cameras were not allowed into the venues. With cellphones, photos were easier to take. My very best opportunity for photos was the *25th Anniversary* tour in Australia, although I'd already seen the show in Denver. I was on a tourist trip to Australia in March 1994 and just arrived in Melbourne after an overnight flight. On the way to the hotel, I saw a huge advertisement for the 25th anniversary tour in Australia and realised my trip coincided with the tour dates. I was excited to be able to see the show in both Melbourne and Sydney. I had my camera with me, and was allowed to take photos without flash. I was able to meet Ian after each show, and he was kind enough to sign an autograph and take a photo with me. I was finally able to have the Red Rocks with Jethro Tull experience during the *40th Anniversary* tour back in Denver in August 2008.

CIVIC AUDITORIUM

14 JANUARY 1977, PASADENA, CALIFORNIA

LINDSAY WOOD

A long-time grammar and high school friend and I attended this concert. We sat on the fifth row of orchestra, left centre. Great seats, and as an added bonus, tickets were free from a friend of a friend. Halfway through the set, the band had a short intermission and we went outside to smoke (not just cigarettes) and have a beer or two. They started the rest of the set, all the members playing different instruments. It was freaking awesome. I only know of a select few nowadays that could pull that off. They did this for two or three songs, then went back to the original instruments. One of the best concerts I have ever been to, and I'm so sorry it was the only Jethro Tull concert I ever attended.

CITY HALL

3 FEBRUARY 1977, NEWCASTLE, UK

PETER SMITH AND NORMAN JONES

In 1977 Jethro Tull released *Songs from the Wood*, their 10th studio album, and the first of a trio of folk rock albums. Of course, folk influences had always been apparent in Jethro Tull's music, but on *Songs from the Wood*, they particularly came to the fore. At the time I much preferred the rockier, blues-oriented side of Tull and was a little unsure about this change of direction. Looking back, this album and *Heavy Horses* were two of their best, and the 1977 tour was also excellent. Tull's set included a few songs from *Songs from the Wood*, along with old favourites. Songs like 'Jack-in-the-

Green' and 'Songs from the Wood' stand up against some of Tull's best.

There were also some line-up changes in the Tull fold. David Palmer, who had worked with the band from the early days as their orchestral arranger, joined full time on keyboards, and John Glascock joined on bass. Glascock was familiar to me; I had seen him play alongside Stan Webb in Chicken Shack in the early Seventies.

APOLLO THEATRE

5 FEBRUARY 1977, MANCHESTER, UK

RICHARD CONNELL

Richard Connell first saw Tull at Manchester's Apollo Theatre

Growing up in a house where music was everywhere (my dad was a semi-professional pianist) was a great start to life, but it gave me a bit of a conservative outlook. Seeking to broaden my horizons, I was fascinated after getting an answer to the question 'who invented the seed drill?' wrong to discover there was a rock band called Jethro Tull. I acquired a copy of *War Child* from a remaindered bin in HMV, and a rather wonderful (but poor quality, probably unofficial) sweatshirt with Ian resplendent in his codpiece. After hearing an interview with Ian (I think on the *Insight* programme on Radio 1) I was hooked.

At university my friend Keith was losing interest in the band ('Too Old to Rock 'n' Roll' was too autobiographical for him!) I acquired his entire Jethro Tull collection and he arranged tickets for my first concert at Manchester Apollo in 1977 and the *Songs from the Wood* tour. I was captivated by Ian's stage presence and his humour, often at the expense of band members.

ODEON THEATRE

6 FEBRUARY 1977, BIRMINGHAM, UK

MARK BILLINGHAM, AUTHOR

Though I remember hearing *Living in the Past* on the radio and maybe even seeing the band on *Top of the Pops* (who's that mad-looking bloke in the scruffy old coat?), the first Tull album I went out and bought was *Too Old to Rock 'n' Roll* in 1976, when I was 15. I was instantly a superfan. I immediately set out to save up and buy, borrow and on one occasion shoplift (sorry, but I was desperate) as many of the previous albums as possible. It was a glorious thing to lie on the floor with my head between the speakers, poring lovingly over the lyrics to *Minstrel in the Gallery* or the mighty *Aqualung* and then striking the traditional teenage air-guitarist poses when Martin Barre cut loose on 'Locomotive Breath'. I'm not sure that listening to music has *ever* given me more pleasure.

Around this time, we had a record player in the sixth form block at my school and there was always a frenzied scramble to get your record on to it at break. My schoolmates were coming into school clutching albums by The Damned or The Clash or X-Ray Spex and, though I liked that stuff too, I would be the one fighting to get the needle down on *War Child* or *Thick as a Brick*. I saw them play for the first time in 1977, at Birmingham Odeon, and was mesmerised by Ian's skills as a musician and frontman. I was equally thrilled and gobsmacked ... ahem ... *several* decades later, seeing them play the whole of *Aqualung* live, by which time I was lucky enough to have met and got to know Ian a little. I was asked to write some programme notes for Tull around this time and Ian was generous enough to give me a namecheck on the cover of *TAAB2*. It's probably cool to be blasé about stuff like this, but all I could think about were those nights devouring the music in my bedroom or out of my head with excitement watching Tull play it live.

If anyone could have told my 15-year-old self ...

GOLDERS GREEN HIPPODROME

10 FEBRUARY 1977, LONDON, UK

NICK BAYLEY

I had to wait until February 1977 to see the band in concert again. By then I was in my upper-sixth year at school and living in Aylesbury as my father had retired there. I remember sending off to the BBC to be part of the audience for the *Sight and Sound* show recorded at the Golders Green Hippodrome. Ian was suffering from a terrible cold and was struggling with his voice (eerily prophetic perhaps?). Four days later I saw the full *Songs from the Wood* show at the Hammersmith Odeon.

In May 1978, during my year out before going to teacher training college, I went to see the band three more times during the *Heavy Horses* tour. I remember hanging around the stage door at the end of one of the shows at the Hammy Odeon and some guy coming out, presenting me with his backstage pass sticker. He literally slapped it on my chest and said, 'Good luck.' The bouncer at the door shrugged his shoulders and let me in. Five minutes later I was standing chatting to John Evan and John Glascock, and before I knew it I was sharing a beer with Martin and Barrie and very briefly having a conversation with Ian about him getting the train from High Wycombe into Marylebone on a regular basis. My girlfriend at the time was doing her Art Foundation year in High Wycombe. Throughout that previous autumn, she had seen Ian on numerous occasions getting out of Shona's Landrover at the station to catch the train up to Marylebone. On one occasion she even told Ian, 'My boyfriend loves you,' and he had asked whether I was insane.

I spent about an hour backstage that night and all the guys were fantastic. They even signed my programme.

Spinning down through the years and numerous tours and line-ups have passed and while the venues and the audiences perhaps have dwindled somewhat, I am still fascinated by Ian's drive and desire to play his music and reach out to an audience.

Of course, I was devastated when Ian and Martin parted ways, but from what I have heard from Joe Parrish, one can only hope that his youthful exuberance and quality will give Ian some renewed vigour. Ian's vocals back then were nothing short of magnificent, even after leaping about the stage and playing the flute or sax at full pelt.

SONGS FROM THE WOOD

RELEASED 11 FEBRUARY 1977

UK CHART POSITION 13

US CHART POSITION 8

FIONA WOOD

I was brought up on a diet of classical music and Gilbert and Sullivan (parents) and ELO, Status Quo and Led Zeppelin (brother), but my first musical purchases were The Wombles and 'Killer Queen'. My close friends all went to different universities and my then boyfriend introduced me to *Songs from the Wood*. I was enraptured.

Fiona Wood

The crispness of the singing, the intricacies of the melodies, the humour, the filth (but thank you, 'Hunting Girl', for confirming I was no deviate) and the soaring guitars of Martin Barre. 'Pibroch' made me cry. When he turns and walks away, you can hear his heart breaking. It gets me every time.

It was the same boyfriend who also introduced me to *The Broadsword and the Beast*, with 'Broadsword' perfectly encapsulating my love of all things medieval – real hairs standing up on the back of the neck stuff.

At Christmas, I met up with my friends when we were all excited to share our new musical discoveries only to find that three of us had independently discovered Jethro Tull (the fourth had become a New Romantic – we never forgave him) but all had different favourite albums. *Songs from the Wood* was mine, with *Heavy Horses* and *Aqualung* being the other offerings. We spent many a happy hour discussing the merits and defending our choices. Except for the New Romantic – he had to make the coffee.

I love many, many other Jethro Tull tracks, but *Songs from the Wood* still retains a special place in my heart and recalls those heady first days of independence – and of being able to play my music LOUD!

TRACY DESHAIES

I stumbled upon Jethro Tull in a thrift shop. The album was *Songs from the Wood*. It was 1977 and I was 11. This album was the gateway drug that hooked me into becoming a Tull fan for the rest of my life. There are so many songs that have provided the soundtrack of my adolescence and young adulthood and continue to enrich my crone years. A pivotal moment that stands out in my memory was first hearing 'Elegy'. It conjured memories of my father, who I lost when I was a young lass of a mere eight years. I felt a connection (my dad has continued to send me musical messages for most of my life). At the time I didn't know what 'elegy' meant, so I looked it up. When I learned that it's a song for the dead, I realised Jethro Tull are so much more than a band, so much more than a soundtrack. The kitchen prose and gutter rhymes are the grit of life, the magic of light at the gloaming of the day, the notes that elevate spirit.

BRUCE HAWKINS

Bruce Hawkins (left) with fellow Tull fans David Drescher (centre) and Stephen Jones

In the late Seventies and early Eighties, several high school and college friends and I would regularly take backpacking trips to Shenandoah National Park. It became a ritual to start the *Songs from the Wood* album when we turned from Route 29 south onto Route 211 west, about a half-hour from our destination. It only seemed fitting.

I kept up with many of those friends, and we still occasionally make backcountry trips. In March 2019, one of those friends and I stopped on our way to the park at a fancy grocery store near that intersection to pick up some last-minute supplies. As we walked past rare cheeses and expensive wines, 'Songs from the Wood' began to play on the store's sound system. We stopped and looked at each other. 'I'm glad you're hearing that too,' said my friend. 42 years after it was released, the album still had a little magic in it. And yes, we did start the album up as we left the parking lot.

ROB HASKELL

I got my first Tull album in 1977 when I was 15. I joined a record club and got 10 records. The album in question was *Songs from the Wood*, and I instantly fell in love with them. Coming from a Scottish heritage and playing the bagpipes, Ian's songs spoke to me in a special way. I've seen them live almost 30 times. I've met Ian several times and have two pictures with him. I'm still a big Tull fan and still haven't figured out how to play 'Aqualung' on the bagpipes.

Rob Haskell has the band's autographs on his jacket

HAMMERSMITH ODEON

11–13 FEBRUARY 1977, LONDON, UK

PAUL ALEXANDER

I first discovered Jethro Tull in 1969, at the age of 13 with the release of the 'Living in the Past' single. I was introduced to the first three Tull albums in the summer of the following year by a family friend and from that day on I have been an ardent fan. I remember how impressed I was with the *Benefit* album, that had not long been released. From that point on, I would eagerly buy each new album on its release date.

It wasn't until I could drive and get to London that I first got to see Tull in the flesh. However, it was worth the wait as it was Hammersmith Odeon in February 1977 on the *Songs from the Wood* tour. Since then, I have seen them on 19 occasions. Having followed Tull and their music since my early teens (I am now 65), they have played a huge part in my life and largely supplied a musical soundtrack to it. *Thick as a Brick* has always been and remains my favourite album. I am pleased to say my eldest son shares my passion for the music of Jethro Tull. He was seven when I first took him to see the band in 1990 and he will in turn, I hope, pass on this passion to his own children.

SEATTLE CENTER COLISEUM

3 MARCH 1977, SEATTLE, WASHINGTON

RONALD HINZE

Ian was really jamming on his flute and the crowd was just mesmerised. Suddenly someone out in the concession area set off a cherry bomb. Ian stopped playing and said, 'Whoever did that was fucking rude,' and suggested someone should find the culprit and mess him up. He then proceeded to get back to his flute solo. It was epic.

ST JOHN'S ARENA

19 MARCH 1977, COLUMBUS, OHIO

RANDY JENNINGS

Arriving well after the doors opened at the Riverfront Coliseum in Cincinnati at a general admission Jethro Tull concert, and a little worse for wear, I found myself sitting in the last row of the nosebleed section. There was no chance of taking any photos. But after a few cups of liquid courage, or stupidity in my case, I grabbed my trusty Nikon and made my way down near the front of the stage. The photos were so-so, but at least I had a good time.

A few days later I was in my favourite record store and my friend asked if I'd like some record company 'comps' for the Columbus show. I said 'sure', figuring that maybe I could stay coherent enough to get decent photos. I knew 'comps' were generally great seats. I was out with a couple of friends the night before the show in Columbus and said, 'Hey, let's go see Tull in Columbus tomorrow night.' It being a little after 2am I figured I'd have no takers.

About 10am the next day there was banging on the front door. Who the hell? There were my two friends, ready to go to Columbus. It took me a few minutes to realise I was amongst the living. After a quick shower I grabbed my Nikon F2 with a 50mm lens, a roll of Kodak Vericolor II and a roll of Tri-X. The first stop was, of course, beer, as we needed a little hair of the dog on an early Saturday morning.

Being unemployed at the time and having no cash, I figured I had the tickets covered so my friends could pick up the rest of the day. We made it to Columbus with too much time to spare, so we had some kind of fast food to deplete more of the financial resources. As we sat in the car outside the St John's Arena waiting for the box office to open, my friends were checking the cash situation to see if there was enough to buy a third ticket just in case the comps were only a pair.

The box office opened so I went up and, much to my chagrin, I had no tickets at the box office. The lady in the box office said the road manager had not arrived with the 'comp' list yet. Okay, well that was a positive. After scraping the floor and seats of the car for change, there was about enough for a ticket and a half. While contemplating panhandling for money to buy tickets, that parking meter could probably fund the tickets. Whilst weighing my options of picking up a felony in Columbus, two stretch limos pulled up to the venue. That had to be the band. I jumped out of the car, heading in that direction.

There I was, standing about 10 feet away from Ian Anderson and the rest of the band. Oh, and two rather large and surly-looking bodyguards. I froze while Ian Anderson gave me an intense glare, me weighing in at 108 pounds of mostly hair, bones and teeth, and maybe a few beers too. I didn't say a word as they entered the building and I headed back to the car.

After about 30 minutes I headed back to the box office. The lady had the envelope with tickets, passes and press credentials. Unfortunately, she didn't have my name on the list anywhere. I asked her to check again. Nothing. I walked back out to the '67 Chevy and broke the bad news.

The parking meter option was all that was left. A few concertgoers were starting to arrive and we picked up a little more ticket funding money. We were parked outside of the arena by what turned out to be a stage door. About that time, two guys walked out and were going to be passing by the car. I recognised one as John Glascock, the bass player. I popped out and in desperation told him the story of the Chrysalis Records rep failing to come through. He just kinda looked at me like, 'Uh, okay.'

They walked over to the hotel across the street. About 15 minutes later they were returning to the venue and I popped out again to remind him. He said he'd see what he could do and entered the building. Another 15 minutes passed and out they came again. I was already out of the car and inquired about the tickets. By this time, I could see he was becoming frustrated by me. He said, 'I've got to go to the hotel to get some shit.' As they returned to the venue, I just looked at him and didn't bother asking again. He gave me a casual wave and headed in. This was beginning to look hopeless.

As the doors opened and the venue began filling up, John came out again but this time alone. He motioned for me to come over to him. As I was almost running to him, I could see he had his hand slightly cupped as if he had something in it. He asked how many tickets I needed. I very sheepishly said 'three.' He extended the cupped hand and said, 'Front row centre, enjoy the show.' I thanked him profusely and almost danced back to the car as my friends were already out jumping up and down.

We looked at the tickets and they had 'balcony' on them, along with some black marker numbers. Oh well, at least we were in. As we made our way in and through various ticket checkpoints, we were getting closer and closer to the stage. Finally, we arrived at the last checkpoint at the edge of where the two wings that jetted out from the stage were located. The usher guided us to the front of the stage, where we found three folding chairs in a row of their own, labelled 1 A, B, and C.

The usher commented, 'These weren't here earlier, you've got the best seats in the house, enjoy the show.' It was one of the greatest shows of my life, after quite the journey getting there. Thank you, John Glascock!

A couple of years later, I returned to see Jethro Tull in October 1979. As the show started I noticed there was a different bass player in the shape of Dave Pegg. Personnel changes aren't really unusual with bands, so I didn't think much of it. I was deeply saddened to hear, less than a month later, that John Glasscock had passed away. I will always remember that evening in Columbus and his kindness and generosity to help me out with tickets to the show. I was still very early in my music photography career, but these were definitely my best concert photos after only a couple of years of trial and error. Once again, thank you John, may you rest in peace.

BOSTON GARDEN

28 MARCH 1977, BOSTON, MASSACHUSETTS
EVAN MARC LONDON, AGE 14

This was my first concert. I was 14 years old and absolutely the happiest kid there. By then I had all their albums and thought Martin Barre was a genius. I would meet my best friend at prep school a few months later and, lo and behold, he was a flute player and I had dreams of doing Tull-like music for a while. I saw Martin Barre in 2019 at a very small venue - a hotel bar - in Cambridge, Massachusetts. I am not a big smiler, but from the second I sat down to the standing ovation at the end, my face hurt from all the smiling.

MARTIN FIORETTI

It was my first time seeing the band. Just before the concert started, a guy sitting near me shouted, 'Jet-ro is gonna get down on his flute!'

FESTIVAL HALL

12 SEPTEMBER 1977, MELBOURNE, AUSTRALIA

IAN HOSKEN

During 1977, Jethro Tull toured Australia, playing at Festival Hall in Melbourne. After the support act, the lights were down when a single spotlight lit up on a guy sitting on the edge of the stage, feet dangling over the edge and dressed like a leprechaun, complete with green bowler hat. He had a guitar or ukulele and, with a strong accent, apologised for the band being delayed and said he was going to fill in. As he started, he span around and stood in one motion, reaching out. A light flashed across the stage following a golden flute which he - Ian Anderson – caught. Whilst still spinning, he started to play. Other lights were added and revealed the rest of the band as they started to play. The performance was worthy of a much larger location, which was good for those watching as the hall made it more intimate.

HORDERN PAVILION

14 SEPTEMBER 1977, SYDNEY, AUSTRALIA

COLIN BRISCOE

As a long-time supporter and programmer and radio presenter of Jethro Tull on volunteer community radio 2RRR 88.5FM, I recall my very first Sydney concert at the

Hordern Pavilion on the *Songs from the Wood* tour with the incredible John Glascock. Ian was quite annoyed at the start that some university students had created a fake news story that the band was to do a live concert in Sydney's Hyde Park.

My friend Rob is also a Tull fan and he arranged a rare meeting at the concert with Ian and the whole band for his 11-year-old son, James, and myself at the Enmore Theatre in May 2005. It was a memorable evening and so special to meet everyone in person.

JAI-ALAI FRONTON

4 NOVEMBER 1977, MIAMI, FLORIDA

JOHN GOLDACKER

John Goldacker first saw Tull in Miami

I first saw Jethro Tull in concert in Miami. There was nobody between me in the stage and Ian kept teasing us with his bowler hat. The next year I saw them in Long Beach, California. I would never have imagined that it would've been as exciting from nearly as far away as you could get from the stage as it was from being upfront. That was an amazing show. And an unannounced Uriah Heep opened.

I took my wife to see the band in Kissimmee, Florida in 1996. Ian had injured himself in South America, and performed this whole show in a wheelchair, spinning around maniacally in the way he would if he was jumping on one foot. We were about nine rows back and the whole performance, especially the material from *Aqualung*, felt as if we were looking in on a psychiatric ward.

Ten years went by and I stumbled into radio. An interview was scheduled with Ian but for some reason he had to bow out and I was offered a photo-pass instead. That started off about 15 years of concert photography – so far. Over the next few years, I've had the distinct pleasure of interviewing Mr Anderson twice.

IRA SCOTT LEVIN

Ira Scott Levin created a piece of artwork, because he was such a fan

I was 13 when my cousin Larry turned me onto *Aqualung*. The song sparked a story in my imagination that I would play out in the movie theatre of my mind. I remember feeling this music was an extension of my innermost being, opening me up to potential vistas yet to be explored. I took up the guitar soon after and 'Locomotive Breath' became the fiery engine that drove my rhythmic style and desire to play and sing out with complete conviction and an abandon that bloomed, 'like madness in the spring'.

I did a deep dive into the group's back catalogue and was genuinely ecstatic when *Songs from the Wood* was released. My cousin Larry took me to see them at the Jai-Alai Fronton in Miami. The band transcended my expectations that they were larger than life. The level of musical mastery, the camaraderie and the theatrical prowess imbued with grandeur and good humour did more than blow my mind; it beckoned me to the quest of committing to the creative life.

In college I wrote a paper for my theatre history class proclaiming Jethro Tull a modern Greek satyr chorus. The earliest elements of what we know as drama came from what were called dithyrambs and satyr plays - fertility dances which were ecstatic revels performed by a group whose bearded leader played the flute, wore big boots, an old cloak and a phallus - the codpiece had yet to be invented - and sang epic poetry of heroes and gods. This leader and his satyr chorus mixed comedy into tragedy with ribald jokes and interactions with the audience to lighten their hearts and raise them up with song, above the commonplace. The goal was to get those witnessing the spectacle to forget themselves and become a part of what they saw; to become part of the pageantry and experience the wise, noble and true virtues woven into the play.

Ian Anderson said in the *Rock Book of Quotes* that 'an honest man who laughs must surely be a god.' Having experienced Tull in concert myriad times, and having watched classic clips from *Thick as a Brick* and *A Passion Play*, Ian seemed to possess a Promethean strength that he brought like freshly-stolen fire into the Tullian universe. It ignited my sense of what could be embraced and actualised within my own life.

Jethro Tull synthesise drama, music, dance and the potential of art itself to infuse the immortal within the temporal. The legacy of the group stands as a beacon to those that can hear, to take up the mantle of their own song and elevate it for the benefit of those around them.

BAYFRONT CENTER

6 NOVEMBER 1977, ST PETERSBURG, FLORIDA

PAUL KENNY

I started undergraduate studies in Florida in 1977 and saw my first Tull concert on my birthday that fall. I came back from the performance thinking I was Ian Anderson. I learned to balance on one leg, kicking the other while simultaneously playing an 'air flute' with one arm. I saw the band every year close to my birthday until graduating, and many

Paul Kenny has won frisbee world titles, with Tull as his background score

more since. My favourite song at the time was 'Teacher'. I grew my hair out along with a scratchy beard and practised Mr Anderson's bug-eyed look.

I have since seen Tull all over the US and Europe. I was the typical American tourist, doing my stand-up imitation during shows - sometimes with good seats, sometimes not so good and sometimes getting encouragement and sometimes having folks telling this old man to sit down.

I am a professional frisbee freestyler and have won two world titles playing to Tull songs. While I am still trying to work *Songs from the Wood* and *Heavy Horses* into my shows, *Thick as a Brick* will always bring back the emotions of winning a title I never expected. I get emotional thinking about it.

MUNICIPAL AUDITORIUM

13 NOVEMBER 1977, KANSAS CITY, MISSOURI

GEORGE DAVIS, AGE 15

I was 15 and we had got our hands on some bottles of alcohol that night. I'm afraid most of my memory of the evening is of eating a peanut but thinking it was the stalest Cheeto I'd ever been handed. I recall Ian was very animated and never stopped jerking about, as was his style. And I remember the balloons being thrown out and them seeming like magic to me. I thought they were something other-worldly but, after the show, learned they were simply huge balloons that behaved strangely. Very wobbly.

NASSAU COLISEUM

20 NOVEMBER 1977, UNIONDALE, NEW YORK

BARRY GOLDBERG, AGE 16

What started as a raid of my older brother's record collection more than 45 years ago has turned into a lifetime of stories and

Barry Goldberg with Ian

memories. At the impressionable age of 14, I was looking to be cool, trying to find my own style, my own music. I came home from school one day and snuck into my older brother's room to look through his albums and stumbled upon *Aqualung*. The cover was super-cool. I grabbed it, ran to my room and put it on the turntable for a listen. I turned the volume up and sat on my bed, holding the album cover. That opening guitar lick instantly catapulted me into another universe. Holy crap, what was this? I was floored. 'Eyeing little girls... Snot running down his nose ...' Then that scathing guitar solo. That's all it took. I couldn't wait for the next song. Suddenly some guy screaming, 'MARY!' Add a flute and more sizzling guitar, some intense bass and pounding drums. Damn, my head was about to explode.

After catching my breath, I hear this soft little acoustic guitar sound and some powerful guitar riffs, then the haunting 'My God'. Life as I knew it was forever changed. I raided my brother's album collection again and grabbed *Thick as a Brick*. What the fuck? This shit was brilliant. Next up, *Benefit*. Mind blown.

Back at school, I tried telling my friends about this Jethro Tull band, but was dismissed because they were all getting into Led Zeppelin, The Who, the Stones, Lynyrd Skynyrd, and so on. They just didn't get it. As the years passed, it seemed I was very alone in my love of music.

In early 1977, I heard a radio promo announcing a new album and tour for Jethro Tull. I was 16 years old. I camped out overnight, waiting for tickets to go on sale. There were hundreds if not thousands of people in line waiting to buy tickets. I was not alone. The band, the music, the professionalism, everything was greater than I could have ever imagined. My friends who I dragged along weren't so impressed. For weeks, I tried telling people about this Tull thing. No one gave a shit. But I was on a mission. I purchased every album, every magazine, every poster. I read every article. I called every radio station requesting more Tull. I couldn't get enough. Nassau Coliseum. Madison Square Garden. I didn't and wouldn't miss a show.

CAPITAL CENTRE

21 NOVEMBER 1977, LANDOVER, MARYLAND

MIKE REISKIS, AGE 15

It was a great night. I was 15 years old. I never used that ticket stub for the free Coke at Roy Rogers, and I'm happy about that.

HEAVY HORSES RELEASED

10 APRIL 1978 (US)/21 APRIL 1978 (UK)

UK CHART POSITION 20

US CHART POSITION 19

JESSICA HAWKER

Growing up in South Africa in the Nineties, my father introduced me to their music. I have fond memories of listening to *Heavy Horses* and *Aqualung* on CD whilst being driven to school in my dad's truck. We sang along together to 'Heavy Horses' and 'Locomotive Breath'. I remember being

Jessica Hawker and her husband danced to 'Moths' at their wedding. Photo: Rebecca Claridge Photography

captivated by the artwork for *Aqualung*. I still am, but I could never pinpoint what it is that draws me to it. In 2019, my husband and I danced to 'Moths' at our wedding. It was, and still is, one of my most favourite songs of all time.

Brad Bishop thinks his love of Tull was passed on by his Tull-loving father

BRAD A BISHOP

My father was such a huge fan that if my mother had lost the argument, I would have had the initials IAB, with my first name being Ian and middle name Anderson. I was born 10 years after Tull's first album, *This Was*, which means there was a very good chance that *Heavy Horses* was playing on our stereo when my mom breastfed me. My folks didn't last much longer, divorced in the mid-Eighties, and my relationship with my father was then tenuous at best. After a few more years of seeing him on weekends twice a month, we really didn't bond too much, especially about music. Especially about old peoples' music. Me and my brother made him listen to top-40 stuff on the long car ride to his house in Pennsylvania.

But as I approached my teenage years, my curious mind finally awoke and I discovered 'classic' rock and quickly devoured The Beatles, the Stones, Zeppelin, The Who, Queen, Pink Floyd ... and Jethro Tull. I raided whatever tapes and LPs my old man had left at our house, mostly mix-tapes he'd made. My mom helped guide me through these and I remember her introducing me to 'Aqualung' and 'Locomotive Breath'. I was fascinated by this new (to my young ears) music. This was the early Nineties and I hadn't yet got into the alternative grunge scene. All I cared about was the music of my elders.

My mom started dating again and her new boyfriend gave me his old LP collection. He had quite a few gems in there, including *Warchild*, *Songs from the Wood*, *Heavy Horses*, and *A*. I got a part-time job and started spending my hard-earned dough on curating my own CD collection. Around this time, the Jethro Tull *25th Anniversary* cigar-shaped box set came out and I treated myself to that and the companion lyric book.

My new fascination and admiration for Tull compelled me to wear a t-shirt to further solidify my new obsession (as well as confuse most of my peers, who didn't have a clue as to who or what Jethro Tull was). I had to make a t-shirt since I couldn't find one that was professionally made. On the back of a white Hanes undershirt, I used a black Sharpie to enlarge the line drawing of Ian from the *M.U.* album while I drew the Tull logo from *Under Wraps* on the front. It wasn't half bad, if I say so myself, but sadly it has not survived. I had maybe two friends who liked Tull enough to join me a couple of times in going to concerts, and I finally got a few actual professional t-shirts in the merchandise tent.

Fast forward 20 years and I have become evermore familiar with Tull's catalogue. I graduated from mere novice fan to appreciate practically every song. If someone asked me to name my top five bands, Jethro Tull would easily be on that list. Being a young fan of Jethro Tull could be a lonely endeavour but that was part of its charm – it was more personal and exclusive to me. Nowadays, I have maybe one friend who would be gracious enough to join me to see Ian Anderson in concert. My lovely and accommodating wife joined me a couple of times.

When autumn rolls around and forces me to rake the yard multiple times, I only listen to Tull while working. I actually look forward to that tedious task of cleaning up the yard in November because I know I'll be listening to many hours of Tull. Emotionally, autumn just feels like Tull to me. *Songs from the Wood*, *Heavy Horses*, *This Was* and *Benefit*, with its wood-carved LP cover, all evoke the fall season to me. So many references to forests, trees, leaves, farms, hunting and skating evoke a very timeless English countryside feeling.

But how did I get so into Tull without any help or influence from my highly Tull-devoted father? He never played the records after the divorce nor talked about music in general. I never got a story of him seeing Tull in concert. My mom just told me Tull was my dad's favorite group, so much that he wanted to name me after Mr Anderson. Maybe Jimmy Page or Pete Townshend was his second choice.

I really don't have much memory of the man, nor did I like him enough to want to be like him, and we didn't even talk for 15 years until he died. But if I got the Tull DNA from him, that's something positive. Only time will tell if my children will appreciate 50-plus-year-old rock 'n' roll in a few years' time. However, my eldest daughter is playing the flute in her middle school band, and I keep teasing her to play me 'Bourée' or 'Thick as a Brick'. Perhaps one day she will, and I'll fantasise that my ol' man is laughing somewhere in the afterlife. But while the jury is still out in trying to figure out if genetics has any role in me being a devoted Tull fan, I have a much better hypothesis. Who needs genetics when the music is just so brilliant?

APOLLO THEATRE

3 MAY 1978, MANCHESTER, UK

CHRIS ION

I saw Jethro Tull only once, in the late Seventies. It was at the Apollo in Manchester. I just remember being mesmerised by Ian Anderson's antics on stage. It was a great night, as you would expect from Tull.

APOLLO THEATRE

4 MAY 1978, MANCHESTER, UK

STEVE COWEN

I remember us turning up at the Manchester Apollo looking forward to the much-anticipated gig. A handwritten note for fans from Ian Anderson was pinned inside a poster casing. It explained that the gig was cancelled due to a hand injury sustained by John Glascock, but would be rescheduled. On the bus journey home, we all pondered as to what was the real reason for the cancellation.

RICHARD CONNELL

I met Keith (and his wife to be) for a meal before the gig. It seemed strange that there was little activity outside the former cinema, but I was new to this sort of thing and it looked as if the gig had been postponed. Moving to the side I saw a hand-scrawled note from Ian explaining that they had plied bassist John Glascock with drugs (until he was virtually flying above the stage), but he still had no feeling in his fingers. The note went on to say they would cancel a *South Bank Show* appearance to do a gig after the tour, and if I went round the other corner I could book for that gig. I must have been one of the first round there, as I was in the middle of the sixth row when I attended that show.

FESTHALLE

28 MAY 1978, BERN, SWITZERLAND

ALDO 'WAZZA' PANCOTTI

40 years have passed since I decided to take my girlfriend to see live, in flesh and beards, the legendary Jethro Tull. We had been dating for a few years and I was indoctrinating her about this group, but no words or records would have the same impact as a live concert. Because of public order issues in Italy, foreign groups did not tour in Italy. I went into a black depression. I had to see Jethro Tull live again. Just listening to the records was not enough for me. Then, a ray of sunshine.

I read in *Ciao 2001* – the *Melody Maker* of the poor – an announcement:

Medianova Spectacles was organising a bus plus ticket for the Jethro Tull concert at the Festhalle in Bern, Switzerland. Going to Bern was like going to the moon, but I had to go. I booked the tickets.

I involved my usual accomplice, 19-year-old Gemma. But what were we going to tell her parents? It was certainly not the time for a girl to say, 'Listen Dad, I'm going to Switzerland to see the Tulls and I'll be back!' I convinced the in-laws this was a rare bus trip organised by my employer to go and see an exhibition of new machine tool technology in Milan. 'We'll travel at night, see the exhibition and come back the next night.' They bit.

We took the Rome-Milan train, stayed overnight in a hotel in Milan and in the morning two buses departed from Piazza Castello towards Bern. These were filled with every variety and fauna of Jethro Tull fans, especially from northern Italy, fans who later were to become the hardcore of the Itullians: Dino Tinelli, Mauro Croce, Loris, Frighetto. It was a great atmosphere. And there were no cellphones, so the parents couldn't find us!

In the afternoon we arrived at the Festhalle, a big hangar of a place. Many people were already bivouacking, long-haired in elephant-legged trousers and smoking, and relaxing on the lawn. I headed behind the stage, where I found the Maison Rouge, a red caravan that served as a mobile studio. We discovered later they were recording a live album. Suddenly Ian came out, dressed as on the cover of *Bursting Out*, and peered inside a black Ford. I called out to him, and we looked into each other's eyes, like Clint

Eastwood and Gian Maria Volontè in *A Fistful of Dollars*, while I tried to get my Super 8 camera out, but he disappeared into the theatre. I recovered and called the others, 'A regà, cè stà Iananderson!' Anderson did not re-emerge and we settled for Barre and Barlow, who were very helpful, giving autographs and allowing me a few minutes of shooting.

The doors of the Festhalle were opened. The first places inside were all taken by Italians. Seeing the stage got the crowd excited, and when a technician positioned the flute, a roar started. Claud Nobs' presentation was thrilling, complete with 'Welcome Italy'. The lights went out and they started with 'No Lullaby' and 'Sweet Dream'. For me, this was the best Tull line-up: the double keyboards of Evan and Palmer, Glascock on bass, Anderson, Barre and Barlow. Barlow imitating Ian on the flute, Anderson throwing the bowler hat at Evan, attacking him during 'Wind Up', Martin on marimba, the cannon-firing confetti, two encores, two and a half hours of concert, all standing, stadium choirs, feet that beat on the ground like drums. The lights came on and we hugged each other. All those kilometres were worth it.

We arrived back in Milan and I greeted the friends of the 'Magical Mystery Tull'. But - how could we get back to Rome for 9am if the train was going to take six hours? We needed to fly. I found two seats on a flight to Rome at 7.30am – half my salary – but it was either that or the father-in-law's cazziatone. We headed towards the boarding. Gemma was exhausted and I hadn't washed for two days – a long-haired bum in jeans, walking alone with posters under my arm. If it had happened today, they would have taken me to Guantanamo. We arrived home by 9am, and to complete the deception I brought along some brochures of machine tools. We only confessed to him years later.

40 years later, an incredible thing happened. With the 40th anniversary version of *Heavy Horses - News Shoes Edition*, of the many live concerts they played in 1978, they released the one recorded in Bern.

APOLLO THEATRE

5 JUNE 1978, MANCHESTER, UK

RICHARD CONNELL

None of the tour regalia, alas, but a great show, opening with a cracking version of 'No Lullaby' (not my favourite) and the rather wonderful 'Dambusters' finale, with Ian's closing remarks wrongly pieced together on the original pressing of the Italian version of the *Bursting Out* album. Ian's reference to 'thrashing John Glascock, ever so slightly ...' before 'Hunting Girl' was particularly pointed.

MAISON ROUGE STUDIOS

SUMMER 1978, LONDON, UK

SCOTT OSTROW

In 1978, shortly after graduating high school, I travelled to England. I got the address for Chrysalis Records, where they told me Jethro Tull were recording in London and gave me the band's manager's name and number. I called him to ask if I could meet the band and he said he would check with Ian. I was told to meet them at the Maison Rouge recording studio. It meant staying in England about a week longer than I'd planned, and because I was running low on money I had to sell my camera. But I was able to meet Ian and the rest of the band, and spent about 15 minutes talking about the band and showed them my (then pretty new) tattoo of the *Too Old to Rock 'n' Roll: Too Young to Die* album cover.

Scott Ostrow met the band in 1978

A PUB

SUMMER 1978, BUCKINGHAMSHIRE, UK

SUSAN VADENCOURT

I love the flute and started playing it in school, in the suburbs of Washington, DC, from about the age of 10. I wasn't allowed to practise at home so used to go into the woods to play. The animals and birds didn't seem to mind, unlike our neighbours. So, I was an early lover of all things connected to the flute.

A few years later, now a teenager, I was sitting in the back seat of someone's car and heard an interesting song with a flute being played and a deep velvet male voice doing the vocals. I was transfixed. As a true romantic, I even loved the words. It was 'Living in the Past'. I made everyone stop talking in the crowded, teenager-filled car, while I listened to the rest of this song. I suddenly blurted out that one day I would meet the man singing this song … whoever he was, wherever he was.

Fast forward about eight years. I was just out of university and backpacking my way around Europe, complete with Eurail pass, staying in youth hostels across the continent. I was in no hurry to return to the US and was taking casual jobs in places I loved, usually waitressing as no work visa was required.

I was meant to do my Europe trip with a childhood friend, but he had backed out in the end so I did the trip solo. My first stop was London. I had no idea of what to see first but as I knew every lyric of every Jethro Tull song I thought I would visit the places Ian sang about. And so my adventures with this free tour guide began. On my days off from waitressing I covered all of London. I saw all the sights as well as visiting every area Ian Anderson ever wrote about. My favourite was Hampstead Heath.

After a few months in the city, it was time to venture out into the countryside. I went to all the usual tourist spots, even went to Blackpool - the first place I really didn't like. After a time in Scotland, Cornwall and Wales, I made my way back towards London. I would need to be leaving in a few months.

I arrived one rainy afternoon off the train at Seer Green in Buckinghamshire and walked a short way to the youth hostel in Jordans. I loved the area so much that I got a job at the guest house next door and helped with their various summer events. I was in my element and thought I would never leave. I bought a bicycle and began riding around the beautiful Buckinghamshire countryside. On my days off I went ever further afield, mostly to sketch the Chilterns Hills, old pubs and country houses. One hot afternoon, I parked my bike and myself outside a pub in the heart of the Chilterns, got some lunch and began sketching. When a man stopped to look at my artistic efforts before entering the pub, I didn't really pay any attention. I didn't even look up, but clearly remember he and several other men went into the pub. I continued sketching.

An hour or so later, these men now left the pub, but one man was clearly peering over my shoulder to look at my nearly-completed sketch. He said something about it being better than his, or words to that affect. I thanked him without looking up. He kept talking. I was about to become annoyed but looked up to find the man admiring my work was none other than Ian Anderson. Having seen Tull concerts, heard everything Ian had ever written and been such a fan for years I recognised him and his voice, instantly. Suddenly, I was speechless - not something I usually experience.

I wanted to tell him so much while he was right in front of me, things like 'thanks for being my tour guide around parts of London, and for the best love songs ever written', but I remained in awe and speechless, perhaps mumbling something like, 'Do you sketch?' The encounter was all too brief.

I had my camera with me, but it never occurred to me to ask for a selfie. As I glanced around, I saw that the other men with him were the rest of the band. I think I smiled. I certainly did inside. Time seemed to stand still. I suspect all famous people recognise when someone is in awe of them, but Ian held my gaze just long enough to make a soul connection, said something polite, smiled, then they all walked on down the road.

As I watched in disbelief I thought, 'No one back home will believe this. In fact, I don't believe this just happened.' I got out my camera and took a shot of the five of them walking away down the road, then went into the pub to pay my bill and ask the man behind the bar if that really was Jethro Tull that had just been inside. He laughed and said, 'Yes, Ian Anderson lives in the property next to this pub!'

Over the years, I have often told this story to my friends. Years later I married a man from Watford and we ended up living near Jordans for a time. Every so often we would go back to that pub. I never ran into Ian Anderson again. Maybe one day. I would so love to do a flute duet ... and, perhaps, see some of his sketches.

MADISON SQUARE GARDEN

8 OCTOBER 1978, NEW YORK, NEW YORK

LOU CORUZZOLO

My earliest discovery of Jethro Tull came in 1971 when I was 11 and introduced to the album *Aqualung*. The artwork and lyrical content of the album had a profound effect on me. The words and music of Ian Anderson and the good boys became the

Lou Coruzzolo has been a fan since the age of 11

soundtrack of my life. Listening to Jethro Tull's music became a daily occurrence for me, and still is. Whether it is a thought of a lyric, hours of listening and relistening to albums and songs, or a natural occurring reminder, the music is very much alive in my daily life.

My first live concert was at Madison Square Garden. From the 13th row I was in awe of the level of musical mastery I witnessed that night. The band was larger than life and simply memorising. How could these men transfer the complex sounds from the studio so precisely into a live performance? It was truly a spiritual experience to see them deliver such a personal, extraordinary performance. After that show I was lucky enough to attend the performances on October 9th and 11th. The first show was broadcast live on the BBC.

Another memorable experience was when my wife, Janice Coruzzolo, and I were able to gain entrance through a promotion to rate the not yet released album, *Crest of a Knave*. We, along with other attendees, were able to hear the entire album and were asked what songs we liked the most, and what would make a good video. Later, my wife and I received a promotional *Crest of a Knave* album from Chrysalis. Our names were printed on the inside of the paper sleeve. What a truly special way to thank the fans.

In November 1992 I was lucky enough to be one of a number of fans invited to witness a live recording of *Living in the Past* at the St Denis Theater in Montreal, later released on the *25th Anniversary* boxset.

I had the good fortune to share truly great experiences with different fans, seeing Jethro Tull many times in many different American cities, but one memory that will always have a special place in my heart is when my best friend, Gerry Adessa, planned an extraordinary tour of Europe in 1993. With the assistance of Kenny Wylie, Gerry banded together 23 avid Jethro Tull fans to see four European shows.

All in all, I have been able to see over 70 live performances in three different countries and 20 different American states. Thanks to the band, I have had many memorable vacations and have seen parts of the world I thought I'd never see. I want to thank Ian, Martin and all the members of the band and valuable team members behind the scenes for allowing me to relive the best times of my life over and over again.

GEORGE PATCHHEAD

This was night two of a three-night run at the world's most famous arena. It's been said that this afternoon gave birth to the satellite broadcast live concert feeds that we all enjoy today. It was quite something to see an audience of 20,000 - most of whom were quite tanked up - filing into the building, taking their seats and not knowing what to expect. Cameras were in place throughout the orchestra and floor areas, excitement was in the air and a test run occurred when the Madison Square Garden audience was briefly introduced to the European viewing audience. Maybe one day, if all the

George Patchhead was at MSG for a show that was filmed

footage can be located and cleaned up, this can be released as a full start-to-finish concert. This really was an amazing evening for the musical arts.

MADALENE LAUDANI, AGE 18

Back in 1978, Jethro Tull played Madison Square Garden on October 8, 9 and 11. I attended all three days as I was a huge fan. A friend's sister entered and won a contest for 10 groups of two to meet Ian Anderson after the last concert. She didn't really follow Tull so I did everything I could to persuade her to let me have both backstage passes, or at least one, but she wouldn't budge. When the concert was over and it was time for the winners to be brought backstage, I decided I would follow the group of winners and see how far I could get. My friend and my brother followed. When we got to the room where Ian Anderson was to be brought in, they did a

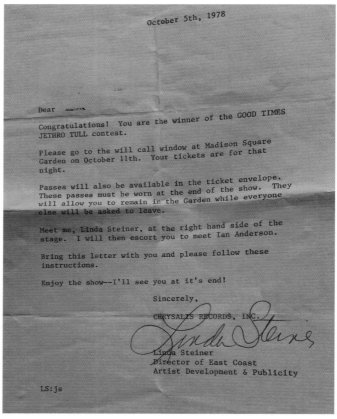

Madalene Laudani got backstage access for a Tull gig that was broadcast across the Atlantic

headcount. There were 11 people, which meant two winners didn't show. They asked who was there that shouldn't be. My brother told me to be quiet. Instead, I dropped to my knees, put my hands into prayer and said, 'Please, please don't make me leave!' I think if all 10 winners had shown, the story might have ended differently, but someone said, 'It's just one more person, let her stay.'

When Ian entered the room, I couldn't have been more excited. We were told he would sign an autograph and answer one question for each of us. At the time, I was very into trying to decipher his lyrics, so any question regarding those would have been perfect. But when it was my turn, the question I asked was, why did you play *Aqualung* twice on the 9th? His answer was that they had been streaming the second half of the show live and wanted *Aqualung* to be part of the stream. The live album, *Bursting Out*, was recorded over those October days. To this day, I can't believe that was my question.

Even thought he had just played his third concert in four days, Ian was very friendly and took his time with each of us. He had his pipe and hat and let everyone take as many pictures as they wanted. I did get to ask a second question. He had signed an autograph for me, 'Best wishes, Ian Anderson and Mistletoe,' and I asked who Mistletoe was. He said it was his cat.

After the meet and greet was over and we were brought back up to the street, we decided we were special for having met Ian Anderson and treated ourselves to a taxi ride home to the Bronx. At every traffic light and stop sign, we told anyone who would listen that we had just met Ian Anderson. A night I will never forget.

MADISON SQUARE GADEN

11 OCTOBER 1978, NEW YORK, NEW YORK

ED TREMBICKI-GUY

Aqualung was one of the most influential albums of my formative years, though my favourite may be a toss-up between *A Passion Play* (my second CD to vinyl replacement after Joni Mitchell's *Court and Spark*) and *Heavy Horses*. I saw them twice at Madison Square Garden, for the *Songs from the Wood* and *Heavy Horses* tours. For one of those shows, we were sitting in temporary bleachers that I thought would collapse as we stomped along to 'Locomotive Breath'. And I remember Allison Steele, aka 'the Nightbird', of the flagship AOR radio station in NYC at the time, WNEW-FM 102.7, once interviewed Ian Anderson. He was so thoughtful and engaging. It was the only time I found her lost for words.

This concert was the first ever transatlantic simultaneous TV broadcast.

MID-SOUTH COLISEUM

20 OCTOBER 1978, MEMPHIS, TENNESSEE

CHRIS BOHRMAN

Chris Bohrman (right) with his brother Andy

Songs from the Wood was the first rock album I ever owned, a gift from my oldest brother Andy for my 16th birthday in March 1978. I immediately became a lifelong fan. Later that same year, Andy took me to my first concert at the Mid–South Coliseum. It took some work on my brother's part to convince my mother to let him take me. In the end, she gave in. Thanks to Ian Anderson and Jethro Tull for a fantastic night, filled with amazing sights and sounds.

CHICAGO STADIUM

23 OCTOBER 1978, CHICAGO, ILLINOIS

STEPHEN DWYER, AGE 16

This was my second time seeing Tull. Uriah Heep were support. Some dingus, or 'cunt' as Mr Anderson so vividly put it, threw an egg and it either hit Barriemore Barlow or landed right next to him, leaving shell fragments to be removed from his eye before the show could (thankfully) go on. Ian was ready to take on the entire stadium, and who could blame him? 20 minutes or so later, they came back out and picked up right where they left off ... blowing us away. Quite the experience for a 16-year-old.

CENTENNIAL COLISEUM

9 NOVEMBER 1978, RENO, NEVADA

ANNETTE NYLANDER

Annette Nylander paid tribute to Jethro Tull at a Californian draft horse show

My older brother introduced me to Jethro Tull in the late Seventies by playing songs from *Aqualung* and *Songs from the Wood*s. I did a lot of house cleaning to the *Songs from the Wood*s album in those days. Then came a chance to see the band live – it was shortly after the *Heavy Horses* album came out. I bought six tickets and invited my brother and friends of ours. I had already heard songs from the album on the radio and couldn't wait.

The show was spectacular but much to my dismay the song 'Heavy Horses' wasn't played ... until the encore. As the album cover image was projected and the song played out, I thought to myself, 'Someday I will be walking those big horses.' I acquired the horse bug early in life and had a riding horse, but nothing like those big guys.

Fast forward many years and I acquired my first draft horse. She was a rescue that I trained to ride and drive and an absolute love. A year later I was contacted by a lady who had two big draft geldings and asked to work with them. Shortly later she moved and gave me those big boys. As I was leading them down out of the pasture one day, it hit me – I was walking them just like the photo on the *Heavy Horses* album cover.

I started a wagon/carriage business and began participating in a big draft horse show in Northern California. It seemed only fitting to do a tribute to Jethro Tull, as that had been my inspiration so many years before. While doing my research I discovered Jethro Tull the agriculturist had invented the horse drawn cultivator, so used that for my farm class entry. For the big Saturday night Americana class, I hooked three beautiful Percherons to the front of an old Massey Harris tractor with a sign off the back: 'When the oil runs dry, they'll be there, Heavy Horses - a tribute to Jethro Tull.'

The crowd loved it, and I took the people's choice award.

LA FORUM

13 & 14 NOVEMBER 1978, LOS ANGELES, CALIFORNIA
GRANT RICHARDS

I was introduced to Jethro Tull in 1973, aged 13, when my older brother gave me a copy of *Living in the Past*. It was the second album I received from him, the first being *Sgt Pepper's Lonely Hearts Club Band*. I loved the album and the pictures on the inside. When I was old enough, I went to my first Tull concert in LA. They were supported by Uriah Heep. It was my first near contact high and a glorious experience. I'll never forget Ian introducing the band and, when he got to John Glascock, calling him 'old brittle dick'.

Grant Richards saw Tull supported by Uriah Heep

ACTIVITY CENTER

2 APRIL 1979, TEMPE, ARIZONA

KAOIME MALLOY, AGE 14

Jethro Tull was the first concert I ever saw. I had just turned 14 the month before and it was a big deal, because my mom let me go by myself. I remember all the t-shirts in my size were sold out. The concert was better than I could have ever imagined, even though I panicked the first time Ian tossed a flute offstage. Tull were as wonderful live as on their albums. At one point, during 'Songs from the Wood', Ian's daughter popped up from behind the drum set to play the flute solo, dressed just like he was on the album cover.

I've seen them another five times since, once

Kaoime Malloy was in awe that the flute could be used in rock'n'roll

with Procol Harum, which was amazing. As a flute player, I was in awe that the instrument could be used in rock 'n' roll music. I used to spend hours playing along with the albums and trying to master Ian's epic flute technique and solos, putting my own spin on them. Learning to play like him dominated my junior high, high school and early college years, and I'll still pull out my flute and play 'Bouree' from time to time.

STORMWATCH

RELEASED 14 SEPTEMBER 1979

UK CHART POSITION 27

US CHART POSITION 22

MAPLE LEAF GARDENS

5 OCTOBER 1979, TORONTO, CANADA

DAVE PEGG

Richard Digance plays the Cropredy Festival every year. He opens up, doing the twelve o'clock lunchtime spot every Saturday, and it's fantastic what he does. He's as much a part of Cropredy as the Fairports are. Three years ago, it was a lovely sunny day and I watched his set then went backstage and caught him as he was coming off stage. I said, 'Hey Richard, that was really good. Well done. Come on, I'll buy you a pint. I owe you a pint.' He said, 'You don't, actually. You owe me a house.' I said, 'What do you mean?'

Richard said that in 1979 he was recording an album at Barrie Barlow's home studio. Barrie was Tull's drummer at the time and told Richard that John Glascock was poorly and couldn't do the American tour. Tull needed a bass player to dep for John until he got better. The Fairports were on TV on one of the nights after they'd finished in the studio and Richard said to Barrie, 'You should check out Dave Pegg and see if he's available, because Fairport are splitting up and he'd be good.' That's how I got the audition. Richard said, 'It was me who got you into Jethro Tull.'

I only had about 10 days to learn all the material that might be played in the set. Ralph McTell had invited my family down to his cottage in Cornwall for a holiday, and I spent the whole of the holiday learning the Jethro Tull set, and all the songs from *Songs from the Wood* and *Heavy Horses*, my two favourite Tull albums of the ones I wasn't involved in.

My live debut with Tull was at Maple Leaf Gardens. There were about 16,000 people there and I was absolutely terrified. But at the end of the night, I was presented with a pipe or a meerschaum by Ian, which was a sign of acceptance (Ian and David Palmer were perpetual pipe smokers) and I stayed with them for 15 years. It was the last gig of the North American tour, in San Francisco, when we heard the news that John Glascock had passed away. That's when I was invited to do the tour of Europe. But then that line-up split up and I was invited to stay on and do the *A* album.

MADISON SQUARE GARDEN

12 OCTOBER 1979, NEW YORK, NEW YORK

IAN ANDERSON

A female fan rushed forward to the front of the stage to give me a bunch of roses. But at that moment I happened to be blinded by a spotlight and was leaning over the front of the stage. She was grabbed by a couple of security guards and in her desperation to give me the roses, she thrust them towards me and unfortunately my cornea was sliced by the thorn of a rose. That was deeply unpleasant.

I managed to get some treatment in New York and further treatment in Boston and was able to continue with the aid of a large temporary covering to my eyeball, like an enormous contact lens, which protected my eye while the cornea began to heal. But it troubled me for many months afterwards, and periodically would split open again and give me terrible pain. But it wasn't the fault of the person trying to give me the roses. It was just an unfortunate accident.

At Shea Stadium, a plastic pint mug was tipped over my head from the seats high above. Someone had obviously drunk their beer, managed to pee the whole lot into the mug they'd been drinking their beer out of, then quite deliberately tipped it over

Jethro Tull live on stage. Photo by Bruce Mironov

me. I had to go on stage with urine dripping down my face, and sing and play the flute. There was no time to get cleaned up or change as I was literally waking out there to the centre of Shea Stadium, which was a big grass field in a baseball arena. That was not particularly enjoyable and made me a little pissed off.

On another occasion, a steel spike was dropped on our bass player Glenn Cornick's head, but luckily just missed him and impaled itself in the wooden stage next to him. And darts like you would play in the pub were thrown on the stage. It was Glenn who was the target again. There was obviously something about his mannerisms that people didn't like, because I remember seeing his double-stack Marshall array behind him with playing darts sticking out of the speakers. He was terrified - it was just luck that they didn't hit him.

Being hit by a bloodied tampon, on the other hand, was very deliberate and very calculated and the result of someone with unswerving accuracy of aim. Unless, of course, they were actually aiming for the bass player again.

CIVIC AUDITORIUM ARENA

9 NOVEMBER 1979, OMAHA, NEBRASKA
DAVID TRZECIAK, AGE 17

David Trzeciak is a lifelong fan

Growing up in Iowa, my buddies and I had access to some really great artists touring through Omaha's Civic Auditorium Arena - Neil Young, Bob Dylan, Tom Petty, Yes and The Kinks, just to name a few! Alas, Jethro Tull announced their 1979 tour with a November 9 stop in Omaha, Nebraska and tickets quickly sold out. But somehow we scored tickets at our local department store, JL Brandeis. The ticket office was upstairs by the men's clothing department, around the counter by children's shoes.

So began the anxiety and heart palpitations awaiting the upcoming show. November 9 rolled around and, after pitching in on gas, me and my buddies were off to the show with the newly-released *Stormwatch* record in tow (you never knew if Ian Anderson or Martin Barre might happen by after soundcheck for an autograph). Since this was a general admission show, we had to arrive early and wait in line for the doors to open. As crafty veterans - I was 17 at the time - we knew how the system worked. Arrive early, form one huge line and wait ... then wait ... then wait some more ... then wait even more.

It was a bit chilly waiting in line but, luckily, some nice fella shared some of his peppermint schnapps with us. It was just enough antifreeze to keep the system running. When the doors finally opened, we shot through the turnstiles and made our way to the third-row centre. Wow, it was finally going to happen. My first Tull show and we were up front and centre.

UK opened the show and were amazing for one song, after which I promptly fell asleep. I was probably just tired from the whole road trip, the line wait thing or maybe the schnapps? When my buddies woke me up, the house lights were on and the show was over. Really, my first Tull show and I slept through it. I was so disappointed and hard on myself as I reached for my coat.

My buddies laughed and asked where I was going, to which I said 'home.' Again laughing, they told me it was intermission and Jethro Tull were to take the stage in 20 minutes. Whew!

Jethro Tull blew the frickin' lid off the joint that night in Omaha. To this day it remains the best concert I have attended, the high watermark against which all concerts have been measured since 1979. I do regret not seeing the entire UK show and of course, Eddie Jobson, who later joined Tull on their next record, *A*. If you see Eddie, would you apologise to him for my behaviour that night? And could you thank Ian Anderson for the show of a lifetime?

LONG BEACH ARENA

13 NOVEMBER 1979, LONG BEACH, CALIFORNIA
STEVEN WESKIRCHEN, AGE 16

I had been a fan since I was 10, admiring those dramatic album covers that sat in front of my sister's record player. I learned all the words to *Thick as a Brick* and drew on my own interpretation of the story. Now, I was cruising in my poppy red '65 Mustang coupe with my friend, Tony, to the Long Beach Arena in Southern California, on my way to my very first Jethro Tull concert. The feeling was electric. Our seats were in the lower loge section, straight on, middle stage, for the *Stormwatch* tour. Ian Anderson didn't disappoint. We watched in teenage awe through the hazy

Steven Weskirchen saw the Stormwatch tour and was front row in 2007

fragrant air, soaking up every one-legged note and stretched-out passionate stance that he and the band put out for us.

It was a full decade later that I saw them next, on the *Rock Island* tour at the Universal Amphitheater in LA. I took my sister and my friend, Mark, for their birthday present. What a setlist! They seemed to have only gotten better, performing with theatrical precision.

*Live shots from 1980 taken by
Bruce Mironov*

In 2002, I was a fresh transplant to Southern Oregon, and newly married. Ian was celebrating the play on words *Living with the Past* tour. We saw this show at a smaller outside venue, among the trees and friendly fans. It was like sitting with family and hearing all the classics, Tull now refined – so clear and at perfect pace. 'Budapest' was a high point and left me with goosebumps in the young summer air.

In 2007, we finally got to see Tull from the front row at a beautiful quaint arena in Oregon. I'll never forget Ian's energised eyes locked into mine, as he spat through that flute three feet from my precious point of view. After the show, I was handed the set-list from this everlasting musical memory. It was well worth the 300-mile round trip that October evening.

It was 2016 before I saw my next Jethro Tull concert, this time with a friend and fan since childhood. Ian manoeuvred the songs to protect his voice, concentrating more on hitting all those musical accents, delighting the crowd to the end with perhaps the most furious version of 'Locomotive Breath' I have ever heard him play.

I will surely snag tickets to the next Ian Anderson's Jethro Tull concert as soon as they go on sale. Until then, I still play all the music, view the poster that adorns my wall, wear the shirt, and relish the precious memories with family and friends that Jethro Tull have provided throughout my life. Thank you, Ian Anderson and bandmates alike.

DEE PALMER

There were very few dedicated holiday opportunities during my years as a group member; we were either on the road or recording. It was a punishing schedule but if you're doing what you like and liking what you do, in and with your life, I can think of nothing better. I can't remember one tour when I was not, in my 'free' time, working on material for the next album. In fact, I had a second suitcase filled with music reference books, MSS paper, etc. to service the need (if only for myself) to maintain a creative output.

Life as a member of Tull was demanding – that's unarguable – but you know, time flies when you're having fun, and a lot of the time we all spent together was truly rewarding, and in many different ways too. Knowing (almost nightly) that, coming off stage, we'd once again delivered the goods to expectant audiences of more than 10,000 gives a great lift to one's heart and mind and a salve to the body, howsoever exhausted it might be.

We went horse-riding on one day off on an American tour, and I remember quite clearly having great fun on one night off in LA at a roller disco. However, the pitch and rhythm of life began, noticeably, to change from 'easy' to 'not at all easy' as we moved through 1979 until the denouement in the spring of 1980.

Where and when that chain of causation began, I have no precise idea, but its onset and path became quite palpable. The light – once a shining beacon emanating from each one of us – was not summarily extinguished. We were still turning in some superb performances and quite memorable gigs, but a dullness had started to hold sway. Was it because of too much of the same thing, ie. work, work, work? I don't know. Regardless of what was expended and for what was gained, suffice to say I endorse those immortal words of George Harrison, 'All things must pass'.

WILLIAM NEWTON

I was a Jethro Tull fan as far back as *American Bandstand* in 1970. Oh, the challenge, obtaining a bootleg with no releases in US and the havoc it caused in my house. Mom was not happy. My father did business with Jagger and even Mick wasn't happy about my adoration of Tull. Anyway, the band became my all-time favourite and when people were gaga over the Stones I was fully mesmerized by Anderson. I missed most of the Seventies and Eighties as I was focused on Tull.

Being a teenager, I walked out of the house to do whatever it took to obtain an album as my mother was yelling, 'I don't ever want to see that garbage in this

William Newton has kept the Anderson-style beard he grew in the 1970s

house!' Within 36 hours, I had a bootleg copy in my hands, a white album with Xerox paper glued on it. I survived my mother's wrath, but the album didn't.

When I entered college in 1970, I became a Deadhead-like follower, hitchhiking across the country whenever I heard about a Tull appearance. It was all about the journey, not the destination. Those days were mostly fond memories that I owe to the band.

Eventually my mother got hip, when she realised the music was more classical than rock. But her visual from those early years remained, as I have sported a beard my entire life, beginning around 1969. It reaches my belt now and has been white for a long time. Poor woman. She passed away over a year ago now but, 'To tell the truth, I'd scare me too'.

APOLLO

8 APRIL 1980, GLASGOW, UK
KEN GEBBIE, AGE 15

My first ever concert was Tull at Glasgow Apollo on 8 April 1980. I was 15 years old and there started my love affair with the band. I've seen Tull many times but this and one other time – the classic rock festival in Malta in August 2004, where Tull played a blinder in the heat – are very special memories.

Ken Gebbie first saw Tull at Glasgow's legendary Apollo Theatre

HAMMERSMITH ODEON

10-12 MAY 1980, LONDON, UK
SIMON HATHAWAY

My first Tull gig was *Stormwatch* at Hammersmith Odeon. I had been into Tull for a few years and travelled from Rotherham with friends. It was a great gig, with amazing musicianship and a great performance. It was their first tour with Dave Pegg.

A

RELEASED 29 AUGUST 1980 (UK)/1 SEPTEMBER 1980 (US)

UK CHART POSITION 25

US CHART POSITION 30

CHECKERDROME

26 OCTOBER 1980, ST LOUIS, MISSOURI

KERRIE 'CONCERT' HALL BURKE

Patricia Fitzgerald photographed Tull at the Checkerdome in St Louis. Photo Patricia Fitzgerald

I was sitting in my guitar class as a senior in high school in 1980. I looked down and there was a student with these incredible Jethro Tull pictures from a recent concert. I had to ask to see them. They were incredible pictures. After talking for a while, the girl introduced herself as Patricia Fitzgerald. Patricia, her sister Wendy and I became fast friends, going to many concerts afterwards. Today we are still rock 'n' roll sisters ... all because of Jethro Tull.

WENDY SUE FITZGERALD

I was lucky to have a contact that helped us get great seats to all the concert venues in St Louis. My sister loved to take photos and I always made sure she got that 'money shot'.

PATRICIA FITZGERALD

I would never have been able to get my front-row photos without the help of Kerrie and Wendy. We had a plan to get my camera, lens and film into the concert venues one way or the other. The early photos were taken using a 110 camera in the late 1970s, and I took more at the Checkerdome in October 1980.

MUNICIPAL AUDITORIUM

28 OCTOBER 1980, KANSAS CITY, MISSOURI

DANNY CAREY, TOOL

I have been a huge fan of the band for pretty much as long as I can remember, stemming back to the early Seventies when I would steal my older brother's copy of *Aqualung* when he was out and about to sneak a few forbidden listens in. This nearly always ended in a good old-fashioned brotherly ass-whipping, as he always remembered what order he placed his records in. In retrospect, I'm sure it was a finely-laid trap. But it was a small price to pay for such a wonderful musical journey.

Many years and album purchases later, I recall one special evening. The *A* record had just come out and I was lucky enough to score tickets to the show at Municipal Auditorium in Kansas City. I had shown up well prepared, with a beautiful girl I wanted to impress, a quarter-ounce of fine Columbian, and a flask of Jack Daniels. It sounds like a recipe for disaster but believe it or not, it was one of the most perfect nights in my life. I was studying percussion at the time at UMKC Conservatory of Music, so I was in absolute drum-nerd mode, and she actually put up with my obsession and even joined in with my gasps of astonishment. The weed and booze helped, I'm sure.

I knew I was in for a drumming treat that night, because I had just bought UK's *Danger Money* album and I was very excited to see Terry Bozzio play. I was already expecting a fantastic show, which was the Tull standard by my few experiences, and then to my surprise Mark Craney was drumming for the band. He lifted my inspiration to a new height. His double-bass work and new interpretation of the classic songs made an impact on my playing that has never left me.

If that wasn't enough, while walking back to our car, a huge black limousine came flying up from under the arena and the window rolled down and there literally five feet in front of me were Eddie Jobson and Ian Anderson. I said something ridiculous like, 'Holy shit! You guys fucking rocked. That was incredible.' They gave a polite wave and merged into traffic, putting a beautiful golden seal on the evening. To this day, I long for moments of inspiration like that.

Thank you, gentlemen, for showing a young and impressionable musician how it's done.

ROYAL ALBERT HALL

20 & 21 NOVEMBER 1980, LONDON, UK

RICHARD CONNELL

Reliant on friends in London to get the ticket, I ended up in a box high above the stage, watching the show through the lighting rig. It was not the greatest view, so I missed some of the show's visuals, but it was a wonderful sound, nonetheless.

This was a one-off opportunity to see two massively-talented musicians (with egos to match) combining on the same stage. The best moment for me was 'The Pine Marten's Jig', which sadly did not make it on to the *Slipstream* video. Ian introduced the song as, 'A duet for flute and electric violin: two minutes 39 seconds of ridiculous musical leaps in unnecessarily complex time signatures, which we start together, but finish all over the place.' It was, of course, note-perfect and precisely delivered.

Then there was David Palmer, suddenly dashing up to play the great Albert Hall organ. This was clearly unplanned, as Ian looked furious. It was an excellent rendition of an underrated album, though the traditional material at the end did not in my opinion come across so well.

HIPPODROME DE PARIS

23 FEBRUARY 1981, PARIS, FRANCE

SERGE HERIOT

I remember they were dressed in white. It was the *A* tour and their suit had a sort of target with a red 'A' in a circle. I don't remember the set-list, but remember they played 'Aqualung' and 'Locomotive Breath'. My secret hope was that they would play a part of my favourite Tull album, *Thick as a Brick*, but they didn't. I remember Ian standing on one leg to play the flute, like a minstrel from the Middle Ages.

Serge Heriot saw Tull at the Hippodrome in Paris

THE BROADSWORD AND THE BEAST

RELEASED *10 APRIL 1982*

UK CHART POSITION *27*

US CHART POSITION *19*

SUSIE LARGE

In 1991, I met a guy in a rock club. We chatted and danced and the DJ put on this track I really liked. 'He plays it every week, but I don't know who it's by,' I told him. 'It's 'Pussy Willow' by Jethro Tull,' says he, 'I've actually got the tape in my car right now.' Naturally, I didn't really believe him – it was way too much of a coincidence – but sure enough, he had *The Broadsword and the Beast* on his tape deck. He loaned it to me, mainly, he reckons, so he'd have a reason to see me again if only to get it back. We've been married 30 years next year. *Broadsword* is still one of our favourite albums.

ION RILEY, AGE 18

The first time I'd ever heard of Jethro Tull, let alone heard one of their songs, was Christmas 1982. My parents bought me the album *The Broadsword and the Beast*, their reasoning being that I was a massive Tolkien fan and the album artwork had runes and a fantasy theme. Even they didn't know who Tull were. I was 18 at the time and have been hooked ever since. *Broadsword* is still my favourite album, with *Under Wraps* a close second.

PALAIS DES SPORTS

19 APRIL 1982, MONTPELIER, FRANCE

LUC VANDENBUSSCHE

I discovered Jethro Tull with the album *Benefit* in 1970 and have followed the band ever since. I have only seen the band live once. It was on the tour for *The Broadsword and the Beast* in 1982. It was great.

TEATRO TENDA (PIANETA SEVEN UP)

2 MAY 1982, ROME, ITALY

FRANCESCO GIUFFRÉ–LEGNANO, AGE 17

I was 17 when I finally succeeded in getting permission from my parents to travel eight hours by train to get to Rome to see Jethro Tull. Once in Rome, I met several people making their way to the concert and joined them, since I was alone and a bit afraid of the big city. The concert was scheduled to start at 5.30pm. Around 2pm, Ian and the boys appeared on a TV soccer programme and performed 'Aqualung' and 'Pussy Willow', with an interview in the middle.

The show was very emotional for me, and it was more than 35 degrees Celsius in a crowded tent. I was not (and am still not) that tall so had to fight my way to see the stage, even though I was around the 10th row. But my heroes were there. I couldn't ask for more. Rushing away at the end of the show, I lost many personal effects due to the crowd, even my ticket stub, but I saw another one lying on the floor and picked it up. I looked at the ticket again recently and noticed the ticket number was 1965, the year of my birth. How strange.

WEMBLEY ARENA

13 MAY 1982, LONDON, UK

RICHARD CONNELL

I next saw them on the tour for *The Broadsword and the Beast*. They played a great atmospheric version of 'Broadsword', but for me the highlight was 'Watching You, Watching Me' towards the end, with an ever-extending conga of roadies, merchandisers, Uncle Tom Cobley and all, bobbing up and down in shining miners' helmets.

ROBERT STEEL

I was serving in Northern Ireland at the time, and had flown over for the gig. We couldn't afford a hotel and were loitering around the car park when Ian and Martin came out the back door, so we raced across and had a chat. Some years later, when we met Ian again and we relayed the story, he was more interested in what it was like serving in Northern Ireland at the time than in answering any of my questions about touring and the band. I used to love the big balloons and the 'Dambusters March' at the end of gigs. Being a squaddie serving in Germany, it was quite ironic. I'm not sure if it would be viewed as politically correct these days.

CITY HALL

15 MAY 1982, NEWCASTLE, UK

PETER SMITH

The next time I saw Jethro Tull was in 1982 at Newcastle City Hall. I went with Norman Jones and Doug Walker. They had just released *The Broadsword and the Beast*, their 14th studio album. The line-up of Tull at the time was Ian Anderson on vocals, flute, acoustic guitar, crazy dance and cocked leg, Martin Barre on wondrous electric guitars, Dave Pegg (ex-Fairport and friendly folkie) on bass guitar, Peter-John Vettese on keyboards, and Gerry Conway on drums. There was no support act and the ticket made sure we knew, 'Please note. No support. Jethro Tull on Stage 8pm prompt.' This was quite a theatrical show with lots of props, the band wearing medieval clothing.

   The set was a mix of old and new, with quite a few acoustic songs. I was still concerned about the folk influence at this stage, but enjoyed the show as always. Yes, the band had continued to move into a folk-rock direction. However, having thought about it, the roots of early Jethro Tull always lay within folk, rock and blues. If you listen to their first album *This Was*, you can hear all these influences coming through. I was not let down. The band continued to perform an excellent show, with a collection of songs from throughout their career. Tracks like 'Locomotive Breath' were becoming firm favourites and remain in the set (usually as the encore) to this day. And 14 albums by 1982 was pretty impressive, giving a massive back catalogue of songs to draw from, Ian Anderson and his family of musicians continuing to impress.

DAVID SNAITH

A couple of months ago a recording of probably the best concert I've ever been to in my life came on YouTube. It was the *Broadsword* tour at Newcastle in May 1982. I was there. Tull hadn't been here for a while. The album was a fantastic album, and the concert was out of this world. You can tell that by listening on YouTube, witnessing the atmosphere. I was part of three couples that went to that show.

   Afterwards we were walking on air. We went to an Italian restaurant, 50 yards away, and my wife tapped me on the shoulder and said, 'You'll never believe this.' In walked the band with their families. She ran over to Anderson, pulled him over to us and said, 'My husband has always wanted to meet you, blah blah blah ...' and he said, 'Well, who is he? The local mayor or something?' It was a totally embarrassing situation. But he was fine. You hear stories of him not necessarily being the most approachable person, but he came over for a couple of minutes and talked to us. I said, 'You must get sick of people like me who want a word', but he said not and that the only place he really disliked was Italy where, in that situation, people would paw him with their hands.

CORNWALL COLISEUM

17 MAY 1982, ST AUSTELL, UK

MICHAEL MACGREGOR

I saw the band during the tour for *The Broadsword and the Beast*. It was an utterly fantastic concert, one of the best I've ever attended. Afterwards, we lined up outside Ian's dressing room trailer to get an autograph. He was extremely gracious and took the time to talk to everyone. He signed my *Broadsword* poster which, unfortunately, I have long since lost. Great memories.

NICK GARRETT

My outstanding Tull memory is of the *Broadsword* show at the Cornwall Coliseum, 1982. It was during the height of the Falklands War.

THEAKSTON MUSIC FESTIVAL, NOSTELL PRIORY

28 AUGUST 1982, WAKEFIELD, UK

HOWARD LAYHE, AGE 17

My uncle had a Bang & Olufsen stereo. At the time it was the best you could buy. When I turned 15, he let me look through his record collection and trusted me enough

Howard Layhe was at Nostell Priory in 1982

to use it. I am so grateful for that. I remember there were records by The Strawbs, Steeleye Span, and ELP. But one record registered with me. It had a yellow sleeve and a cartoon inside. I just had to play it. That moment in Prescot, Liverpool changed my life.

I first saw Jethro Tull at the Theakston Music Festival at Nostell Priory. My dad said I could go. I was only 17. I travelled by train from Chester to Wakefield. I've still got the pictures. Most of the kids at school liked Iron Maiden, The Grateful Dead, and Genesis, but Tull were the only band for me. I think they'd passed the label of being the biggest band in the world, but I regarded them as the underdog or black sheep, which attracted me. I remember walking down a country lane outside the festival with steep sides and high hedges, looking for a pub to enjoy an underage pint. Jethro Tull were doing a soundcheck and I could hear 'Jack in the Green' whilst walking through this amazing countryside. The best of days. I next saw then on the *Broadsword* tour at the NEC. I always wanted a jacket like Ian's. I've seen them 34 times since. I've got Mr Anderson's signature on a poster in my lounge. They're such a big part of my life. Oh, and I've managed to push one of the balloons into the air. Thank you, Jethro Tull.

NEAL DAVIES, AGE 16

I'd just taken my O-levels and we'd been away for a family holiday. Back at home I was made to open the dreaded envelope, then off we went to relatives in Yorkshire. Saturday night and we went to Nostell – me, my cousin and her boyfriend. I heard Tull's guitar and vocals across the stately gardens. I've been a fan ever since, out of step with my peers but ahead of them in taste. I love the lyrics, the variety, the theatre, the short ditties, the epic classics. And I've explained horse-hoeing husbandry to many people.

SIMON HATHAWAY

My second gig was the *Broadsword* tour at the NEC, another great gig, and shortly after I saw the same line-up at a mini festival at Nostell Priory, near Wakefield. Marillion and Fairport supported them, as did Wang Chung. I slept under a big plastic bag. This was easily one of the best concerts I have seen, and I have a tape of this somewhere. It was a real return to roots, with lots of acoustic stuff, including tracks off the first album. At one point a band member came on as a green man in a leafy suit and various members came onstage and faked throwing up. Anderson started the gig walking onstage playing the bagpipes. My mate took a swig of a wine bottle that was passed to me, but it wasn't wine - it was piss. And I remember it took an age to get home on public transport from there to Rotherham.

RICHARD CONNELL

This was the only time I saw Tull perform outdoors and I believe it was their first outdoor gig in the UK in nine years. It was a beautiful sun-drenched day. First on the bill were Marillion, a late replacement for someone. Led to expect early Genesis stuff (they had been on Tommy Vance's *Friday Rock Show*) I really enjoyed them, though I was a little disappointed with Fish, who clearly thought he was more of a charismatic Peter Gabriel-like talisman than I did. His later cult following as a solo artist clearly saw much that I missed.

There followed an eclectic range of acts, from the horrific erzatz jazz of Wang Chung (although I did like 'Dance Hall Days'), through a strangely subdued Lindisfarne to an excellent set from The Blues Band. Then the interminable wait in fading light for the main act.

Suddenly, in that joint way that only an utterly focused and committed throng can muster, there was complete silence, eyes focussed totally on the pitch-black stage in hushed expectation (I had osmosed to the front and middle of the crowd by then). Then, again, in that way only a united crowd can bring, everyone knew the moment was imminent.

In a flash stage, left was Ian as a tartan-clad piper, wailing away on his bagpipes. There was darkness again for an instant, and lo, centre-stage bathed in the spotlight there was Martin Barre wailing away on his guitar. As the opening chords of 'Something's on the Move' reverberated across the stage, various band members emerged, adding bass and drums, climaxing with a reclothed Ian sidling in stage right. One snatched flute intro and Ian's vocals are underway. Oh, what a joy it was in those far-off days to hear him in full flow.

There were too many highlights to count in what followed, but it was great to hear 'Jeffrey Goes to Leicester Square', the only time I heard it done live. 'Broadsword' was immense and 'Aqualung' brilliant, but the highlight of the show was again 'Watching You, Watching Me'. This time the ever-extending conga line (including festivalgoers who tagged along) was even more impressive, bobbing in and out of the gathering gloom. For goodness' sake, I even enjoyed 'Seal Driver', which I thought was a bit of a dud on the album.

Traditional folkie Gerry Conway had been the drummer at Wembley Arena, but he was replaced by Paul Burgess from 10cc. I later saw a recording of Ian on Yorkshire TV recounting how he'd been auditioning drummers in preparation for the festival ('while all the other guys were on holiday ...').

I think this was the only time I have seen or heard a continuity disruption during a Tull show. For what seemed like an age, but was probably only 20 or 30 seconds, the sound failed during 'One Brown Mouse'. It was quite amusing watching everyone frugging about on stage in complete silence, although I did have visions of Ian firing the sound engineer on the spot when he next left the stage.

I'd given no thought on how I was going to get home to Leeds after the gig, not having a car (or even being able to drive at this point) so I merged with the deliriously happy crowd as it left the grounds, vaguely thinking of hitching a lift home.

We gradually thinned out into a small band of fellow travellers, and it emerged that one of us, believing there was a 3.25am train from Wakefield Kirkgate station, led the way. After huddling together outside the unmanned station - we weren't dressed for these cooler hours - the stationmaster finally arrived. With a hearty guffaw he gleefully announced, 'That train stopped running 30 years ago.' So we trooped off to Wakefield Kirkgate Station for a train at 4.30am, which duly arrived but was only for passengers leaving the train. By now in hope rather that expectation, we traipsed off to Northgate Bus Station. With a bus to Leeds at 6.30am, we settled down for a short nap before eventually returning to Leeds.

BLOSSOM MUSIC CENTER

11 SEPTEMBER 1982, CUYAHOGA FALLS, OHIO

STAN COCHEO

In the summer of 1981, I was introduced to the music of Jethro Tull. Sitting on the floor between speakers, I was getting an education. This was the beginning of a summer romance between me and the girl that gave me this music education. We had already shared an interest in music, yet there were gaps in my knowledge. She put on the *Aqualung* album, and I had no idea what I was in for. At first, the riff of the song 'Aqualung' hit me, and I was thinking it was a later Seventies-era hard rock album. As the album played on, and my observation of the music developed, I realised it was much more than that. It was then pointed out to me that it wasn't even a later Seventies-era album.

I was completely hooked as the album was turned over to side two, and the ideas presented both lyrically and musically in 'My God' began to unfold over me. The relationship with the girlfriend only lasted the summer between my junior and senior year of high school. But by the end of that summer, I had been turned into a fan of Jethro Tull and their music. At that point, my only concert experiences had been a couple of regional artists that played in my high school, plus one who could be labelled a 'regional act'.

My first international touring artist concert was Jethro Tull at Blossom Music Center. I'd already spent over a month away from home at Kent State University, so coming home for the weekend was just to make it to the concert. It was a struggle as my friend Gordon, who knew the way to get to the beautiful outdoor venue, was on a parentally-imposed restriction to not go, yet I needed him to drive. He and I took our two dear friends - me taking Paula, the girl that got me into Jethro Tull, and him a girl that had no idea about the band, named Brooke.

We didn't know that there was to be an opening act. They were added at the last minute, and even though their show was exceptional and memorable, only recently did I recall that I'd gotten to see Saga on their *Worlds Apart* album tour.

The position we selected on the lawn was good. Blossom Music Center has only a few spots that aren't optimal and where the support pillars block some parts of the stage. We didn't have any blocking in our view. We did have binoculars and were able to swap back and forth to get a better and closer view. I was watching through those binoculars when it appeared that Ian, whilst swinging his flute around, hit himself in the head. According to the review written by Jane Scott in the *Cleveland Plain Dealer*, it seems Ian reopened a wound he had gotten a few years earlier when he was hit in the head by a rose thrown onto the stage by an attendee at Madison Square Garden. What I saw was him rushing off stage and coming back after a moment, with a towel that had an increasingly large blood stain on it.

Having not been fully versed on the music of Jethro Tull, when they played an instrumental version of 'Living in the Past', I thought that was the original form of that song. Much to my surprise, a few years later I heard the original version, with lyrics included.

The stage show was something to admire and set the standard for me. Though this show didn't have the tall ship they were reported to have due to size restrictions (although the Blossom Music Center has a huge proscenium stage) that prop was not missed, or even noticed by me. Again, it was Jane Scott's review that told me this. And though the ship was missing, the acting out of songs included Ian walking back and forth across the stage, and each

Ian Anderson on stage in 1982. Photo (this and opposite page): Bruce Mironov

time he came near the edge of the side-stage another person in a full jumpsuit would add to the line, following him. That was during the song, 'Watching You, Watching Me', and at the end of the song, a cold ending, the lights went out, only to come back on a second later, the stage being cleared.

Another part of the performance had what looked like a park bench and a trash can, Ian digging through the can and pulling out concert t-shirts and other bits of merch, throwing them into the audience, finally pulling out a mandolin and performing 'Fat Man' on it.

I'm ever so grateful to my friend Gordon, and the two girls that went with us, for making that night a special memory, and of course to Ian Anderson and Martin Barre, plus the rest of Jethro Tull, for really giving me a great start to my concert-going existence.

I attended a high school that had a vocational programme that centred on a fully student-run broadcasting radio station. WKHR, the Voice of the Chagrin Valley, will always be in my heart as it really made me who I am today. My pursuit of a career in radio broadcasting was thwarted for a long time, but when I found that I could create an internet radio station, and also interview musicians on that station, I truly found a place for my passion.

Back in 2012, when Ian Anderson's publicist, Anne Leighton, was spreading the news about the upcoming *Thick as a Brick 2*, I reached out to see if I could get a copy to review, and hoped that maybe I'd be granted an interview. I was, and I spoke to

Ian one early morning after he landed late the night before in the United States. This became my first phone interview, and what a place to start!

The struggles began when I was called early in the morning that Ian would be ready to talk, if I could call him at his hotel. The flight had been delayed it seems, and that meant that Ian, or others on the tour, hadn't yet been able to acquire American cellphones, so calling me was not possible. Yeah, my first phone interview and I'm having technical issues. On top of that, I had a broken ankle, and my mobility was greatly reduced. I was hobbling through the house, nervousness increasing and really wanting to do a good interview.

Thankfully Ian is an amazing interviewee, gracious, understanding, interesting and appreciative. We talked for a good length, touching upon many subjects including songwriting, performing in the Middle East where he had just flown in from, and of course the upcoming album and how it was returning to the subject of Gerald Bostock and his possible futures or history over the previous 40 years. Then Ian gave me what has become a prized possession, a station ID for my show, *Musical Conversations*.

I've had the pleasure of speaking to Ian a few times since, and do look forward to talking again. As always, I thank Ian, and also Anne for making that connection happen.

SUMMIT

14 OCTOBER 1982, HOUSTON, TEXAS

BRIAN DENNISON

I had the opportunity to see the band in 1982 for the tour of *The Broadsword and the Beast*. I was living in Leesville, Louisiana and the concert was in Houston, Texas. That in itself was a big obstacle, but I really wanted to go, so I bought tickets. I was partying hard the night before, playing quarter-bounce - a drinking game - and had possibly the worst hangover of my life, my stomach burning all day. But myself and two friends went on the long road trip anyway, enjoying one of the best live shows I've ever seen.

I really love that album and loved the live performance of 'Watching Me, Watching You', the guys in the white coats creeping behind Ian during the song. The t-shirts being sold read, 'I humped to see Tull', and given the events leading up to going, I certainly did.

OAKLAND COLISEUM ARENA

19 OCTOBER 1982, OAKLAND, CALIFORNIA

STEVE RUSSEY

1982's musical climate was definitely changing. Punk, new wave and modern rock were challenging the classic rock acts, which were beginning to be described as dinosaurs, overblown, pompous and out of touch with the people and their audiences. My response to that ... nonsense! Progressive rock is still relevant and has an audience. A year after I graduated from high school, I was an aspiring musician myself in what could be described as a progressive hard rock band, deludedly believing I would be on an arena's stage one day.

This show was a truly excellent pairing of bands. Opening act Saga were receiving airplay due to their recent release, *Worlds Apart*, so I was familiar with their FM rock radio 'hits', and they provided an excellent opening set. Then the usual redressing of the stage took place, a compilation of well-known rock tunes played for our enjoyment over the PA as the technicians busily and carefully set up Tull's gear ...

Then the recorded music stopped suddenly, the house lights disappeared, the assembled crowd erupted with cheers, and Ian Anderson with his new musical recruits lit into 'Something's on the Move' from my favourite Tull release, *Stormwatch*, and for the next two hours or so, he dazzled us with his tireless and unprecedented stage presence, wielding and spinning that flute like a rapier, then standing still on one foot as he played. His precision acoustic guitar playing was fantastic, his between-song banter always a laugh, and of course Martin Lancelot Barre ripping and shredding his guitar with razor-sharp prowess, skill and cunning technical ability. Priceless. This was all backed by the always-outstanding musicians Ian works with, and a very impressive set-list, including the title track off *Broadsword* as well as 'Beastie' and 'Clasp', all pristine. 'Black Sunday' was impressive and then they gave us one of the definitive Tull gems, 'Heavy Horses', and album companion piece 'One Brown Mouse'. These were followed by the condensed 'Thick as a Brick' (was this really a parody of progressive rock?) and the usual *Aqualung* material, which is always a joy, then a surprise for me - that odd, non-album track with the even more strange video, 'Sweet Dream', which new visual medium MTV featured.

I had two gripes. Ian did not play my favourite Tull tune, 'Skating Away on the Ice of the New Day', while *Stormwatch* was under-represented. 'Dun Ringill' and 'Orion' would have been very welcome. But this was truly a progressive rock concert which could summon the splinters of the apocalypse.

I left the arena that night believing progressive rock would reign and dominate as the years advanced. It did neither, but it did remain. One can still enjoy versions of Yes and Carl Palmer's ELP legacy, and we must applaud Marillion for staying with us against the odds. And, by golly, gee willickers, Jethro Tull had a new album out in 2022.

CHRYSALIS RECORDS

DECEMBER 1983, NEW YORK, NEW YORK

DOANE PERRY

It's like that old adage; success is when preparation meets opportunity. I studied and practiced quite hard as a teenager. I didn't get any encouragement from my school or much from my family. My father was quietly supportive and my older sister more vocally so, but music in general wasn't considered a viable career option ... and with probable good reason. But music drew me powerfully and by the time I was a young teenager, I knew I *had* to do this. In New York City I was up against strong headwinds and understood that I'd better get as good as I possibly could, because I had a lot of competition. Miraculously, when I was 19, I got the gig playing with Teo Macero, who was Miles Davis' producer and the architect of Miles' sound. He composed and conducted the music for a large multi-day, multi-cultural event at Lincoln Center and I performed with his big band at that. It was exhilarating and terrifying at the same time, playing with people considerably older, established and far more experienced than me ... and thrown headlong and wide-eyed into the deep end of the pool.

I was working professionally on the weekends in bands by the time I was 15 or 16 and began working in studios occasionally while I was in high school. In my early 20s I started going back and forth between New York and Los Angeles but found myself working more and more in California. One day I got a call from my old friend, guitarist Larry Saltzman, in New York. He said, 'You know I just heard about this ad in *The Village Voice*.' Larry had been on the phone with another friend, Marc Shulman. Just before the end of their phone call, Marc casually said, 'Hey, check this out. Let me read this to you.'

"Fairly well-known British rock band suffering from standard male pattern hair loss requires drummer with faultless timekeeping, vigour, creativity and warm personality to accompany the above on world tour through drug-free zones and various time signatures. Tapes and details of hat size in confidence to Ian Anderson, c/o Mary Smith, Chrysalis Records, 645 Madison Avenue, New York, New York, 10022."

Marc didn't know I was a Tull fan, but Larry did and said, 'That *must* be Jethro Tull. I have got to call Doane and tell him about this.' It was a very cleverly worded ad and if you didn't know who Ian Anderson was, you would have no idea it was Tull. So Larry called me in California and read the ad to me.

It seemed like quite a long shot but another part of me felt, 'I should do something about this.' I called a friend at Chrysalis Records who I had known when I was working with Pat Benatar, who was also signed to Chrysalis. He said that Ian had recently called and asked, 'Do you know anybody in America that might be suitable for the band? We've been looking and haven't found anyone yet.'

My friend at Chrysalis said to me, 'I can't believe you called. I just told Ian Anderson that I know this one guy. I don't know if he's available. I don't even know where he is right now or if he'd be interested.' He also didn't know that I had been a young fan and had followed Jethro Tull over the years. He just felt I was a really good player and could cope with the music. It was a Tuesday in mid-December 1983. He said, 'We're closing up for the Christmas holidays and the band don't want us sending any more solicitations over to the UK. If you could get me something by Friday, I'll make sure to pull it and tell them to look out for it, because they're swamped with tapes and letters.'

At that time I was signed to Warner Brothers and had done one album with a great band called Maxus, which has since gained some cult status. It was a good album and I was proud of it but we were one of many casualties of Warner's unsuccessful attempt to try to break the payola scandal in America. Up to that point, I'd performed on a couple of hit singles but had also played lots of jazz, rock, pop, R&B, fusion, classical, folk, Celtic, latin and even some Middle Eastern, Brazilian and Indian music. I put various excerpts of some of these tracks from different records on a cassette and sent off a letter with that tape, plus a copy of the Maxus album to Chrysalis.

A week or two later I was on Long Island visiting my aged aunt and uncle. The phone rang one afternoon and I picked it up because my aunt and uncle were having a snooze after lunch. I was expecting it to be Mrs. Yehudi from down the road, and this distinct English voice said, 'Hello, is Doane Perry there? This is Ian Anderson calling.' I wondered how he would find me or even know I am here. I had an answering service in New York who would pick up the line if you didn't answer and get a message to you at whatever studio you were working, but I did not recall leaving this as a forwarding number for the two days I was going to be out of town. Normally I would just check in with them when traveling. This was a little before everyone had their own answering machines, which you generally had to be home to access anyway, so answering services were much more practical for working musicians who were out and about. Later I found out my answering service apparently did *not* give Ian my number, nonetheless he had mysteriously tracked me down at this obscure residence on Long Island.

We talked for about an hour. He asked lots of questions about my general background, if I was available and familiar with the music, did I play double bass drums, etc. He wanted to get to know me a little bit to see if he felt I was potential material to even consider, musically and personally.

Then he said, 'I really like your playing.' However, he had only heard the Maxus record, although that seemed to be enough to persuade him to give me a call. Somehow the LP got separated from the cassette tape and I think Ian got the record and perhaps the other guys got the cassette tape. I don't know who got the letter. He said, 'Look, I'll call you back in a week or so and we can talk about songs to learn.'

He called me back soon after and we talked some more. Perhaps he had heard the tape by then. He asked if I could learn a number of specific songs and come over to the

UK to play with the band in January. Some of the songs I knew reasonably well but I practised, studied the music in more microscopic detail and did my homework.

AUDITION

25 JANUARY 1984, UK

DOANE PERRY

They flew me over. There were a few other people being considered, although I didn't know who those people were at the time. Knowing who was the competition was not going to help anyway. I just needed to be well prepared and play it the way I would want to naturally interpret it, while observing the important aspects of the existing arrangements and drum parts. I knew it would be a mistake to go in and attempt to imitate any of the incredible drummers who had preceded me.

Kenny Wylie was the band's production manager and said, 'If you want to bring over a trap case with a favorite snare, cymbals, pedals, sticks and whatever, then go ahead and do that.' But my trap case never made it through Heathrow customs, who held it up for the entire day of the audition. I didn't even have my own drumsticks.

Everything I used was completely borrowed from the rehearsal studio where we were having the audition. The drum set had been very, very well used by people and was considerably past its 'sell by' date. I didn't like the way the pedals felt, didn't like the snare or the cymbals and didn't even have my own drumsticks. There were a lot of things that would have made it far more comfortable if I could have had some of my own essential equipment. But they *weren't* there, and I had to transcend that limitation immediately. I had to work with what I had in front of me.

We played all the songs Ian had requested me to prepare, then he asked, 'Is there anything you'd like to play?'

'How about Black Sunday?'

'You can play that?'

'Yes, I think so.'

'Black Sunday' is a fairly tricky song, but I picked it because I loved that it was a big, dynamic piece and although complex, it felt quite natural to play. We got through that fine and Ian asked, 'How are you in odd time signatures?' So we did some things in three, five, seven, nine and various permutations of those time signatures. Following that he asked about soloing. So we played something and I did a solo.

'We've got this new piece of music' he announced. 'Let's see what you can do with this.' This was something from the yet to be released *Under Wraps*. There were no vocals on it, just the backing track. I had brought my music staff notebook and said, 'Could you give me a couple of minutes, go have a cup of tea and I'll work on it,' While they did that, I transcribed the piece very quickly so I could read it back. They returned and I was able to play through that, pretty much from top to bottom, and keep the form together. I think they could see that I could learn things fairly quickly and write them out and read it back if necessary. Being able to read music wasn't a prerequisite to the gig, but it was certainly an asset. I'd often do that if we had limited rehearsals or were recording and working quickly.

Finally … the trap case rolled in literally five minutes before the audition finished. Kenny Wylie, Tull's production manager drove me to the airport the next day and I vividly recall him saying to me, 'You'd *better* get this gig, because it cost us £500 to get this over here.'

That was part one of the audition.

Then they took me out to dinner. It happened to be Burns Night. 'We're having dinner at a Scottish pub,' Ian said. 'Have you ever had haggis?' I didn't know anything about haggis, apart from having heard the name.

'I don't think so,' I warily replied.

'Great, you're going to love it. It's like Scottish health food.' This was still a little unconvincing and he later told me he'd pegged me as a nuts-and-berries kind of guy.

When they brought out the haggis, they handed it to me and had me ceremoniously cut it. I didn't realize that strange black balloon I was carving into was actually a sheep's stomach. I'm glad I didn't. I remember cutting it open and this oatmeal-like substance, in addition to things that looked suspiciously like small body parts with a reddish tint, began to ooze like lava out and over the top, spilling down the sides. I'd never seen anything like this. It did *not* look like health food to me … Scottish or otherwise. I wasn't immediately horrified … that came later when I discovered what it actually contained. It didn't smell bad but it did look very strange. Accompanying the haggis were these slightly conical, Kliban looking cartoon-like, amorphous food masses, which turned out to be some sort of unidentified vegetables served on the side. I didn't know what those were exactly, but they looked a little less threatening than the oozing lava from the black balloon. I know all of them took some slightly perverse delight in knowing I had *no idea* what I was eating or where it came from. But I've always been a pretty adventurous eater. I tried it. I ate it. I've had haggis several times since but certainly wouldn't go out of my way to have it again.

Ultimately the haggis experience wasn't totally satisfying, and I was still a little hungry. Martin was sitting directly across from me. They had served this wonderful garlic bread (at least *something* recognizable to me) and Martin's unloved and uneaten portion was sitting forlornly on the side of his plate. He had apparently finished his meal, so I leant across the table and quietly asked, 'Martin, are you going to eat that garlic bread?' Whereupon, he looked up at me in mock horror and said, 'Doane, I *hardly* know you!.' But being the kind, compassionate soul he is, he momentarily pondered the question then gave his garlic bread to the hungry American … or maybe he was just trying to give up carbs.

We got through dinner and then they passed around a book of Robert Burns poems. Everybody read a stanza. Even though I was a 10-year-old American kid when *Mary*

Poppins came out, I recognized Dick Van Dyke's English accent as an absolutely hideous caricature. However, I *could* do an equally poor imitation of it so when it came to my turn to read a stanza of Robert Burns, that's exactly the way I read it, which at least made them laugh. Maybe that's why I got the gig ... so thank you Dick.

In retrospect, the social part of the evening was probably as important and equal a part of the audition process. 'OK, he seems to be able to handle the music and be able to play and he's enthusiastic about the music and appears to know it. Let's see how we like this guy. Can we get on with him for the next six months on the road?' Most touring musicians would probably agree that you don't want to work with somebody who can play your music but might be difficult or unpleasant to be around when you're all out on the road together.

CAIRD HALL

30 AUGUST 1984, DUNDEE, UK

DOANE PERRY

When we were doing pre-production rehearsals on these insulated sound stages and later full production rehearsals with the PA and staging in a bigger place, they were still somewhat insulated and didn't quite prepare me for what I was about to hear. My first show was in Dundee, Scotland at the Caird Hall. I could not believe how *loud* it was ... and I'm the drummer! This was the loudest music of which I'd ever been a part. There was no discernible acoustic treatment in the Caird Hall, and this was some serious volume.

Peter Vettese, Tull's incredibly gifted keyboard player, was on the riser to my right, immediately next to me. He had a small apartment block of speakers that were his monitors and I had one small floor monitor. How was I going to get over the top of this? This was long before in-ear monitors, and monitoring was much more basic back then. Dave Pegg had his own separate cabinet right behind me as well, which was simply dedicated to bass monitoring. The rest of the band plus a little bit of my bass drums came through the single floor monitor wedge. But from where I was sitting, it wasn't nearly enough to make it a well-balanced sound. To everybody's relief, particularly Ian's, the onstage volume got much quieter over the years as the monitoring technology substantially improved.

The first concert was incredibly exciting and exhilarating, but I *was* astonished how loud it was in a live, bright hall with the full PA at concert levels. I wasn't all that nervous, probably because I felt reasonably well prepared and was ready to bring everything I had. It was a great gig. I remember I was soaked from head to toe and needed a complete change of clothes afterwards, which became the norm, post-concert. It was athletic, cerebral and challenging ... and I loved it. We went back to the hotel after the concert and had a celebratory drink. I felt good about my maiden voyage with the band. There were no train wrecks that night, although we had a few train wrecks or minor derailments other times over the years.

The whole *Under Wraps* tour was great fun, but not without its difficulties. There were drum machines on the album and Ian and Peter came up with some great drum programming. They were thinking about what would sound good and not necessarily concerned with whether it would be difficult or not to play by an actual drummer, although Peter is actually a very good drummer and I'm sure that aided in some of the programming. I clearly remember saying to Ian, 'You'd have to have at least two drummers at certain points to accomplish all you've got on this album. These are creative and wonderfully layered parts, but there's no way I can play all of them as one human being.' Out of necessity, I created hybrid parts, referencing what was on the record in the main. Sometimes we would play back certain isolated parts of

Ian in 1984. Photo: Bruce Mironov

the programmed drum machine on backing tapes and I would play along, either on my stand-up electric kit or acoustic drums to fill in the rest of the parts. It was like double drumming on stage and was fun to play along with, giving us the ability to re-create the parts on the record more accurately.

One of the nightly highlights of the set for me (and probably also the others but

Live shot from 1984. Photo: Bruce Mironov

for different reasons, in that it gave them a needed pee break), was when Peter and I would play this intense and complex duet, a challenging 11-to-12-minute piece to perform. Like the rest of the Tull set, it was *a lot* of notes to get in the right order every performance. We did our best.

IAN ANDERSON

For the *Under Wraps* tour, newspaper print wrapping decorated the whole stage. The drums, the guitar, everybody was literally wrapped up in what came off these enormous industrial rolls of newsprint paper. We would carry those around in a truck and rip off big chunks of it when we were setting up and wrap people up in a deliberately loose, untidy and messy parcel, out of which the band members would burst out and play. And it worked, because the newspaper wrapping couldn't really go wrong. You could burst out of that. Even a drummer could flail his sticks around and it would all shred and fall away to the side.

But the final bit of wrapping paper left on stage remained through the second song, looking intact, and people were beginning to wonder, 'Why has that one not revealed its contents?' And within the context of a strobe light, which made it really difficult to see what was going on, a completely naked lady burst out of the packaging and ran behind me across the stage and into the welcoming arms of a roadie carrying a white bathrobe to wrap around her and escort her back to her dressing room, where somebody gave her the probably $100 fee, and back she went to work in the strip club or wherever she came from.

CITY HALL

2 SEPTEMBER 1984, NEWCASTLE, UK

PETER SMITH

This tour was to promote the new album, *Under Wraps*, which introduced an Eighties electronic/synth pop sound, to a mixed reaction from fans and critics. But the concert was a big success, with quite a long set drawing from many of Tull's 15 albums and a couple of tracks from Ian Anderson's solo album *Walk into Light*.

The band at this point consisted of Ian Anderson (flute, vocals and part-time detective for this tour concept), Martin Barre (guitar), Dave Pegg (bass), Peter-John Vettese (keyboards), and new man Doane Perry (drums). The programme consists of photos of the band members, depicting Ian Anderson as a super-sleuth (the subject matter of the songs on *Under Wraps* was heavily influenced by Ian's love of espionage fiction), and lyrics from some of the songs which were performed during the concerts.

NATIONAL EXHIBITION CENTRE

6 SEPTEMBER 1984, BIRMINGHAM, UK

SIMON HATHAWAY

My next gig was the *A* tour at the NEC, a great hard rock gig with the band all dressed in white jumpsuits. I have the DVD. Next was *Under Wraps*. The band were all wrapped up in paper at the start, Anderson tapped them with his flute and they burst out of the wrapping. I was right at the back of the NEC. It was a bloody awful view, but great guitar from Barre.

UNDER WRAPS

RELEASED 7 SEPTEMBER 1984

UK CHART POSITION 18

US CHART POSITION 76

CHARLES BARNES

I really, really like *Under Wraps*. In my opinion, *A* and *Under Wraps* showed Tull to be a progressive rock group which successfully adopted the new wave trends, as did King Crimson, Genesis and Rush. And 'Hot Mango Flush' off *J-Tull Dot Com* is the happiest song I have ever heard. I just want to be there, in the world conjured by that song: it makes me hopeful that wholesome joy and happiness are attainable.

Charles Barnes is a big fan of Under Wraps

HAMMERSMITH ODEON

8 SEPTEMBER 1984, LONDON, UK

STEWART WOOD

I have had at least three Jethro Tull epiphanies. The first was when I fell in love with Tull in 1982. It was at my brother's urging: he had an instinct that I would like them. Aged 14, he played me *Stormwatch*, borrowed from the school record library, and made me buy *This Was*. But my Road to Damascus moment was on June 9, 1983, aged 15. I was on my third listening of *Aqualung*, and told myself to pay proper attention to the next song. It was 'Cheap Day Return' and it made my jaw drop. 90 seconds like nothing else I had heard - multiple tunes, unorthodox song structure, unique arrangements, stunning guitar playing, sung with poignancy and wit. I must have played the album *Aqualung* five times that day, and was knocked sideways by the range of sounds, the variety of types of songwriting, the punch, the subtlety, the attitude ...

My second epiphany came when I bought *Thick as a Brick* a few months later. I ran home with it, played it straight through and knew immediately I had finally found my music. It was touching, funny, silly, philosophical, playful, complex, beautiful, and made me cry just a bit. It was all drenched in musicianship and energy that took my breath away, and still does.

My third epiphany was on September 8, 1984, when I sat in Row D of Hammersmith Odeon and saw Tull live for the first time, on the *Under Wraps* tour. I remember almost every moment: the opening theatre of the science lab, with Martin Barre bursting out of a paper shroud; the pulsating energy and musical perfectionism of the performance; the sadness when we had to rush for the last train home.

Jethro Tull are my band. The band that provides the soundtrack for my life. Their songs are my constant companion I carry around inside me every day. To say they are unique is an understatement. No other band combines folk, blues, rock, classical and many more musical threads in such an original way. No other band reinvented itself so constantly, always staying true to the faith of being different, innovative, challenging and unobvious. No other band manages to make complex, sophisticated music that is so emotionally direct. And absolutely no one plays the acoustic guitar like Ian Anderson.

CONGRESS ZENTRUM HALLE

2 & 3 OCTOBER 1984, HAMBURG. GERMANY

CARL SPRINGER

I had already seen the group two years before, at the same venue. And I had observed the rules of the security personnel: during the main part of the show, they would watch out that the audience remained sitting. They'd guard the stage after the main act, when people were shouting for the encore. But a few moments into the encore, they would start to leave. So when, after an already exciting show, the group came out for the encore that night, I kept an eye on the security guys, and at the moment I saw them walking away, I rushed to the open triangular space in front of the stage. The band was right before and slightly above

Carl Springer got to shake Ian's hand

me (the stage floor was less than a metre in height), playing 'Locomotive Breath'.

I was a skinny 19-year-old in my old t-shirt, lit by the lights of the stage, and standing in front of the band it was as if the band was playing only for me. I felt their amused eyes on me, and spontaneously - hopefully gracefully - bowed to them. And Ian, never shy for the appropriate response, made a gesture as if seeing an old friend. Singing, he came up to the edge of the stage and held out his hand to me. I reached up and we shook hands, musician to teenager, prime entertainer and artist to teenage boy not yet able to decide what to do with life. It was a great two seconds before dozens of other fans arrived from behind, and submerged the scene like a wave.

COW PALACE

1 NOVEMBER 1984, SAN FRANCISCO, CALIFORNIA

JASON ROBERTS

My first college roommate, Dan Cisco, turned me on to Tull in 1975. My first Tull concert was at the Oakland Coliseum in the spring of 1977. I remember the red bowler and tights Ian wore. We ate marijuana brownies for the occasion, so the memory is a bit hazy. We had awful seats, but the show was uniquely theatrical, with sets and dramatic entrances and exits. All very thrilling. 20 shows later, I rarely miss a tour. For the *Under Wraps* tour at the Cow Palace in San Francisco, the stage had two giant white paper-covered sculptures on each side of the stage. I remember being shocked when a naked lady burst out of one and ran off stage at the end of the first song. This was another good show, despite the fellow in front getting quite annoyed because I clapped along with the songs so much.

Thanks for all the good shows, boys, and all the great memories.

UIC PAVILION

4 NOVEMBER 1984, CHICAGO, ILLINOIS

ROB WINTERCORN

I saw the *Under Wraps* tour in Chicago with my brothers. I am blessed, being the youngest of seven and being able to dial in such a mix of music interests. I remember having pretty good seats on the main floor. I also remember always turning the volume up whenever Tull was played on the radio in my car in the early Eighties, and spinning my brother's Jethro Tull albums when he wasn't home to beat me up for it, as older brothers do when you touch their stuff. There's something about playing 'Locomotive Breath' or 'Aqualung' when you're about 10 years old and get home from school 37 minutes before your older siblings to play their records on their equipment.

CONVENTION CENTER

9 NOVEMBER 1984, SAN ANTONIO, TEXAS

ROB FRIEDENBERG

I was 14 years old when I first heard a Jethro Tull album. I was a Beatles fan from a young age, but in my teenage years my brother introduced me to most of the other music I listened to. Living in a small town in Georgia in the late Seventies, I used to steal into the converted shed outside our house where he lived and listen to his albums. I discovered Pink Floyd, The Who, Mike Oldfield and Neil Young, and also more contemporary bands like The Police and Tom Petty. I was also a history buff from a very young age, and when I came across his copy of *Songs from the Wood*, I thought it was medieval music. The fusion of medieval music with rock mesmerised me. I recorded the record onto a cassette tape and listened to the album incessantly. I even tied my little tape recorder to my bicycle so I could ride around the neighbourhood to the sounds of 'Velvet Green' and 'Hunting Girl'.

Rob Friedenberg saw Tull in Texas

In the spring of 1981, I ordered cassettes of *Aqualung*, *War Child*, *Thick as a Brick* and *Stormwatch* from a mail order music company. The music was so complicated and the lyrics so dense. As a fan of the acoustic guitar, I loved that Ian Anderson always wove acoustic elements into the harder rocking side of the music. I soon caught up with the full back catalogue, collecting every album.

I left Georgia for military school in New Mexico, then college in Texas, all the while remaining an ardent fan. I first saw Tull in concert in San Antonio, Texas. I was a college student in Austin and rode a Greyhound bus alone to get to the concert. I was expecting a great show, but when I saw Ian Anderson almost explode onto the stage, I was again mesmerised. I remember sitting in the audience, wishing I'd been older so I could have had the chance to see Tull live in the 1970s.

In over 40 years, through an army career, living in numerous countries, and seeing Tull live in concert seven times, my passion for the band has never waned. Throughout the years, with numerous changes in musical style, Anderson's inventive songwriting and flute and acoustic guitar playing keep me coming back album after album. Ian Anderson's music has been a positive influence on my life. I know I am one of many fans who, given the chance, would thank him for the joy and inspiration throughout the years.

HOLLYWOOD AMPHITHEATER

22 NOVEMBER 1984, LOS ANGELES, CALIFORNIA

TIM QUESNEL

I had been a Jethro Tull fan for several years before I ever got the pleasure of seeing them in concert. It all started when one day a classmate of mine in high school brought in *Thick as a Brick* and played it in its entirety in class (thankfully the teacher was very lax). I was completely hooked. Since then, there is not a piece of music that any of the boys have produced I have not heard. But I never had the opportunity to see them live in person.

But I was in the US Navy, watching *American Bandstand* one Saturday morning on board the USS New Jersey, I caught Honeymoon Suite doing their hit, 'New Girl Now'. The interview that followed stated they were the opening act for Tull on their *Under Wraps* tour and were going to be in Southern California soon. It turned out that Tull were going to be playing the Hollywood Amphitheater for three nights, starting on Thanksgiving Day.

Tim Quesnel has seen Tull over 20 times. Photo: Tim Quesnel

Being a poor sailor and not having my own vehicle, I had to get 11 people to go with me because 12 was the minimum to use the ship's van. Truth be told, there was only me and another shipmate that wanted to go. Even then, I'm not so sure he really wanted to. Fortunately, I got the van anyway and we were on our way to musical bliss! The other person I got to go with me was from Providence, Rhode Island and his favourite artist was Bruce Springsteen. But I think I made a Tull convert out of him that night.

Not knowing for sure if we could get there, we aimed to purchase tickets at the door. Fortunately, as it was Thanksgiving, there were plenty of seats available and we got aisle seats in the eighth row. I really don't remember even seeing Honeymoon Suite, but Tull I remember vividly, starting the show by 'bursting out' of all the 'wrap they were under'.

Ian was just coming off his hiatus after suffering a strained voice. Numerous people in the first two rows were smoking pot and about two thirds of the way through, Ian had to stop the show to firmly let them know to 'put the shit out!' Unfortunately, the damage had been done, Ian's voice started to plummet, and by the end of the show it was all but gone and he had to fill in with flute for the vocals that should have been there. Consequently, they wound up having to cancel the other two shows. But it was a night I will never forget.

I have had the pleasure of seeing Tull or solo Ian Anderson almost 20 times. Each one is a great thrill, especially the time I took my daughter (13) and son (10) to see Tull for their very first concert. Sadly, they are not big fans like their ol' man, but they do appreciate the band's music abilities. My daughter is now a music teacher, and my son an awesome guitar player. I'm looking forward to my next show, but for now I'll be 'Living in the Past' ...

The band concluded 1984 with the seven-date *Down Under Wraps* tour of Australia.

FESTIVAL HALL

13 DECEMBER 1984, BRISBANE, AUSTRALIA
DEAN TUMMERS

It was serendipitous, really. For us at least. Not so much for Ian Anderson, who had been forced to do the unthinkable and postpone a Tull concert leg due to illness. I think it was unprecedented for them at the time. But there we were, the band tuning up on a Thursday night in Brisbane and my two mates and I with a few dollars spare. With the prior knowledge of one Tull song between us ('Living in the Past') we bought tickets and filed into what was recognised as one of the worst venues in Brisbane for acoustics, the now defunct Festival Hall. We three teenagers had no idea what to expect. But we knew the venue was licensed and that was enough for us. We could tolerate plastic cups for the beer and armed ourselves with the same before settling into seats not too far from the stage. On the stage were what appeared to be mannequins and equipment covered in sheets, being checked over by technicians. Interesting ...

Dean Tummers first saw Tull in 1984 and still has his 25th anniversary tour tickets

The lights went down, a saxophone played. A spotlight played over us before settling on someone sat a few rows in front of us. Was that Ian Anderson? Playing saxophone? We had no idea, but the theatrics were an eye-opener. Whoever it was looked up in feigned surprise, may or may not have cried, 'Oh shit, sorry!' then raced onto the stage. The sheets were whisked off, revealing the band, and it was on!

It was a fantastic show, the *Under Wraps* tour. The three of us loved every minute of it. Within weeks I had most of the back catalogue on vinyl, driving the owner of my local record store to distraction as he tracked down album after album.

Ten years later they were back, and so was I. This time it was the *25th Anniversary* tour. My two mates had long since moved on, but now I was a fully-fledged fan the concert went differently for me. A decade prior I was sitting listening intently to songs I'd never heard before. This time around those same songs were old friends.

Since then, I've run into fans in the strangest of places. An 'Orphan's Christmas' function in Papua New Guinea where Tull were playing on a compilation Christmas CD. An inebriated evening in New Zealand where someone put on the just-released Rolling Stones *Rock and Roll Circus*, and there they were again.

I still have the concert programmes. I don't know where the ticket stubs from 1984 went, but the 1994 stubs are now a fridge magnet. I still have most of the vinyl, I've updated some to CDs and still share a knowing smile with anyone wearing the band's shirt or even mentioning them in passing. We are everywhere. It's been nearly 40 years since that Brisbane show and my memory may not be the greatest. And if I've misremembered any of the above, the inaccuracies are purely my own. But I'm grateful that the tour was held up, that we heard about spare tickets on the radio, and that we got to see a show that would herald a whole 'next generation' of fans.

HOWARD THRIFT

I was looking for different music from the mainstream that was around back then. The FM station was the very first FM station in Queensland at the time and they played so much new music that no other station would touch. Seeing Tull was a memorable experience as their show was groundbreaking at the time. My girlfriend (now my wife) was mesmerised by Ian Anderson standing on one leg like a minstrel playing the flute. Their live shows were usually staged around their latest albums, so the staging was always something different.

The *Under Wraps* album and subsequent show had some memorable things happening on stage. The lights went down and a guitar solo started with all the band covered in white wrapping paper. As the first song finished, Ian Anderson went over to a wrapped-up person on the stage and ripped off the paper to reveal a completely naked young woman. He led her across the stage to the side, where she disappeared from view. Back then that was pretty shocking. Live nudity wasn't something the authorities liked at all.

Music-wise, their live concerts easily matched the sound of their albums. In fact, they are a group that even today no one tries to imitate; their music is so complex it's hard for anyone to try and copy. The last concert I saw, Ian was having trouble reaching the high notes. He even had a sort of backup singer to share the vocals. A lot of the original members have now moved on, but Ian has maintained the band's music, even with new members.

SOMEWHERE OVER NORTH WEST USA

JUNE 1985

GABRIELE BANASZAK

Gabriele Banaszak mixed pre–flight cocktails for Ian Anderson

It was the summer of 1985 and I was a flight attendant for Republic Airlines, a small regional airline. We were boarding a flight from Madison, Wisconsin to Detroit, Michigan with intermediate stops in Chicago, Grand Rapids, Kalamazoo and Lansing before finally landing in Detroit. Boarding in Madison were a group of guys who looked like they were a rock band.

They were flying to Detroit but unaware of all the stops before Detroit. Because all these flights were so short in length, we were unable to have a beverage service. However, we would be on the ground for about 30 minutes before we would take off again. After two stops, some of the band members were getting antsy for a cocktail and we explained that the flights were too short to have a beverage service. On the ground in Lansing, one of the band members came up to the galley and asked if he could please order a few cocktails before take-off to our last stop in Detroit. Feeling bad that they were unaware of all the stops to Detroit, I agreed. While making the drinks, I asked this man if his group was a rock band. He said 'yes.' He explained that his band's name was Jethro Tull, and his name was Ian Anderson. I nearly dropped the cocktails to the ground before handing them to Ian. I couldn't believe it. I was so star-struck I didn't know what to say and what came out of my mouth was, 'Oh yeah, I heard of you.'

To this day, I can't believe I said that to Ian Anderson. We continued to talk, Ian graciously offering me tickets to their concert in Detroit. I regret that I wasn't able to go but cherish my short conversation with Ian. To this day, whenever a Jethro Tull song comes on the radio, I say, 'Yeah, I heard of these guys.'

JETHRO TULL
IS WAXING LYRICAL
ABOUT THE NEW
VIRGIN MEGASTORE

Chrysalis

KARL EISENHART

I discovered Jethro Tull by accident during the summer of 1986. I heard an instrumental song on the radio which featured yodelling and, significantly, a flute solo. I had no idea who it was but in asking around one of my friends informed me that Jethro Tull was the only band he knew that had flute in it. I picked up *Original Masters* at the local record store. Not surprisingly, the song I sought was not on it. It was by Focus! But I was stunned by the songs that were. I used that album as a road map to diving into the back catalogue over the next year

Karl Eisenhart heard a flute and bought Tull's greatest hits on the strength of it

EWS..NEWS..NEWS..NEWS..NEWS..N

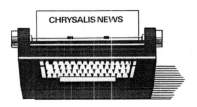

CHRYSALIS NEWS

JETHRO TULL and DAVID PALMER single
****

JETHRO TULL and DAVID PALMER are to release a new single on 16th June.

Entitled "CORONACH", it is the main theme tune to the Channel 4 series 'The Blood Of The British', and is being released due to huge public demand when the series was first shown last year, and to coincide with the first repeat showing on Channel 4, which commences on 18th June at 8:00 p.m., and runs for eight weeks.

"CORONACH" (TULL 2) was written and produced by former TULL member DAVID PALMER, who has continued to be the band's orchestral arranger. The track was originally a 90-second piece of music, but has now been re-recorded and runs for 4 minutes.

'The Blood Of The British' is a documentary series tracing the ancestry of the British people through the ages. It is an archaeological story gleaning facts from monuments and artefacts left behind all over the British Isles by our forefathers.

On the B side of "CORONACH" is a track called "JACK FROST AND THE HOODED CROW", a song written by IAN ANDERSON, which is previously unreleased.

"CORONACH" is performed by IAN ANDERSON, DAVID PALMER, MARTIN BARRE, DAVE PEGG AND GERRY CONWAY.

On the live front, JETHRO TULL are Special Guests of MARILLION at the Milton Keynes Bowl on Saturday, 28th June. Press inquiries to JUDY TOTTON on 01 403 1274.

For further info: Press Office &
Radio/TV Promotion Dept.

4th June, 1986   Chrysalis Records   01 408 2355

Chrysalis

12 Stratford Place London W1N 9AF Telephone 01-408 2355 Telex 21753 Fax 01-409 0858 Cables Chrysalis London W1

JETHRO TULL SUMMER RAID 1986 MILTON KEYNES BOWL

28 JUNE 1986, MILTON KEYNES, UK

STUART ROBINSON

In the summer of 1986, I found myself with my brother Andy gearing up for a trip from Fife, Scotland to Milton Keynes, England via Langholm to watch Jethro Tull perform at an open-air festival. I was about to turn 21. I had my own car, a Ford Escort Mk. 2 which I had completely rebuilt and in which I had installed a good stereo cassette player. I was enjoying the songs from a newish band to me called Marillion, who'd had some recent success and just released the album, *Misplaced Childhood*. As a long-time Tull fan, the opportunity to see Marillion and Tull together live was too good to miss, even though it involved a road trip of some 1,000 miles there and back.

We headed south to Langholm first to meet friends and continued our journey, leaving early the next day. The trip south was reminiscent of the great summer of 1976, with wall-to-wall sunshine and big blue skies. We arrived at Milton Keynes with our tickets for Marillion's *Welcome to the Garden Party* festival, with special guests Jethro Tull along with supporting artists Mama's Boys, Gary Moore, and Magnum.

Arriving early at the Bowl we searched out the merchandise area, a must at gigs in those days, cash in hand. I picked up a superb Jethro Tull *Summer Raid* t-shirt and a programme and made friends with some other *Garden Party* goers. As is the norm, national pride spurned us on to play a Scotland vs England football friendly on the Bowl's grass, which we won ... honest! Then came the music and the bouncing rock sound from Mama's Boys and especially 'Runaway Dreams', Magnum and their clear keyboard rock sounds like 'All of my Life', and Gary Moore expertly picking his axe for 'Parisienne Walkways'.

And so to Jethro Tull, featuring Ian Anderson, Martin Barre, Dave Pegg, Peter Vettese, and Doane Perry. They played well that day and sounded good in the 'Bowl', essentially a large outdoor sunken grass oval. If you were anywhere near the back, the wind carried the sound away. Fortunately we had camped down near the middle and thoroughly enjoyed the day, along with 60,000 other fans, helped by wall-to-wall sunshine. I took my camera, an old Pentax ME Super with a 500mm mirror lens, and got some great shots of the band playing, including during 'Fat Man' and 'Living in The Past'.

It was a great day, capped off by Marillion playing to the crowd well into the evening, and ending with fireworks. For us it was a long trog back home, slightly tanned and tired. But I'm very glad we made the effort.

DAVID FLINTHAM

The first time I remember hearing Jethro Tull? That's an easy one. June 1981. I was in the sixth form of my senior school. The head of sixth form, Mr Otterwell, deserves the credit as he was a great Tull fan and would attempt to educate us accordingly. On this particular day, it was *Bursting Out* on the cassette player in the common room, and the first song I remember hearing was 'Hunting Girl'. Mr Otterwell was also a great cricket fan, so is ultimately responsible for two of the three passions in my life, the other being malt whisky, for which he can take no credit.

It wasn't until the next year that I bought my first Jethro Tull album, the superb *The Broadsword and the Beast*, which remains my all-time

David Flintham first saw Tull at Milton Keynes Bowl

favourite Tull record (and when the legend who is Dave Pegg signed my copy, he mentioned it was his too).

I first saw Jethro Tull at the Milton Keynes Bowl on their Summer Raid in 1986, supporting Marillion's *Welcome to the Garden Party*, but it would not be until 29 October 1987 that I saw them in concert proper. I didn't have a ticket but managed to buy a fan's spare under the nose of a tout.

I've only met Ian Anderson once, and that was briefly. I took my then eight-year-old son to see the concert at St Bride's in Fleet Street in December 2012 and met Mr Anderson by the toilet at the interval (he was coming out, we were going in).

There are so many other memories: cycling to Strathaird on Skye to visit Dun Ringill, and the connections of particular albums with particular places - *Songs from the Wood* always takes me back to the Yorkshire Dales, whilst *Stormwatch* is Lerwick on Shetland. Then there are the Christmas concerts, which are always memorable, and finally the countless times I've explained to people that Jethro Tull is the name of the band, not the one-legged flute player.

JERRY FLAY

My lifelong love affair with the music of Jethro Tull began one wintery afternoon in 1979, in a boarding house in a boys' school in Berkshire, as the beguiling notes of 'Acres Wild' seeped through the wall from the room next door. Immediately I sensed this music was closer to the land, something which had been important to me since as long as I could remember. It wasn't until 1986 that I got to see them, playing second fiddle (in starting order anyway) to Marillion at Milton Keynes Bowl. They were superb. As darkness fell, they illuminated the entire crown with their performance.

Tull became a yardstick for my love life. I would take a new girlfriend to see them, and if she didn't get it, we would swiftly be no more.

So many gigs, so many memories. When I moved to New Zealand in 2001, I assumed that was that, but to my delight I saw them twice, in Wellington. The last time was 2017. By this stage the band's career was at a time when only diehard fans would go to see them, and the audience embraced them with everything they had.

My relationship with Tull's music has always been intensely personal, evoking thoughts of another time and another life, a place in the past which I could never hope to see except through the flights of fancy their lyrics and tunes inspired within.

I'd like to say thank you for the music, but that wouldn't really do it justice. They have been so much more for me than that. So I'll just say cheers, to all the band members, and Ian in particular, for all they have given, and for the indelible memories I have.

DAVID LARGE

I went to see Marillion. Tull were in the line-up, playing *The Broadsword and the Beast*, and were tight. Mr Anderson and his famous one-legged stance was a joy to watch. It was a lovely warm summer's day, sitting on the banked stadium drinking snakebite. At the end of the evening, everyone was leaving and trying to get to their cars. Ray, the friend who had driven us there, was getting quite upset that he could not find his car. Nearly in tears at this point, I had to tell him he was sitting on the bonnet of his own car. I laughed so much I nearly died. On the way out, the police were just flagging cars to move them on. There were no attempts to stop any drink drivers in those days.

Jethro Tull's Summer Raid tour also took in Tel Aviv, Budapest, Ringe, Dinkelsbuhl, and Lorely.

MTK STADION

2 JULY 1986, BUDAPEST, HUNGARY

BOGDÀN GOMILKO, PROMOTER

I spent my first 25 years in Ukraine, then in the Soviet Union. Access to Western music was very limited. It was out of the question to see a Western band performing live – they were forbidden to come here. There was one illegal music source – the BBC. On Fridays, the BBC would broadcast about rock music in Russian. From there, people could learn about what was new in rock, although the KGB frequently interrupted the broadcasts. Records by Western artists were not sold in shops but a black market existed for such things. There you could buy many things for sky-high prices. For one month's salary, you could buy two or three LPs.

Music fans would buy albums and trade them. In 1979, after such a trade, I acquired *War Child*, Jethro Tull's album from 1974 (later confiscated among my other records by the police during a raid). It was really something else – unique, new, interesting. With the prog-folk-rock elements and the flute, no other band sounded like Jethro Tull. I started to search for the band so I could get my hands on more albums, but that wasn't easy, since it was not mainstream. But then I bought *Aqualung* and from there on, Jethro Tull became one of my favourite bands. In 1980, I started university in Kyiv, where it was easier to get hold of Jethro Tull records, although they remained rare.

My first Jethro Tull concert was in Budapest in 1986, when they first performed behind the Iron Curtain. It was a huge experience. There were 30,000 people in the audience, and I was 10 to 12 metres away from the stage. The rain was falling. We were soaked and standing in mud. But it didn't matter. At the end, Ian was throwing giant white balloons into the crowd. I've kept my ticket ever since. Hungarian television recorded the show. I have the recording, and although it's not very good quality I still watch it from time to time. In 1987, *Crest of a Knave* came out, with the song 'Budapest' on it – one of my favourites. I became a huge JT fan and a collector (and later, a promoter) after this first show in 1986. I've seen them in many other setups with excellent musicians, but I remember the first the most.

In 1999, during a show in Vienna, I got much closer to Ian Anderson. I was standing in the second row and was repeatedly taking photos with a flash. At the end of a song, Ian quite angrily said to me, 'Hey you! Switch off your fucking camera!" This was the first time Ian 'talked' to me, and I'm very proud of it.

I first met Ian properly in 2004, backstage during an interview a friend of mine did with him. I have my first photo of the two of us together and my first autographs from that time. Six years later, I started to work with Jethro Tull. Since then, I've organised many Jethro Tull shows in Hungary, Slovakia and Ukraine.

In 2017, we organised a show with my Ukrainian partner in Kyiv. Ian wanted to come three days early and visit Chernobyl and asked me to go with him. My partner arranged it and we went into places where a regular tourist could not visit, including inside the nuclear power plant itself. It was a huge experience for everyone. Ian was really glad he could be there.

DOANE PERRY

In 1986 we played in Budapest for the first time on the *Summer Raid* tour. That's where the song 'Budapest' had its roots. This was before perestroika. We were playing in a packed soccer stadium and the people were just so delighted we had simply turned up. A lot of acts just didn't go behind the Iron Curtain back then. We played to a huge, enthusiastic, responsive crowd that evening. It was one of those nights where it felt like everything came together in the right way. Sound on stage can be such a variable situation, even with your own gear, but it seemed we could all hear each other well, and everything gelled. It was outdoors so we didn't have a lot of distracting slapback, which can really be a problem at times. In those situations it can often sound like there's another band at the other end of the arena playing something that resembles what you're doing, only slightly *later* in time. Not ideal for accuracy. But it was a special occasion for us and for the Hungarians, and everybody played brilliantly that night.

The first time we played in Tallinn, Estonia was also exciting, and a bit unnerving. I believe that was just prior to the end of perestroika. The audience was huge but quite reserved compared to most Western audiences. They didn't know *how* to appropriately respond at a rock concert, plus the military attempted to brutally swat people back at times, not wanting anyone to get overly excited. They would get out their billy clubs, menacingly brandishing them and threatening people, even hitting an unfortunate few. At one point Ian stopped the show and said, 'If you do that once more, we're going to stop playing.' The billy clubs were put away, with militaristic resignation and disdainful looks shot in our direction by the guards.

We played in India numerous times but under far more cheerful conditions. On several occasions we were also paired with some celebrated Indian musicians, one being Hariprasad Chaurasia, master of the Indian Bansuri flute. We had to learn to play a raga and basically had one afternoon in Dubai to rehearse two ragas. They didn't have things written out in the traditional Western way, but we made our own notes. It was quite a challenge playing with Hariprasad's group, just as it was with Anoushka Shankar, the brilliant sitar-playing daughter of Ravi Shankar, whom we played together with on a separate Indian tour. Primarily, we were going over to their side of the musical playing field and learning their music, although Anoushka did play some Tull music with us as well and rose to the occasion beautifully.

With Hariprasad there was always a segment at the end of each show where we would come down front and Tull would play together with his group. I would play a pair of bongos and various hand percussion. They played very quietly, so I'd use multi-rods on the bongos or brushes on a snare drum. The stage was hollow so what I normally played with my bass drums or hi-hats would naturally resonate under my feet (sans pedals) as I played on the boards of the stage, which also served to help keep me where I needed to be.

When I engaged my feet, Hariprasad would jump up, start smiling and laughing and dancing for joy, as I would begin doing trade-offs with his extraterrestrial tabla player, Vijay Ghate. In traditional Indian style, we had to play these gradually diminishing phrases, starting at 16 bars then going to eight, four, two, one bar, half a bar then one beat each. It was one of those 'holding onto the table with the last digit of your pinky' kind of performances. Indian classical music has almost nothing to do with the way Western song form might be interpreted and we were playing in crazy compound time signatures as well. You had to think differently, in a more linear, more classical way. It was a little scary but fun and exhilarating. In particular, those stood out because they were very challenging gigs. However, we were able to bring something of our own identity as Jethro Tull to the Indian audiences and didn't feel the need to show up wearing turbans. They clearly got that and also got our humor, which made it a genuine fusion of East meets West. Those tours with Hariprasad and Anouska were very well received and remain personal highlights for me with the band. And the after-concert curries were amazing!

Tull had a tradition of occasionally guesting with some of our support acts or having them guest with us during the course of an evening. Notable ones where there was meaningful musical and personal intermingling would *have* to include Fairport Convention, Willy Porter, Emerson Lake and Palmer, Lucia Micarelli, and Procol Harum. They were all phenomenal, accomplished musicians and great people with equally developed senses of humor - some understated, others wicked, but unquestionably an absolutely necessary character prerequisite to help sustain personal and group sanity over the course of a demanding tour.

We had one particularly memorable night performing in London with, amongst others, Gary Brooker from Procol Harum for a UK benefit at the Clapham Grand called Friends of the Earth, in support of environmental awareness. Gary simply seemed to possess one of the most soulful, timeless, resilient, uniquely identifiable voices in music, equally matched by his utterly surreal sense of humor and deadpan between-song delivery. We were happily his backup band that night, playing some of that sublimely melancholic and moving Procol Harum music. I think that was a musical highlight for each one of us.

CREST OF A KNAVE

RELEASED 11 SEPTEMBER 1987 (UK)/16 SEPTEMBER 1987 (US)

UK CHART POSITION 19

US CHART POSITION 32

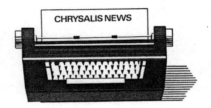

On the 7th September IAN ANDERSON and JETHRO TULL release
their twenty-first album for Chrysalis Records and embark
on a world tour on the 4th October, kicking off in Edinburgh.

The new album titled "ON THE CREST OF A KNAVE"(CDL 1590) was
completely written and produced by ANDERSON, and a single from
the album will be released early October.

The nucleus of the band, besides, of course, IAN ANDERSON,
are guitarist MARTIN BARRE and bassist DAVE PEGG, who are
heavily featured on all tracks, and who will of course play
the world tour.   The drums on the album are shared between
GERRY CONWAY and DOANE PERRY, both of whom have worked with
TULL before.   Doane will do the tour, and keyboards for
the dates will feature old friend of the band DON AIREY.

It is three years since the last album, and TULL are back
with a vengeance.   "ON THE CREST OF A KNAVE" is one of
their finest masterpieces to date!

Further information:

BERNI KILMARTIN
01 408 2355
25th August 1987

Chrysalis

12 Stratford Place London W1N 9AF Telephone 01-408 2355 Telex 21753 Fax 01-409 0858 Cables Chrysalis London W1

LISA LAMPANELLI, PODCASTER/RETIRED STAND-UP COMEDIAN

I was really into progressive rock when I was in high school. I wasn't a 100 per cent nerd but it was my way of connecting because I was smart. I always figured that if you were a smart person, you'd be into something complicated, and progressive rock was soooo complicated. I was into Tull, Yes, and bands like that. I remember being in the West Village and buying a copy of *A Passion Play*. It was soaked in cat piss, but it was an original pressing and I said, 'I don't care if this stinks my house up for the rest of my life. I want this fucking album.' I was that kind of a fan.

I went off to journalism college and did interviews as a way to meet bands, not because 'I need to meet famous people' or 'I need to bang rock stars'. I was a chubby fucking college graduate and that's not what I was looking for. 'I'm not trying to fuck the band. I just want to talk to them and be intellectual about it.' I was always well researched in the days before you could look things up on the internet and you had to go to the library to research it. And I used to lie and say I was a photographer to try and get into the front row at concerts. I still have the shots I took of Ian Anderson and Jethro Tull.

I was obsessed with *Crest of a Knave* and Ian must have been doing a phoner tour, so I pitched to some local music publication in Connecticut that I wanted to do an interview with him. I wasn't a comic yet. I was a journalist, and I say 'journalist' in quotes because I wasn't a hard-hitting investigative journalist or some shit. It was effectively just interviewing bands. I was living in the East Village, on Ludlow Street above a fucking bar that was so loud. And I was thinking, 'I'm going to interview fucking Ian Anderson. He's calling me at my house!'

At the time I was reading Ayn Rand, because Rush were really into Rand and I interviewed Rush so many times, and there was a phrase that she always used which was 'a sense of life'. I just loved Ian Anderson's sense of life. I didn't really know anything about him except that he's a great musician. He was an inspirational guy. On stage, twirling that fucking flute, he made a nerdy instrument appear badass. That was really cool. And he was a farmer and had a salmon farm and…. 'Oh my god, what a great guy this must be, and his sense of life seems so unique and different.' I wanted to be like him.

When he called me, from Scotland I think, I was super-prepared. I asked some questions that weren't just 'surfacey' but was thinking, 'Oh my God, I'll probably never talk to this guy again. I just have to tell him he inspires me, and I aspire to live the way he does.' And you know how in your 20s you're just so emo that you say whatever you want, even if you tear up or something? I said something like, 'Mr Anderson, I just want to say…' – and could hear my voice cracking like a big fucking emo douche – 'I'm very inspired by you. And I see your lifestyle and you have such a great sense of life and I hope to emulate that someday.'

That must have been so uncomfortable for the poor guy. There was dead silence for a while and I thought, 'Oh my God, he's fucking hung up on me. I'm such a geek'.

Then he said, really slowly, 'Okay, well then, thanks', and hung up.

Needless to say, it didn't lead to the emotionally fulfilling conversation I thought I wanted in my 20s. I was just such a goofball. I thought, 'Well, you've got to write about what just happened, and that's what just happened.' So I wrote about it in the article I wrote on him, and what a douche I was at the beginning and how silly it must have seemed to him, poor thing. I was cracking up. 'Lisa, do you have to be emotional with everybody?'

I continue to be a great fan.

BEN BARCLAY

It was the early 1990s. I was in high school. My younger brother and I had just received our first CD players for a Christmas present. That was cutting edge technology. My dad checked out Jethro Tull's Grammy award winning *Crest of a Knave* CD from the local library. I never heard of Tull prior to that, or didn't care. But that CD left such an impression on me. It was returned to the library and I began my journey, purchasing Jethro Tull CDs based on their cover art. *The Broadsword and the Beast* was next. *Stormwatch* followed. Yep, I was hooked. Before I started college, I had amassed the full collection of Tull in CD form. To this day, Jethro Tull is still my favourite band, and 'Budapest' my favourite song.

Ben Barclay was introduced to Tull via Crest of a Knave

Crest of a Knave **was supported by the** *Not Quite the World, More the Here and There tour.*

APOLLO THEATRE

7 & 8 OCTOBER 1987, MANCHESTER, UK

RICHARD CONNELL

This was the *Crest of a Knave* tour and a great gig showcasing a fine album. All the shenanigans around the 'heavy metal' Grammy tended to obscure this. It was a great finish to the concert with one of my favourites, 'Wind Up'. I was an Anglican lay-reader for 20 years, and did actually manage to preach on the meaning of the song once. Oh, and the 'Not the bloody balloons again' finale was great.

CRAIG HUGHES

I first recall getting into Tull when I heard 'Living in the Past' on the car radio whilst on a family holiday in the mid-Seventies. Later I bought *M.U. The Best of*, which contained many songs I was unfamiliar with. In the early Eighties I bought my first house. My new neighbour was a bit of a metal head and had a huge vinyl

Craig Hughes has an array of Tull memorabilia

collection and we used to lend each other records to listen to. I borrowed *Bursting Out*, which gave me a renewed interest in Tull, and started buying various albums and singles.

In the late Eighties and early Nineties, I was involved in the music business as a sound engineer and worked with a lot of big bands. This gave me the opportunity to make contacts while an increase in my earnings allowed me to buy more obscure Tull items. I have limited editions, coloured vinyl, foreign release singles and albums. Through my contacts I have managed to source many British and European tour posters. I have signed photos given to me by someone who was working with Fairport. I have numerous records and CD releases and promotional material like a *Rock Island* 3D counter display, a *Heavy Horses* mirror, and dozens of tour programmes.

The pride of my Tull collection is the platinum disc awarded to Ian for £75,000 worth of sales for *War Child*. Someone who I got to know asked if I wanted to buy any Ian Anderson awards. I was sceptical but said I would have a look. I went to his house, only a few miles from where I lived, and on entering his living room he started pulling out many award discs from behind the sofa, all awarded to Ian Anderson. He said he was only prepared to sell the platinum disc and a *Heavy Horses* gold disc. To this day, I kick myself for not having enough money to buy both. I asked where they had come from as I thought they could be fake. He told me he was Ian Anderson's nephew. I was very sceptical until he offered to give me Ian's phone number, which I declined.

When Tull were playing the Apollo in Manchester on the *Crest of a Knave* tour, Ian's nephew phoned and asked if I would like to meet Ian after the gig. He met me and took me to the stage door, where I had a short chat with the man himself and so confirmed I had indeed been dealing with Ian's nephew.

Working in television has opened doors for me. Recently I was invited by one of the top motorcycle teams to a race day and had the opportunity I could only dream of meeting. I hope one day to meet Tull … and see at least one last gig by them.

LE ZENITH

26 OCTOBER 1987, PARIS, FRANCE

AJAY MANKOTIA

A college friend offered to sell me *Stand Up*, *Benefit* and *Aqualung* for a sum of 100 rupees in my first year of college in 1974. I laughed him out my house. Jethro Tull? Who the hell were they? What kind of band had a name like that?

I made amends two years later when a friend gave me a spool of the very same albums of Jethro Tull I heard on my Wallensak tape recorder. A few months later, I wished him a long and healthy and happy life. Mind you, it was not easy at first. Like Marmite and caviar, Jethro Tull is an acquired taste. I think the precise moment when I bit the bait was probably the introductory music of 'With You There to Help Me'. It was pure magic, and Martin Barre entering the arena unexpectedly with the lead guitar (although Ian Anderson had already given us a glimpse of the riff on the acoustic guitar earlier) was perfect icing.

Tull live on stage. Photo by Bruce Mironov

I had unnecessarily lost two years but now I had to make up for it. Albums had to be taped from friends, colleagues and acquaintances who had the immensely good fortune to possess these precious commodities. Recording them was rudimentary, with my cassette player placed in front of their loudspeaker. Some albums I would

Tull live on stage. Photo by Bruce Mironov

hear about and seek. Some would just announce themselves by sheer serendipity. At
a Himalayan hill station in 1977, sleeping in a friend's university dormitory, I heard
the soothing strains of 'there's a haze on the skyline' at two in the morning. My
addled brain recognised the band immediately and started floating on the melody. At

an engineering institute in a desert town to participate in their cultural festival, I was supine on the green lawns staring at the night sky through a stupor brought about by the excesses of the past three hours, when I heard the opening notes of 'Hunting Girl' from the hospitality tent.

In 1979, I read the review of *Heavy Horses* in an English magazine at the British Council library in New Delhi. In 1982, on an overnight train journey in Central India, I did not get a sleeping berth and had to spend the night sitting on a seat. My co-passenger was listening to music on a Sony Walkman cassette player. His face wore the serenity of Buddha. On enquiry, I learnt he was listening to the newly-released *The Broadsword and the Beast.* We met like long-lost friends.

I heard the opening piece of 'Living in the Past' as the theme music to current affairs analysis programme *Perspective.* It is a mystery how Jethro Tull appeared on state-owned television when it was not available to the public in record stores. But De Mello undoubtedly had excellent choice.

In 1980, a sailor friend was in London when he recorded Ian Anderson talking about his favourite bands on the BBC. Ian's measured, articulate presentation and choice of songs and reasons made it an absolute joy to listen to.

I finally saw the band live in Paris in 1987. I was sent there on a one-year training programme by the Income Tax Department, where I was working. The band was on the *Crest of a Knave* tour. The opening act was Fairport Convention, led by then Jethro Tull bassist Dave Pegg. My wife and I, along with some colleagues I had converted, reached the venue five hours before the show. The seats were not numbered and there was no way we were not going to be sitting right up front.

The climax after 11 years of complete surrender to the band had been willed by God

Tull live on stage. Photo by Bruce Mironov

to take place on foreign shores. But being just a part of the audience was not enough. The band, and Ian in particular, had to be met. But how? God had a plan and sent forth some of the travelling crew members to check out on the swelling queue. This was my chance. I got talking to one of them about my passion for the band and he was intrigued by the details I was throwing at him. A group of Indians in Paris for a Jethro Tull concert, one of them completely deranged and spewing factoids which only the most committed would know? What clinched the deal was when I asked if he had heard *A Classic Case* featuring the London Symphony Orchestra playing Jethro Tull. The album had been released two years earlier and I had obviously heard it. 'There is no such album,' he said, dismissing me. 'Of course there is,' I persisted. He then enquired from another colleague, who concurred with me. That was enough to secure for all of us a backstage pass to meet the band after the show.

No words can describe the show, or my emotions. It was a dream fulfilled; I could die now. We met Ian after the show and spent a considerable time with him, me blabbering away like a lunatic with zero hold over tongue and sentiment. But Ian was patient, having probably handled thousands like me in his career. We met the other band members too, including Martin, the only remaining member from the early days. The photograph of that most cherished and precious meeting adorns the wall of my drawing room. I show it to visitors to this day with a swollen chest.

The North American leg of the 1987 *Not Quite the World...* tour saw Fairport Convention supporting Tull.

ARENA

11 NOVEMBER 1987, BALTIMORE, MARYLAND

MILLIE LANDRUM-HESSER

I saw them with Fairport Convention in the mid-Eighties and it was an incredible night of music by both bands. Ian Anderson danced the whole time as he played the flute, often hopping on one foot. He looked like he had stepped straight out of *Lord of the Rings*.

CENTRUM

21 NOVEMBER 1987, WORCESTER, MASSACHUSETTS

GREG THOMPSON

Greg and Bubba Thompson with Ian Anderson

My first real date with Bubba was at the Worcester Centrum on the *Crest of a Knave* tour, with Fairport Convention opening. It was winter but we camped out all night on the street in front of the box office to get tickets. We wanted to be first in line. In the morning, we were surprised to find out they had given out wrist-bands and we ended up at the back of the line. We did get tickets and the show was sort of a pre-nup or test for our relationship, either she liked me *and* Jethro Tull or this thing was never going to work out. Lucky for me, Tull put on a superb show that night and Bubba became an instant fan (and has been my girlfriend and wife ever since). We have been side-by-side on our Tull and life adventures ever since.

We are very lucky to live in a very Tull-centric part of Massachusetts, between (not kidding) Tanglewood, Barre, Palmer, Tully Lake and Doane Falls, and the farm where Jon Glascock worked is close by. Our central New England location has allowed us to see over 100 Jethro Tull shows over the years.

In 1990, we had just seen the documentary *Of Fish Sheep & Rock 'n' Roll*. After seeing Ian's salmon operation on the Isle of Skye and thinking about how much I enjoyed fishing and my time in aquatic environments, I was inspired to go back to college, earn a degree in Wildlife and Fisheries Biology and pursue a career in conservation. I have worked for the US Fish and Wildlife Service ever since. One of the key driving factors behind for the career move was undoubtedly seeing the documentary and Ian's work in aquaculture.

We used our honeymoon in 1996 to go see the Strathaird salmon operation for ourselves. We stayed in a guest house on Skye with a clear view of the salmon pens in the documentary, climbed the Cuillins, visited the local Tull-related sites, saw Broadford and Dun Ringill, and experienced the true magic of the place for ourselves. Many people go to Scotland for a honeymoon and go on whisky trails, but we made our honeymoon the Jethro Tull salmon trail!

UIC PAVILION
HARRISON AT RACINE

29 NOVEMBER 1987, CHICAGO, ILLINOIS
SKIP BENNINGHOUSE

Skip Benninghouse first saw Tull in 1987

Like a lot of people my age, I first encountered Jethro Tull on classic rock radio in the first half of the 1980s. Stations seemed to play mostly songs from *Aqualung* – the title track plus 'Locomotive Breath', 'Hymn 43' and 'Cross Eyed Mary'. I also remember hearing 'Living in the Past' and 'Bungle in the Jungle' and perhaps 'Bouree', that two-or-three-minute edit of 'Thick as a Brick', 'Teacher' and 'Skating Away on the Thin Ice of the New Day' – the standard classic rock fare.

It wasn't until 1987 that I looked beyond the radio appetisers and searched their back catalogue for the main course. I had been a Genesis fan for five years and more than one elder proghead had given me the 'If you like old Genesis, then you need to check out...' speech. It was an interesting year as prog stalwarts Yes, Pink Floyd, Rush and, of course, Jethro Tull all released albums that year. I recall seeing ads for *Crest of a Knave* in *Kerrang* and other music 'zines that I read at the time. I said to myself, 'Now is the time for me to get into Jethro Tull.'

I began by getting a copy of *Crest of a Knave*. Most older progheads seemed more interested in what the band had done in the Seventies. I was interested in that too, but I was also keen to hear what they were up to now because they were still around and still flexing their creative muscles. It was only a matter of days before I had thoroughly consumed, absorbed and fallen in love with *Crest of a Knave*.

Sure, Ian Anderson's voice was quite different from what I was accustomed to. I was unaware of the throat problems in 1985/86 that had narrowed his range and made it raspier, grittier. Having not yet heard *Under Wraps*, I had no conception of *Crest of a Knave* having any atavistic qualities. To my ears, Martin Barre's guitar had never played second fiddle to keyboards.

While the drum machine and synths on 'Steel Monkey' brought ZZ Top's mid-Eighties stuff to mind, the album as a whole just sounded like the quirky Jethro Tull that I had enjoyed on the radio. It had plenty of loud electric guitar that was usually doing some twisty-turny pas-de-deux with the flute. There was the expected acoustic guitar but also a guest violin courtesy of some gentleman named Ric Sanders. A clutch of more straightahead rockers was complemented by songs like 'Budapest' and 'Farm on the Freeway', which balanced acoustic and electric, fast and slow, loud and soft. These longer songs took melodic detours and went the scenic route full of dynamic playing.

The next step for me on my journey into Tull was to return to the source of many a musical discovery for me – scouring my older brother's tape collection. Eager for more flute-laden proggy goodness, I found a tape with 1982's *The Broadsword and the Beast* on one side and *Thick as a Brick* on the other. I immediately took to *Broadsword*, its loud guitars sharing space with synthesizers plus the occasional mandolin. *Thick as a Brick* took longer, but I eventually fell under the spell of its bouncy folk melodies and crazy time signatures.

That fall I went to see them in Chicago with a friend who was also a prog neophyte trying to catch up with the back catalogue of many a progressive rock band. While there were no codpieces to be had, it was rockin'. The set-list had a good variety of songs from the band's career and the new stuff sat well alongside Seventies classics.

I would go on to gobble up the rest of Tull's records, see the band or Ian Anderson in concert several more times, and write a goofy essay in which I attempted to tease out some meaning from Ian's lyrics. I was even allowed backstage before one of their shows and got to have Martin Barre and Shona Anderson poke fun at me – all in good jest, of course. It's hard to believe it's been 34 years since I got into Jethro Tull and discovered their music in a meaningful way.

A few years ago I was able to find a copy of that very first Tull show I attended back in 1987, along with the opening set by Fairport Convention, whose fiddle player was one Ric Sanders.

UNIVERSAL AMPHITHEATER

14 – 16 DECEMBER 1987, LOS ANGELES, CALIFORNIA

GUY DIESSO, AGE 20

I've been a Jethro Tull fan since the age of 11. Their sound was unlike anything else available. 'Teacher' was the first song that hooked me. I first saw Tull in 1987 at the Universal Amphitheater. I had money and a car by then, or I would have made it sooner. I have a painting of Ian Anderson done by an artist named Mike Nisperos. It was given to me by a co-worker who knew I was a huge Jethro Tull fan. It currently hangs in my room.

RED ROCKS AMPHITHEATER

7 JUNE 1988, DENVER, COLORADO

PAM SCOOROS

It was 1970. I was a sophomore in college. I was listening to the radio and heard a most wonderful song. It was different from the rock 'n' roll being played in those days. It was like I had been waiting to hear this all my life but didn't realise it until then. I didn't catch the name of the song nor the band. I listened as much as I could to the radio until I heard the song again. As soon as I did and heard it was by Jethro Tull, I immediately went to the store and bought *This Was*, *Stand Up*, and *Benefit*.

Pam Scooros saw Tull at Red Rocks

In 1988 I had plans to go to England for a vacation. I contacted the UK fan club to see if Jethro Tull were playing any concerts during my trip. I was told they would be in the US and was given the name and number of the head of the US fan club. I called and she told me Tull would be in concert at Red Rocks in Denver, where I lived. She planned to drive from Kansas to Denver for the concert, inviting me along. When we were driving to Red Rocks, she told me she had backstage passes for us. I silently screamed. After the concert, we were backstage. She and bassist Dave Pegg were talking, and I just stood there in shock, not hearing a word. Ian Anderson walked by within a few feet of us. Wow!

POPLAR CREEK MUSIC THEATER

12 JUNE 1988, HOFFMAN ESTATES, ILLINOIS

BARRY ROSE, AGE 17

The third time I saw Jethro Tull was probably the most memorable for me. The concert was at Poplar Creek, an outdoor venue in the western suburbs of Chicago. A few hours prior I was at my high school graduation, and after graduating most people are out getting drunk and wasted at graduation parties. I was having a much more enjoyable time.

I went with David Feinberg and Steve Lim. We had pavilion seats. We may even have missed a class or two when tickets went on sale (shh! Don't let my dean know). Two days after the concert, I was on a tour bus myself, as I was playing minor league baseball - another reason why we didn't party. It was a great way of transitioning from childhood to adulthood.

Since then, I have seen Jethro Tull seven more times. My daughter has been trying to duplicate Ian on the flute. She also thinks he's amazing. Thanks for the memories.

MUD ISLAND

17 JUNE 1988, MEMPHIS, TENNESSEE

TERESA BARNES EVANS

I discovered Jethro Tull when my father heard me listening to country music on the radio. He commented, 'Oh, good, you like country too?' I immediately started scanning radio stations to see what other kind of stations there were. It hadn't occurred to me to do that before then. One of the very first rock songs I heard on the radio was 'Bungle in the Jungle', and I was hooked.

I was at Mud Island in Memphis for the 20th anniversary tour with my then 21-year-old daughter, who if anything is a bigger fan than me. My uncle is a huge fan too, although he's one of those people who insist on calling Ian 'Tull'. Ian opened this show by riding out in a wheelchair, but soon demonstrated he could still kick above his head. We were unfortunately seated behind an extremely inebriated woman who kept starting to take off her shirt. Her companion repeatedly sweet-talked her out of it by telling her what a pretty shirt it was, so it'd be a shame to take it off. Two men a few rows back took pity on us and offered us vacant seats near them, so we could still see the show and not have to see her.

RIZOUPOLI STADIUM

15 JULY 1988, ATHENS, GREECE

COSTAS KATSOUDAS

The concert started with a theatrical performance of 'Too Old to Rock 'n' Roll, Too Young to Die', Ian and the group entering the stage in prams pushed by nurses. Since then, I have seen Jethro Tull many more times. I will always remember the concert at the Monastery Lazariston in Thessaloniki. It was an open-air theatre but Ian banned people from smoking because it was bothering him.

GINASIO GIGANTINHO

2 AUGUST 1988, PORTO ALEGRE, BRAZIL

ROGER STOLTZ

I worked as a translator for Jethro Tull in 1988 when they visited Porto Alegre in southern Brazil. At the press conference, I recall a reporter asking about the Mark Knopfler guitar playing style on their latest album, *Crest of a Knave*. I could see Martin, who at all times was silent and shy, gulp and prepare to move his lips to reply, but Ian jumped right in to answer, defending Martin and explaining that he and Knopfler were both

Roger Stoltz (right) translated for Jethro Tull when they visited Porto Alegre

inspired by the same guitarist, whose name I don't remember. Apart from this slight frustration, Ian was very relaxed, taking it easy during the whole visit. In a car driving down Avenida Farrapos in Porto Alegre, he mentioned how at home he felt in the city. When I asked why, he said there was something about the (uninteresting) view that reminded him of his hometown.

Martin was somewhat bashful all the time, while Dave Pegg was as cheerful as a jumping schoolboy on vacation. There were no cell phones then to take hundreds of pics, so I settled with just a few shots in order not to annoy them, even though they did not seem bothered. The entire band looked like schoolboys on a field trip. Smiles and good humour were a constant. When Ian saw the Guaíba River in Porto Alegre, he asked if I could find a way for him to get a small boat, even a rowing boat, so he could go fishing. But the time schedule did not permit it.

  I had a swell time in Ian's company. He didn't care for anything fancy or sophisticated. He wanted to go somewhere simple and cozy to have a bite and drink some beer. Conversation was light and loose. As a translator I avoided showing how big a fan I was to keep things smooth, but did ask him to sign some album covers.

ROCK ISLAND

RELEASED 21 AUGUST 1989

UK CHART POSITION 18

US CHART POSITION 56

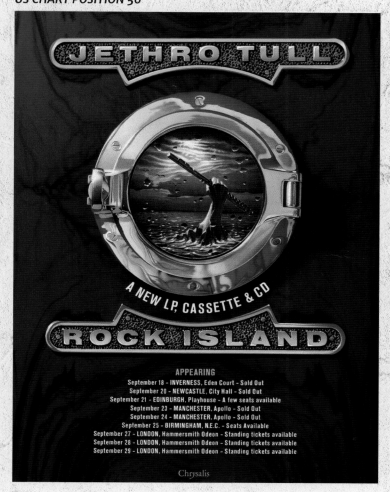

ED LUCAS

I was a 15-year-old listening to San Diego radio station KFMB-FM, which was known for playing the hits - Michael Jackson, Richard Marx, Madonna, Debbie Gibson, and so on. There was a four-hour show called the *B Morning Zoo* with four jolly, goofy disc jockeys. On 22 February 1989 the topic turned to the *Grammys* the night before.

'Guess who won the Best Heavy Metal award?'

'Who?'

'Jethro Tull!'

And the laughing was uncontrollable for a moment. No, it went on and on.

I had no idea who Jethro Tull was. I had never heard the name, but clearly there was some irony here. It happened that my social circle was drawing me closer to listening to local rock

Ed Lucas was led to believe Tull were heavy metal

station, KGB FM. KGB had a metal show. Within a week I was listening to KGB with an ear out for this Jethro Tull and a few other things I knew the station played. There was also the fact that I had no real knowledge of what heavy metal really sounded like. I knew some of the band names, but never really heard the stuff. Would I know what I was listening for?

And then it happened. A Jethro Tull song came on. I don't remember if it was announced before or after the song, but I was pretty amazed at what I heard. Not because I liked it so much but because I was trying to square in my mind how in the world this song I just heard was heavy metal. Then another song came on and it sounded nothing like the first. And another that sounded unlike either of those. There must have been a few more that did nothing to clarify what heavy metal was, but the B Morning Zoo jokes were starting to make sense.

And these were *all* Jethro Tull songs? I later learned the names of the songs I'd heard – 'Bungle in the Jungle', 'Steel Monkey', 'Farm on the Freeway', and 'Locomotive Breath'.

It was equal parts brain static and endorphins. Who or what was this band that made these diverse songs? I was a kid with endless questions. I had to know more. None of my school friends knew anything about this band. The folks that got me interested in KGB FM could indulge me more. And they did.

By the end of the summer, I was given a hand-copied version of the *20 Years of Jethro Tull* box-set. I thought that was all there was to the entire catalogue, so trying to take it in and make sense of it was just as strange a thing as the first experiences earlier in the year. I started hitting the local record store. I got the newly-released *Rock Island.* Then I was off and running, spending my weekly allowance on one or two albums most weeks for the next couple of months. It took me ages to really unpack what I had on my hands. Even now, I find new things that reveal themselves in familiar material.

That same summer I started to return to playing drums, this time with new excitement and drive, fired up by my newfound love of music. Doane Perry became an early drumming hero.

Over the course of 30-plus years, Jethro Tull's music has become the gateway to my broader education. Being an American, I had to try harder to figure out what the various place names, historical references and other lyrical bits all meant. Following the band members' comings and goings introduced me to more music. My musical development was egged on repeatedly in stages and, being a listener with the freedom from older brothers' or uncles' ideas of what I should like, I found myself drawn heavily to the *A* and *Under Wraps* albums, and the thought exercises of what *Under Wraps* might sound like in more traditional sonic colours became a topic that sparked a whole new musical birth after dropping out of music for several years.

So while the Grammy win was to some a thing of dubious notoriety, or a joke, to me it was the call to my future. Had that *B Morning Zoo* conversation been had even one hour later, I might have been sitting in my classroom at school, missing out on - well, everything. Nothing would have been the same.

HAMMERMITH ODEON

27 – 29 SEPTEMBER 1989, LONDON, UK
PAUL ALOYSIUS MURPHY, AGE 18

This was my first ever gig. I turned 18 four days earlier. The band were on excellent form - I remember how unusual it was to see the late Maart Allcock coming out from behind his steampunk keyboard bank at the start to add additional guitar muscle to 'Steel Monkey'. But it was the anticipation of the gig that really stays warm in my heart; the hour beforehand spent in the boozer beside the venue was an exciting new world to me, seeing mostly older and more grizzled Tull-heads, many of them with huge beards and long hair, all with often ancient (or at least well-loved!) t-shirts of bygone tours. They seemed like ancient, companionable

Paul Aloysius Murphy saw Tull at his first ever concert

warriors to my callow teenage eyes. I remember wondering if one day I'd ever become one of them (spoiler: I did).

I also remember hearing a distinctly pished gentleman roaring 'Kissing Willie' in a broad Scots accent with gusto as the band came on stage that night. He then proceeded to shout 'Kissing Willie' between every... single... song. I think he carried on even after the band played the bloody thing. I like to think he too went home more than satisfied by the overall evening.

It was the start of a lifelong love of Ian Anderson and Jethro Tull.

JERRY EWING, EDITOR, *PROG* MAGAZINE

I grew up in Australia so didn't know very much about Tull or prog rock. Being an Aussie kid, I was into guitar-based music like AC/DC. In Australia, if it's got a loud guitar in it, it's going to be cool. I came to England in 1980, when the New Wave of British Heavy Metal was kicking off, and got totally into that. Then I went to see Asia at Wembley Arena on their first tour with my mate.

My mate's brother had bought Marillion's first 12-inch, 'Market Square Heroes', with 'Grendel' on the B-side, this big 17 minute song. At that point I didn't know bands could write songs that long. We listened to it before we went to see Asia and it completely blew me away. I thought, 'Wow, what is this sort of music?'

I'd always been an avid reader of *Sounds*, which I'd get three months late in Sydney, and devoured the music press. I knew that working in the music press was what I wanted to do. I remember going to see Marillion at the Marquee, getting a copy of their newsletter, *The Web*, reading it on the train back. I thought, 'I can do something like this.'

I set up a prog rock fanzine, *Court Jester*, largely inspired by what was happening with bands like Marillion in the Eighties. But I was also going through a learning process of discovering the rich history of rock music from the Seventies, and Tull's *Broadsword* was their latest album. As a kid inspired by that sort of music then, the album cover spoke to me a lot and I absolutely loved the music. It's probably still my favourite Tull album. Then it was probably *Aqualung*, as it was for many people, and *Too Old to Rock 'n' Roll*. I'm a massive folk music fan as well and loved the way they married those different styles together. There was a bit of hard rock in there, there were folk inflections and bits of progressive music, and by '82 they were even experimenting with electronics.

Rock Island was the first album they released when I was actually a professional writer, working for *Metal Hammer* magazine. The first time I saw them was at Nostell Priory. They were phenomenal. They put on a show, and I've always been somebody who likes to see something a bit more visual from a band on stage than them just standing there playing their music. Tull were a great live rock band. They could whack it out quite heavy but also had those moments where they could drop it down and the music got more intricate and you'd be listening to it. They were so dynamic live, and Ian was quite mesmerising.

I also saw them on the *Rock Island* tour at Hammersmith. At that point there was still an element of Monty Python-esque sketches to their stage show that they'd done in America in the Seventies. I enjoyed the frivolity of it – it was almost like they were breaking down the fourth wall. They weren't taking themselves completely seriously. Ian is incredibly, deadly serious about what he does but there was that slightly more tongue-in-cheek side to them. It's part of what Ian's about.

WORCESTER CENTRUM

28 OCTOBER 1989, WORCESTER, MASSACHUSETTS

BRIAN PAONE

I was born in 1976 and was fed a healthy amount of prog rock at an early age. I had two older brothers and a mother who loved the late Sixties and Seventies progressive music movement. I remember sitting on my bedroom floor,

Brian Paone went to see Jethro Tull with his uncle Ray

somewhere around six or seven years old, listening to *Thick as a Brick* over and over while looking at the foldout vinyl sleeve. I read all those 'articles' so many times, wondering if they were real stories or not. Then *Rock Island* came out when I was 12 and blew me away. It became my favourite Jethro Tull album, and still is to this day.

I had only gone to one concert in my life when Tull started touring this album, but my Uncle Ray thought it was important for me to see them live, on what was my favorite album. He took me to see them at the Worcester Centrum. I only had one other concert to compare Tull's live show to, but I was awestruck from the middle of opening song, 'Strange Avenues'. That they opened the show with the final song from the album blew my mind.

My uncle bought me a *Rock Island* sweatshirt at the show with the front cover artwork. I wore that thing to death. I am now a published novelist, but wrote a short story called 'The Whaler's Dues' in 2016, a loose adaptation of the *Rock Island* album, as if the album was a true concept album. For my birthday last year, my uncle sent me a *Catfish Rising* sweatshirt and a *Stand Up* t-shirt.

LAKEFRONT ARENA

28 NOVEMBER 1989, NEW ORLEANS, LOUISIANA

KEN GREEN

I consider myself in the upper echelons of Jethro Tull fans from around the world. I have been a fan since 1973, when I was 13. Since then, I've seen over 175 Tull/Ian Anderson/Martin Barre concerts in two countries (US and UK) and 12 states in the USA. My first was in March 1975 in New York City on the *War Child* tour.

I am a retired journalist who has interviewed Ian in person, one-on-one, three times for publication in three major US newspapers. I also interviewed Martin Barre for *A New Day* magazine. I own a formidable collection of Tull memorabilia that runs the gamut.

Ken Green was featured in Rolling Stone because he's such a Tull fanatic

I had a full-page article in the 21 September 1989 edition of *Rolling Stone* magazine (with Madonna on the cover), that magazine running a feature on fanatic fans of different bands and musicians, and I was selected. The photo was taken by now renowned photographer Mark Seliger, who flew into my hometown in Texas and took pictures of me for three days. At that time Seliger was in the early stage of his career. Ian and the band were thrilled at the time of the *Rolling Stone* picture and it helped me develop some great and lasting friendships with band members, crew and fellow fans.

In 1989, during the *Rock Island* tour stop in New Orleans, I was selected by then tour manager Gerd Berkhardt to be a guest 'air guitarist' on stage with Martin Barre during the playing of the title track. Tennis racket in hand, it was the most exciting two minutes of my life. Martin later referenced my appearance with him in the Tull '90 tour programme - I was singing the guitar line loudly in his ear!

I consider Ian Anderson and Martin Barre to be two of the greatest musicians in the history of popular music. Ian is a musical genius. Tull have been the soundtrack of my life and will be until the day I die. How Jethro Tull are not in the Rock and Roll Hall of Fame is an absolute joke and kills the credibility of the Hall of Fame.

THE SUMMIT

29 NOVEMBER 1989, HOUSTON, TEXAS

DAVE STEWART

I grew up in Southern California and was 14 in 1972, the year I heard 'Aqualung' at a friend's house, his dad playing it on the record player. I was awestruck by that and 'Locomotive Breath'. In 1974, 'Bungle in the Jungle' was a hit on AM radio. Soon, I started listening to FM, and heard 'Thick as a Brick', and around then I started buying LPs. *Aqualung* was my first Jethro Tull album. I played it over and over and loved every track. 'Cross Eyed Mary', 'My God' and the others were mind-blowing. I've loved them ever since, especially what I consider the comeback, *Crest of a Knave.* In 1989, I finally got to see Jethro Tull at the Summit, touring the album *Rock Island.* It was a fantastic show.

UNIVERSAL AMPHITHEATER

5 & 6 DECEMBER 1989, LOS ANGELES, CALIFORNIA

KEN MCNEILL

As college took up my time and other bands were enjoyed (Genesis and Gentle Giant spring to mind) I lost touch with Tull. I didn't enjoy *Stormwatch* or *Broadsword* nearly as much and was disappointed in the line-up changes. I began to again play music myself and quit school to perform for a living. My travels took me to a five-year stay in Santa Monica, California, and in 1988 I got a chance to see Tull during the *Rock Island* tour at the Universal Amphitheater.

This was of course after the Grammy win for *Crest of a Knave.* Ian's voice had slipped quite a bit and the volume of the stage was lower. It was still a great show.

EMPIRE THEATRE

6 MAY 1990, SUNDERLAND, UK

DAVID SNAITH

In 1989 they released *Rock Island* and I went up to Edinburgh with friends to see them. We were having a pint after the concert and a couple of German lads were there. They'd come over from Germany to see Tull and we must have exchanged addresses or whatever. In 1990, the band did a mini-tour of English and Scottish places they played in the early days to promote the *Rock Island* album, with one of the shows at the Sunderland Empire. I got a letter from the German lads saying they had tickets for the tour. I don't know how they managed to get them but the next thing I knew, two or three days later they turned up at my house, one of them with a flute. I didn't know these kids from Adam, but they stayed at the house and I thought, 'Yeah okay, we'll go for a pint before the gig.' They had other things in mind, and said, 'We want to go to the soundcheck. We want to do this. We want to do that...' I thought, 'For crying out loud!' I said, 'Look, we can't go to the soundtrack, but we will try our best.'

We went along to the pub next to the Empire and then went and stood outside the stage door. There was no movement and then, blow me, Ian Anderson came out of the taxi to do the soundcheck. There were various fans stood around. The friend I was with said, 'Look, these two lads have come all the way from Germany to see you. Is there any chance of them getting into the soundcheck?'

Ian could've been frazzled by all the hassle but said, 'Hold on a minute', and two minutes later someone came out and said the German lads and myself could go in. They were over the moon. They came all the way from Germany, got to see the soundcheck, and had their photograph taken with Anderson. Their day was made. I was blown away by it too. For all his reputation of being standoff-ish sometimes, on the occasions I've come into contact with him, he's been absolutely brilliant.

I've seen lots of different bands but Tull's music, lyrics and performances not only entertain you and give you a buzz but give you something to think about. I wouldn't say it was all thinking man's music, but it covers every angle.

From the fans' point of view, we scratch our heads and wonder how somebody as intelligent and articulate as Ian Anderson can leave a sour taste in the mouths of certain band members and of fans by the way he mishandles situations. Over the years there have been fans' favourite band members who left in unceremonious ways. It doesn't add up. He understands life. He's a very intelligent man. He seems to have a broad view of life and of people. Yet the way he seems to have treated some band members is a huge mystery.

When Glenn Cornick left at the end of an American tour, Anderson wanted him out but, by all accounts, instead of saying 'your rock 'n' roll lifestyle is too much for the band', they all went to the airport to fly back to Britain and Anderson asked the manager to hold Glenn back so he missed the flight and the manager told him he was sacked.

In the late 1970s, when John Evan and Barriemore Barlow left, they were just told Anderson was making a solo album. It turned out to be a Jethro Tull album. We're talking about managing people. It's about sitting down with people, explaining things, showing concern and valuing people. I've heard Anderson talk about these occasions, saying he regrets one or two things. But he's such an intelligent, articulate man, I can't imagine him getting into these situations. It was never a rabble-rousing band that threw televisions into swimming pools and all this kind of stuff. It wasn't a case of falling out and maybe getting back together in 10 years. Anderson has got more about him than that.

PETER SMITH

I went with a group of mates - Norman Jones, Bill Gillum and Doug Walker – and it was some 19 years since we first saw Jethro Tull at the same venue. The late Eighties and early Nineties saw Tull return to rock and the blues for the albums *Crest of a Knave*, *Rock Island* and *Catfish Rising*. This was much more familiar and welcome territory for me. I always secretly worried about the folk-rock influences.

The one thing that sticks in my mind about this gig is Ian coming on stage with a massive searchlight, which he proceeded to shine at all of us. He crept around the front of the stage sneering as he shone the light. It was pretty menacing.

Looking back at the set-list reminds me Tull played some great old favourites that night, including 'Living in the Past', and taking us right back to the start and early hit single 'Love Story', still a big favourite of mine. This was Jethro Tull back on top form and it was great to see them back where we all saw them for the first time, in our hometown.

CIRCULO MILITAR

8 SEPTEMBER 1990, CURITIBA, BRAZIL

FELIPE AUGUSTO, AGE 17

The first CD I heard was by Jethro Tull. There were stores that rented CDs, and that's how I got it. On 8 September 1990 I watched Tull at the Palácio de Cristal in Curitiba. I was 17. During the show there was a break. There was the sound of a phone ringing. A girl brought on a phone on a tray. Ian answered it. The music continued. At the end of the show Ian threw balloons at us. One was over my head. Someone with a cigarette popped the balloon. A piece fell on me. I caught it and kept it inside my shirt.

CANECÃO

13 & 14 SEPTEMBER 1990, RIO DE JANEIRO, BRAZIL

WILLY FALKENHEIN, AGE 14

I've seen Jethro Tull three times, all of them in my home city, Rio de Janeiro. I'll never forget the band entering the stage in 1990. The stage was pitch-black. They all had headlights on their helmets, like coal miners. Then they burst into music. I was 14 and went with a friend and his father. What a show! I've been a fan ever since.

Besides the all-time classics such as 'Aqualung', 'Locomotive Breath' and 'Thick as a Brick', I was also quite impressed by songs from the album from the previous tour - 'Crest of a Knave', 'She Said She Was a Dancer', 'Farm on the Freeway' and 'Budapest' were fantastic and remain favourites of mine to this day.

ADOLFO VIAL

The first time I listened to Jethro Tull was in 1972, at the age of 14, when a school classmate lent me the album *Aqualung*. It captivated me. I couldn't stop listening to it for days. Since then, I have continued to follow Jethro Tull and Ian Anderson, collecting 45s on seven-inch singles, albums released in different countries with different labels or covers, books and all kinds of souvenirs of the band. Now I have a room in my house dedicated 100 per cent to the band, where I can exhibit and keep my collection.

The first Jethro Tull concert I saw was in 1990 in Rio de Janeiro, Brazil and it was a coincidence, or rather incredible synchronicity! I was attending a seminar in a town near Rio. The day it finished, a bus picked us up to take us to our hotel. During the bus ride, I leafed through a local newspaper and was surprised to see in the entertainment pages Jethro Tull would be playing Rio that night. I couldn't believe it.

I arrived at my hotel, left my suitcase in my room and rushed to the theatre to see if I could get a resale ticket. I found a very expensive one, but would have paid any price for it. Never in my wildest dreams did I imagine I would see Jethro Tull live. It was a spectacular show in a small theatre, with some little tables at the side where they served snacks and beer (I got one of those). I remember they played a lot of the album *Rock Island*, and Maartin Allcock (RIP) was there playing with the band.

However, the most remarkable and incredible thing that happened to me was having the opportunity to meet Ian Anderson, Shona and James. It all started when in May 1992 I got an address to write to Ian and try to tempt him to come and play in Chile. Besides the invitation, I offered to take him to visit some salmon farms, as I knew he had some in Scotland and I knew the president of salmon farming in Chile. To my great surprise, in September I received a reply from Ian with an autographed photo, saying he would be interested in coming to play in Chile, as they were coordinating some shows in Brazil and he would like to take advantage of adding another one in this part of the world. He said he was very grateful for the invitation to see salmon farming, but he had already seen too many and if he had any free time he would prefer to sit in a cafe and watch people to learn a little more about Chile.

To coordinate the proposed concert, Ian asked me to contact his road manager by fax. I did so and began to make good progress in coordinating the production of the show, contacting the theatre manager, the sound and light guys, a radio station that specialises in progressive music in Chile, the British Embassy, the subsidiary of the record label in Chile (EMI), and a couple of potential sponsors. Unfortunately, or maybe fortunately, everything was cancelled, as the producer in Brazil decided not to go ahead with the shows, deciding the economic situation in Brazil was too risky.

I say 'fortunately' because the following April, 1993, the person from EMI Chile I contacted a few months before called to tell me EMI was coordinating a Jethro Tull show in Chile and Ian would be doing a promotional visit to Santiago in a couple of weeks. They invited me to pick him up at the airport. So I went with the EMI people to pick Ian up. I introduced myself, telling him I was the one who sent him a letter inviting him to Chile, and he immediately said, 'Ah, you are the banker' (I used to work in banking). I accompanied him to a couple of radio stations and TV channels. In October, Ian returned to Chile to play with the band, and I again accompanied him to some radio stations and a TV channel. And on October 29th he gave his first concert in Santiago and on October 30th in Viña del Mar, the only time Jethro Tull has played twice in Chile.

Ian returned in 1996, giving a press conference at the Sheraton Hotel and a show on March 6th. I got a backstage pass from a local radio station and went to say hello after the show. Two days after the concert in Santiago, he played in Buenos Aires and I went to that show too.

In March 2004, Ian came back to Chile, and a local radio station invited me to watch the interview they were conducting. Knowing he was coming, I had sent an email beforehand inviting him to dinner at my house. He hadn't replied.

After the radio interview, I went over to greet him and told him about the dinner invitation. He said he never received it but, if it wasn't too late, he would be happy to accept. Of course, I immediately said yes. As it was three o'clock in the afternoon and I now had to organise a dinner for the band at my house that evening, I warned him we would do something simple, like cheese and wine or sushi, to which he replied he loved sushi. I immediately called my wife.

That night the whole group came to my house, including Ian's son James. During dinner we talked about my wife and I visiting the Cropredy Festival and taking the opportunity to visit the Anderson family home. Later that year I flew to the UK with my wife and daughter to attend the show in Cropredy. The day after the show, we went to the family house and were invited to have lunch at a nearby restaurant with Ian, his wife Shona and son James.

I have seen Jethro Tull and the Ian Anderson band in several countries ... several times in Brazil, Chile, Argentina, Peru, Scotland and England. The last time I saw them play was April 2018 at the Royal Albert Hall, celebrating 50 years of Jethro Tull. A great show as always.

At every show, Ian and James have been kind enough to provide backstage passes for me, my wife, daughter, and a couple of friends. I have many other unforgettable and unimaginable anecdotes and stories for something that started when I was 14 years old after hearing *Aqualung*, stories I will treasure for the rest of my life.

WNEW-FM
ELECTRIC LADYLAND STUDIOS

20 AUGUST 1991, NEW YORK, NEW YORK

CARMELA DAMANTE

My husband and I have been to about 20 Jethro Tull concerts, but meeting Ian was the greatest. I was at work, listening to WNEW-FM radio, when they announced a contest for free Ian Anderson tickets for a live show at Electric Ladyland, New York City, that evening. I kept calling and finally got through. My husband Bill and I are huge Tull fans, and this would have been a wonderful gift. When I won the tickets, I called Bill at work and told him I won the tickets and to grab our copy of *Stand Up* and meet me at the venue. I then called my son and asked him to tape the concert.

The show was fantastic. Ian was as charming and funny as he still is. It was about an hour of music and talk. After the show, I met him and he was so gracious and fun to talk to, asking us where we lived. When we told him we lived on Staten Island, he said he liked our island and thought it was as nice as the Isle of Wight, but had too much traffic – which is still true to this day. Ian signed our album and Bill was so excited. He had seen Tull way back at the Fillmore East in 1969 or 1970, before he and I met.

It was Bill who introduced me to their music, and I haven't been the same since. Tull's music is on repeat in my car.

Sadly, Bill has passed, but we shared a lot of wonderful things, including our love of Tull and this spectacular memory.

Carmela Damante met Ian at WNEW–FM in New York

CATFISH RISING

RELEASED
10 SEPTEMBER 1991 (US)
23 SEPTEMBER 1991 (UK)

UK CHART POSITION 27

US CHART POSITION 88

APOLLO THEATRE

4 OCTOBER 1991,
MANCHESTER, UK

RICHARD CONNELL

The *Catfish Rising* tour. This was an under-par gig. Ian's voice was dodgy, the album material wasn't great (when the best song live is the weakest on that album, 'Tall Thin Girl', at the expense of Doane Perry, it's not good). The local colour/character interlude just didn't work. I could go on, but I just put it down to experience.

HAMMERSMITH ODEON

7 OCTOBER 1991, LONDON, UK

PHIL MAWSON

My recollections of Tull gigs are so numerous since I became a follower in 1969. However, one particular memory is forever etched in my mind. I tried to get two tickets for the Hammersmith Odeon gig, and living in Pembrokeshire, West Wales had no choice but to use spurious ticket providers. However, I only managed

JETHRO TULL

CATFISH RISING
THE NEW CD, CASSETTE & ALBUM
AVAILABLE NOW.

ON TOUR
3,4 OCTOBER · MANCHESTER APPOLLO
5 OCTOBER · BIRMINGHAM NEC
7,8,9 OCTOBER · LONDON HAMMERSMITH ODEON

Chrysalis

to get one ... at a vastly inflated price. I really wanted to take my six-year-old son, already a rabid Tullian. Unbeknown to me, a friend contacted Chrysalis Records to explain my predicament and somehow a very kind and sympathetic Ian Anderson got to know about the situation and was moved to instruct one of his PAs to contact me. She told me Ian had instructed her to confirm two complimentary tickets would be provided for us to be collected at the box office on the night, the night preceding the performance I already had a ticket for. We travelled up to London a day earlier than planned, so I gave my first (and expensive!) ticket to a young bank clerk the next day and asked her to go and see the band too. Hopefully, she became an avid fan as a result.

I will never forget Ian's thoughtfulness. He's a real human being and true gentleman and, yes, we remain loyal Tull fans to this day.

DOANE PERRY

Dave Pegg and Maartin Allcock used to take great delight in trying to undermine my reasonably sober touring disposition. On the *Catfish Rising* tour, Maartin Allcock had what fittingly looked like a Jules Verne-designed steam-punk English pub set-up, which disguised his keyboard rig. There was the top of the bar with a row of beer pump pulleys and his keyboards were under 'the bar'. I was set up stage right, Maartin was stage left, and there were stairs which went up to this elevated section behind me where Ian, Martin or Dave could do acoustic numbers. This particular evening, Ian was doing an excerpt from 'Minstrel'. While that was happening, I went over to the English pub part of the set and played darts. I used to drink Gatorade on stage, which looked vaguely like the color of questionable whiskey. They had eight little shot glasses lined up on the bar and I'd take these eight shots of Gatorade in quick succession but it would look to the audience like I was taking eight shots of straight whiskey... except on this particular night it was Gatorade, probably mixed with some highly potent vodka.

I started playing darts. I'm not a great dart player to start with but suddenly the darts were going off into Martin Barre's speaker grill or off into the monitor desk area. As I had taken the eight shots quickly, I was substantially altered by the end of my dart game. Unfortunately, I still had to go back to my office in this 'new altered reality' and play the last hour and 40 minutes of the concert. I felt rubber-limbed and far too relaxed. Whoever spiked my drink (nobody *ever* confessed) probably got quite a big laugh out of that as I wasn't much of a drinker, even off stage, but I did get through the gig ... somehow. Rescued once again in this time of wobbly-legged distress, courtesy of the reliably embedded musical DNA that somehow intuitively knew when to take over when the engine room was flooding.

FOX THEATRE

26 NOVEMBER 1991, DETROIT, MICHIGAN

MICHAEL G FARLEY

I was a huge Tull fan and had contacts in the entertainment business, so I called in every favour and asked if anyone could get me backstage at the upcoming Tull concert to meet Ian Anderson. After what felt like an eternity, I ended up with 'meet and greet' passes for the show. The contact from the band said I shouldn't be disappointed if it didn't happen; Ian rarely met fans after shows, and the band was tired from being on the road so long. He said every discouraging word short of 'you don't have a chance.'

I attended the concert with my wife, brother-in-law and sister. The programme was titled *Unpacked* and displayed the contents of each player's suitcase. I remember Martin having running shoes.

It was a great evening, we had fifth-row center tickets, dined fancy and arrived by limo. With the possibility of a 'meet and greet' a million to one, I kept the secret to myself to avoid any additional disappointment. The plan was that after the show we were to remain in our seats. If it was going to happen, someone from the group would contact us. It felt as if we sat there for months, convinced they had forgotten us, until someone peeked from behind the curtain and gave us the signal.

We were going to meet Ian Anderson! My wife graciously offered her pass to my brother-in-law, another dedicated Tull fan, then we were led to the side of the stage and told to wait. Ever since I had learned of the possibility of meeting Ian, I had begun compiling questions and rehearsing what I would say. I knew the script by heart and was ready to go.

Eventually, Ian Anderson approached and stopped no more than 24 inches from us. This was it. I reached to shake his hand, but he nodded to the ace bandage wrapping his wrist. Concerned, I had to ask how he hurt it before we launched into our conversation. I looked up at the face of Ian Anderson, and couldn't say a single word. Through my job I have met a gaggle of stars without incident, but I stood there like a starstruck teen, until Mr Anderson said, 'How about if I give you an autograph?' Then it was over and Ian was gone. All those great questions and comments lost.

It took a few minutes to compose myself before returning to our wives in the theatre. We were led back on stage, ducked under the curtain, and what do you think we saw? The rest of the band sitting and talking with my wife and sister - Martin, Doane, everyone. They were talking as if they were regular people, asking about their hometowns and families. It was crazy. We ended up collecting autographs and talked with the guys for over 30 minutes.

When it was over, we slid into the limo, poured a drink and sat back to rekindle the memory. I looked at the concert programme again, eventually landing on the page that had Ian's suitcase unpacked. That's where I learned Ian carries an ace bandage to avoid shaking hands. It was an evening I will never forget.

Oh, and the show was awesome.

MCNICHOLS SPORTS ARENA

7 DECEMBER 1991, DENVER, COLORADO

JORGE PICABEA

I got the green Aqualung cassette when I was about 18 in Argentina. Since then, I have always wished to play the flute like Ian. For me, Tull is more than the music; it makes me travel to mystical, timeless places. Later, living in Denver, Colorado, I heard at work that tickets were going on sale the next morning at the stadium. I went home, ate some food then went to the stadium parking lot on my ratty Honda Interceptor 500. There were lots of people waiting to buy tickets the following morning. I spent the night there, hanging with the others. There was a great feeling. We were like brothers, sharing food, beer and tales. Next morning, I made the queue, got the tickets at about 7am, rode to the Waffle House for breakfast then went to work.

Jorge Picabea does his Ian Anderson impression

It was a great concert. Ian was shooting darts at a dartboard, there were big balloons with the Tull logo, and there was lots of pot smoke.

UNIVERSAL AMPHITHEATER

14 & 15 DECEMBER 1991, LOS ANGELES, CALIFORNIA

JAMES BRANAGAN

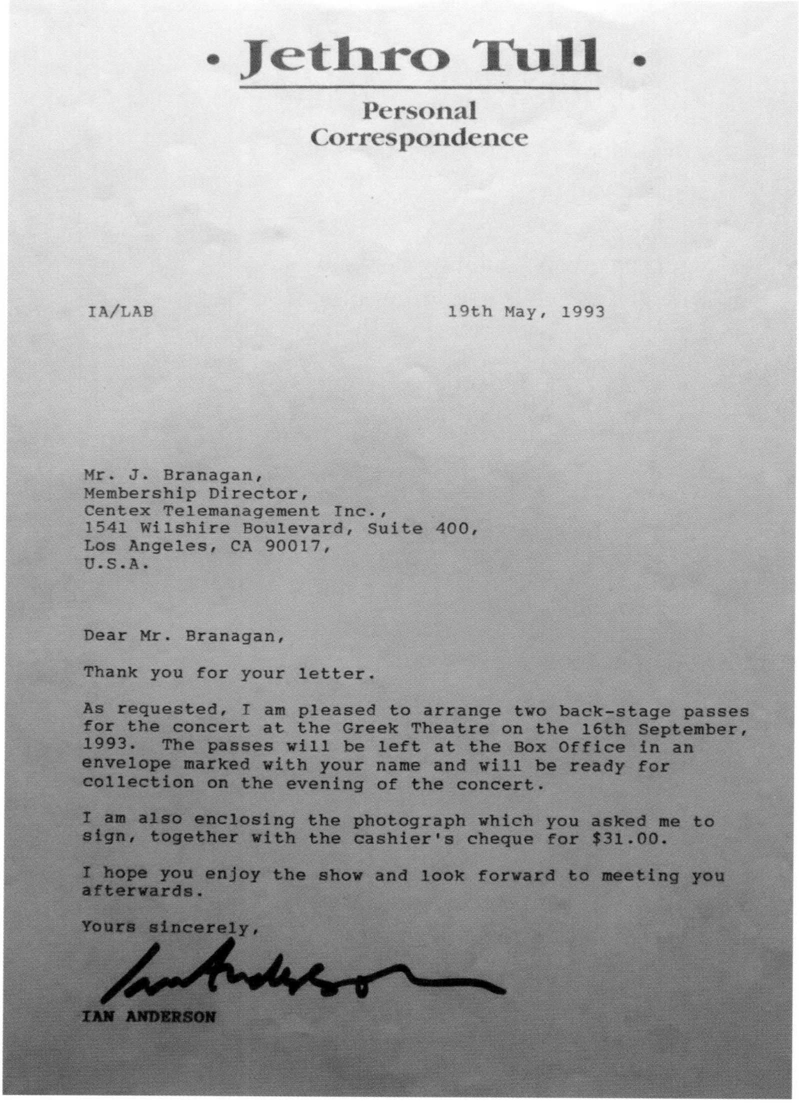

In the early Eighties I was immersed in the metal revolution ongoing at the time. One of my best friends introduced me to Jethro Tull and it was like a sword cutting through the past and present. Leading up to 1991, Tull were about to release *Catfish Rising*. Tickets went on sale and I bought great seats.

Off we drove to catch this amazing band. We were a large group, including my friend and two girls. I was so excited and immersed in the show that I lost track of them. I was endeavouring to snap a photo of the band in action and moved to the front, next to the stage. I was able to catch a front-row view of a rocking show. Song after song the band tore into their catalogue, delivering a powerful performance. Finally, at the end, I removed my camera and took a single photo. When the sound dissipated and lights went on, I could not find my friends. Where had they gone?

I went to the car and waited, only to find out later that my buddy and the two girls

· Jethro Tull ·

Personal
Correspondence

IA/LAB   19th May, 1993

Mr. J. Branagan,
Membership Director,
Centex Telemanagement Inc.,
1541 Wilshire Boulevard, Suite 400,
Los Angeles, CA 90017,
U.S.A.

Dear Mr. Branagan,

Thank you for your letter.

As requested, I am pleased to arrange two back-stage passes for the concert at the Greek Theatre on the 16th September, 1993. The passes will be left at the Box Office in an envelope marked with your name and will be ready for collection on the evening of the concert.

I am also enclosing the photograph which you asked me to sign, together with the cashier's cheque for $31.00.

I hope you enjoy the show and look forward to meeting you afterwards.

Yours sincerely,

IAN ANDERSON

James Branagan's friends were on stage with Tull and he didn't notice

had been invited to take part in the show, acting as a butler and two maids serving drinks to the band, cleaning up the stage and being part of the show. Afterwards the entire group was invited backstage to meet the band. While I was immersed in the performance, I had not noticed that one of my best friends was feet away from me on the stage along with the two girls. This is an event that my friends love to roast me over to this day.

I developed the photo and realised it was a really good image of Ian in his element, focused and intense with intent during the performance. I thought maybe if I sent it to him with a payment, he would sign it for me. I drafted a letter with a brief review of my experience and sent the check, photo and letter to an address I found. To my surprise, the check was returned along with the photo, signed by Ian and personalised to me, along with a letter from him saying I would receive backstage passes to the *25th Anniversary* shows on their next tour. I was speechless.

I took my buddy (the bartender I never noticed on stage) to the shows and was elated to meet Ian. I made sure to express my appreciation, thanking him for going so far for one fan in the entire world. I also met the rest of the band, who are incredible musicians and really nice people - Andrew Giddings, Doane Perry, Dave Pegg, and, of course, Martin Barre.

I cannot express enough the impact Ian has had on me over the years. He is one of those guys who does not get the acclaim for his ability to play the guitar and craft an amazingly diverse span of compositions. I am so grateful to have been introduced to the band. They have and continue to enhance my life. I am also humbled and grateful for Ian Anderson to make the time for me the way he did. He is one of the nicest, hardest-working artists in the business.

CITY HALL

19 MARCH 1992, NEWCASTLE, UK

GARY STAFFORD

I got into Tull in September 1989. I was 15. I heard 'Strange Avenues', 'Kissing Willie' and 'Rattlesnake Trail' on a local radio rock show. I was blown away. I thought they were old men. It seems strange to think they were younger than I am now.

I bought the *20 Years of Jethro Tull* box-set and video and was amazed at the range of music and the characters in the band. I first saw Tull at Newcastle City Hall in '92 and waited outside from 10am hoping to catch a glimpse of the band. When Ian pulled up in a white car, I couldn't believe he was right there in front of me. He got out and politely signed autographs. I wish I'd had a mobile phone with a camera back then.

They have provided me with some great memories over the years. Their songs are very poignant at different times in my life. The best thing I ever did was switch on the radio that September night in 1989.

PALACIO MUNICIPAL DE DEPORTES

8 APRIL 1992, BARCELONA, SPAIN

GUSTAU SOLÉ DIAZ, AGE 15

Gustau Solé Diaz is a huge fan

I was born the year the *Songs from the Wood* album was released, and 13 years later discovered an old tape my sister had recorded with *Aqualung* on the A-side and *War Child* on the B-side. It was quite common in Spain to share music through recorded tapes. It wasn't right, but in this case we could say that tape became a good investment for Jethro Tull, something that definitely changed my life. I remember listening to that tape over and over again on my walk to school. I was absolutely fascinated by the music, so different from everything I had listened to so far. 'My God', 'Wind Up', Sealion' and 'The Third Hoorah' were some of my favourite songs. 'Locomotive Breath' wasn't on the tape. *Aqualung* wasn't released in Spain in 1971 because of censorship. When it finally came to light in 1975, 'Locomotive Breath' was left out because of the '...has got him by the balls' line. It was one of the last acts of censorship of the Spanish dictatorship. 'Glory Row' was in its place, a good song from 1974 not included in the *War Child* album. I was a teenage fan of Jethro Tull in the early Nineties. My friends knew nothing about the band. The majority considered the music slightly weird and I was seen as a bit of a freak. But I loved that music. And following my own path, despite it being far from the mainstream, had a key role in forging my personality. I remember perfectly the first time I bought a Jethro Tull album. I was in a small music shop managed by an old rocker. I asked him for 'something by Jethro Tull' and he abruptly said, 'This is the first decent request I've had the whole day!' He suggested I take the *Bursting Out* live album. It was a good recommendation that linked me to the band forever. Going to see them aged 15, in Barcelona, was probably the first time I went out at night. I went alone and felt like I was the youngest in the venue. I took a taxi there and home afterwards. It was worth it. In 1992, Virgin opened a megastore in Barcelona, as CDs were starting their hegemony in the music industry. You can imagine how my eyes opened wide when I saw so many different albums in the Jethro Tull section. As soon as I had saved enough money, I bought another CD. It was like they Tull had released a new album every few weeks just for me. At that time the internet didn't exist, at least for me, but when it did arrive in 1998, it brought with it the Jethroweb from Albert Villanueva, where I could learn everything about the band – its history, discography and its members. Most importantly, I could meet other Spanish fans with whom I

281

could share my passion for Jethro Tull and from which the Spanish fan club Tullianos emerged. I've never again gone alone to a Jethro Tull concert. I've been fortunate enough to help organise the annual convention of Tullianos many times. I've had the pleasure of greeting and chatting with many musicians from Jethro Tull. The most exciting experience was being the assistant of Ian Anderson, John O'Hara and Florian Opahle on their visit to the IX Tullianos Convention in 2011. While organising everything I had the chance to share some experiences with the band during the weekend. Fortunately, the event was a big success for everybody and it's something I'll never forget. Neither will I forget the big hug Ian Anderson gave me when I dropped him off at the airport. The 13-year-old boy at the beginning of this story never imagined that one day this might happen.

REGENT THEATRE

22 SEPTEMBER 1992, IPSWICH, UK

LINDA ROGERS

l saw them in Ipswich about 30 years ago and nearly fell asleep. It was probably not the band's fault, to be fair. The sound there was rubbish.

PARAMOUNT THEATER

13 OCTOBER 1992, DENVER, COLORADO

PAM SCOOROS

I was going through some hard stuff – the death of my father, relationship woes. I was in a constant funk. I found out Jethro Tull was going to be in concert in downtown Denver. The concert was sold out. I was taking a class downtown that ended about two hours before the start. As a lark, I decided to go to the concert hall instead of home. People were outside, selling tickets at much higher prices. A man pointed out this guy who was quietly off to the side and said he might have a ticket. I asked this guy and he did have one to sell for the same price he had paid. I bought it and only glanced at the ticket. I had been on my bicycle so had to deal with the box office as to where to keep my backpack.

When I was finally being led to my seat by the usher, I started to realise we were getting closer and closer to the stage. I was in shock to be put in the first-row centre seat. It was a great concert. The guy who sold me the ticket was in the next seat and really nice. I bought him a drink. I was so close, I could see the wrinkles on Ian Anderson's forehead. There was a moment when I think he looked at me with recognition - maybe from me seeing him in concert in 1988? The man who led me to the ticket seller came to me at intermission and marvelled at my great fortune. I thanked him for his part in it. After that, my funk was completely gone, and I was a tiny step closer to believing in God.

LONESTAR ROADHOUSE

26 APRIL 1993, NEW YORK, NEW YORK

BARRY GOLDBERG

Barry Goldberg rubbing elbows with Ian Anderson

Jethro Tull were about to embark on their *25th Anniversary* world tour. They decided to play a small pub in New York City at lunchtime. The only way to get in was win a contest hosted by WNEW-FM radio in New York. I tried and tried to no avail. However, that morning my younger cousin called and told me he was on his way to pick me up for the hour drive into the city. I had broken my leg and was in a full leg cast. I tried to explain that I couldn't fit in his Jeep in such a condition. Well, we put a sock over my foot, rolled the window down and drove into the big city, my leg hanging out the window, with absolutely no assurances we would get into the pub.

Upon arrival, there were about 20 people lined up outside. None of them had won the radio contest, but these guys were true fans. I couldn't believe there were others like myself. Half an hour before showtime, the front door swung open and the girl with the clipboard told us management would allow us to come in. Everyone scrambled for tables.

I hobbled over to a payphone to call my wife and tell her I got in. While waiting to make my call, I heard a very recognisable voice coming from down the hall. When I looked up, it was Ian Anderson. He was walking directly towards me, two flutes in hand. I stepped in front of him and asked if he would be so kind as to sign my leather Indiana Jones styled hat. He explained that he had to get ready to go on stage shortly, but if I hung around after the show, he'd be more than happy to say hello and sign my hat.

Then I heard another very recognisable voice. I hobbled down the hall and came to a doorway with police tape across the opening. Inside was Martin Barre seated at a table finishing up an interview. I ducked under the tape and approached him to ask if he would sign my hat. The interviewer was obviously annoyed and said, 'Excuse me, I'm doing an interview here,' to which I replied, 'I don't give a fuck what you're doing. This is Martin Barre!' Martin was amused. He got up from the table, pulled up a chair for me to sit in, and I sat there while he completed his interview. And this was all before noon.

Ian and the band played a full show in this small bar and, as promised, after the show when all the contest winners had left and returned to work, many of us remained and the band came out to say hello. They raised a few glasses, everyone signed my hat and I was a happy guy.

In 25-plus years since that incredible afternoon in New York City, I have seen over 200 shows featuring Tull or Ian or Martin solo, travelling across the USA and seeing them in Germany, England and Spain. It has become my passion. I've met so many wonderful people along the way.

In November 2014 myself, Dennis Landau and Michael Grin hosted the USA Jethro Tull Convention in New York, an incredible three days where everything was about Tull, with attendees and musicians from around the world performing non-stop Tull

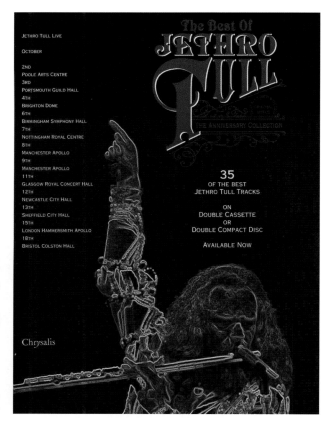

JETHRO TULL LIVE

OCTOBER

2ND
POOLE ARTS CENTRE
3RD
PORTSMOUTH GUILD HALL
4TH
BRIGHTON DOME
6TH
BIRMINGHAM SYMPHONY HALL
7TH
NOTTINGHAM ROYAL CENTRE
8TH
MANCHESTER APOLLO
9TH
MANCHESTER APOLLO
11TH
GLASGOW ROYAL CONCERT HALL
12TH
NEWCASTLE CITY HALL
13TH
SHEFFIELD CITY HALL
15TH
LONDON HAMMERSMITH APOLLO
18TH
BRISTOL COLSTON HALL

Chrysalis

The Best Of JETHRO TULL

THE ANNIVERSARY COLLECTION

35
OF THE BEST
JETHRO TULL TRACKS

ON
DOUBLE CASSETTE
OR
DOUBLE COMPACT DISC

AVAILABLE NOW

NATURBÜHNE

11 JUNE 1993, ELSPE, GERMANY

DAVID REES

Since the Rainbow gig in 1974, I've never missed a tour, have bought every album on day of release and have managed to see the band in nearly 20 different countries ... but that's not particularly unusual, as there are thousands of dedicated hardcore fans out there. The real life changing event began in 1985 when I decided to 'knock out' a photocopied attempt at a Jethro Tull fan magazine, in the hope that someone might pick up the reins and run with it properly. That never happened, so I stuck with it, and still do, with 2022 seeing publication of #141 of *A New Day*, the Jethro Tull magazine.

David Rees has at least one avid reader of A New Day magazine

I've had countless wonderful and memorable experiences over the years, largely as a result of the magazine, both in terms of the readership – many of whom have become good friends – and the members of Jethro Tull, all of whom have been very friendly and helpful along the way. I still remember the day in 1987 I received a call from Kenny Wylie, Tull's then road manager, asking if I would like to interview Ian Anderson at home for the magazine. Would I like to?!

It was the start of an ... interesting relationship. Ian has been incredibly supportive of the magazine, even when the content has not been particularly gushing. It was immensely gratifying to hear him say, during a concert at a fan's convention, 'I'd like to thank David Rees and the people at *A New Day* magazine for their support and their honesty. When we are shit, they say we're shit, but in the nicest possible way.'

I've had a couple of other honourable mentions from Ian at concerts; once, in Ipswich, when they played 'Jack-a-Lynn' and followed it by saying, 'It was a track that would never have been released were it not for the efforts of David Rees.' And in Prague, maybe not such an honourable mention, when Ian told the audience, 'We are sorry to say that a good friend of ours, David Rees, is really quite ill at the moment, so we dedicate this next piece to him as it is one of his favourites.' They went on to play 'From Birnam Wood to Dunsinane', a tune I previously criticised in the mag. I wasn't ill of course, I was in the audience, so it was something of a rebuttal, but still quite pleasing to think Ian at least read the magazine, and cared enough to be pissed off about it.

I've been to far too many gigs to pick a favourite, but I have definitely got a favourite memory, derived from our attendance at a gig in Elspe, Germany, in 1993. We had three maps of Germany with us, but only one had Elspe in it – yes, that's how small and insignificant the place is. Pre-internet days of course, we used to roll into town, find a hotel and crack on. Elspe, however, was something else. One road, a few houses, one bar and no hotels for miles and miles around. We did what any group of Englishmen would do, headed to the bar to make some kind of a plan. As we stared forlornly into our beers, Martin Webb, co-conspirator in the Tull mag, went back to the bar. He had always maintained he could speak fluent German, although we had never seen any hard evidence of it.

He returned after a few minutes, scratching his head and looking fairly bewildered. 'I think I understand what she said, but it can't be right. I think she said there are no hotels within 20 miles or so, but we have rooms. You probably won't like it here though because the bar is open all night and it gets very loud.' That is exactly what we were looking for. Turns out she thought we were Jethro Tull, and would probably like a good night's sleep.

The gig itself was incredible, with probably the most spectacular natural backdrop for the stage, as it was set in a huge cowboy-themed park (yes, in Germany!). Both Tull and support band Procol Harum were on fire that night, as they were throughout the entire tour.

Two days later we saw Tull at a huge festival in Jubeck, where our lives were threatened by a very large group of drug-fuelled thugs ... but that's another story.

MERRIWEATHER POST PAVILION

30 AUGUST 1993, COLUMBIA, MARYLAND

GWENDOLYN THOMPSON

When I was a little girl, my father used to put us to bed and play DJ with his album collection. I always asked him to play his Jethro Tull albums. When I left home as a young adult, the first CD I bought with my first real paycheck was *Songs from the Wood*. I took my future husband to see them play in 1993 at Merriweather Post Pavilion in Columbia, Maryland. Now I play Tull for my kids on our Alexa for special occasions, like roasting marshmallows by the fire pit, at Christmas (I love the *Jethro Tull Christmas Album*), or just whenever I'm feeling nostalgic. Tull has serenaded three generations of our family, and when my kids have little ones, I will play it for them too. Jethro Tull have been the theme music for my life.

MANN MUSIC CENTER

31 AUGUST 1993, PHILADELPHIA, PENNSYLVANIA

CHRISTINE RITCHIE

Christine Ritchie's ticket collection

I distinctly recall the exact moment I became a Jethro Tull fan. I was a freshman college student in 1991/92 and listening to the local classic rock station when 'Skating Away on the Thin Ice of the New Day' came on. I was blown away by the overall song itself but in particular Ian Anderson's voice and phrasing. The next day, I went out and bought *Original Masters* (the only CD in the shop that had 'Skating Away' on it), *Stand Up*, *Aqualung* and *Songs from the Wood*; Tull have been my favourite band ever since. My first Jethro Tull concert was in 1993 for the 25th Anniversary tour, and my last concerts were Ian's and Martin's respective 50th anniversary tours.

KINGSWOOD AMPHITHEATRE

4 SEPTEMBER 1993, TORONTO, CANADA

MICHAEL LASHAM

Michael Lasham tied a work trip in with a Tull concert

The first time I heard Jethro Tull I was on a scout camp. My friend played me the opening of a song and asked what I thought. I said, 'It sounds like a train.' Then he played the rest of the song, 'Locomotive Breath'. I was hooked. I went looking for Tull records and found *Stand Up* at a jumble sale, bought *The Broadsword and the Beast* and have been listening ever since.

The first time I saw Tull live was on a work trip to Canada. My colleague and I went to Five Flags over Canada, near Toronto, where Tull were playing on their *25th Anniversary* tour. Procol Harum were the support band, followed by Jethro Tull, who came out with miners' hats on, saying that was their light show. I loved it.

WORLD MUSIC THEATER

12 SEPTEMBER 1993, TINLEY PARK, ILLINOIS

PAUL HURST

Paul and Anne Hurst's first date was at a Jethro Tull show

The first conversation I had with the girl I eventually married was about our favourite band, Jethro Tull, and specifically 'My God' and 'Hymn 43'. On our first night out as 'friends', we found 'Rainbow Blues' on the jukebox and played it all night long, laughing at how everyone tolerated us. Our first actual date was the *25th Anniversary* Tull Concert in Tinley Park, Illinois. We snuck up to claim some better, empty seats, only to find one being claimed by a late arrival, so we shared one seat for the rest of the concert. Before long, we were at our wedding, dancing our first dance as man and wife: 'Reasons for Waiting'.

Many incredible performances later, including amazing concerts like Ian's *Divinities* tour, we celebrated the 25th anniversary of our first date at Tull's *50th Anniversary* concert at Ravinia Festival in Highland Park, Illinois. We're still in love with each other and the music of Jethro Tull. Thank you to all the members over the years and our favourite musician of all, whose work we're so grateful for - our lifelong friend (who we've never actually met), Ian Anderson.

APOLLO THEATRE

8 & 9 OCTOBER 1993, MANCHESTER, UK

RICHARD CONNELL

I saw the blues–heavy *25th Anniversary* tour twice, at Manchester Apollo in 1993 and again in 1994 at Bradford St George's Hall. I don't think they'd sold enough merchandise on the 1993 leg, and that's perhaps why it continued into '94. It was well played, but ironic given that they'd been very much an electric rock band for the years since Martin Barre joined.

ROYAL CONCERT HALL

11 OCTOBER 1993, GLASGOW, UK

RAB STRAITON

After the *War Child* tour, my next Tull gig wasn't till 1978 and the *Heavy Horses* tour. This was another awesome gig, with the band in excellent form. I then got a gift of a ticket for Tull's *25th Anniversary* gig in 1993 at the Royal Concert Hall in Glasgow. The stage was done up like a sitting room. Easy chairs, rugs and fireplace adorned the stage. It was a relaxing atmosphere compared to the Seventies. But the music wasn't so relaxing as they ripped through a back catalogue of gems, one after the other bringing back memories from the Apollo years. I've seen a lot of bands live but definitely Jethro Tull are one of the best live acts I've had the privilege to watch.

HAMMERSMITH APOLLO

15 & 16 OCTOBER 1993, LONDON, UK

STEFAN NORDENG, AGE 20

I was living in Sweden when me and my girlfriend at the time purchased tickets to see Tull at Hammersmith Apollo. The day before we were due to leave home to travel to

London, we couldn't find the tickets. Getting rather stressed, we realised they might have been put in the garbage bin and thrown out. We lived in a flat and shared a garbage room with many other people, so the search began, going through 10 to 20 paper bags filled with garbage, finally finding the correct bag ... and there were the tickets.

VICTOR GUSEV, SPORTS COMMENTATOR, RUSSIAN TV

I remember sitting on the floor in the middle of a wild party at my friend's apartment in Moscow in 1972. Headphones on, I didn't care what was happening around me. All the vodkas were passing me by, my girlfriend dancing with another. I was 17 and listening to a strangely-named album by a strangely-named group I'd never heard of. I kept turning the record over and again until very late at night when it was time for the guests to go ...

Aqualung, my first Jethro Tull album, was an easy catch. It was brought from outside the Iron Curtain by my friend's father, a diplomat. For *Benefit*, *Thick as a Brick*, *This Was* and *Stand Up* (bought in this strange order) I had to go to the black market, getting each one for 40 to 50 roubles, the size of my monthly scholarship.

What happened next was like a lesson of geography and a dream come true. I bought *Minstrel in the Gallery* the day it was released in 1975 during my stay in Albany as an exchange programme student at the State University of New York. I instantly fell in love with the album, which I still consider the best in the history of rock. A bookstore in Addis Ababa, the capital of war-torn Ethiopia, where I was stationed as a military translator from 1977 to 1979, surprisingly had a copy of *Songs from the Wood*.

THE JOLLY JETHRO 1993 WINTER UPDATE

MERRY CHRISTMAS EDITION

A stopover in Wellington, New Zealand in 1985 helped me finally get hold of *The Broadsword and the Beast*, also unavailable in the Soviet Union (very fittingly – 'cold spray flying in' - I was on my way down to Antarctica on board a rescue mission ice-breaker). 'Steel Monkey' from *Crest of a Knave* came to me from the English radio in Seoul in 1987 on my pre-Olympic media tour. I soon bought the album as the first CD in my collection, together with my first portable CD player.

Perestroika made it possible for me to get a tourist visa and fly to London for a JT concert in 1993. I spoke to Ian Anderson for five seconds at the Hammersmith Apollo exit. Ten years later, we met at a lunch organised by my friend at Pushkin restaurant on the day of Tull's first ever Moscow concert. Thanks to Ian's invitations I enjoyed many more gorgeous shows in LA, Magdeburg and London ... and proudly translated the brilliant *TAAB2* lyrics into Russian for the album's special edition booklet in 2012.

I'm 67 years old now, and I am putting on my headphones again, just like that boy half a century ago. The world stops and I dive deep into *Heavy Horses* and *Stormwatch*, *Roots to Branches* and *The Zealot Gene*. The heavenly music of Jethro Tull. The soundtrack to my life.

RANG BHAWAN

16 & 17 FEBRUARY 1994, MUMBAI, INDIA

AJAY MANKOTIA

A few months before Jethro Tull played Mumbai's Rang Bhawan as part of their *25th Anniversary* tour, Ian Anderson had visited Mumbai. A large billboard on Marine Drive showing Ian (a leaner, balder version of his Paris show) welcomed him. No rock band, certainly no band member, had ever been heralded in this manner. Perhaps my college friend, then heading the International Music Division of HMV (a fellow Tull freak) was responsible. He invited me to the press conference. Ian must have been pleasantly surprised to hear 'Pibroch (Cap in Hand)' when he entered the conference room. Attired in a multi-coloured quilted jacket, he spoke for a bit, then switched on the music track, took out his harmonica and launched into 'A New Day Yesterday'. What followed in the next half-hour, with Ian now on the flute, was something very few have had the good fortune to see – a small, compact concert with 50 people in attendance, sitting just a few metres away from Ian.

Then followed the press conference. Jethro Tull were still relatively unknown, the press was not quite up to speed regarding the band's details, and there was no internet in those days. Ian answered the basic and banal questions patiently. India was still virgin territory for the band.

Then I got up and asked Ian why he was so fascinated by Jeffrey that he actually composed three songs for him on the very first three albums. Further, Jeffrey was the narrator of 'The Story of the Hare who lost his Spectacles', and also wrote it, which was highly unusual since he (Ian) wrote and sang all the songs himself. Ian was flummoxed – he never expected this kind of query from this part of the world. The press members were clueless. Ian smiled. He saw a fanatic – he'd seen hundreds and thousands like me – and proceeded to answer the question. I met him afterwards and mentioned our Paris meeting. He remembered!

Months later, a day before the two shows, there was yet another press conference and the same story repeated itself. Ian asked me to join him at the dais and the conversation between us (unintelligible to most of the gathering) happened before the throng. By then Ian was convinced he was dealing with a mad man.

I attended the concert both days (naturally). Rang Bhawan was an open-air theatre with limited seating. Both days saw a packed crowd. Anywhere in Europe and the US, the band would have required a much bigger venue. The shows were, needless to say, absolutely fantastic.

BANGALORE PALACE GROUNDS

19 FEBRUARY 1994, BANGALORE, INDIA
VINOD KUMAR GOPINATH

One of my friends had a mix-tape consisting of songs by the groups The Doors, Deep Purple, Pink Floyd and Jethro Tull. He named the cassette 'Classic Rock'. That's how I discovered Jethro Tull. *Songs from the Wood* was the first Tull album I purchased.

In 1994, Jethro Tull played in Bangalore. A month before the concert three of us decided to not miss the opportunity to see the greatest band on the planet. A week passed and I did not see any interest in the other two in booking the tickets. I confronted them and said it was time we

Vinod Kumar paid 200 rupees for a ticket

purchased the tickets. They no longer exhibited the excitement of the previous week. I felt like a child asking for an ice cream from a 'you-shall-only-have-one-ice-cream-every-six-months' type of parent. The guy who owned the tape called the idea ridiculous. The other fellow agreed. The mix-tape friend said, 'It's 200 rupees da! That is a lot of money.' The other friend agreed. 'Yes da! It's one ninth of our scholarship.'

The money talk hit me hard, 200 rupees was a lot of money. The last Jethro Tull cassette I bought had only cost 50 rupees, so 200 rupees would buy four cassettes I could listen to whenever I wanted. The argument sounded good and I could not find reasons to push for purchasing the concert tickets. I said 'bah!' and forgot about the concert.

As we walked into the games area of our college on the day of the concert, we saw a group of friends leaving the campus. One said, 'We are going to the Tull concert.' Our shoulders drooped. We did not look at each other. A voice in my head shouted, 'Four cassettes, you moron!' The mix-tape friend got up and declared, 'Let us go to M G Road'. MG Road was the heart of Bangalore, where one could watch movies, have ice cream, visit restaurants, buy t-shirts or just hang around. That evening, we planned to hang around.

We boarded a bus from the college gate. In a few minutes, the bus passed by the concert ground. We heard Ian Anderson singing and the audience cheering. For a few seconds, it felt as though someone had pierced a knife through my heart. I shook off the feeling and said, 'It's too loud.' The other two repeated in agreement, 'It's too loud.'

I have never attended a rock concert in my life. Frankly, there were not too many opportunities. But every time a group decided to have a concert in the city where I lived after that, I argued, 'I missed Tull's concert to save 200 rupees. What is the point in going to this concert?'

Four years ago, a young colleague visited the US during the summer and came back with stories that she offloaded onto colleagues. She had a narrative for me too. 'Guess what? I went to a concert in the US. Guess the group!' I looked at her with disinterest and asked, 'The Beatles?' 'No! Not The Beatles. I went to a Jethro Tull concert .' I did not want to hear the rest of the story but did not have a choice, so I continued to listen. 'I went to the concert with my uncle, and it was fantastic. Ian Anderson sings so well, and when he plays the flute … My uncle explained everything about the group and the song. It was great.'

I faked a smile and said, 'Great! Tull are great!' She continued to talk about the concert, but I only heard the words '200 rupees' looping through my head.

YMCA GROUNDS

20 FEBRUARY 1994, MADRAS, INDIA

MURALI MENON

Madras is balmy but not hot in February. But on 20 February 1994, Jethro Tull landed in Madras and turned on the heat for over two hours with a blistering performance. It was the last leg of their *25th Anniversary* India tour, after playing in Bombay and Bangalore. And what a show it was.

The concert ambience was something new to me. As we walked past the large parking bay at the YMCA arena, one could hear music screaming out of car radios.

Much of it wasn't just from the Tull catalogue, but classic rock nonetheless. The bonnets of the parked cars served as makeshift bar counters and the evening sea breeze wafted in with copious whiffs of spliff. My cousins and I were buzzed to the brim, waiting for Ian Anderson, Martin Barre, Andy Giddings, Doanne Perry and Dave Pegg to start the magic.

The stage was sparse. A clothesline hung across the front with some underwear and t-shirts. A lady walked in and swept the front of the stage. The band members appeared next, welcomed by a rip-roaring reception from the crowd. With a hint of British humour as he picked the undies from the line and threw it aside, Ian announced, 'We didn't even have time to wash our underwear, as we flew in from Bangalore just now. Now that's out of the way, how are you doing, Madras?'

I don't remember every song they played in that two-hour set. 'Songs from the Wood' was the opening number and they segued into the *Crest of a Knave* album and performed American social justice anthem, 'Farm on the Freeway' before sauntering back in time to earlier records and played 'A Song For Jeffrey' and 'A New Day Yesterday.'

The crowd waited in anticipation for the one-legged flute maestro to whip out his favourite instrument and play JS Bach tribute, 'Bouree.' And he did it so brilliantly that the crowd was mesmerised and jubilant in equal measure. Another crowd favourite, a tale about an old biker who refuses to change his old familiar ways, 'Too Old to Rock 'n' Roll, Too Young To Die' was a splendid singalong piece for the ecstatic audience.

As the crowd was getting rapturous and overwhelmed with all the great music, we realised Tull had already been playing for over an hour and a half. We weren't sure at that time how long the show would go on. Ian Anderson then swiftly harked us back to his life on the farm with Martin Barre's opening riff of 'Heavy Horses'. A personal favourite, this song much like the ones from *Songs from the Wood*, has a nostalgic take on farming and the disastrous effects of modernisation. The full panoply of pastoral songs Ian wrote during the late Seventies are testimony to Jethro Tull's powerful commentary on society's rampant, capitalistic sojourns.

Finally, the show reached its crescendo with two of their finest songs serving as an appropriate coda to a stellar evening. The crowd went absolutely delirious when Martin Barre played the stupendous opening riff of 'Aqualung' – 'DA DA DA DA... DAA DAA!' Barre slowly ratcheted it up a notch higher and skated through the fretboard with wonderful precision, as Ian and the crowd sang along. The next one, their closing number, brought in a maelstrom of emotions in every single fan who watched them that evening. It was the fantastic 'Locomotive Breath', a saga about how we are on this frenetic runaway train of unbridled capitalism and feverish debauchery. Where do we get off? That's a pertinent question.

After 27 years, I am still reminiscing about that evening, a whirligig of time that promises not to pause.

FESTIVAL HALL

9 MARCH 1994, BRISBANE, AUSTRALIA

JOHANNA MENSO

My father Clyde Holtom has been infatuated with Jethro Tull for as long as I remember. He first saw them in 1970 at the Isle of Wight festival, before I was born. When we emigrated to Australia in 1972, he brought the album *Stand Up* with him. This is the album that was on high rotation and was my introduction to Jethro Tull at a young age. The album

Johanna Menso's father Clyde (left) passed his love of Tull on to his three children

artwork mesmerised me and I reproduced it on paper as a teenager. We had *Bursting Out* on cassette and played it so much that the tape stretched. We just then sang the stretched version instead.

In 1994 I was a young adult and working, so I surprised my dad with tickets for the Festival Hall show in Brisbane. What a magical evening. We attended three more shows after that, two in Brisbane and one in Sydney. Each time I had to fly more than 1,000km, but it was worth every penny.

My dad kept buying any Jethro Tull album he could get hold of and was so proud of his collection he listed them on a record collecting website. In 2021 I surprised him with the news that I had pre-purchased a signed copy of *Silent Singing* for him which would arrive later in the year. To say he was happy was an understatement.

Unfortunately, he passed away that June, but his collection will be played, treasured and appreciated by his three children for many years to come. And the copy of *Silent Singing*? Well let's just say it will stay with me and my growing collection of Jethro Tull albums.

FESTIVAL HALL

9 MARCH 1994, BRISBANE, AUSTRALIA

MARTIN ROBINSON

I was born in 1973 and heard my first Jethro Tull album, *Songs from the Wood*, at my mate's house at age 18. It was his father's original vinyl edition of the album. It was late at night, at full volume and we were drunk. I have explored every album and love their music dearly. I have been lucky

Martin Robinson was at Brisbane's Festival Hall in '94

enough to see them live once so far, at the Festival Hall. I saved up to buy the ticket, the most expensive I had bought at that time, but could not convince any friends to go with me. I was certainly the youngest in the audience, and one of the few not in a suit, such was the average age of the attendees. That said, it was the first time in my life I saw anyone older than myself passing joints around the seats.

The stage was set as an apartment and the opening scene was a frumpy maid dusting the rooms. She wandered around dusting different instruments, before eventually picking up a flute, which was played, starting the first song. It was Ian, in all his mischievous nature. Such a vivid memory still. Play on, play loud.

AFTER DARK

16 MARCH 1994, HONOLULU, HAWAII
CHRISTOPHER VAN DYKE

After high school, wanting a bit of excitement and a break from academics, I found myself enlisted in the US Army. My duty station was in Oahu, Hawaii, which was not as great and exotic as one might believe. But there was a small local venue there, After Dark, and sure enough Jethro Tull was going to play it.

Happily, we weren't scheduled to be out running up and down the Hawaiian mountains, so my roommate and I scored tickets and headed on out. We made it to the concert sober, but that slowly slipped away as the night wore on. It was a memorable concert, and I loved the great music in a smaller venue where we could get up close. After the concert, my buddy and I headed to a bar near the venue and upon walking out we ran into Ian Anderson. I was perhaps a bit too enthusiastic in seeing him and wanting to buy him a beer, and he quickly turned away. I went after him and he went faster. After a moment, my buddy pointed out that we were actually chasing the poor guy and we promptly stopped. I still regret my behaviour a bit, 28 years later. Perhaps a cooler, calmer and sober me would have ended up having a beer with Ian Anderson. If I ever have the luck to run into him again, I'll be sure to offer that beer. Just not so insistently.

SHEA'S THEATER

2 APRIL 1994, BUFFALO, NEW YORK
SCOTT DEMAYO

Tull have literally been part of the soundtrack of my life. Blessed to have older sisters with great taste in music, some of my earliest musical memories are of listening with my sister, Vickie, to her *Living in the Past* double-album. From the age of four, I was already entranced by the music. I was eight when she went away to college and she gave me her album, which I still have today, along with all the others, CDs, box-sets, etc.

I first saw the band in Rochester, New York in 1982 and went on to see them five more times - in Rochester, Buffalo and Toronto - along with multiple solo shows by Ian and Martin. My favourite Tull show was in 1994 at Shea's in Buffalo. My sister was very ill at the time, fighting for her life. The band played my favourite song that April night, 'Life's a Long Song', and I remember how beautifully it was performed and how hard it hit me. We lost my sister four days later to leukemia.

I've never stopped loving this band and I'm known among friends and even casual acquaintances as a Tull fanatic. Thank you to all members in the band's long history for making this world that much more interesting to live in.

TYPHOON HALL

6 MAY 1994, TURKU, FINLAND
HANNU BJÖRKBACKA

Ian Anderson in action in Turku. Photo: Hanna Björkbacka

I was 14 in 1970 when I heard Jethro Tull for the first time. It was 'The Witch's Promise' playing on Finnish Radio Yle. Ian Anderson was wooing me with the siren's call opening of 'Lend me your ear/While I call you a fool.' A bit later I saw an item on Finnish TV news that said Jethro Tull were coming to Finland for the first time, showing a clip of Ian Anderson dancing like a dervish in his long coat. I so wanted to see them. In 1994, Jethro Tull came to Turku's Typhoon Hall. I was the film reviewer for the newspaper *Keskipohjanmaa* and persuaded them to send me to cover the concert and interview the band. There were five journalists present. Ian Anderson came and seemed a bit irritated at first, but relaxed when he saw we had prepared some half-intelligent questions. I also got to talk to Martin Barre, nice and shy, as always. He had his new solo album out. For the concert, we got the permission to take photographs in front of the stage for the first two songs. I got one I really liked of Ian playing his flute with the coloured stage lights just right behind him. Afterwards, Jari Petäjäniemi from EMI Finland asked me to go backstage again. I was the only one left with a camera and they needed someone to photograph the fans who had won the prize of a meet and greet with the band via a competition arranged by the local radio station.

Backstage I got to talk with all the band members, especially Andrew Giddings, who was very friendly. I got all their autographs. I took photos of the fans, mainly with Ian, who after the show was in a jovial mood. I am not a professional photographer

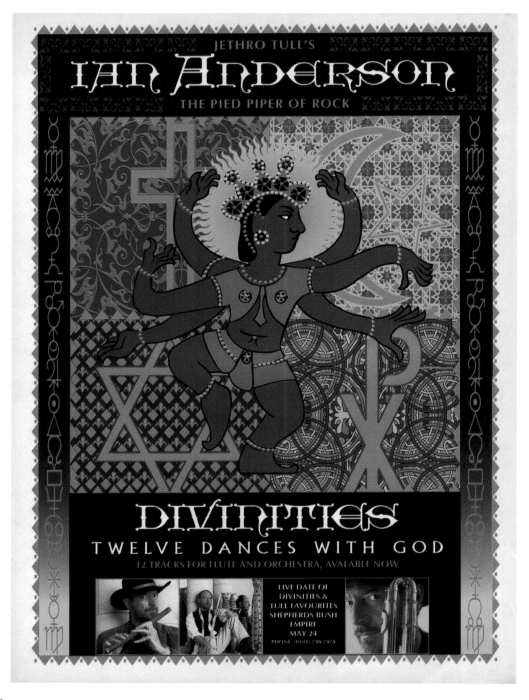

and Ian seemed to notice. He finally asked what aperture and shutter speed I was using and, of course, I did not know what he was talking about. Despite my lack of technical knowledge, the photos came out pretty well. I got my photos printed in the *Keskipohjanmaa* newspaper with a review and an interview, and I sent copies of the photos to EMI for them to send to the fans, receiving a copy of double-CD compilation *The Best of Jethro Tull* in return. It was a dream come true for a lifelong Tull fan.

TUTBURY CASTLE

16 JULY 1994, TUTBURY, UK

ADRIAN HAMMOND

The first Tull track I ever heard ('Song for Jeffrey'), was on Island sampler, *You Can All Join In*. I have bought almost every album ever since, and spent a lifetime following Tull. My favourite Tull concert was a small gig at Tutbury Castle in Staffordshire.

VOLKSHAUS

21 MAY 1995, ZURICH, SWITZERLAND

FRANCESCO GIUFFRÉ—LEGNANO

I had spent many days and much money on Tull over the years and in Zurich in 1995 decided it was time to try to meet and shake hands with the band. As it was a solo concert and not a Tull concert, I thought the security might be more relaxed.

On the afternoon of the show, I entered the theatre via a door that had been left open and sat in the hall while the band were soundchecking. When this ended, I followed them to the dressing rooms. I met Mr Giddings, who was very kind to me and told me about the evening show. I knocked on the door marked 'Mr Anderson's dressing room' and his wife, who I recognised from photographs, opened the door. I introduced myself and told her I wished to have a picture with Mr Anderson. She said, 'Sure, come here after the show'.

I enjoyed the show, the fabulous set-list, and the musicians. After the show I started to walk in the opposite direction to the rest of the audience, moving toward the dressing rooms. After a short wait I saw Mr Anderson coming down the corridor with his wife. I was there and clearly waiting for him. He looked at me with a quizzical expression and I thought he was concerned about his security. But Mrs Anderson shouted, 'You are Franco, I know you!'

Mr Anderson joined us for a couple of pictures, then moved through the main door while I left via the back door. On the outside was a group of fans waiting for him. Instead, they got me.

CITY HALL

22 SEPTEMBER 1995, SHEFFIELD, UK

RICHARD CONNELL

The *Roots to Branches* tour saw a fairly low-key but enjoyable gig. It was notable for my first experience of the acoustic version of 'Aqualung', which is sadly now the norm with Ian's failing voice. It was played early in the set and Ian whispered, 'Some of you may recognise this one.' It came across well because it was so different.

MUELLE UNO

19 MARCH 1996, LIMA, PERU

JAVIER VEGA GRIS

This was my first night out, leaving my wife at home with our son, born just 11 days before, so it wasn't easy for me but I could not miss this epic opportunity to

Javier Vega Gris remembers Ian injuring himself on stage

see Jethro Tull in concert for the first time, in Lima as part of the *Roots to Branches* tour. The night was reaching its climax. To end the concert came 'Aqualung'. It was a magnificent performance and Ian made his classic jump to finish the song but ... 'Ouch!' he shouted, falling down on the floor. An uncomfortable silence followed. The audience were petrified and immediately the crew helped Ian to recover and leave the stage. He had hurt his ankle.

My God! What had happened? What the bloody hell had I seen? Ian Anderson? Noooo! It is not possible. Everybody waited anxiously for what seemed to be an eternity and for any announcement. Then Ian appeared on the stage, assisted by the crew and sat down on a chair. We were astonished. The piano sounded familiar because it was the encore, 'Locomotive Breath'. People went completely mad. Ian sang with a really broken voice that made that performance surreal. In the middle of the song, Ian stopped singing and apologised. He said he could not continue because of the pain.

The concert ended with all the audience stood up and clapping for several minutes because of that special moment. It was hard to leave the place and come back home with all those mixed feelings. It was an unforgettable night.

IAN ANDERSON

My jump was perfectly timed. But it was a slippery stage because we were down by the Pacific Ocean in an outdoor amphitheatre stage and, with the time of the day, the condensation that had formed meant the wooden stage had become like an ice rink. Unfortunately, I slid sideways when I landed from that big jump and snapped the anterior cruciate ligament, an injury common amongst footballers, skiers and other elite sportsmen. The guys in the band claim that over the sound of that last perfectly timed chord, they heard a crack that they assumed was gunfire, and they thought I'd been shot!

The crack they heard was actually my ACL going off. I tried to get to my feet and realised I actually couldn't walk. I hopped on to do the encore without really being able to put my foot on the ground, and was in huge agony. It was only when I got to the hotel that I realised just how bad this injury was. I had it ill-advisedly strapped up by a local doctor and plastered and was told not to move it. That was absolutely the wrong thing to do, because strapping it up means the injury is locked in place. Keeping mobility is the first and foremost thing to do in modern medical science.

DAR CONSTITUTION HALL

26 MARCH 1996, WASHINGTON DC

FRED RIDLEY

The DAR Constitution Hall is an old theatre near the monuments in Washington DC. I had awesome seats, maybe 10 rows from the stage. What a surprise when Ian Anderson appeared on stage in a wheelchair. He explained he had fallen from the stage in South America. He did that show like he had always been in a wheelchair. He is a true professional in every way.

KEN MCNEILL

The next show I attended was the *Roots to Branches* tour in 1996. Ian had blown out his knee and rather than cancel the show he performed in a wheelchair, spinning it around like he'd been in it all his life. To this day that is one of the most incredible and courageous stage performances I've ever seen.

I attended three more Tull shows after that: 2001 at the Norva in Norfolk, Virginia; 2006 at the Ferguson Centre in Newport News, Virginia; and 2008 at Chrysler Hall in Norfolk, Virginia. Ian's voice unfortunately made it difficult to listen and it pained me to hear, although the musicianship and stage shows were all spot on. There are so many things that come to mind about Tull live shows, but one of the most enduring was their punctuality and professionalism. So many bands in the early Seventies were drunk or late to arrive onstage, and sometimes incredibly sloppy in their dress and performance. Tull set the standard back then. I never saw them arrive late in all the shows I saw.

It's unfortunate that there is so little quality audio and video of Tull live shows from *Aqualung* to *Minstrel in the Gallery*. The 1976 Tampa show, the 1978 MSG show, the 1977 London Hippodrome show and 1977 Maryland Capital Centre show are about it.

But it was during the *Thick as a Brick* and *A Passion Play* era where the band was at the peak of its powers. To this day, when I talk to people fortunate enough to see Tull between 1971 and 1975, they all say the same thing. 'Those were the greatest live shows I ever saw.' And this sometimes from people who don't even listen to Tull much anymore. Although well loved by many, they are so often overlooked regarding their impact on rock music and live stage shows, when rock was in its embryonic live era.

BRONCO BOWL

6 APRIL 1996, DALLAS, TEXAS
KEITH KINKLE

I loved Tull from an early age. My parents had *Thick as a Brick* and *Aqualung* so I knew the tunes as a child of hippie-era parents. I first saw Tull in the mid-Eighties at Dallas Convention Center Arena. When Ian Anderson came out, he was rolled out by a nurse in a wheelchair. He looked so weak and decrepit and I was wondering what was going on. Suddenly he popped up out of the chair like a madman and pulled his flute from the side of the wheelchair. The crowd went nuts and I was blown away! I thought that was such cool theatrics.

When Jethro Tull returned a few years later to the Bronco Bowl, a medium-sized venue in the Oak Cliff area of Dallas, I brought a friend along. Out came Ian again in a wheelchair. I kept telling my friend, 'Watch, he's going to jump out of the chair like a madman.' It never happened. As it turned out, Ian had broken his leg or foot at a previous show and was in a cast, performing the whole show in a wheelchair. It didn't stop him from being his usual flamboyant self, doing spins in the wheelchair and hot-rodding around the stage.

Keith Kinkle saw a wheelchair-bound Ian

JOE SHELBY

I started rediscovering the prog scene in the mid- to late-Eighties. By the summer of 1990 I was in college, having had my fill of Yes (having listened as a little kid to my dad's collection) and discovered King Crimson. I knew Tull sort of fitted into that vein, having picked up *Aqualung* as one of those Columbia House deals for cheap. The depth of the *Aqualung* lyrics (particularly 'My God' and 'Wind Up') didn't actually hit me until many years later. Once I got a job and could afford video rentals, I checked out the *20th Anniversary* VHS tape, complete with videos from all the eras of Tull up to that point (there was an unbalanced excess from *Under Wraps*, but never mind, videos were new then).

The 'folk' era (*Songs from the Wood* through to *Stormwatch*, plus the shortened version of *Thick as a Brick*) and 'Steel Monkey' caught me the most, though in the end, my next big plunge was to get the 20th Anniversary boxed set on cassette (I picked up the CD version years later) and I just drank it all in. By the time I left college I had everything from *Stand Up* to what was the latest, *Catfish Rising*.

I didn't get to see the band until the wheelchair tour, when Ian hurt himself in a fall on tour and later had the DVT (deep vein thrombosis) scare, and I also caught the *Roots to Branches* and *J-Tull Dot Com* tours in the States. Even in that show with the wheelchair, I was astounded at Ian's stage charisma and energy. That energy remains a mental image.

STATE THEATRE

12 MAY 1996, SYDNEY, AUSTRALIA

JOHN KANELLIS

My wife and I saw Tull at the magnificent Sydney State Theatre on the *Roots to Branches* tour, with Ian performing in a wheelchair following his Peruvian injury and knee surgery. We eventually realised it was no joke. Ian seemed in discomfort but did an amazing job, wheeling around on the stage in typical energetic fashion, and it was a great concert featuring one of my favourite albums. I just love the Eastern vibes on it, plus loads of flute.

The following day the Australian concerts were all cancelled as Ian was hospitalised with deep vein thrombosis. A few days later, a nurse friend of ours who worked at St Luke's hospital in Potts Point, Sydney mentioned she had been looking after a musician and I realised from her description of him - charming, witty, handsome – that it was none other than Ian. While I was majorly tempted to find some way to pay him a visit, I was also mindful that this would certainly be an imposition. Instead, our friend took my vinyl *Thick as a Brick* album and my *25th Anniversary* CD cigar box set into the hospital and Ian very kindly signed them. These are hugely treasured pieces in my music collection and my kids will inherit them some day. My flute-playing 17-year- old daughter is a big fan of Tull, so they'll most likely be hers.

IAN ANDERSON

Some weeks later, having soldiered on to do the tour in a wheelchair, I had surgery back home in the UK. I then went off on an Australian tour when it became apparent that I had a DVT as a result of the inactivity in my leg that resulted in a hospital stay of some urgency.

In fact, I think my death was reported in the UK – wrongly! – but one particular night it came close. It was the night Damon Hill won a Grand Prix race, as I remember I was watching it in my hospital room when I began to become seriously concerned. My heart rate and I became really short of oxygen. It was all the classic symptoms of a DVT breaking loose and causing an embolism, and a short step towards either your brain being shut down or your heart ceasing. They got me onto oxygen, and I had scans and X rays during the night and luckily it passed. Some of the DVT broke up without terminal injury. I got away with it, but it was a close call.

A New Day #53

GRAHAM WHITTINGHAM

Ah, the Tull tales. 1974 at the Opera House, Jeffrey resplendent in zebra stripes. 1977 at the Hordern Pavilion. Big Tull. John Glascock and Barrie Barlow. Wow! The bitter disappointment of 1984 when, after being savaged by critics in Melbourne, Mr Tull edited the set-list so no music post-1978 was played. The thrill of Doane Perry inviting me into the soundcheck in Brisbane in 1994. The abominable sound in Brisbane in 2005. The brilliant sound at the Enmore two days later. The palpable onstage tension at Bluesfest in 2011. Six tours. Five bass players. Five keyboard players. Two drummers, Martin and Ian. I own every official release and dozens of bootlegs. I guess you could call me a fan.

And there's my friend Mac at the State Theatre in 1994, jumping onto the stage and offering Ian five bucks to buy a new tin whistle. And the two Metallica boffins who walked in late, with a show-us-what-you've-got attitude, who were within minutes smiling and tapping their feet. It's a shame they didn't see Tim Finn.

I was going to crew for the Tulls in 1996 to satisfy a course requirement at university. I had struck up a friendship with (tour manager) Kenny Wylie and (sound engineer) Leon Philips on the previous tour and they graciously allowed me to work with and pick the brains of their regular crew. Sadly, the tour was cancelled because of Ian's life-threatening DVT. I was able to satisfy my course requirements later that year when Fairport Convention played, of all places, Lismore Workers Club. It was a delight to work and play with those guys. Peggy remembered me from '94 and warmly accepted the many ales I bought him that night.

The remaining Australian concerts were cancelled because of Ian's condition. In August 1996, Jethro Tull embarked on a joint tour with Emerson, Lake & Palmer.

IAN ANDERSON

Emerson, Lake and Palmer had nothing to do with American music other than the version of 'America' that Keith came up with, based on Leonard Bernstein's 'America' from *West Side Story*, which got them a little bit of notoriety and gave them a shot at fame and fortune, and which they rather threw away due to their own excesses and perhaps not being a very user-friendly band. When it came to relationships with promoters and venue operators, it took a nose-dive really.

They came back once to play the USA as an opening act for Jethro Tull, later on, and they were as good as gold. They absolutely were just so professional and totally easy to work with, really great guys. That was after a time where they'd not been able to play America because promoters didn't want to book them. In half the country they were not that successful, and in the half they were successful in, promoters shied away from them because they were notoriously difficult.

But when they were with us it was completely the opposite. They were really well behaved and really good guys to have along with us. But Keith was suffering badly from hand injury problems at that point, and it hampered their ability. Keith said to me, 'After 40 minutes I am in agony, in pain and struggling to finish off the set.' 45 minutes was all they could do. So it was a poignant finale to Emerson, Lake and Palmer before it briefly became Emerson, Lake and Powell, when Carl Palmer threw in the towel in favour of Cozy Powell.

MERRIWEATHER POST PAVILION

23 AUGUST 1996, COLUMBIA, MARYLAND

TOM FLAVIN

This was a multi-band concert with ELP and Meatloaf. Jethro Tull followed ELP and between some of the first songs, Ian was making comments about how the members of ELP still had all their hair. He said, 'God bless them …' then proceeded to pull his stocking cap off to reveal he had absolutely none left on his, prompting the crowd to laugh.

GREAT WOODS ARTS CENTER

26 AUGUST 1996, MANSFIELD, MASSACHUSETTS

RUSSELL BASTONI

Emerson, Lake and Palmer opened for Tull with a one-hour fabulous set. Tull opened their set with a fiery version of 'Aqualung', after which Ian Anderson commented that it was great following a band that still had all their hair.

STAR PAVILION, HERSHEY PARK

29 AUGUST 1996, HERSHEY, PENNSYLVANIA

STACEY LOOSEBONES

I saw Jethro Tull for the first time, playing in Hershey, Pennsylvania with Emerson, Lake and Palmer. Both bands were phenomenal. I heard Tull for the first time in 1989, when my brother played me 'Jack Frost and the Hooded Crow'. Since then, they've become my favourite band. I even named my son Ian.

ST GEORGE'S HALL

25 NOVEMBER 1996, BRADFORD, UK

RICHARD CONNELL

This was the *Aqualung 25th Anniversary* tour and the show was in aid of Shelter, the homeless charity. In the bar prior to showtime I gently wondered, 'What will Ian's voice be like tonight? It wasn't great in '91 …' The atmosphere instantly changed. How dare I question Ian's vocals? In the end the set included 'Bungle in the Jungle', with all its vocal leaps, the only time I have heard it live, and Ian's voice was great.

I loved hearing Jonathon Noyce and Martin Barre on recorders at the intro to 'Mother Goose' and was frustrated that, after the rest of the album in full, they only played a truncated version of 'Wind Up'. I was also frustrated (although not surprised, as it didn't make it onto the actual album) that they didn't play my favourite from the *Aqualung* sessions, 'Lick your Fingers Clean'.

I really thought I'd seen them for the last time.

DACORUM PAVILION

3 JUNE 1997, HEMEL HEMPSTEAD, UK

TERESA KUEMPFEL

I was clearing through some of my mum's old singles when I found 'The Witch's Promise'/'The Teacher'. I was 14 at the time and blown away. I was genuinely excited by what I heard. It turned out they were singles that belonged to her brother, my godfather. When I next saw him, he played me *Thick as a Brick* and I was then on a mission to buy all the albums I could. We actually saw them together at Hemel Pavilion in 1997. It was amazing. Now I am a devoted fan. There's nobody else like them.

Teresa Kuempfel found an old copy of 'The Witch's Promise'

COLISEUM

10 JUNE 1997, WARSZAWA, POLAND

LUKAS WAS

I am pretty sure I was dancing around to particular parts of the *Aqualung* album when I was just four or five years old while my father played it. When I played it myself, aged 11, the 'Aqualung' guitar solo, the percussion on 'Up to Me' and surrealistic sounds on 'Wind Up' were strangely familiar, and archaic memories started to fly!

But my Jethro Tull adventure really started around 1994, when the band was completing its *25th Anniversary* tour and Ian was working on his *Divinities* solo record. My mother recorded the 'Bungle in the Jungle' off a Polish classic rock radio station onto a cassette so we could listen to it in our car. I was truly impressed by the strength of Ian Anderson's vocals, Martin Barre's tasty guitar parts, the catchy melodies, and Dee Palmer's string arrangements. I had to ask my parents who we were listening to.

As someone born in 1983 in a Communist country, I missed all the glory years. In June 1996, three Tull gigs were booked for the band's first visit to Poland, including an open-air festival in Wrocław for which my mother and I bought tickets. A friend broke the bad news that the concerts were being cancelled because of Ian's accident in Lima and subsequent DVT issues in Australia. Can you imagine the warm salty tears on the face of this 12-year-old?

They came in 1997, and my first Tull show was very solid. I went with my father, brother, and mum's friend. It was an interesting set-list of very familiar songs but also rarities like 'Acres Wild' and 'Teacher', during which drops of the audience's sweat – which had condensed on the ceiling - poured onto the stage from the roof, to the surprise of Ian, the band and the crew. Yes, it was hot inside that circus tent. One of the roadies came out and mopped it up.

The band was in great form. Some people complained about the acoustics, but from my position close to the stage, it sounded really good. Or was I in shock and didn't realise?

GUILFEST, STOKE PARK

3 AUGUST 1997, GUILDFORD, UK

PEGGY DEAN

When Jethro Tull were playing our local park, I could hear them from my house. I'd just had my daughter and my son said, 'Stick her in the pram!' and we ran all the way to the park so we could watch through the fence. I was so excited, I couldn't breathe.

GRANT PARK CHICAGO JAZZ FESTIVAL/NATIONAL FLUTE ASSOCIATION CONVENTION

14 AUGUST 1997, CHICAGO, ILLINOIS

KEN LUCAS

I went to my first Jethro Tull concert in 1975. Over the years I have seen them 26 times, the most memorable of which being when they played the National Flute Association's free concert at Grant Park. It was a beautiful summer's night and the concert was at the bandshell in the park. Each act played three or four songs. James Galway and other flute musicians played songs like 'Birds in Flight' and Moonglow'. Jethro Tull closed the concert with 'Cross Eyed Mary' and 'Locomotive Breath'. What a way to bring down the house.

After the concert we went over to the Hyatt Hotel, which was hosting the National Flute Association convention, figuring that's where they might be staying. We were in the bar and before long Martin Barre walked in, so I went over, talked to him, and he signed my *Thick as a Brick* t-shirt. Then we walked to the other bar at the hotel and Ian Anderson was standing outside the convention hall. He talked to us and signed my shirt. Thank you, Ian and Martin, for being so nice.

The autographed shirt is now under glass, hanging on the wall, along with a set-list and ticket stub from a 2003 show in Fort Wayne, Indiana, where Ian handed instant cameras to people in the front row after he had taken their pictures. Pretty neat.

CHRIS GREEN

I was introduced to Jethro Tull courtesy of the Government of Québec, whose Ministry of Education decided 'Locomotive Breath' would be required for study by all Grade 11 music classes in the 1974/75 school year. But within weeks, someone discovered the word 'balls' appears in the lyrics (and not in reference to sporting equipment) and complained. The Government abruptly changed the required study piece to 'Aqualung'. I ignored the government and listened to the entire album about 500 times that year. Aged 15, I became a fan.

Two decades later, sometime in the 1990s, visiting Chicago, a friend and I were walking through Grant Park on our first evening in

Chris Green listened to Aqualung around 500 times in 1974/75

the Windy City. Off in the distance, we could hear a rock band playing … a rock band with a flute. I only knew of one such band but, come on, what were the odds? We gradually neared the band and what should appear out of the gloom but Ian Anderson and a small band, playing to a very appreciative audience of maybe 50. Apparently, he had been hired to play in the park by a flautists' convention that happened to be in town that week. I will never forget.

MUSICA IN CASTELLO, CASTELLO SFORZESCO

17 JULY 1999, VIGEVANO, ITALY

ANDREA FEDELI

1999 was a very important year for me. I attended my first ever Jethro Tull gig. I was young and went with my parents. The gig was in a wonderful medieval castle. The energy was overwhelming. This was a very different concert to others I was used to. At nine o'clock an attendant brought Ian's flute onto the stage, he lifted it to the sky and the audience went crazy. Then Ian took the flute and the magic began. A few months later Tull played a concert in Milan. It was a Wednesday and the next day I had school, but I couldn't miss the opportunity to see them again. A friend and I waited a whole afternoon for the gates to open and at the gig we were in front of the stage. I have attended many more Tull gigs since 1999, and I never miss an opportunity to listen to them live. Ian's determination and energy led me towards a career in music.

JONES BEACH THEATER

2 SEPTEMBER 1999, WANTAGH, NEW YORK

MICHAEL AXELBAUM

My father loved Jethro Tull and introduced the band to my brother and I at an early age. He would play 'Aqualung' on the way to the store and we'd stay in the car to hear the end of the song before we could get out. He'd play *Minstrel in the Gallery* and have a listening session in the basement. He took me to see Ian Anderson play at Carnegie Hall and encouraged my brother to play the flute in high school, because nothing was cooler than flute in Tull. My dad passed away in 2020 and on the anniversary of his death, as we pulled up to the cemetery, 'Locomotive Breath' came on the radio. It couldn't have been more perfect.

CENTENNIAL GARDEN & CONVENTION CENTER

2 OCTOBER 1999, BAKERSFIELD, CALIFORNIA

RACHEL WOLFE

Rachel Wolfe took her flute when she went to see Tull

I was first in line for tickets and got a seat, second-row centre. I could not have asked for a better view. I can't find the ticket stub, but still have the t-shirt. I even brought my flute and stood outside the stage door in hope of getting an autograph on the case. Alas, it was not to be.

I was first introduced to Jethro Tull as a child. Before I even started school, I was listening to the band. The rhythms, time changes and lyrics - that I didn't understand - made their way into my being. When I started studying music and learning flute, my models were not the classical musicians, but Ian Anderson and the way he makes his instrument speak. Not that I learned to play that way, but I absolutely love to listen to his fabulous playing.

Now that I teach music in primary schools, I've introduced my flautists to this music. I have to make sure the YouTube videos are school appropriate. One girl loves to try to imitate Mr Anderson's style, especially his eyes in the younger concerts. She'll burst out into random tunes, fingers flying, eyes starting and proclaim, 'I'm Ian Anderson!'She's in middle school now. I wonder what that teacher thinks of her?

Thank you so much for being such an inspiring group of musicians. I can't name a favourite song, as I love them all. Maybe 'Songs from the Wood', 'Skating Away', 'Thick as a Brick', and 'Solstice Bells'. Beautiful tunes, all.

CITY HALL

23 NOVEMBER 1999, NEWCASTLE, UK

PETER SMITH

It had been nine years since I last saw Jethro Tull. I'm not quite sure why, but I had lost touch with them and missed a few concerts, which I now regret. By this time the line-up had changed a little (again) to: Ian Anderson (flute, vocals), Martin Barre (guitar), Andrew Giddings (keyboards), Jonathan Noyce (bass), and Doane Perry (drums). They had just released the album *J-Tull Dot Com*. The new material displayed Eastern and World music influences, but as usual the concert featured a mix of Tull material from throughout their career.

I now realise how eclectic Ian Anderson's taste in music was and how he steered the band through many different incarnations and many different musical styles. Throughout this he was the guiding factor and clear leader of the band. This concert reminded me how great they were (and still are), and how much I had enjoyed their music. It was great to see Ian Anderson and Martin Barre in particular. Ian was ever the showman, although his voice was not as strong as it had been. Martin's guitar playing and quiet presence were as excellent as always. And they played classics like 'Living in the Past', 'The Witch's Promise', and 'Fat Man'. Great stuff. I was hooked again, starting to attend Tull concerts more regularly from this point onward.

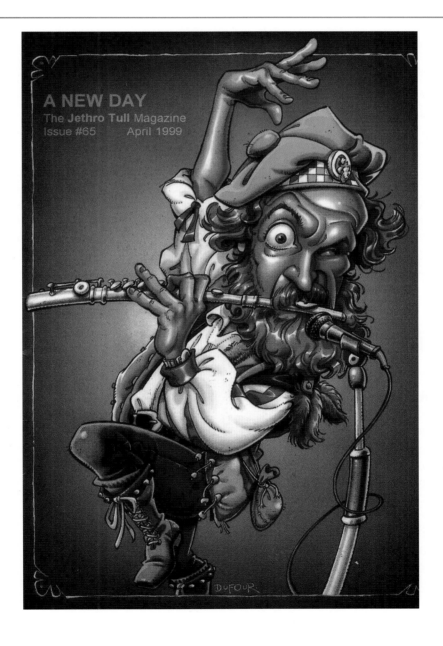

CITY STAGES FESTIVAL

17 JUNE 2000, BIRMINGHAM, ALABAMA

CAROLYN SWINNEY TRAPANI

This was a three-day event in Birmingham, Alabama. I was excited to see Ian Anderson and Martin Barre performing on the Hardee's Stage and was blown away by Ian's talent and energy and the excellent performance he gave us that night. I had no idea this would turn out to be one of the best live concerts I have ever seen.

BLOCKBUSTER PAVILION

2 JULY 2000, CHARLOTTE, NORTH CAROLINA

BRENT ROBINSON

In 2000, I was fortunate enough to do a phone interview with Ian while on-the-air at a small FM rock station in Asheville, North Carolina. He was charming and gracious as ever. Maybe, even a bit too verbose, I had to apologise and cut the interview short as I was truly doing my air shift and playing other music while recording Ian for a later playback. He gave me about 25 minutes of genuine, intelligent, humorous and what I believed to be honest answers to my queries. Meeting him, pre-show, backstage three days later is one of my fondest memories of being in radio.

DELAWARE STATE FAIR

22 JULY 2000, HARRINGTON, DELAWARE

FRED RIDLEY

Tull came to the Delaware State Fair. This show was great for me because I only had to drive 17 miles. The other great thing was that Joe Bonamassa was on first and played an excellent set, including a great version of 'A New Day Yesterday'.

When my son was born, we named him Jason Ian Ridley, after Ian Anderson. The men at the place where my wife worked knew he was a Jethro Tull fan. Their job was working

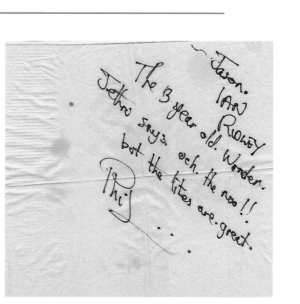

Fred Ridley's son has a set of autographs from the band

on emergency generators all over the country. They were in a hotel bar in Norfolk, Virginia when they met the lighting man for Jethro Tull. They told him about my son's name, and he got autographs from the band, who were also in the bar.

THÉÂTRE SAINT-DENIS

26 JULY 2000, MONTREAL, CANADA

DENIS CHIASSON

I arrived early to see them in Montréal at Théâtre Saint-Denis and decided to go in the coffee shop in front of the theatre. Waiting in line I realised Martin Barre was in front of me. After getting my coffee I went to his table to ask for an autograph. He was really nice and signed my ticket. I asked him what the first song of the show was going to be. He said, 'For a Thousand Mothers.'

After they played 'For a Thousand Mothers', Ian said, 'And now we are going to play 'For a Thousand Mothers'. Oh wait, we just played that. It was the first song of the show!'

Denis Chiasson got his ticket signed by Martin Barre

Denis Chiasson

FINGER LAKES PAC

28 JULY 2000, CANADAIGUA, ROCHESTER, NEW YORK

NIK MAGILL

I've been a Tull fan for over 20 years now. Tull was my very first concert. My best friend and I bonded over our love for the band when we were 15, back in 2000, and in 2019 created the first

Nik Magill does a Tull podcast with the friend he saw a 2000 show with

Jethro Tull podcast, which we proudly call *Talk Tull to Me*. There are now at least two more. Each week we discuss a track off an album in chronological order, one song a week, including bonus tracks and random bits and bobs. We started with 'My Sunday Feeling', and just recorded the episode for 'Living in These Hard Times', the bonus track off *Heavy Horses*. We've been fostering a growing and loving Tull fan community.

BALLOON FESTIVAL
BROOKHAVEN CALABRO AIRPORT

17 AUGUST 2001, SHIRLEY, NEW YORK

MARY ELLEN LARCY

My father and sister were at this concert on Long Island, New York. She was sat on his shoulders when Ian pulled out a disposable camera and took a photo of the two of them, saying my sister was the 'youngest attendee at a show'. My father was absolutely obsessed with Jethro Tull, which led to my four older sisters and I loving the band from as far back as we can remember. My father died in 2003, and it's still hard for us to sit through some songs, because we miss him so much. My sister has been longing for a copy of the photograph Ian took ever since. We don't have many photos of him, and this memory is an unbelievable experience that nobody else believes happened.

SOUTH SHORE MUSIC CIRCUS

22 AUGUST 2001, COHASSET, MASSACHUSETTS

JOHN MOSTACCI

I first heard Jethro Tull on the PA system when I was at Woodstock. The music was somewhat haunting and I wanted to hear more. When my father passed, it was the music from *Benefit* that got me through that period. Over the years I went to 33 concerts. In the mid-Seventies I started to film concerts with my Super 8mm sound camera. I was lucky enough to be friends with a person who sold tickets and was able to get seats in the third row, centre, perfect for filming. I would slice the footage together and invite friends to a 'Tull Night'. It was a blast. The filming went on for four or five years.

I never had any luck getting backstage until they played the Orpheum in Boston. I was invited to go to a soundcheck, where we met the band. I did not know you could take pictures. I remembered the old days, when Ian even paused during a sound due to the flashing of cameras. I had brought a disposable camera with a flash. As we talked and took pictures, he said the pictures would not come out. He was right. I vowed that if I ever had a chance again, I would be ready.

That chance came again during this small venue tour. At South Shore Music Circus, I got to take pictures with Martin and the next day at the Beverly North Shore Music Theater, three miles from my home, I got my redemption ... or so I thought. I managed to get a returned ticket at the box office – third row. I had to wait for them, so I sat for a few hours.

All of a sudden, the band pulled in, came over to me and asked if there was a beach nearby. They only had an hour to spare. We sat down and I listened to Perry, Giddings and Noyce. We took some great candid shots, including of Perry tweaking his nipples. We were standing in the parking lot and a car screamed through the ropes and jammed its brakes six inches from my knees. It was Martin.

When the boys went inside to get ready for the soundcheck, I was standing in the back and a limo pulled up. It was Ian and his wife. Out of the blue, Ian looked over, pointed to me and said, 'Do you want to take some pictures?' We took some shots together, and it was the perfect ending ... or so I thought.

My plan was to go to CVS, have the film developed in one hour, show the pictures to the manager, and maybe get them signed. But when I went to CVS, the person said, 'The developing machine broke and we lost your pictures. But don't worry, you will receive a free roll of film.'

I went to the show and had a great time. I brought a picture of Ian my sister took in 1977, found the manager smoking at a back entrance and asked if Ian might sign it. I waited 30 minutes and he came back with it signed.

I have a lot of great memories, thanks to Ian and the Tull boys. Now I am 70 and 'Too Old to Rock 'n' Roll, Too Young to Die.'

TINA PAINE

John's my big brother. After our dad died, when I was 11 and John 19, I looked to him as a father figure. As I got older, he let me tag along with him and took me to my first concert, Jethro Tull at the Boston Garden. I was the girl in school with the 'cool' brother, so not only do I equate Jethro Tull with great music, but also to the comfort and love my big brother gave me during that time.

PIER 6 PAVILION

31 AUGUST 2001, BALTIMORE, MARYLAND

DONALD WARNICK

Ian Anderson was playing flute with one leg propped up, resting on the opposite knee, as he has done so often. As the song concluded, he raised his flute

Donald Warnick remembers Ian channelling thunder from the skies

heavenward at the exact moment a burst of thunder rolled across the water and through the facility. Of course, the crowd went wild.

BARBICAN

16 NOVEMBER 2001, YORK, UK

PETER SMITH

My interest in Jethro Tull had been revived by the great show I attended at Newcastle City Hall in 1999. I was therefore quite disappointed when their 2001 outing missed out Newcastle, so I persuaded Marie to come and see them with me in York, the nearest show on the tour. Tull were on grand form as usual, and I enjoyed the show, although there were quite a few songs which were unfamiliar to me. At least four of the songs were Ian Anderson solo tracks. Ian had released three solo albums by 2001. Marie and I had a friendly argument about Ian's flute solos. When he started a solo, he would press a foot pedal. Marie was convinced that the solo was on tape and Ian was switching the tape on with the pedal. I was equally convinced there was no use of tapes, and the pedal was merely an effects pedal.

MEADOW BROOK MUSIC FESTIVAL

18 AUGUST 2002, ROCHESTER HILLS, MICHIGAN

MARK CIPOLLETTI

My most memorable Tull show, on the hill at the Meadow Brook amphitheatre, exposed to a very comfy, bugless night and Perseid meteor showers before moonrise. The second best? The surprise streaker on the *Under Wraps* tour!

In October 2002, Ian embarked on the *Rubbing Elbows with Ian Anderson* tour, combining live music and a talk show format.

PERISTYLE THEATRE

11 OCTOBER 2002, TOLEDO, OHIO

BARBARA DAILEY

Jethro Tull has been a part of my life since 1975. At the age of 74, I can remember all the words to 'Minstrel in the Gallery', but don't ask what I had for lunch yesterday. I saw Tull in concert twice and also played the kazoo with Mr Anderson in Toledo on his *Rubbing Elbows* tour. Even now, every once in a while, I *have* to listen to 'Minstrel in the Gallery' all the way through.

AUDITORIUM STRAVINSKI

4 JULY 2003, MONTREUX, SWITZERLAND

DOANE PERRY

Even if I went on stage sick, I tried not to let it show. Usually, I could transcend almost any discomfort during a show. I might feel terrible before and after but could usually muster my energy to get through the gig. The music would carry me and thankfully I generally wouldn't notice much physical distress that I might have been in until it was over. Ultimately, the audience probably doesn't care if you've been out on the road for months, travel was rough, you had a bad meal, not enough sleep, etc. That shouldn't be their concern, nor should they have to know about it. They've paid their money and perhaps waited quite a long time to see you perform, so it is our obligation to go out there and give everything we have … or we have no business being there.

In Montreux we were filming and recording a live album, released as the *Live at Montreux* CD and DVD, in addition to it being broadcast live across Europe, as it was the opening night of the festival that year. I refer to that gig as my 'kidney stone concert'. I'd always sweat a lot and occasionally get a bit dehydrated, and unfortunately also had a genetic propensity for developing kidney stones. I'd had them before. It is a deeply unpleasant experience, probably not dissimilar to being shot in the stomach with a gun, and it can be all consuming when it hits. I didn't tell anybody in the band because I thought it would unnecessarily worry them, and part of my job is to hold things together onstage. The day of the concert the pain really started ramping up and I thought, 'No, this *can't* be happening today.' The concert was done in two halves and I said to myself, 'If there is a God, please be playing attention, give me a hand, and don't strike me down in the middle of this gig.'

Prior to the concert, I tried my best to get into a zen-like state of mind and transcend my corporeal problem, but despite my best mind over matter efforts, I began to develop excruciating pain. Miraculously, I somehow got through both halves of the show. After the show, having temporarily dodged the worst of the stone bullet, I went back to my dressing room and dissolved, just so incredibly relieved that I did not get struck down mid-song, because when it really hits, you can't think about *anything* else. When I look at the DVD now, I remember how much pain I was in, but I actually played fairly well that night. I don't think I made any mistakes, somehow remaining reasonably focused.

The next day we had off in Montreux. Claude Nobs, our colorful promoter, had a little lunch for us at his chateau, and I felt well enough to go but began to start to feel poorly again mid-afternoon. I believe he called a doctor I saw when we went back to the hotel. But the next day, after traveling to Italy, I got taken to the hospital. We had a gig that night and I was worried it might get cancelled or that I could miss it entirely.

In the hospital while waiting to get wheeled in, I passed out from the pain and woke up four or five hours later. Hallelujah … *I'm cured!* I thought they had gotten the kidney stone, but bless those Italians - they had given me just enough prescription medication to make it so I didn't *feel* the kidney stone until after the gig. Somehow it must have gotten out into the crowd about what had happened, because at the beginning of the concert all the people lit their lighters the moment we came on stage, rather than traditionally at the end. Ian knew I was in a lot of pain and said, 'Look, if you get into trouble, just whack the snare drum a couple of times and I'll go into 'Mother Goose' or something.' But I got through it. The band kept turning around and looking at me, like, 'Are you okay?'. I was, but I was also on some serious painkillers.

It was in that moment that I realized how deeply embedded in my musical DNA the music of the band was, as I could still go onstage, play and navigate the complexities of the arrangements and not make any egregious mistakes … at least that I can remember. The band seemed a little surprised that I didn't fall apart. But … the Italians timed it just right, because about 10 minutes after we got off the stage and I was changing in my dressing room, the pain really kicked in again. The miracle cure was over.

Anticipating this, the hospital *had* given me a little brown paper bag, like you would put your lunch in, and it was filled with all kinds of wonderful and mysterious potions and elixirs, which they provided to keep me relatively out of pain. Thanks to them I got through the rest of Italy and Greece, then flew back home and had unsuccessful kidney stone surgery the day after I got back. I should have just stuck with the Italians' more reliable medical solution.

PALACE THEATER

5 NOVEMBER 2003, CANTON, OHIO

JOHN KISTE

The music of Jethro Tull has been part of my family for as long as we've been a family. When I married my wife Lonna, the organist claimed she could not play 'Skating Away' or 'Thick as a Brick', even though I had given her the sheet music, with lyrics. Thinking back, the dear old lady was probably uncomfortable with 'Your sperm's in the gutter ...' and 'Your pants were undone ...' My best man remedied all by exclusively blasting Tull on the tape deck as we drove around after the service – Hallowe'en 1981!

John Kiste and his daughter Gwendolyn remember trying to play kazoo to accompany Ian

I've seen some permutation of Tull or Ian Anderson 13 times, the last being in Greensburg, Pennsylvania, just before I had a double-lung transplant in 2014. There were strong odds I would not survive, but my son-in-law Bill had never seen the band live and very much wanted to go with us. He graciously pushed my wheelchair to and from the venue. Afterwards my body, just as graciously I thought, accepted the new lungs.

My favourite time seeing Ian Anderson was the *Rubbing Elbows* tour at the Palace Theater in Canton, Ohio. I was the county's head of tourism, and though I paid full price for our tickets, I used my position that one and only time to procure front-row seats. Ian wanted someone with whom to play 'Locomotive Breath' on the kazoos we had received. Many tooters were far more musical, but I played it straight and he put his arm around me and gave me his microphone. He also tried to get my daughter Gwendolyn to play, but though she could play bass guitar, piano and clarinet, she placed the kazoo in her mouth backwards, and dear Ian eventually gave up tutoring her to toot.

As we left the concert, I saw a fan I had met at other Tull concerts who shouted, 'That must have been awesome!' I replied, 'It was the greatest moment of my life', to which Gwendolyn sneered and said, 'What about the birth of your daughter?' ... to which I laughed and responded, 'Shut up and learn to play the kazoo!'

FERGUSON HALL TAMPA BAY PERFORMING ARTS CENTER

22 NOVEMBER 2003, TAMPA, FLORIDA

DEBBIE LIEBERMAN

To celebrate my husband Larry's birthday in 2003, I surprised him with front-row seats to the *Rubbing Elbows with Ian Anderson* show in Tampa, Forida. An avid fan, he was elated. Showing up in original vintage *Thick as a Brick* t-shirt, he was accosted by fans, who all wanted it off him. The show was fantastic, but what happened during 'Locomotive Breath' was a memory of a lifetime. Ian Anderson passed out kazoos to random audience members to play along. My husband was dejected he didn't get one. He sang along

Debbie Lieberman's husband saw Tull on the Rubbing Elbows tour

as if he was the performer. When the song was over, Ian leaned forward off the stage and handed his kazoo to my husband. You would have thought my husband had won the lottery.

HOMI BHABHA AUDITORIUM

31 JANUARY & 1 FEBRUARY 2004, MUMBAI, INDIA

AJAY MANKOTIA

Jethro Tull started touring India fairly regularly. I saw them at two concerts they played with Pandit Hariprasad Chaurasia, the greatest living master of the bansuri (the Indian flute) and met Ian on the first day. Then I saw them in Mumbai in 2006, and performing with Anoushka Shankar, daughter of Ravi Shankar, in New Delhi in 2008. My children, having heard Jethro Tull all their lives at home, insisted on coming along to this one, and seeing Ian in concert sealed the deal for a 19-year-old girl and 16-year-old boy. And I saw Ian play to a packed house at the Royal Albert Hall in June 2013 - *Thick as a Brick* in the first half and *TAAB* 2 in the second. Playing two albums back to back is no mean feat, and my respect for Ian, even without any headroom left, went up even more.

PALAIS THEATRE

7 MAY 2005, MELBOURNE, AUSTRALIA

AIDAN PHELAN

I was introduced to Tull by my dad playing a cassette of *The Broadsword and the Beast* when I was about 14. It left a mark. A couple of years later I started looking for more Jethro Tull music, because I wanted to hear what else there was. I discovered that when my mum was the same age Jethro Tull was her favourite band and she still had her copy of *Aqualung.* I put it on and even though the stereo was dodgy and the sound wasn't crash hot, I was hooked!

In my penultimate year of secondary school, studying media and film, for my major assessment I made a short film that was perhaps a little too ambitious, a medieval fantasy epic inspired by the song 'Broadsword'. But it turned out alright for something made with literally no budget on borrowed equipment from the school.

The first concert I ever saved up and made sure I was in line to get tickets for was Jethro Tull's show in Melbourne in 2005. To this day, it is probably the very best concert of any act I've seen. I manage to take some photos on a crappy old digital camera, so when my memory grows dim, I'll at least have those to jog it.

A few years ago, I was going through a really rough time, my father dying and my marriage falling apart. What helped get me through was *Minstrel in the Gallery.* Songs like 'One White Duck' helped me find a voice for the feelings I was struggling to express. Since then, I've often retreated into Tull's albums to help me through various rough patches. I find *A Passion Play* is the one that can get me through the roughest of times and which never gets old, no matter how many times I put it on repeat.

Ian Anderson's lyrics are as profound and deeply human as anything sprung forth from the Bard's quill. The seeming ease with which he can flit from the bawdy to the sublime is incomparable, and he always surrounds himself with the absolute cream of the crop where musicians are concerned. Tull's music, for the most part, has a timeless quality to it that many try to achieve and fall short of. Though it shifts and shimmers like a cuttlefish as members come and go, there can only ever be one Jethro Tull, and one Ian Anderson to captain the ship.

THEBARTON THEATRE

8 MAY 2005, ADELAIDE, AUSTRALIA

JACK WEBSTER, AGE 21

My dad tells a story of seeing Jethro Tull at the Apollo Stadium in Adelaide on the *Thick as a Brick* tour in 1972. The crowd were getting restless and tired of waiting and a jester walked out on the stage, wandered over to the microphone and started dinging his hat bell into the microphone. After a few minutes of this, as expected, someone shouted 'GET OFF THE STAGE', at which point Ian leapt from behind a speak stack and screamed, 'FUCK YOU, THAT'S MY LINE!', and the band then proceeded to rock the house down. A magician without a hat.

In 2005, I was working as a dish pig. The young lass who worked with me split her time working the kitchen and the counter at the local ticket sales office. When I heard Tull were coming to Adelaide and would be playing Thebarton Theatre, I couldn't believe it. Living in the bottom end of Australia, I never thought I would get the opportunity to see them live. I blew my whole week's wage on the ticket and when said young lass handed it over to me, she winked and told me I would love my seat.

When I turned up for the concert, I was working my way through the crowd out front and copping a lot of stares. I was the youngest attendee out of a crowd consisting of mostly 50 to 60-year-old Scots. When we got let into the theatre, I had my ticket in my hand and was winding my way through the aisles looking for my seat. Thebarton Theatre had a mixture of flat seating leading out from the stage, grandstands behind and alcove seating on the walls. My friend had picked me a seat behind the flat, two rows up and directly behind the sound box. It was the best seat in the house and my eyes and ears had the best night of their life.

I spent the first part of the night getting stranger and stranger looks from the people around me as I stomped my feet and sang my heart out with every song. Eventually I settled into the background for them, but I didn't care. No shame, no regret, I was having the time of my life. I started to despair when they left the stage and still hadn't played 'Locomotive Breath', but then the lights dimmed again, I heard that beautiful chocolatey piano lead in and I settled back into my seat. All was right with the world.

The *Aqualung* shirt that I blew another half week's wage on still hangs in my closet. My kids won't listen to Tull, and my wife's not a fan, but any time I'm out driving with my dad, it's the only thing to hit the speakers.

KOUKAIDOU

11 & 12 MAY 2005, TOKYO, JAPAN

CHRIS DIXON

I first encountered Tull in late 1982, shortly after I turned 17. I was attending an independent school in the UK and had been made a prefect over the youngest three grades. There was a prefects' room, and the custom was that each of the six prefects should provide something for it. My contribution was the most important: a toasted cheese sandwich maker. Somebody else brought a kettle, and Andy Rupp provided a record player. Andy also had a few LPs: Joni Mitchell's *Blue*, Neil Young's *Harvest*, and – more importantly – an album I didn't know by a band I'd never heard of, *Heavy Horses* by Jethro Tull.

Andy and I did not get on terribly well, so it was difficult for me to ask him if I could listen to said Tull album. So I waited until he was at class one day and had a free hour. I put this interesting-looking, clearly agrarian album on. Woah, blow my socks off or what? This is what I had been searching for. This was the stuff! I had been a Beatles fan since the age of 12 – who hadn't? – and conditioned by their genius into assuming there simply wasn't any other popular music worth listening to. Now I understood how wrong I was. This was something totally new. This was challenging, intricate, sophisticated, mature music, a bizarrely drab album cover giving no hint of the luscious, powerful, beautiful music inside. I wondered if anyone else in my class had any other Tull albums I could copy illegally to cassette tape? Yes, Mike (or Jules or Julian - he seemed to want to be called something different every week) had a veritable smorgasbord of Tull records, which I spent the next few weeks copying on the only record player the school had with a tape recorder connected to it.

But what the hell was this? Surely *This Was* couldn't be the same outfit. And *Benefit* was surely not by the same band that made *Heavy Horses*. So began a journey of discovery and pleasure I have walked for 40 years, and with news that we were about to be graced with not one but two new Tull albums, it was a path I walked with a newfound joy in my step. Just six short years after this Rupp-assisted life-altering epiphany I found myself, post-university, living in Japan. Struggling with the language and in a pre-Internet world, in those early years I missed a lot of band visits. It was not until May 2005 that I first saw Tull in concert, when they came to Japan and played two nights in a row (May 11 and 12) in a rather decrepit old venue in Shibuya, Tokyo, called Koukaidou (公会堂). And it was only recently, via *A New Day* magazine, that I discovered this was the same venue they played during their first visit to Japan, way back in July 1972. Plus, ça change ...

The line-up was Messrs Anderson, Barre, Noyce, Giddings, and Perry. On the first of these shows, we were so far up at the back that they were issuing oxygen tanks at the doors, but as this was the first time for me to see the very best band in the world, nothing could detract. During 'Mother Goose', the audience burst out laughing as one. Since the band were no bigger to my distant eyes than twinkling stars in the night sky, I had no idea what was going on. It was not until the following night, better seats having greatly improved my proximity to the action, that I understood the cause of this hilarity: Ian was doing his lead thing, the rest of the band lined up at the front of the stage and playing their recorders with their noses. I nearly peed myself.

Later, Ian Anderson toured *Thick as a Brick 2*, performing both *Brick* albums in their entirety, back-to-back. Talk about stamina! I saw this show on 16 April 2013 at Tokyo Dome City Hall, the last time I saw Tull or mainman Ian perform live in concert. But with the imminent release of *The Zealot Gene*, I was again on the edge of my seat with anticipation, albeit a little sad that Martin Barre was nowhere to be seen.

I remember once hearing Ian Anderson in an interview say something like, 'It's meaningless to me when someone comes up and says, 'Hey, man, thanks for the music; the soundtrack to my life', finding it a little strange he couldn't empathise with the joy people derive from his music. Surely there must be artists he loves and respects and whose existence has made his own significantly more enjoyable and satisfying. Whatever the case, this is how I feel about Tull's music. Through all the crap we have to deal with in life, the hardships and heartaches, disappointments and stresses, there is one constant that will never let you down; on the contrary, it will lift you up: the music of Jethro Tull.

And what of Andy Rupp? After a successful career in the City, he's now one of only 18 permanent members of the BBC singers. He and I were able to overcome our differences and have been good mates for many a decade now. He introduced me to Jethro Tull. How could we not be friends?

ANFITEATRO DE LA FERIA

31 AUGUST 2005, SAN SALVADOR, EL SALVADOR

ANTONIO ARREAGA

Antonio Arreaga saw Tull's first visit to El Salvador

Due to work, in April 2005 my family and I went to live in El Salvador. I was at a social gathering after work when a colleague commented, 'Do you know Jethro Tull is coming to El Salvador?' 'Seriously?' I asked. 'It's my favourite rock band since I was 15 years old!' When I got home, I told my wife.

Soon after, I was overly-excited to hear the concert's promo on a local radio station, with emblematic songs in the background including 'Living in the Past', 'Aqualung', and 'Thick as a Brick'. Fast as I could, I went to buy tickets, wanting to be as close to the front as possible. I bought tickets for my wife, a great friend from Guatemala who was also a fan, and myself. On arriving at the CD store, they told me the best seats available at that moment were $45 each and in Row G, central VIP. The first five rows were reserved for special guests.

The store was going to be selling CDs signed by Ian Anderson and if I wanted, I could have one set aside for signing. I asked them to put away *Crest of a Knave* for me, as that album was not in my collection. I hoped I might get to meet the band, and Ian in particular, and ask for an autograph or perhaps a photograph. But I had to make it happen. It was not going to happen because of a 'magic flute'!

Jethro Tull arrived in El Salvador a couple of days before the concert. A press conference was held and through that I found out where the band were staying. The day before the concert, I went with my wife for drinks at the hotel bar they were staying at and hoped Ian or one of the band might show up. I took some CD covers with me, just in case. Sadly, we didn't see any of them.

After work on the day of the concert, I went to pick up my friend who had travelled from Guatemala from the bus station. He left his things at my house and without further ado, the three of us headed to the venue. It did not matter that we had our seats numbered and reserved. The emotion of listening to our favourite band since adolescence was magnetic and drew us to this the musical encounter. Following my hunch, I took the same CD covers I had taken to the hotel the night before.

As it was still early, there were no other people in line. We handed over our tickets and went inside to our VIP seats. After a few steps, strategically placed to attract the attention of the fans, there was a kiosk where a couple of attractive young women were offering rum for sale. My friend, enthusiastic about the girls, went straight ahead to talk with them. I continued my way, leaving my wife a little behind.

Shortly before lining up to look for the seats, I could not believe what I saw.

Right there, alone, watching like a feline, at a distance from the kiosk and the rum-selling movement of the girls, was a man wearing a black staff t-shirt without anyone noticing him - Ian Anderson! People were going to their seats, not recognising him. I stopped a few feet from Mr Anderson, took the CD covers out of my bag and started walking slowly towards him. He was staring at me. 'Mr Anderson,' I said. Feeling finally discovered and realising my intention to request an autograph, he shook his head in denial and began to walk slowly towards the stage in search of his dressing room, his final refuge.

Not knowing what to do and what to say, I exclaimed, 'I am from Guatemala.' I don't know why I said that, and why would he care where a fan was from? But he stopped and said, 'I was in your country yesterday, I liked it a lot. I'll sign your CD.' I gave him one of the covers for the band's *20th Anniversary* CD trilogy. Within seconds there were three people around us, also wanting an autograph. He used the same pen I carried to sign for these people. 'It's really great that Jethro Tull has come to Central America,' I told him. As Ian had almost finished signing the autographs, my friend from Guatemala appeared, grasping Ian's elbow. He withdrew it firmly, indicating he did not want people making physical contact. Autographs over, he returned to his dressing room.

The concert began with 'For a Thousand Mothers' and carried on with 'Thick as a Brick', 'Mother Goose', 'Bouree', 'Budapest', 'Aqualung', and 'Locomotive Breath'. After the concert we went to celebrate, joining other friends who had come from Guatemala to listen. We didn't finish until around 3am.

Next day was a business day so, after a huge cup of black coffee, I went to my office to work. Before I sat down and turned on the computer, a colleague exclaimed, 'Antonio, you are in all the newspapers!' He showed me the two main newspapers of San Salvador and, in the concert reviews, my wife and I were in the photos.

A few days after the concert, I returned to the CD store where I had reserved a copy of *Crest of a Knave* with Ian's signature on it. 'In the end, Ian Anderson didn't sign anything for us,' said the man from the store. 'So it's lucky you got your CD cover autographed at the show.'

MAURICIO ZARRUK

If I were forced to live by myself on a desert island and could only choose one band's discography to listen to for the rest of my life, it would surely be Jethro Tull. I started with a *Best of* compilation, which left me numb. I remember being deeply affected by the song 'Heavy Horses'; Ian Anderson's lyrics constitute one of the most beautiful poems I've read, its melody unadulterated artistic expression at its highest level.

I live in Honduras, and in 2005 travelled with a friend to see Jethro Tull live in El Salvador. We got on a bus the day before to make our dream come true. Being then a newlywed and father of my firstborn son, I made the mistake of not buying a front-row ticket since I was

Mauricio Zarruk witnessed Tull's first ever performance in El Salvador

taking care of my money. This was my first big show outside my country and I didn't know what to expect. Now I regret not paying whatever the price was to see the band up close. The concert was cut short because of an incident generated by a fan who managed to climb on stage to get close to Ian, who was startled by this invasion of his space and decided after to play just a few more songs and leave. Still, I was able to see a little more than an hour of live music, and my soul was blessed. Jethro Tull's music is an integral, permanent part of my life and I hope wherever I go after I die, I can take their music with me, hopefully for eternity.

MASSEY HALL

4 OCTOBER 2005, TORONTO, CANADA
LORNE MURPHY

I saw Ian hop out of a taxi to head into the venue for the soundcheck. He was already late. Jon Noyce ran inside, but Ian stopped for a few moments to chat and allowed my wife to take a photo. Great memory!

Lorne Murphy met Ian outside Toronto's Massey Hall

CITY HALL

3 MARCH 2006, NEWCASTLE, UK
PETER SMITH

I saw Jethro Tull at the City Hall in 2004 and 2006. Tull were involved in a number of projects during these years. In 2003 they released the *Jethro Tull Christmas Album*, a collection of traditional Christmas songs, along with some more they'd written. The album was a big success and their bestselling release since *Crest of a Knave*. The set for the 2004 concert included quite a few Christmas songs as well as some old favourites like 'Beggars Farm' and 'Nothing is Easy', taking us right back to the very early days. I went with Norm Jones and Will Gillum and we enjoyed seeing the old guys again.

In 2005 Ian Anderson released live double-album and DVD, *Ian Anderson Plays the Orchestral Jethro Tull*. A DVD recorded live at the Isle of Wight in 1970 and a live album, *Aqualung* Live (recorded in 2004) were also released in 2005. There were further lineup changes in 2006, bassist Jon Noyce leaving to be replaced by David Goodier, and keyboardist Giddings leaving to be replaced by John O'Hara. The 2006 tour was billed as the *Aqualung* tour, Tull playing that LP in its entirety. They were accompanied by electric violinist Lucia Micarelli for this tour, and she fronted the band for a couple of songs, notably covering Queen's 'Bohemian Rhapsody' and Zeppelin's 'Kashmir'. Electric violinists featured alongside Ian on a couple of Tull tours around this period. The 2006 concert was a sell-out, proving the band retained their popularity and they still have a loyal fan-base.

BILKENT ODEON

22 JUNE 2006, ANKARA, TURKEY

CENGIZ BOZKAYA

When Ian Anderson played with Bilkent
Youth Symphony Orchestra, I was there
with my son, Deniz.

MERRILL AUDITORIUM

30 SEPTEMBER 2006, PORTLAND, MAINE

CHRISTOPHER DELISLE

*Cengiz Bozkaya and his son, Deniz, saw the
orchestral Tull in Turkey*

I first experienced Jethro Tull when I was around 10. My big brother Darryl took me
to a rope swing for a swim in Rutland, Massachusetts. He had a Westfalia camper van
with *Thick as a Brick* on 8-track. I was enthralled, becoming a lifelong fan.

   I took my teenage son Ian - in part named for Mr Anderson - to see Ian at the
Merrill Auditorium in Portland, Maine. It was his tour with a 15-piece chamber
orchestra. The room was amazing, one of the best halls I've ever seen a show in. I was
in the cheap seats for a classical show there once, and you can hear a triangle from
the balcony.

TOWN HALL

4 APRIL 2007, MIDDLESBROUGH, UK

PETER SMITH

In 2007 came the release of *The Best of Acoustic Jethro Tull*, including some of the
band's best known acoustic tracks from 1969 onwards. To promote the album, the
band toured an acoustic show which called at Middlesbrough Town Hall, an historic
and lovely old venue with a great hall which can be set out in either standing or seated
format. This evening we were all seated, as befitted the quieter, softer form of the
concert. Norman Jones, Bill Gillum and I had seats quite close to the front and we all
wondered what this acoustic format would be like.

   The lineup of Tull for this tour was Ian Anderson, Martin Barre, David Goodier,
John O'Hara, and James Duncan Anderson. They were accompanied by special guest

violinist Anna Phoebe, one of a series of electric violinists who joined the band over this period. Ian would have great duets, which became almost duels between himself on flute (and, of course, on one leg) and the lady on violin. Excellent.

I'd grown to like the folkier side of Tull as time passed, and I certainly enjoyed this gig, which presented a mix of songs from throughout the band's career via the softer, folkier acoustic side of the band, befitting the ornate surroundings of the Town Hall.

THE LUNA PARK

20 APRIL 2007, BUENOS AIRES, ARGENTINA

JUAN IGNACIO QUESADA

I discovered Jethro Tull back in 1989 when I was 17. A friend had several records featuring prog rock, which I was getting into and he had no clue about. Among them was *Thick as a Brick*, so I borrowed it, played it when I got home, and loved it from the first listen. Those first minutes with the acoustic guitar and Ian's voice and flute got me - who on earth writes a 45-minute rock 'song'? – and I started buying all the Tull albums I could, beginning with *War Child*.

After that I went to every concert Jethro Tull did in Buenos Aires, Argentina, the last one being in April 2007. This one was almost a miss for me. I was having issues with my right knee and, after an MRI, the doctor concluded I needed surgery for ligament repair. We scheduled the surgery for 20 April, and the day after I learned Jethro Tull was coming to Buenos Aires. I went to buy tickets for me and my wife, and when I arrived home, she said, 'You have your surgery that day!' My response? 'Screw my knee, Jethro Tull is way more important.'

So there we were that day, not at the hospital but at Luna Park Stadium, Buenos Aires, on Row 20, once again watching Ian Anderson, Martin Barre, and the rest of the band. That was the first time I heard Tull playing with a violinist. There's a bootleg of it, *Aqualuna*, which sounds amazing because it's recorded right from the mixing board.

And the knee? Well, I had the surgery a month later, and it's totally fine now.

PATRICIO BERNABÉ

I'm a big fan since 1968 and have seen the band live many times in Buenos

Patricio Bernabe has seen Tull several times in South America

Aires. I also had the chance to speak briefly backstage with Ian after one show. He's a true gentleman and a wonderful musician.

WASSERSCHLOSS KLAFFENBACH

8 JUNE 2007, CHEMNITZ, GERMANY

MARTIN WEBB

Martin Webb was invited onstage with his newly-purchased digital camera

I have genuinely lost count of the number of Jethro Tull and Ian Anderson shows I have attended over the last seven decades. Inevitably, some are more memorable than others, perhaps because of an unusual venue, the live debut of a new band member or a new song, or some onstage or offstage incident. And very, very occasionally you have an out-of-body experience you subsequently doubt could actually have happened. But you know it did, because you've got the photos.

One such extraordinary moment in my longstanding Tull fandom occurred in June

2007 in the picturesque, cobbled courtyard of moated 16th century Saxon castle, Wasserschloss Klaffenbach, near Chemnitz, Germany (it's so much more attractive than Manchester Apollo...).

The evening began unremarkably, as I stood in the front-of-stage photographers' pit alongside the local press, adorned with my official photo-pass and listening to promoter Alex's familiar list of rules - first three songs only, no flash, don't stray beyond the marked point, etc. I was a tad excited as, after years of using film, I had finally succumbed to the lure of digital and was debuting my new Canon EOS 400D with f2.8 28-105mm lens. On a previous tour I had been in a similar front-of-stage position in Luxembourg when a pro photographer with a lens the size of a bazooka looked at my camera, raised an eyebrow and, a little too kindly, said, 'Hmmm, useful for learning on at art college.'

In Chemnitz, on strolled Ian Anderson and Martin Barre for a bluesy 'Some Day the Sun Won't Shine for You', followed by the rest of the band for a lively 'Living in the Past', at the end of which Ian ran to the photographers, pointed at me and beckoned, saying: 'Martin, come here ...' Oh, gawd! My life spiralled before me, as I wondered whether I'd accidentally been using flash without realising, or was standing in the wrong place, or had been committing some other photo-pass faux pas.

He said, 'Martin, can you do me a really big favour, and come up on stage and take some photos of Martin and Doane?' Well, you don't argue with that, do you? I ran round to the side, hotly pursued by the promoter, who hadn't heard what Ian had said, through security, up the stairs at the back of the stage, and popped up in front of 2,000 people.

Production manager Chris Archer calmly inquired, 'What are you doing here, Martin?' 'Er, I don't really know,' I said. Martin Barre then spotted me and deadpanned, 'Martin, grab a guitar - you're on next!' He also pointed meaningfully at me while instructing Chris to keep an eye on his bottle of wine ...

I started taking pictures of Martin Barre and Doane Perry as instructed, although I was very confused. A couple of songs later Ian took advantage of a guitar solo to pop over to the side of the stage and explain that there was a live DVD coming out of the 2003 Montreux Jazz Festival show, and he needed extra photos for the cover/insert, particularly of Doane, who tends to be hidden from 'first three songs' photographers behind his expansive drum kit. Ian said I could shoot the whole show, and go anywhere on stage 'for the first and last time ever!' Wow.

What a good job I now had digital camera - a week or so earlier, I'd have had to say, 'Sorry Ian, I've run out of film.' In fact, a couple of songs later I was crouched down, lining up a shot, and was suddenly aware that Ian was peering over my shoulder. 'Aaaargh,' he shrieked, 'you've gone digital! No excuses now, Martin' Right, no pressure, Ian.

Meanwhile, my mates in the audience were naturally puzzled as to why *A New Day* fan magazine's chief/only photographer was onstage, waving his fancy new lens at the drummer. So naturally they tried to find out. There I was, carefully positioned to one side of Doane, when my mobile phone went off! For a brief second, I thought it would be really cool to answer it. Then I realised it would be one of the least clever things I'd ever done at a Jethro Tull concert, and I hurriedly switched it off.

Now, I'm sure many of you are wondering what it's like being onstage with Jethro Tull. Well, I have to admit the gig itself largely passed me by, as I watched a lot of what seemed like an extended drum tutorial through the viewfinder. But it was extraordinary how quiet it was up there, a bit like listening to a CD with the volume at number six. It was perfectly possible to chat to the band without raising one's voice – indeed, I was concerned during one of the acoustic numbers that my stage left conversation with Doane would be audible to the audience. It was also great fun to be able to see the audience – possibly also a bonus for the band, it being an outdoor gig in the June dusk rather than an indoor gig with blinding spotlights – and to get a feel of what it's like to play to that many excited people. There was also a palpable sense of onstage professionalism, teamwork, and enjoyment. In a history of rare privileges accorded to me through my *A New Day* associations, this truly was reet champion.

Inevitably there is a sadly predictable punchline to the tale. Ian subsequently advised me that the DVD company had decided instead to use grabs from the film recording to illustrate the cover, which is what they should have done all along. Frankly, that was something of a let-off, as my fledgling digital efforts had been more miss than hit, as I peered uncomprehendingly at the array of buttons scattered around the camera's body – although not all was in vain, as there were enough successes to grace the pages of the less discerning *A New Day*. Of course, within weeks I was totally digital savvy, and haven't looked back, embracing upgrades 'n' all. But Ian was true to his word when he said I'd be snapping onstage 'for the first and last time ever.' My chance of a lifetime came just too soon. And, totally extraordinary though it was, I do know I didn't dream it — because I've got the photos to prove it.

TOWN SQUARE

30 AUGUST 2007, SIBIU, ROMANIA

ILYANA IVANOVA

I saw the band for the first time by chance on TV in my youth and was intrigued by the untypical musicianship and performing. And, of course, it was love at first sight. Later, in 2007, I was on a trip with my sister in Romania and we visited Sibui to find that our favourite band was playing a free show that very day.

PARAMOUNT THEATRE

30 SEPTEMBER 2007, SEATTLE, WASHINGTON
LISA CARPENTER

I first heard Jethro Tull in my dad's truck as he drove me to school. I was a kid in the Nineties and got to listen to a lot of his favourites from his youth. Jethro Tull was definitely amongst them. I grew up playing flute in the school band (all the way through college, where I studied music) and I loved playing Ian's solos from a book I still have today. I first saw the group live in Seattle in 2007. My then boyfriend (now husband) and I took our first road trip together, and we had a blast. I've been to concerts before but couldn't remember being so excited for one, I suppose because my love of Jethro Tull had built up for so long before I could finally see a show. It meant an awful lot to me.

Lisa Carpenter was at the Paramount with her boyfriend (now husband)

Now I'm a mom with a toddler of my own and I get to pass down my good taste in music down to her the same way my dad did with me.

The 40th Anniversary tour featured a variety of special guests and one-off appearances by former Tull members.

COLSTON HALL

18 APRIL 2008, BRISTOL, UK
SETH LAKEMAN, SINGER-SONGWRITER

I was first introduced to Jethro Tull quite late in my teens. I was hanging out with a good musician friend, a massive fan, and he played me *Aqualung*. I was blown away by the musicianship and songs. 'Locomotive Breath' was a first favourite, but I loved the interplay between them all. The real sound that blew me away was Ian's voice and his melodic flute. It certainly planted a seed for me and my future. The way an instrument like that could be used in such a progressive and groundbreaking way. Later, in my thirties, I dived much further into the Tull catalogue with my father-in-law. He has a real encyclopaedic knowledge of the band and really showed me the full extent of their sound. They totally blew me away. We went to see them in Bristol on

CITY HALL

8 MAY 2008, NEWCASTLE, UK

PETER SMITH

2008 was Jethro Tull's 40th anniversary year, and they toured extensively to celebrate this momentous occasion. The tour featured special guests on some of the dates, former Tull members Mick Abrahams, Clive Bunker, Dave Pegg and Barrie Barlow putting in appearances at various venues. Jeffrey Hammond attended one of the gigs but did not appear on stage with the band. A few non-Tull members also joined as guests at some of the gigs, including Greg Lake, Seth Lakeman, and Fish.

There were no special guests at the Newcastle gig, the band being joined by Heather Findlay (vocals) and Brian Josh (guitars) from Mostly Autumn, who started the show with four songs, and were joined by Tull for two of these. The Tull set was, unsurprisingly for an anniversary tour, a selection of songs from throughout their career. This was a great show, with heavy use of video images from the early days. Ian's voice was also pretty good, much better than some of the times I'd seen him recently.

HEATHER FINDLAY, MOSTLY AUTUMN

It wasn't until the mid-Nineties that I saw the *Top of the Pops* performance of 'The Witch's Promise'. I'd just left art college and was getting into playing live music. Though I knew of the song from its radio airplay growing up, I'd never actually seen who created the song. I remember being both instantly mesmerised and a bit disturbed. What was I watching? Who was this incredible Dickensian character? I later learned this was Ian Anderson, who reminded me very much of Catweazle, who I'd loved watching repeats of in the Eighties as a kid. I was covered in goosebumps and a seed of inspiration had been planted.

A couple of years later, I was beginning to get into the Rolling Stones, collecting everything I could, and whilst watching the *Rock and Roll Circus*, there they were again – that band, Jethro Tull! The goosebumps were back. I bought *Songs from the Wood* immediately, and *Stand Up* and *Benefit* a little later.

In the early 2000s, a friend gave me his Tull CD collection, which he was replacing with remastered versions. I remember particularly getting into *Broadsword* and

Crest of a Knave around that time and, much to Angela (Gordon)'s delight, no doubt influenced by my copious Tull listening, began adding bountiful flute breaks to everything I was writing. A lot of songs written at that time ended up on the Odin Dragonfly *Offerings* album, as did our own cover of 'The Witch's Promise'.

Not long after this, Mostly Autumn signed to a record label that were also working with Uriah Heep, Caravan, and others. On one occasion, Bryan Josh and I were invited to a Uriah Heep show in London where Ian Anderson was making a guest appearance. Our record company boss told us to meet him at a restaurant in Leicester Square before the show. We walked in and were shown to a table of many. There were our friends Heep, some record company/industry people and, to my youthful (and secretly giddy) disbelief, there seated at the head of the table ... was Ian Anderson, Himself. I didn't manage to muster up the courage to say much to him personally, but quietly enjoyed the honour of dining with someone who had become such an influence in my world with his poetry, eccentricity and musicality.

Later in 2008, myself and Bryan Josh were invited to tour with Jethro Tull as their integral guests. We opened for them each night, playing a couple of songs on our own, followed by one where Ian Anderson would join us, then the rest of the band would join us for our final number. At the end of the night, we were invited back on stage to perform 'Locomotive Breath' with the band as their closing number.

For fans of Tull at heart, we were awestruck. On accepting the offer, Ian asked us to provide a selection of songs which we felt might be suitable for himself and the band to join us for. I couldn't believe my luck, but the two songs Ian chose to play with us were two songs I had written, 'Yellow Time' and 'Caught in a Fold', full of flute flourishes and inspired by him, of course. The whole band made us feel so welcome. I loved every second of that tour. Looking back, it must have been like playing a part in a dream ...

BRYAN JOSH, MOSTLY AUTUMN

I've always thought music is more than just hearing it. It's a soundtrack to our lives, merging seamlessly into memories. I vividly remember, back in the mid-Seventies, lighting a fire in an old quarry in the Lake District and my brother playing *Stand Up* on repeat. This was my first memory of Tull, and I was totally blown away. It was like hard rock, blues, folk and jazz, but totally unique. No one else sounded like this. For me it was like the music came from the earth, a magical flute-wielding minstrel mystically taking the listener on a journey. The rest is history - we acquired album after album, staring endlessly at the album covers. Every camping trip had Tull on in the background, and still does now.

When we were invited to share the stage with them for a tour, it blew our minds, especially when they joined in on some of our own songs. A privilege such as this is rare in a lifetime and will always be treasured. I raise a glass to the living legend that is Jethro Tull.

GRAND OPERA HOUSE

11 MAY 2008, YORK, UK
RICHARD CONNELL

This was a much better song variety and selection than the *25th Anniversary* tour, and the great way they projected images of old press cuttings around the venue was superb. It was also the last time I heard Ian's voice on top form, which was a real treat. In the bar I chatted to a chap who, like me, was wearing a *25th Anniversary* t-shirt. He remarked, 'We wouldn't want anyone thinking we only turn out to see them every 15 years, would we?' I suspect I may have seen them more often than him.

JONES BEACH AMPHITHEATER

9 AUGUST 2008, JONES BEACH, NEW YORK
DANIEL ADLER

I only saw Jethro Tull one time, at Jones Beach Amphitheater in Long Island, New York. Peter Frampton was the opener. Because it was the group's 40th anniversary, the setlist focused on the early years, the first four albums in particular. While he had trouble hitting some of the high notes, Ian Anderson's flute and guitar playing were still top of the line. For this show, the usual quintet was turned into a nonet with the inclusion of a string quartet that turned the usual rock 'n' roll ambience of Jones Beach into Carnegie Hall, especially when they did 'Bouree'. It was as if the ghost of J.S. Bach was conducting from backstage.

Other highlights included Doane Perry's drum solo on 'Dharma for One', the cocktail jazz of 'Serenade to a Cuckoo', Ian belting out the harmonica on 'Song for Jeffrey', and 'A New Day Yesterday', Martin Barre's electrifying guitar solo on 'Aqualung' and an instrumental version of the rarely performed 'Sossity; You're a Woman'. In all, Jethro Tull gave it all they'd got on a beautiful summer night overlooking the Atlantic Ocean, the aroma of saltwater mixing with the sounds of good ol' rock 'n' roll music.

MUSEUMSMEILE

24 AUGUST 2008, BONN, GERMANY

BERNARD MICHALAK

I was 16 in 1981 when my parents moved house. I bought *Heavy Horses*. Although there was a lot of new wave and punk and young Bowie playing in my room, I was stunned by 'Rover', 'Heavy Horses' and, of course, 'Moth', which alleviated my homesickness.

In 1983 I went away without my parents for the first time, travelling with two friends from Germany to France, where we spent three very chilled weeks in Brittany. One of my mates had *Living in the Past* on tape, and I played it over and over.

In 1986, I was riding pillion with my brother when we had a quite serious motorbike accident. During the next two years I had around 20 surgeries and spent around four months in hospital. On so many

Bernard Michalak saw Tull in Bonn in 2008 after being a fan for years

nights when I could not sleep, I was glad 'Nursie' was there on the sensational *20 Years of Jethro Tull*, a present from my niece's husband. And at university, *Thick as a Brick* came over me like a landslide. This would be my desert island disc.

Not your average concertgoer, I saw Tull for the first time live in 2008. Everything I wanted and hoped that music could be was provided by the flute and this unbelievable artist. Thank you, Ian. You lit up my life and will do so until I die.

AVO SESSION FESTIVAL

15 NOVEMBER 2008, BASEL, SWITZERLAND

DOANE PERRY

At one point I developed some heart issues and got hospitalized for that back home in Los Angeles. Getting out of the hospital, I didn't initially have much energy to play but knew I had to go to Europe to do this tour. For the first time in a long time, I hadn't played in four or five weeks, which felt like an eternity. I may have practised a day or two in my studio prior to leaving, just to make sure I hadn't forgotten everything, but I was still not feeling great. Like the *Live at Montreux* concert, the AVO

Session (the first date of the tour) got filmed for a DVD, and it was another one where I was greatly relieved I had gotten through relatively unscathed. It was a test drive of how well my heart was going to be doing ... and I passed the driving test.

IL LAZZARETTO

4 JULY 2009, BERGAMO, ITALY
LEANDRO PESSINA

The first time I saw Jethro Tull live, I was only 14. It was an outdoor gig and that night we had an incredible storm. We seriously risked the cancellation of the event, but luckily the rain stopped and we were able to enjoy a wonderful concert. I was very close to the stage border, and it was an incredible experience. Sadly, it lasted only 40 or 50 minutes, because of the delay caused by the weather.

Leandro Pessina has met Ian a couple of times

I met Mr Anderson after one of his solo concerts in Milan in 2015. I discovered the exit door for musicians, and waited in the company of Florian Ophale and Greig Robinson, substituting for David Goodier. When Mr Anderson arrived, people waiting for him were invited to form a queue. I gave him my flute case to autograph. He made a nice comment while I was trying to formulate some words to say thank you. I was extremely embarrassed. Everything was so quick.

And in 2017 in Brescia, I had a backstage pass and met Ian again. We had 15 lovely minutes where we spoke about everything except ... Jethro Tull! We talked about geography, the environment, (Ritchie) Blackmore's Night, and Renaissance music instead of *Aqualung* and *Thick as a Brick*. Moreover, I believe he appreciated that I never entered his personal space: no hands on his shoulder during the photo or similar. The last thing I wanted was to appear like an annoying fan. I think he liked our chat, because when I left, he made the first move to shake my hand. I consider myself very lucky. I don't think many people can say they 'made the clasp' with Mr Anderson.

THE CRESSET

15 SEPTEMBER 2009, PETERBOROUGH, UK

RUPERT BOBROWICZ

This was billed as an Ian Anderson concert and not Jethro Tull. I'd last seen Jethro Tull in 2006 at Peterborough's Broadway Theatre, where I saw a somewhat ageing band, with Ian's vocals not as powerful as in his younger days. The new material used included a flute rendition of a well-known Led Zeppelin song, and a Queen song. I was somewhat reluctant to pay for a ticket in 2009. But as the date of the concert came closer, I began to yearn to attend. What sort of concert would this be? Would Tull band members be participating? What music would Ian be doing? Imagine my delight when, a few days before, Helen said she would get me a ticket.

I was over the moon with anticipation and began looking forward eagerly for the venue to begin. *This Was* going to be a special evening, and as I had a ticket for a seat there would be no need for me to *Stand Up*. This was definitely for my *Benefit*.

Arriving at the venue I took a shortcut through the Cresset pub to gain access to the main foyer. It was buzzing, with a refreshments table, bar, and the usual t-shirt stand. My ticket showed 'F23' and the seat was just past the soundcheck desk on the middle end of the left row, a fabulous seat near to the stage by the front of the hall.

On the stage as a backdrop was a large black curtain, in front of which were a pale teak-coloured keyboard/organ (similar in style to John Evan's old brown Hammond organ), a black stool with a couple of tilted microphones for a guitarist, in the middle front of the stage another black stool with a tall microphone stand with a small empty container strapped to the side (to accommodate a thin musical instrument), a third stool and, on the far right, a drum kit with a single bass drum. Gone are the days of the double bass drum.

A shadowy figure came across the stage, sat on the middle stool with a guitar and in the darkness we heard a synthesized sound coming over the PA and some faint words being spoken, followed by the amplified acoustic guitar. Instantly I recognised the first song from the *Stormwatch* album, 'Dun Ringill'. 'Great,' I thought. 'Ian is playing Tull music and especially a song I wanted to hear live, which I hadn't seen live before.'

The spotlight was on Ian as he continued the song, but only the guitar could be heard. I glanced round to the sound desk, where it appeared to be panic stations. Meanwhile those at the back started to whistle and jeer. Was there going to be a riot? Ian, either oblivious to the problem or sticking to a tight schedule, having started 10 minutes late, continued to play. The sound problem was rectified after a minute or so and there was a big cheer from the audience, followed by rapturous applause at the end of the song.

The second song was 'March the Mad Scientist', part of the A-side of the 'Solstice Bells' extended single, not one I expected to hear live. Another short song, but well received. I wondered how many in the audience knew this. The next song, 'Just Trying to Be', was taken from the *Aqualung* era but never quite made the album, and had Dave Goodier on wooden xylophone.

Prior to the fourth song, Ian stated that he about to play the first song he ever wrote about climate change, 'Skating Away on the Thin Ice of a New Day'. He dedicated the next song to a former Tull bass player, adding that he called the current bass player 'Number Seven', being the seventh bass player in line. It was 'Jeffrey Goes to Leicester Square', another song I never heard played live. This was turning out to be a really good concert. It was followed by the *Broadsword*-era 'Jack-a-Lynn', which fitted in well with the new line-up.

'Back to the Family' followed, which Ian described as one of the most difficult songs he'd written and a live rarity. I thought this *Stand Up*-era song would sound strange without Martin Barre and Glenn Cornick, but the new line-up mastered it well, with a slightly different guitar interpretation for the end passage. A classical electrified acoustic guitar does not have the same effect as full-blown electric guitar, but it worked.

After 'Pastime with Good Company', an instrumental with some good flute playing, the concert continued with a new piece, 'Tea with a Princess', an extended version of 'Fat Man' with a good instrumental passage, and wound up the first half with 'Rocks on the Road'.

When the lights went down for the second half, a guy stepped forward to check the main microphone, receiving a cheer when it checked out okay. Ian reminded the audience that when Tull started, they were a blues band, and began with 'Someday the Sun Won't Shine for You', with Ian on harmonica. 'Serenade to a Cuckoo' followed, Ian starting and finishing with cuckoo noises on the flute.

'Mother Goose' was introduced as a 'whimsical one', then we got two new songs, Florian with a wonderful piece of mixed tempo (flamenco-style) guitar called 'Andantino' whilst the other group members watched or took a break, and something called 'A Change of Horses', although Ian admitted the title had changed a few times. This was another lengthy piece, and well received.

Ian announced that the next song was probably the oldest they played, 400 or 500 years old. Adapted from J.S. Bach, and Ian thought he might approve. After a somewhat extended musical introduction, the familiar flute sounds of 'Bourée' came across the PA. The next song was at first hard to distinguish without introduction, but soon developed into the recognisable 'My God', with Ian's flute solo faultless.

They finished with a revamped version of 'Aqualung', Ian extending the original by several minutes. He ran back onto the stage with flute in hand for an encore of 'Locomotive Breath', with a bluesy flute intro before steaming along to the middle section and a bluesy keyboard normally found at the beginning of the song. John O'Hara did his John Evan 'Cheshire grin' impersonation, after which Ian finished the song to rapturous applause amidst the cheerios.

And that was it. What an evening! One that will stay in my memory for all time.

CITY HALL

27 MARCH 2010, NEWCASTLE, UK

PETER SMITH

Norm, Will and I are long-time fans of the band and must each have seen them 15 to 20 times. The City Hall was, as always, packed full of ageing rockers to see Ian Anderson and crew. We had a quick look at the support act, but retreated to the bar, saving ourselves for the delights of Tull. The band took to the stage around 8.40pm and started with Ian on a small acoustic guitar playing 'Dun Ringill'. The set was a mixture of old songs, with quite a few from *Stand Up*. As always, the band delivered, Ian as lively as ever and giving us some great flute playing. It was great to see him still out there doing it at the age of 63! A night of some fine rock and great nostalgia for us; roll on next time.

MICK BATEY

My son absolutely loved *Aqualung* from being little. His first live gig was Tull at Newcastle City Hall at the age of 10. He was awestruck, and I was so proud, as I indoctrinated him. He was so excited at seeing Ian's moves on stage. He was in his element as virtually everyone who passed us told him to enjoy himself. He still talks about how welcome he felt. He's still a big fan of Tull, in between his love of hardcore West Coast rap. Slow shake of the head …

GYPSIES GREEN STADIUM

17 SEPTEMBER 2010, SOUTH SHIELDS, UK

PETER SMITH

This gig had been set up as a special one-off appearance tied in with the *Great North Run*, which was being held that weekend. Martin Barre was running in the race, and thus the opportunity must have arisen for the band to play. The concert was in a large marquee set up within the grounds of Gypsies Green Stadium.

Tull came on around 8.15pm, the massive marquee pretty full, devotees having travelled from far and wide to see the band. First up was 'Nothing is Easy', followed by other early classics such as 'Beggar's Farm', 'Nothing Is Easy', 'A New Day Yesterday', 'Songs from the Wood', 'Bourée', 'Thick as a Brick', and 'My God'. The set centred around the classic Sixties and Seventies albums, closing with 'Aqualung' and the usual encore of 'Locomotive Breath'. Norm and I enjoyed it more than other recent Tull shows, perhaps because of the different venue.

OPERA HOUSE

24 SEPTEMBER 2010, YEREVAN, ARMENIA

ARVIN MAGHSOUDLOU

I met Ian and his band very briefly after his concert in Yerevan, Armenia in 2010. Yes, that is former Armenian Prime Minister Tigran Sargsyan (a huge rock fan) behind us.

SOUTHAM HALL, NATIONAL ARTS CENTRE

17 OCTOBER 2010, OTTAWA, CANADA

JACQUES CANTIN

Arvin Maghsoudlou met Ian when he played with the Yerevan Symphony Orchestra in Armenia

My greatest Tull moment was actually an Ian Anderson moment, when my favourite artist of all time took a few moments after a show at the National Art Centre to autograph my copy of *Thick as a Brick.* I was hanging around the exit of the indoor garage parking garage after the show with very little hope of catching Ian on his way out. At first, I got the chance

Jacques Cantin has his wife to thank for this photo

to catch Florian Opahle, having a cigarette before heading out to the tour vehicle. Florian was very friendly and allowed me a photo op with him. A few minutes later, out walks Ian Anderson, taking some fresh air before heading out. While I was talking to Florian, my wife said, 'Isn't that the guy over there you hope to get an autograph from?' I was almost in a state of shock ... there was Ian Anderson in flesh and blood, mere metres away.

Ian was super-nice and really down to earth. To him, this gesture was probably not a big deal, but to this lifelong fan (since *This Was*) it was a big, big deal. I have the picture framed on a wall in my music room. Every time I look at it, I replay that magical moment in my mind. Thank you, Ian Anderson!

BLEÚ CLUB

24 MAY 2011, MEXICO CITY, MEXICO

ANTONIO ZAMUDIO

I remember falling asleep listening to 'Bungle in the Jungle', 'Skating Away' and many other songs (including a short version of 'Thick as a Brick' – I thought that song was only four minutes long!) on my old Discman. In 2011 I finally had the chance to see these songs performed live when I learned Ian Anderson would be in Mexico. I couldn't afford it – I had barely enough money to support myself – but thought, 'When will he return to Mexico? It's now or never, I have to be there,' and bought the cheapest ticket available when I got paid, even though it meant I would run out of money before my next payday.

Antonio Zamudio saw Ian at the Bleú Club in Mexico City

That night was magical. I had a good place on the second level, right in the centre, with no one to obstruct my view. The performance of the band was excellent. It was when they played 'Thick as a Brick' that I discovered the song lasted longer than four minutes.

Luckily for all of us who enjoyed it, the concert lasted longer than expected. I had to call a friend to come and pick me up after the show because the subway had already closed, and we got lost on the way back because he didn't know the way and I only knew the way by subway.

I could not afford to buy a drink or any memorabilia. But from that incredible night I still have my ticket, and of course the best memories. These are worth more than any souvenir and this remains one of the best concerts I've been to. The band has not returned to Mexico since, so I don't regret deciding to go, making sacrifices to be there that night. Thank you, Ian, for such a wonderful night at the Bleú Club. You have given me memories that will never be erased.

CHICAGO THEATRE

11 JUNE 2011, CHICAGO, ILLINOIS

MICHAEL GILLETT

I took this picture outside the Chicago Theatre in Chicago, Illinois prior to an *Aqualung 40th Anniversary* concert. There was a large group of Tull fans waiting to be let in and none of them noticed that Doane and Martin had come out for a breath of fresh air. Only after I asked if I could take their picture did the fans catch on. That said, one lad kept calling Tull's drummer 'Don Perry'. I wanted to give him a slap.

Jethro Tull's drummer, Doane Perry, Paul Hammer (Hammer Guitars) and guitarist Martin Barre. Photo: Michael Gillett

CHATEAU STE MICHELLE WINERY AMPHITHEATRE

18 JUNE 2011, WOODINVILLE, WASHINGTON

ANON

My wife and I love the Jethro Tull song 'Dun Ringill' from *Stormwatch*. We became curious about the lyrics, and their meaning. It was back in the early 2000s, and we searched for

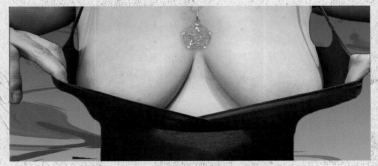

'Dun Ringill' nearly inspired the revealing of naked flesh

'Dun Ringill' on the internet. We learned that it is an ancient Pict ruin on the Isle of Skye. Coincidentally, we were keen on visiting Scotland so hatched a plan to go on a quest to find the mythical Dun Ringill. At the time, hits on that search term were few and there was just one grainy picture. We could not find a map or directions of where it was on the island.

Finally in 2007, our quest began. On the way to Skye, we ducked into Inverness Library. Helpful librarians got caught up in our excitement when we two American tourists described our little quest to find this obscure little spot which none of them had heard about. We pored over maps until we finally found it, a little blip on a map that didn't really show side-road names. We got our photocopy and left for Skye.

The locals we quizzed on Skye had no idea about it. In fact, we learned that ancient ruins were of little interest to the locals. They were too pagan. So we thought we were on our own. On the big day we had also booked an excursion to the Cullen Hills via boat, after which we would search for Dun Ringill. The guide mentioned that Ian Anderson once owned a resort that was visible as we sailed along. On the return trip, I asked the guide about Dun Ringill. He didn't know about the ruin. But when I explained where it probably was, he immediately knew how to describe the turn we needed to take from the main road. He said Ian once owned a house in the tiny village of Kilmarie, right near the area on the map of Dun Ringill. Now, it was no wonder how the song was inspired. Our guide spilled a lot of gossip about Ian, well beyond what we asked about. Sorry Ian, now we know more than you probably wished we did.

Unlike most days we were there, this was a beautiful warm day. We found the road to Kilmarie, parking by the side of the road near a footbridge over a creek that spilled into the sea. The path opened to a field of tall grass, through which someone had mowed a path. Part of the time walking barefoot on the wet spongy velvet green, we followed the path, scanning the shoreline for Dun Ringill ... until we spotted it. And nobody else was there for as far as we could see. We found our way to the top of the ruin, where soft grass had taken root. The sea was lapping against the rocks, and the sun was beaming down. Oh, and I took her quickly, on Dun Ringill.

Four years later, we learned Jethro Tull was performing at the Chateau Ste. Michelle Winery in Woodinville, Washington. We were so excited. Before the concert, I wrote to the fan club, never imagining Mr Anderson would read it. I wrote something like, 'We're excited to see you play at the Chateau Ste. Michelle Winery. Be warned, there are a lot of pagans out here in the Seattle area. If you play 'Dun Ringill', you might just see women taking off their clothes and dancing.'

The day of the concert arrived. It was sold out, everyone happy to be there. But for some reason, the crowd was practically sedated, everyone sitting on their arses watching. Several times, Ian admonished the crowd to show some life. The venue tends to discourage people from standing during concerts there, because it's just a terrible grass lawn with bad visibility. On other occasions when we have attended that venue, people would just ignore the rule, but not this time.

But, oh my God ... About midway through the concert, Ian announced that they had just dusted off an old tune for this night. And he feared it might inspire some naked pagan dancing (in language much more witty than I precisely remember). Holy shit! He read the email. They're playing 'Dun Ringill', and now it was necessary for my wife to show her tits! We had talked about it before, and she said that, in the very unlikely event he played that song, she would flash her tits for the band. But everybody is just sitting there like it's a church service. And Ian deserves to see my wife's tits, but how can she do that in front of this crowd? There was no safety in numbers.

She would have needed to walk in front of the stage, as everyone was sitting at a safe distance watching the show and expose herself as she walked by in front of everybody. In retrospect, she would have found the courage to do it, and it probably would have livened the place up. But in the moment, it was just too much. She was sooooooo close, but couldn't overcome the circumstances she was facing. So we sat through our favourite song, which we are sure was probably only played for that specific set, and never at any other event that year, because it was kind of obvious they hadn't played it in a very long time.

Ian, if you are reading this, we are so sorry. And so flattered that you played our favourite song. If we ever meet you, you would be welcome to ask to see my wife's amazing tits, and no doubt she would oblige.

AUDITORI MARC GRAU

9 JULY 2011, BARCELONA, SPAIN

LUIS DELGADO

Ian was attending a meeting with the Spanish fan club, the Tullianos, and dedicated a few minutes to talk to them and sign discs and pictures. I told him I had nothing for him to sign but had a present for him. I presented him with a print of my girlfriend. She was a classical flautist and the print showed her playing a solo standing on one leg, imitating Ian. She was a big fan of Jethro Tull. Ian was very interested and asked me a couple of questions, even though he was not talking as he had a concert that afternoon. The other musicians, John O´Hara and Florian Ophale, liked the print too. Ian took it up to his room. I wonder if he still has it?

Luis Delgado attended the ninth 'Tullianos' convention

349

SAGE

19 SEPTEMBER 2011, GATESHEAD, UK

PETER SMITH

Ian now seemed to be touring endlessly, sometimes with Tull, sometimes solo. I would have much preferred to see a full Tull show, but a chance to attend a show by the great showman flautist in the smaller, more intimate Hall 2 at the Sage was not to be sniffed at. The set was a mixture of old Tull favourites, lesser-known tunes and a few classical pieces. All of these were done largely acoustically by Ian, a keyboard player and guitarist, Florian Opahle. Florian was a pretty slick guitarist, and with Ian's flute playing, the smaller band setting allowed him to play longer solos than in the context of a Jethro Tull show. It was good see him again, and Norman Jones, Bill Gillum and I met up with our old Tull mate, Doug Walker.

On reflection, Ian performing solo was a signal of what was to come. He was soon to be regularly performing full Jethro Tull shows without Martin Barre and eventually to become Jethro Tull himself, to all intents and purposes. Martin Barre went on to lead his own band, performing his own version of old Tull classics. What went on between them – if anything – has never been revealed. Such is life in the strange game of rock 'n' roll.

CITY HALL

17 APRIL 2012, NEWCASTLE, UK

PETER SMITH

I went with Norman Jones, Bill Gillum and Doug Walker to see Ian Anderson and his merry band play *Thick as a Brick* and *Thick as a Brick 2*, the latter just released by Ian. I was late getting away from work, so arrived 10 minutes after the 7.30pm start time and missed a small part of the show.

It was in two parts, the first set being the old album and, following a short interval, the new album played in its entirety. Ian assembled an excellent band and the show was very theatrical, one guy playing the part of Gerald Bostock, singing quite a lot of the vocals. The additional singer was a good move, giving Ian a break from singing at times. The show was supported by video and the use of props, coming over very well indeed.

The situation around Ian Anderson and Jethro Tull was somewhat confusing, to say the least. While it appeared that Jethro Tull have not formally split, Ian was doing more and more things as solo projects, and Martin Barre had started his own band, New Day, featuring Tull songs in their set. It also seemed strange that Ian had chosen to revisit *Thick as a Brick* and treat it as a solo project, when Martin Barre had been so intrinsic to the Tull sound for so long. This point notwithstanding, we all agreed this was the best we had seen Ian Anderson or Jethro Tull for some time.

CHUMASH CASINO

18 OCTOBER 2012, SANTA YNEZ, CALIFORNIA

JAY RUBENSTEIN

I have been attending Tull concerts since the mid-Seventies. Two really stick out – the orchestral Tull concert at Royce Hall, UCLA, and the *Thick as a Brick 40th Anniversary* tour where I drove to two shows, at Santa Ynez and Long Beach, to watch *Thick as a Brick* played in its entirety. I have told my wife on many occasions that 'Thick as a Brick' is my all-time favourite song and that, when I die, all she has to do is play that one song.

Jay Rubenstein particularly remembers the Thick as a Brick 40th anniversary tour

CHRISTMAS CONCERT
ST BRIDE'S, FLEET STREET

15 DECEMBER 2012 (also 2006, 2007, 2008, 2011) LONDON UK

IAN ANDERSON

I had played in a couple of churches over the years as part of other people's efforts. Greg Lake asked me to accompany him and play the flute on 'I Believe in Father Christmas' at St Bride's Church. I was well aware of his song from hearing it on the radio every year and I'd known Greg from the ELP days, when they were on tour with us. I thought, 'Yeah, that would be fun.' The curate of St Bride's was the newly-ordained George Pitcher, ex-journalist of some repute who had written for both *The Observer* and the *Telegraph*, so both sides of the fence. George was anxious that I should come back and do a fully-fledged Jethro Tull Christmas concert, which I agreed to do.

We played a number of concerts in St Bride's and on one of those occasions Marc Almond, who had recently recovered from some terrible accident, showed up and did a spoken word thing, the beginning of a friendship with Marc. He's played with me on many Christmas concerts since then at cathedrals, and indeed other notable guests have kindly come along to perform as well. It spread from St Bride's to Exeter as the first bona fide medieval cathedral I played.

I've played in Catholic establishments under the radar a number of times in Europe, and that's a little more tricky. You're not supposed to do that sort of thing in the Catholic church by edict of Rome back in the Eighties. You shouldn't be playing anything beyond the strictly religious canon of approved Catholic music, and you shouldn't be charging money for tickets. But if you're raising money to keep the roof on or fix something after an earthquake, as I have in Italy, I think the rules have to be bent.

Once you become aware of the significance of performing in these ancient and magnificent buildings, it's a bit of a badge of honour to be part and parcel of supporting the ongoing reality of the physical place of worship, even if you don't go along with the detail of religious worship and prayer and everything that goes with it. I'm not drawing people in to experience some Damascene moment where they suddenly become born-again Christians. If it happens, it happens. If it doesn't happen it's just an entertaining secular concert, although I do try and find the right balance between the spiritual Christian Christmas and a secular concert.

In honour of Greg, who passed away some years ago, I continue to play and sing 'I Believe in Father Christmas', which to me is one of those songs, rather like my own 'A Christmas Song', which rather points the finger at the secular side of Christmas and the degree to which perhaps the spiritual side of Christmas has been lost for most people.

PALÁC LUCERNA VELKÝ SÁL

21 NOVEMBER 2013, PRAHA, CZECH REPUBLIC

BILLY LEITCH

Billy Leitch and Barbara saw Tull in Prague

I was born in 1951. I remember well the explosion of rock bands when Led Zeppelin, Black Sabbath and many more were breaking through. Jethro Tull was one of these bands and I was totally enthralled by *This Was*. *Stand Up* and *Benefit* also made me appreciate the genre. I didn't manage to see Jethro Tull in their heyday but have been many times since. I saw the *TAAB 1 and 2* concert in the UK. *Thick as a Brick* is one of the finest pieces of music I've ever heard.

My best memory is going to a concert in 2013 in the Lucerna Theatre in Prague. My partner uses a wheelchair but could walk very short distances. When we arrived, we found out that the theatre was old and had five or more flights of stairs to the auditorium, with no lift. It reminded me of the cover of the *Minstrel* album. The concert was sold out, with a lot of people waiting to get in. We were spotted by the band's security or roadies, who could see we were struggling to get in. They came over to ask if we required their help. They then asked us to wait a while until it quietened down. They were so helpful and friendly and managed to get my partner to her seat, albeit with a couple of sit-downs on the way. They said if there was anything we needed, to simply wave over to them and when the concert was finished to wait and they would ensure we got out safely.

The concert was fantastic, mainly due to the superb Tull line-up but also to the theatre being perfect for the *Thick as a Brick* experience.

True to their word, the 'helpers' arrived to assist us out of the theatre. I don't know how true it was, but they said they asked Mr Anderson if we could use the private exit behind the stage. They got us safely out of the theatre thanks to their kindness and caring attitude. I said it had been a fabulous concert and they said it was the same at the previous concert in Brno, where the audience reaction was brilliant.

I've never had the pleasure to meet Ian Anderson, but he remains my favourite performer, mainly due to the uniqueness he brings with the music of Jethro Tull, regardless of the line-up.

BRIGHTON DOME

28 APRIL 2014, BRIGHTON, UK

MATT SMITH

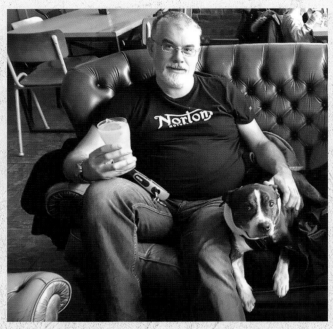

Matt Smith was introduced to Tull by his friend Dan

I came to Tull at a fairly early age. Back in the tail end of the 1970s, I had a great friend called Daniel Shires. He had moved with his family from Doncaster, following his father's job, and they bought a house just down the road from where I lived. Dan was aged nine, the youngest of three boys. His two brothers were much older; 16 or 17. Dan used to knock around on his bike looking a bit bored, and so it was that we got talking and became buddies.

After a while it was common to find us at each other's houses, and of course Dan's was much more interesting, as his brothers had cool stuff like a Honda CB175 and a Yamaha FS1E, an Atari games console, a Soda Stream, air pistols, and an old black Squire Strat that was rumoured to be Noddy Holder's old practice guitar.

They also had quite big record collections and their influence rubbed off on Dan, who was a bit older than his years because of his brothers. Dan would quite often pull out an LP from his brothers' collections. One day, he played 'Too Old to Rock 'n' Roll, Too Young to Die'. I have no idea why, but this song struck a chord with me and has remained one of my favourite Tull tracks to this day.

Dan's family had a VHS video recorder and not long after playing 'Too Old ...', Dan produced a Tull video his brothers had hired from the local video rental shop. 'Too Old ...' was on the tape along with tracks from *Stormwatch*. I was utterly spellbound and not long after, Dan played me 'Flyingdale Flyer', as one of his brothers had just purchased *A*.

I couldn't get enough of Tull at that point: I was 10 or 11 but very aware I was listening to some very grown-up music. More than that, the songs told stories of places I wanted to go to and things I wanted to know more about. When Dan realised he had a fellow convert, he opened up the stops and we spent hours listening to Tull. The two albums we played the most were *Heavy Horses* and *Songs from the Wood*, followed closely by *A*. I started buying my own copies of Tull albums, but my go to favourite was always *Too Old to Rock 'n' Roll: Too Young to Die!*

As I moved through senior school, I would often cycle the mile or so home at lunchbreak, slap *Too Old to Rock 'n' Roll: Too Young to Die!* on my Philips music centre (purchased from Argos with my birthday money) and listen to as many tracks as I could get in before I had to fly back to school. As both parents worked, I often had the house to myself during these lunchtime sojourns, and very distinctly recall listening to 'The Chequered Flag' and really feeling the melancholic, almost nostalgic sadness of the verses, and almost tear-choked chorus with its defiant line, 'Isn't it grand to be playing to the stand, dead or alive?'

I've been a fan now for knocking on 44 years, and fortunate enough to see Tull five times over the years, mostly at Portsmouth Guildhall (and thank you, Ian, for coming to play regularly in a city many bands seem to want to ignore). But the most memorable time was at the Brighton Dome, where the sound quality of the live gig was absolutely like listening to a CD recording. Every instrument was clearly audible in its own right, not overpowered by thunderous drums or drowned by thrashing guitar. It was just a perfect evening listening to songs that have been old friends to me for over 40 years. And of course, Ian's chat to the audience between songs has always made me feel like I just want to go and sit in the corner of a country pub somewhere and nurse a pint or two while nattering away with him about steam trains, or country ways lost to history, or some old mate we once knew who crashed his Triumph Bonneville up on the A1 by Scotch Corner.

To all members of Tull, past and present, thank you for the music.

SAGE

13 SEPTEMBER 2015, GATESHEAD, UK

PETER SMITH

The touring band known as Jethro Tull seemed to have been shelved, with Tull frontman and our manic flautist hero Ian Anderson touring under his own name, and Tull guitarist Martin Barre doing likewise. But Ian Anderson couldn't keep away from the Tull moniker and concept for too long. So, as 'a tribute to the original 18th Century agriculturalist', whose name the band borrowed back in February 1968, our hero had 'imagined a scenario where the pioneering pursuit of improved crop-growing and farming methodology might apply to the world of today and tomorrow.' This led to the development of *Jethro Tull: the Rock Opera*, the delights of which Norman Smith, Bill Gillum and I experienced at the Sage, Gateshead.

Anderson's rock opera concept was to take the story of the original farmer and inventor Jethro Tull and bring it up to date, telling that tale through the songs of Jethro Tull, the band (with a few new ones written especially for the occasion) and creating a theatrical stage show which took the audience through the story.

The show was very much that – a 'show' rather than a concert. The band provided the music, playing in front of a giant high-definition video screen. On the screen appeared a cast of 'virtual guests' who played the parts of Mr Tull and his family, narrating the story and singing segments of the songs.

Anderson explained it thus: 'Instead of spoken introductions to the songs in the show, there will be the use of that operatic device, the 'recitative', where the links are made by short sung vocal segments in a usually simple musical backdrop.' So, the songs were sung in part by Anderson live, and in part by virtual singers on the screen. The songs flowed from one to the next with short video segments as bridges.

The show started at 7.30pm prompt. Parking problems made us a little late, and we had to wait outside until 'a suitable break in the performance', i.e. after the first song, *Heavy Horses*, was finished. The first half was around one hour and there was a short interval before the show resumed.

How did it work? Very well actually. The video was high quality and the sequencing between Anderson and band and the virtual singers was faultless. Anderson's voice may not be quite as strong as it was back in the day, so the use of video allowed him some vocal rest, and gave welcome variety to the performance. However, Ian's flute playing remains as excellent as ever, and his stage presence and antics were undiminished. In terms of the virtual sets, we were transported onscreen to Preston station for 'Cheap Day Return', and deep into the forest for 'Songs from the Wood'. Great Tull fun.

A special mention has to be made for Unnur Birna Björnsdóttir, whose vocals were exquisite and made for great reworkings of Tull classics, particularly 'The Witch's Promise', and Florian Opahle, whose guitar playing was tremendous. A very different and highly enjoyable Tull evening.

THEATERHAUS

27 SEPTEMBER 2017, STUTTGART, GERMANY

BARRY GOLDBERG

My most memorable opportunity came in 2017 when I was invited to attend Martin Barre's 70th birthday parties at the Bayerischer Hof in

Munich, Germany, as well as at his favourite restaurant near his home in England, and at his home. I had to pinch myself to convince this was for real. I then learned that Ian Anderson was going to be performing *Jethro Tull: The Rock Opera* in Stuttgart a couple of days before Martin's party in Munich. I reached out to James, Ian's son, and asked about the possibility of attending the show in Stuttgart. For the umpteenth time, James went above and beyond, providing me with great tickets and backstage passes. And I sat next to Florian Opahle's mom, Renata, and Hubert. We partied well into the night. To this day the details remain foggy.

Martin's party in Munich was simply incredible. His band played well into the night, and the party continued into the morning hours. The next day, I travelled with Martin and the band back to England to celebrate his 70th year in style. Simply an incredible week on the other side of the globe. To this day, it remains the most incredible sequence of events I've ever experienced (besides the birth of my children).

In 2020, I was fortunate again to see Jethro Tull, this time in Barcelona and Madrid, Spain. And again, James Anderson outdid himself, setting me up with backstage passes. I can never thank James, Ian and Shona, Martin and Julie Barre, or any of the band members and crews through the years that have allowed me to accrue so many memories by allowing me into their lives enough. I am blessed.

At this point in my life, there is 'no way to slow down'. And my brother never saw again that *Aqualung* album that I 'borrowed' from his collection over 45 years ago.

TEATRO BRADESCO

10 OCTOBER 2017, SÃO PAOLO, BRAZIL
ANTÔNIO CARLOS

I became a fan after watching the 'Too Old to Rock 'n' 'Roll' music video on MTV in 2007. I was living through a very tough period in my early 20s, all third world socio-political issues aside. Failed attempts to establish a career in music was draining all my hope. During this period, I befriended Camila, who shared the same passions in life and music. When Tull's Brazilian tour

Antonio Carlos meets Ian Anderson. Photo: Camila Veilchen

was announced, Camilla asked if I was going to the São Paulo gig. I said I couldn't because I was broke. She said she would help me out.

On the day of the gig, I arrived at the theatre early, met old friends, had a beer and laughed a lot. The gig was splendid, and I cried a few times because it was my very first time watching Ian Anderson and company. And then it was like Christmas came early that year, as I was invited to go backstage. I entered the room with Camila, her sister and brother-in-law. I am not normally shy, but I was shaking.

Ian entered and chatted with us all. My anxiety passed and we started goofing around. Ian and I joked about each other's hair. I told him I would willingly cut some of my hair to give him a hair transplant. Some weeks later, Camilla told me Ian had sent her an email saying I reminded him of himself when he was young.

That simple comment made me feel reborn and gave me the strength to return to my musical career. It made me want to work hard to make my dreams come true and, most importantly, make sure I never miss a Jethro Tull gig ever again. The connection I have with the art of Ian Anderson helped me overcome many obstacles.

IAN ANDERSON CHRISTMAS CONCERT
DURHAM CATHEDRAL

14 DECEMBER 2017, DURHAM, UK

PETER SMITH

Ian Anderson's Christmas concerts have become a regular part of his calendar. Each year he plays a few of these concerts at selected cathedrals around the country. This time we were lucky enough for him in the majestic surroundings of Durham Cathedral. The concerts take a similar format; a mix of festive songs, songs from the *Jethro Tull Christmas Album*, often a special guest, and a selection of Jethro Tull favourites.

I turned up on a cold winter's night in a taxi with Jackie my carer, dropped right at the door of Durham Cathedral. I was greeted inside by my friends Norman Jones and his sister Barbara, and our old friend Doug.

Durham Cathedral is a wonderful venue for a concert. The audience were seated in the pews in the central nave of the cathedral, with the stage in front of the high altar. I was seated in my wheelchair in the aisle at the end of a row, around halfway back, with a good view of the stage. Ian was accompanied by the rest of his 'Jethro Tull' band.

The concert was in two halves; the first set opening with festive classics 'God Rest Ye Merry Gentlemen' and 'Gaudete', the latter made famous by Steeleye Span. This was followed by a selection of tunes from the *Jethro Tull Christmas Album*, including the great single, 'Ring Out, Solstice Bells'. The highlight was a performance of Greg Lake's' 'I Believe in Father Christmas', and the set ended with the beautiful flute solo, 'Bourée', written by Bach and featured on Jethro Tull's *Stand Up* album.

After a short break, the second set featured Ian's friend Loyd Grossman playing his former punk band Jet Bronx and the Forbidden's single 'Ain't Doin' Nothing'. The set ended with Tull classics 'My God', a particular favourite of mine, 'Aqualung', and closed with the inevitable encore of 'Locomotive Breath'.

Ian was on great form all evening, entertaining us with his usual anecdotes and some excellent flute playing. I couldn't think of a better way of spending a cold Christmas evening than one with old friends, festive music, and Ian Anderson and his band playing Jethro Tull classics. A great start to Christmas.

BRADFORD CATHEDRAL

15 DECEMBER 2017, BRADFORD, UK
JOE ELLIOTT, DEF LEPPARD

I first discovered Jethro Tull, like most people I guess, when I heard 'Living in the Past', probably on the Dave Lee Travis show on BBC Radio 1 way back in 1968. The main difference between me and most people though is that I was only eight years old. A couple of years later my mum came back from town with the five-track single, 'Life's a Long Song', and a lifelong love affair with the music was born. I would further my Tull education throughout my early teens thanks to the likes of *Aqualung* (still one of my favourite albums of all time), *Thick as a Brick* and even - right in the middle of punk - *Songs from the Wood*. My first encounter with the band live was at Hammersmith Odeon on the *A* tour in 1980. Since that time, I've managed to catch them twice in Dublin, a blessing for me considering by then my heavy work schedule meant being in the right place at the right time was always increasingly unlikely ...

Cut to 2017 and I had the opportunity of joining Ian on stage for a fundraiser at Bradford Cathedral, where I got to perform two of the songs from the aforementioned five-track single, an unbelievable honour for me and a closing-the-circle moment for sure. Yes, my life would be a lot poorer if it wasn't for good ol' JT!

BLACKPOOL & THE FYLDE COLLEGE

2018, BLACKPOOL, UK
SOPHIE GORNER

In 2018, Jeffrey Hammond exhibited a collection of his observation landscape paintings at Blackpool and the Fylde College. In an interview with me, a degree student and Jethro Tull fan, Hammond discussed his decision to move away from the

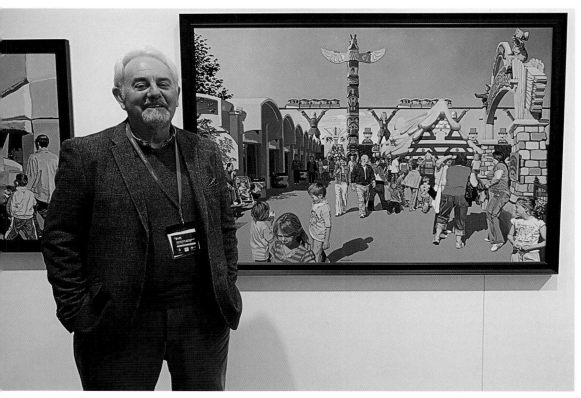

Jeffrey Hammond during an exhibition of his art at Blackpool and the Fylde College. Photo: Sophie Gorner Photography

music scene, stating his heart was no longer with music and he wanted to concentrate on his painting.

Although he did love touring, loved being a part of the band and being creative, Hammond didn't see music as his full life path. He remained in contact with the band and always wished them luck in their future endeavours. Travelling the country, especially the Lake District, Hammond used his surroundings as the backdrop for his art, photographing the tourist hotspots then painting them with vibrant colours, adding crowds to give them edge, even hiding himself in some of them, like a 'Where's Hammond?' Each painting took Hammond three to four months to complete, adding minor details and making his art photo realistic.

Hammond is a true gentleman and was happy to chat about Jethro Tull and his artwork. He found it hard to leave the band, but with his heart no longer in it he decided to move on, opening a space in the band for someone who was dedicated heart and soul.

BARCELONA AIRPORT

2019, BARCELONA, SPAIN

PAVO MAJIĆ

At an early age, many years ago, I became homeless. The conflicts with my family and with society began initially because of my appearance. I dressed in frayed second-hand clothes and had long hair and a beard. At home they told me, 'You look like that homeless man from the *Aqualung* album you listen to all the time.' Hardly anyone's mother wanted her son to look like Ian Anderson.

A couple of years ago, I was waiting for a connecting flight at Barcelona airport. I was returning home to Croatia from Portugal, where I'd had an exhibition of my paintings and the launch of a new book. Ahead of me in the queue was Ian Anderson. Looking closely, I realised my appearance was almost identical to his. We both had relatively short hair and the only real difference was that he was wearing a cap and me a hat. I laughed as I remembered how similar we looked in the 1970s.

We met and talked briefly. Ian was with his young guitarist, and they were flying to Russia where they had a concert scheduled. I showed Ian my new book and he wanted to show me his. He went through all his pockets and his bag but couldn't find it. His guitarist commented with a smile, 'At your age, people seem to have a hard time remembering where things are.'

Pavo Majić met Ian at the airport

THE ODEON OF HERODES ATTICUS

15 JUNE 2019, ATHENS, GREECE

NANA TRANDOU

As a young girl in the Greek fishing village of Agria, I heard magic and limitlessness offered in the music and lyrics of Jethro Tull. The messages written into *Aqualung*, *Thick as a Brick* and

Ian Anderson in Athens meeting the Greek Prime Minister Kyriakos Mitsotakis

Songs from the Wood mixed seamlessly, speaking to and through the mountains and seascapes of the Pelion region where this 15-year-old, without such guidance to gaze up and out, might have default to a limited focus on survival in the village. Ian's songs encouraged me to engage, approach, and see what only they could. Jethro Tull inspired me to dream and to listen to those dreams.

As a young woman in Athens, having followed my dreams and left the village, I became a music promoter - surely a calling not unrelated to my 'Tull exposure'? The apogee-location for performers in Athens (as well as for producers of such events) is the ancient Roman theatre built into the Acropolis of Athens, known as the Odeon of Herodes Atticus. Surrounded by sacred Moria trees and built into sloping limestone at the city's peak, it incomparably facilitates such giving and receipt.

As an international music promoter, I began to dream that the Odeon of Herodes Atticus was built into nature and was, like Tull's music, for all people across time. I had the power to bring the voice which spread such messages to that venue. So it was with Jethro Tull's *50th Anniversary* show on the horizon that such an overwhelming confluence of factors birthed in my mind a vision beyond question; the dream of hosting such epic culmination in such a space.

In June 2019, I brought Jethro Tull to the Odeon of Herodes Atticus during their *50th Anniversary* tour. It was one of the most substantial concerts I've ever organised, and I saw thousands of fellow citizens on the steps of the ancient theatre, listening to Tull's songs with their timeless messages. I endlessly thank the band of Jethro Tull, Ian, his production teams and audiences. Thank you for trusting me to promote all your shows in Greece and for the opportunity to experience a dream by sharing this special event at the magnificent Odeon of Herodes Atticus.

Ian Anderson in Athens. Photos by Nana Trandou

KATHARINENKIRCHE

30 NOVEMBER 2019, FRANKFURT AM MAIN, GERMANY

OLAF LEWERENZ, CITY-PASTOR, FRANKFURT

It was in the late Seventies that my brother bought a copy of *Aqualung*. It was the first time that I listened to the music of Jethro Tull. As soon as possible, I got myself *Heavy Horses*, *Thick as a Brick* and *Songs from the Wood*, which to me has always been the most amazing album. In 1983 I took my final exam at school. For the written exam, I chose music, and I couldn't believe my eyes: I had the choice between two topics, the *Passions* of Bach on the one hand or, on the other, *Songs from the Wood* as a typical piece of progressive rock. Well, I chose Bach, because Jethro Tull was too important to me to be dealt with in school.

During the Nineties, I gave away all my records because I started listening to CDs. Only *Heavy Horses* and *Songs from the Wood* remained of my LPs. In 2015, Ian and I made contact and exchanged several emails until in 2016 we met in Frankfurt, where he invited me to his concert at the Alte Oper. We stayed in touch and in 2019 he finally gave a Christmas concert in my church. It was fantastic.

ROYAL FESTIVAL HALL

10 FEBRUARY 2020, LONDON, UK

MARC ALMOND

It's far back in the mists of time now and it all seems blurry, but I heard Jethro Tull before I saw them. The song was 'Sweet Dream'. I heard it on the radio and loved it. I was becoming properly conscious of rock music at that time, going into my teens. I was starting to save enough pocket money to buy records of my own and I bought 'Sweet Dream'. Its dramatic fantastic chords and brass had a touch of flamenco, I thought, and I credit the Spanish drama of that song (in my mind, anyway) to a lifetime love of classical flamenco gypsy music. And there was Ian's voice, so distinctive and different from the other blues rock singers of the time, winding around the melody, one minute sweet, the next snarling and threatening, and a mix of blues, rock and folk style. But 'Sweet Dream' aside, it was 'The Witch's Promise' that really cemented my love of Jethro Tull. I saw them perform it on *Top of the Pops* and was blown away. Not only did I love the song and the sound of the echoing flute (you just didn't hear a flute so prominently in a rock record, especially played in that way, it was other-worldly), it was the performance itself.

In a time of very hairy blues rockers like Free, Led Zeppelin, Black Sabbath and Deep Purple, Jethro Tull were another level of wild with Ian's mischievous posing, eye-rolling and flute-waving right into the camera stare. It may seem tame by today's standards but at the time it was shocking and startling. *Top of the Pops* of course added a few dozy dancers and chip-solarised, telly druggy effects. My parents, who were young and had grown up in the days of rock'n'roll to psychedelic freak-out rock, were stunned. 'Jesus Christ, what is that!' said my father. My mum just looked bemused and dumbfounded. That made me love it even more. Ian in his old checked long coat like a Dickensian tramp and a ballet-dancing Pied Piper. I was thrilled and excited and rushed out to buy the record soon as I could. Pocket money well spent.

On my 14th birthday my mum said I could choose an LP to buy of my choice. We went to the nearest town of Harrogate, and I chose *Benefit*. I loved that album to death and wore it out on our stereogram until it was scratchy and jumped, and until the sleeve was dogeared and held together with Sellotape.

Tull were never like the other aforementioned bands with a blues background. The music was far more musically interesting and seductive, crossing genres and breaking barriers. Jethro Tull had a mystique. Me and my best school friend Frank were known as the class freaks ,as we both had longer hair than anyone at school and both loved Jethro Tull. I remember him proudly displaying his copy of *Thick as a Brick*. Sadly, Frank is no longer with us. He would have been totally blown away in disbelief and awe to see me singing 'The Witch's Promise' on stage with Ian, where he was the special guest at my Festival Hall concert.

Paul Scott's portrait of Ian

DOME

22 SEPTEMBER 2021, BRIGHTON, UK

PAUL SCOTT

At school everybody went mad about Led Zeppelin, so being the obtuse sod I am, I looked round for something else. A wild man in a tattered greatcoat standing on one leg playing the flute seemed to fit the bill! I bought *Living in the Past* and found I loved the music. In the alcove behind my bed, I painted a picture of Ian. When I moved out and my aunt moved in to look after my dad, she had to paint over it because it gave her nightmares.

Fast forward 52 years and I saw Jethro Tull at the Brighton Dome. They were still terrific.

ESPAI MARAGALL

20 NOVEMBER 2021, GAVA, SPAIN

ALBERT VILLANUEVA, PRESIDENT OF TULLIANOS, SPANISH FAN CLUB

Albert Villanueva arranged a fan event in Spain which Ian Anderson attended

I had just turned 16 the first time I heard Jethro Tull. Until then, I was a child who had practically no access to music. I had no older brothers or relatives to get me into the world of music. I didn't even know there were people who sang in English. But one day, a classmate left me a record that belonged to his brother. It was *Minstrel in the Gallery* and it turned my insides upside down. I always say that was the day I stopped being a child and became an adult. From then on, Ian Anderson's music became the soundtrack of my life.

I didn't get to see a Tull concert until I was 30. I remember going with a girl and when 'Thick as a Brick' came on, tears of happiness and gratitude welled up in my eyes. My friend asked what was wrong with me. All I could say was, 'You wouldn't understand ...'

If someone had said to me, the day that *Minstrel in the Gallery* fell into my hands, one day I would have close contact with Ian Anderson, I would have told them they were crazy. But sometimes dreams come true. Ian came to Gava in 2021 and I was able to make the following speech to him in front of an audience of Spanish Jethro Tull fans:

'Many of us, in our adolescence, were the 'weirds' of the class ... Some bands like Pink Floyd, Genesis, Yes or Supertramp were triumphing, but the band we liked the most was not so known then here ... and had an unpronounceable name in that old 'black and white' Spain. The figure of a gangly musician, who kept his balance on one leg while with the sound of his flute he removes our entrails, became iconic.

Many of us ceased to be children and became adults the very moment we heard a Jethro Tull album for the first time. In my case it was *Minstrel in the Gallery* and each of you have your own moment and your own song. But for all of us, Ian Anderson's music became, since those long-ago distant years, the soundtrack of our lives.

Those 'weird' teenagers now have less hair, more belly and more wounds. But when the music of Jethro Tull caresses our ears, we vibrate, we shudder and we get a thrill in the same way as we did then.

If those 'weird' teenagers had been told we would ever meet in person the creator of all that music – you'll forgive me – but we would have pissed our pants. If that happens today, we surely can blame our prostate for that slip-up. But some of those fans came together as Tullianos and, with work and enthusiasm, made that unimaginable thing come true.

We can only thank Ian Anderson for all the happiness he has given us over the years. And all the happiness he will continue giving us, with his music, his albums, and his kindness towards Tullianos.'

THE ZEALOT GENE

RELEASED 28 JANUARY 2022

UK CHART POSITION 9

US CHART POSITION 10

IAN ANDERSON

I was due to perform in Kiev, Ukraine and St Petersburg, Russia later this year but those concerts are not now going to happen. It's not the first time I've been faced with performance schedules that conflict with trouble spots in the world. On a number of occasions, we have missed by a day or two terrorist attacks which might not necessarily have involved us. I remember being in Turkey where we were due to perform, and a friend who's an ex-special forces guy in the USA had got wind of a terrorist attack from the grapevine in Washington.

He sent me a message saying, 'Just got this information – a terrorist attack is anticipated tonight in central Istanbul.' We had a concert in the theatre right next to the main Government headquarters. I felt dutybound to let the guys in the band and crew know this was information received. 'It might not be accurate. It might be alarmist, but we should be on our guards and everybody be really careful, and if something happened to get the hell out of there and make sure you run in the right direction.' They were all very nervous about it and of course nothing happened. I think somebody got arrested somewhere miles away. These are things you accept as part of the world you live in.

We've never been to China. We've had a presence in most parts of the world over the years, with the exception of East Asia. Jethro Tull has never been popular in China or much of the Far East. We had a brief flurry in Japan in '72, and I've been back a few

times since to play a theatre or two on a relatively small scale. I've played twice in Hong Kong. But we're talking about playing to British and European ex-pats.

Amongst the domestic audiences of most of East Asia, Jethro Tull means nothing at all because they didn't have Western rock music in the early days and they jumped straight from that position to developing a viable and hearty homegrown national music scene. There are a few exceptions - Duran Duran got in during the middle period when western rock music was accepted and domestic music had not developed as the pop music hysteria of today in East Asia. But it was already too late for Jethro Tull. So there's a big chunk of the population of the planet that does not know Jethro Tull. And, of course, even in the countries where we have been successful, if you ask the average person in the street, they're going to say, 'Jethro what?' In some places, people don't even remember The Beatles!

ANNA PHOEBE, VIOLINIST, COMPOSER, PRODUCER, PRESENTER

I was touring in the States with Trans-Siberian Orchestra when an email landed in my inbox - it was a guy called Ian who said a fan of his was also a fan of mine and had suggested we play together. I thought it was a hoax at first, but sure enough, it was real. I went to see him play with Anne Marie Calhoun on violin - and was absolutely blown away by the incredible musicianship from every single person on the stage. I definitely felt under-qualified, but it's not an offer you turn down.

A few months later I was picking up Ian and his flute from Highbury & Islington tube station to bring him back to my house in Stoke Newington, London. We had a jam together (I remember playing 'Griminelli's Lament') and then got sent some tour dates. We've been friends ever since.

The first time I joined him on stage was nerve-wracking, but exhilarating. We'd only had one band rehearsal and I was playing on about 10 or so tracks - I'd come off a huge tour where everyone is on in-ear monitors and you kind of assume no one is really listening to what you're doing. But the next day in soundcheck Ian came over and was so specific about his feedback — literally, 'You know the way you approached the first note of the third verse in 'King Henry's' - maybe you shouldn't slide up to it but hit it straight.' I was shocked, flattered and impressed, all at the same time. Ian knows exactly what he wants and what he expects from his music and musicians - I really respect that. That level of care and attention and detail … to not let that slip after decades of playing the same songs - so impressive.

Also, the fact he was so open and willing to play my own music - not many musicians of his stature would do that, open up their stage time as part of their set to play music from someone guesting with them. He's so open and giving.

I think Ian's endless curiosity, showmanship and innovation shines out, and as someone who lives and breathes music, that is all so inspiring. He's had a career spanning so many years - he knows every aspect of the business and is always looking for ways to evolve. These are all things I admire, and I would definitely see him as someone who has shaped my musical career.

I remember very early one morning (around 7.30am) I got a phone call from Ian. Or maybe it was a text. 'Call me back - I have an idea I want to run past you.' When that comes from Ian, you know it's going to be interesting. And it didn't disappoint. He wanted to come round and film me and my new-born, Amelia, plus my husband (Gavin Esler) in the Aqualung wetsuit … and had this elaborate idea of how in the middle of the concert for his tour, the phone would ring and it would be me - then I would suddenly start joining in with the band. In the meantime, Gavin would skulk in the background wearing a wetsuit. Genius! Who thinks of these things at 7.30am on a weekend? This is so Ian! Not only does he think of these things - he makes them happen. I love his brain.

What kind of legacy will he leave us? Ooph - I don't like to think of him leaving anytime soon. He is one of a kind. He has already left a legacy and shaped musical history, has influenced countless musicians, and inspired and connected with countless music fans.

As for a certain song that will remain with me, I think 'Locomotive Breath'. Just from a personal experience of playing with him - it gets to this point in the set and the audience goes wild and is fired up. It's a defiant, brilliant song and I love playing it. The thumping bassline and Ian's solos always have a magical effect on me.

GAVIN ESLER, WRITER, BROADCASTER, MUSICIAN

I first saw Ian Anderson and Jethro Tull on stage in Edinburgh when I was a teenager. I thought they were wild and crazy - Ian especially. I loved the flute and the way Ian combined folk, rock, and a bit of mayhem on stage. Somehow, I understood that while he took his music very seriously, he was also having a laugh.

The first Jethro Tull record that made an impression on me? This Was, played on an old Dansette record player until it must have been worn out. I used to go to my friend Murray's house in Dolphin Road, Currie, on the outskirts of Edinburgh after school. We'd listen to Tull along with Cream and Pink Floyd, drink really bad instant coffee and believe we were being cool.

Ian won't leave us. Neither will his achievements in music. That's his legacy.

As for certain Tull records that will remain with me, Aqualung and Thick as a Brick are stunning, literate, clever, beautiful. But what stands out for me is something different - Ian's generosity, his charitable work, the fun he brought to playing in Canterbury Cathedral and other great churches ... and the way he could make an audience laugh.

CADY COLEMAN, ASTRONAUT

The first time I talked to Ian Anderson, I was in the living room of my home-away-from-home in Star City Russia − training to fly in space with the Russians and live on the International Space Station. On our six-month expedition, we were able to bring along a few things we thought might be meaningful to fly in space. I'm a flute player so - of course − I brought flutes!

It meant the world to me that Ian had brought the flute to rock music, so of course I asked him if I could bring one of his flutes to space.

Ian: 'So, this flute will come back to earth, right?'

Me: 'Well, hopefully. Never a guarantee, but right now it has a return reservation on the space shuttle.'

Ian: 'I think I'll send my 'mugger's flute' with you.'

Me: 'Your mother's flute?'

Ian: 'No, my *mugger's* flute. It's the one in my guitar case that the muggers will take first, leaving my favourite flute safe and sound.'

And so the mugger's flute came to space, and seemed quite happy floating around inside the International Space Station, wrapped in a navy blue t-shirt (for Great Britain), orbiting the earth every 90 minutes along with two Americans, one Italian and three Russians. Coincidentally, Jethro Tull was playing a concert in Perm, Russia as we were flying overhead. Ian emailed me, 'How about a space duet?' Brilliant!

So, on the 50th anniversary of Russian Cosmonaut Yuri Gagarin's flight – the first time ever that a human left our planet – Ian and I played the first duet between Earth and space.

What I love about Ian is that he is intentional, and somehow ensures that projects he takes on have a way of creating ripples into the future. He didn't just bring the flute to rock music, he taught a new generation of musicians that flute players could do anything.

And with our duet, he has brought so many people to space, a place that belongs to all of us.

PIERRE DUVAL

I've been lucky enough to see Jethro Tull quite a few times and lucky enough to meet Ian twice, but not able to really talk with him. Maybe someday. But I have Jethro Tull in my skin!

RAYMOND NESMITH III

I discovered Jethro Tull via an 8-track of *Living in the Past* in my late father's music collection.

Pierre Duval has Jethro Tull under his skin

It was the only piece I had until I was able to save my allowance to buy *Aqualung*, then *War Child* and *A Passion Play*. During my late teenage years, I listened to almost every Jethro Tull song and record. Many times, I requested to hear them on the radio. In 1993, I took the time to write and ask if there was a fan club, not expecting any response. Months passed and then, to my surprise, I received a letter with subscription information for *A New Day* magazine and a signed photo of Ian Anderson. I am grateful to have a piece of Jethro Tull memorabilia. I have never been to a show. Unfortunately, I lost my father in 2019. We always discussed going to a Jethro Tull concert in Texas.

LIAM HAIR

My love of Jethro Tull started in 2016 when I was 14 and exploring this new (to me) genre called progressive rock. I was intrigued by the flute playing and style of their music on *Thick as a Brick*, so I got a copy of *The Very Best of Jethro Tull* on CD. I've never seen them live, but run a podcast and had the chance to speak with Peter-John Vettese from their *The Broadsword and the Beast/Under Wraps* era, who spoke to me about his time with the band and said Ian Anderson was like a mentor to him and taught him a lot during his time with the band.

And I was talking to a relative of mine in December 2020 about my love for Jethro Tull, when he said that he was related to Ian Anderson. 'My grandmother and his mother were sisters.' It was then that I realised I am partly related to Ian Anderson!

ANDREA DONAHUE

I had a child while I was still in high school in the early 1970s. My family decided that he should be placed for adoption. Fast forward 32 years and we found each other. We had lots of things in common, and one of those was a love of Jethro Tull. Is it genetic? Who knows?

ZOLTÁN SCHMIDT

I met a guy in my little village's pub and we talked a lot about music. I told him what I normally listened to, and we were soon on the same spiritual level. We became very good friends and he introduced me to a lot of music I didn't know, including Jethro Tull. My new friend said, 'Just listen to it, and you will quickly realise it is the greatest music ever!' I started to listen to the music and lyrics and realised he was right. I had found my favourite band and made a very good friend too.

Zoltán Schmidt is a huge fan

JIM JIM

In the late-Seventies there was an old man in the next town who embodied Aqualung. He'd often be seen standing in the recessed doorway of an old shop on West Main

Street, wearing a dirty, heavy, long coat all year round. When we drove past, we'd yell, 'Hey, Aqualung!' at him and wave. Years later I became friends with a local policeman who shared the man's story. He was homeless and had a sad life. It's very embarrassing to recall, and a reminder to be kind to others. More recently, my new wife saw a mechanic at the garage around the corner from her condo. He looked to be in his mid-60s - tall, thin and kind of scraggly and worn out. He was wearing work overalls. His name tag read 'Ian Anderson'. She imagines that they made him wear a name tag but he got to decide what name to put on it.

KARI THUNE

Tull's music changed my life as a teenager. I was raised by parents who had me later in life, and I had a half-brother 15 years older so grew up with a large swathe of musical influences. But as a teenager, I met a kid the grade below named Drew. We became super-close and got into some shenanigans here and there, but I got to be a part of his family over the years. And when his dad Glenn came over for a family event one day, I got to witness him play bass in the living room with some friends and his ex-wife. I was blown away. I had no idea who he was.

Drew shared the Tull albums with me and I was blown away by those too. I'm pretty sure 'Bourée' was the first thing I ever heard, because it's the one that still hits me over the head each time I listen to it. I can literally hear every note in my head as we speak. And holy hell, that man was amazing, and the chemistry you can feel in the music is life-altering.

I remember Glenn invited my guitarist friend to join them for a jam session in that living room and my friend was so nervous because he loved Tull, but as soon as the first bass note hit, everything just flowed. Glenn would drink Tecate beer with us and told us the stories of travelling and playing way back when. We'd sit in the garage and dote on every nuance of each song.

Music is the greatest achievement of humans and Tull the top of the list when it comes to music. RIP Glenn, and thank you to the rest of Tull for creating such depth, wonder and amazement together, and sharing it with us all.

IAN ANDERSON

The band and crew now owe it to each other after two years of unemployment to try and make sure we're not just willing to show up for work but we are able to show up for work. We do all have to take a little extra care. We can't just call in sick and say, 'You know what, I don't think I'm coming into the office today. I might have Covid.' That's not acceptable. We have to get on an aeroplane, go somewhere and potentially risk the legal consequences of knowingly having Covid and not admitting to it. And, of course, some of us might get seriously ill.

As a flute player, my expulsion of fine aerosol droplets extends about something in the region of six or seven metres in front of me when I play a high D on the flute. I can't play the flute with a mask on. I now deliberately set up two metres further back than I used to, because I've aware that when I'm playing the flute or singing, I'm projecting in front of me.

Of course, it works both ways. The people in the front close to me might be coughing and spluttering or shouting, and whatever it is, it's heading my way. I've said to the band and crew, 'If at any time you're a little bit nervous or concerned, put your mask on to perform on stage. It's absolutely acceptable.' I don't have that luxury.

But when I walk out of my dressing room, I put a mask on for the distance it takes me to walk from there to the side of the stage, because I'm going to encounter stage-hands and other folks, not all of whom can be trusted to wear a mask. All of these things are the reality of touring today. And for Jethro Tull fans who've been to see us recently, their recollection will be of two hours of purgatory stewing inside a mask because it was a legal obligation to wear one.

You might hear people saying, 'I met Ian down at the disco. He's a really nice guy and I bought him a drink.' Well, sorry chum, it wasn't me. You were suckered. You bought somebody else a drink. I'm not a clubber. I'm a bit of a loner. I try to be polite to fans but if they interrupt me while I'm eating and start trying to do selfies surreptitiously while I've got a mouthful of food, I get a bit pissed off and think they would feel the same way if it happened to them.

Generally speaking, I try to be polite to people. But at this particular time, I'm not going to get up close and personal and let people hug me, as they will still want to do, in the context of Covid. It's just an unnecessary risk. From behind the face mask I will smile, I will nod, I will try and give them 'smiley eyes' if they can't see my face and I will try and make them feel they had a little one-to-one attention. But don't press me for something I feel uncomfortable about. And I'm not comfortable about shaking hands or hugging unless I've actually seen the result of someone's rapid antigen test with my own eyes.

The band and crew have been testing every 48 hours to try and reassure ourselves as well as each other that we are safe to be amongst. The guys are sociable. They get together and have a glass of wine and sit down to eat in catering every day. Some of them tend to go and sit alone at a different table.

Some sit together and chat. I personally don't, but then I never have. I like to eat alone. I like to be alone. I like to walk around cities and explore alone. I'm not a gregarious person. I enjoy being thoughtful and contemplative about the environment I'm in. I'm a loner. I am Clint Eastwood in a spaghetti Western. With a flute!

I've never found it easy to be sociable on that level, even in the early days of Jethro Tull, which is why Martin Barre and I got on very well musically. It was because we didn't have the social relationship. He was a bit like me. Most of the time he just wanted to be by himself and do his own thing, whereas other members of the band have been more naturally gregarious.

And perhaps the ease with which Martin and I worked for so long in a musical sense without disagreement is because we valued the musical relationship but we didn't ever feel it was clouded by relationships on a more personal level that might be frayed or tense. Sometimes it's really helpful to have a positive professional relationship and avoid the personal ones that sometimes can become abrasive just through repetition and stress of travel and touring.

TIM BOWNESS, NO-MAN

I discovered Jethro Tull via an advert placed on my school noticeboard in 1980. Somebody was selling a copy of *Aqualung* cheaply (always a good incentive to investigate!). Contact made with the seller, I walked across town in the pouring rain with pocket money in hand to collect the album. On returning home and hearing it, I was immediately smitten, and the dark riffs, gentle interludes and eloquent lyrics strongly appealed. The artwork and the music possessed an unsettling sense of otherness and antiquity.

Following this introduction, I quickly became familiar with the band's back catalogue and then current release *A*. I greatly admire the early trilogy of *Stand Up*, *Benefit* and *Aqualung* and the late 1970s trio of folk-rock releases – *Songs from the Wood*, *Heavy Horses*, and *Stormwatch*. The ambition and depth of *A Passion Play* was also something I was dazzled by when I first heard it. Damn the haters!

I've always been amazed by how productive the band was between the late-1960s and mid-1980s and how, despite an excessively busy touring schedule, its sound managed to change so dramatically so frequently.

Jethro Tull always kept abreast of the times while remaining totally true to its idiosyncrasies. From the blues flavourings of the debut through the hard folk-rock of 1969-71, the prog excursions of 1972-73, the slight Roxy/Bowie influences of 1974-76 and the electronic experiments of 1980-84, you can hear the band distinctively reflecting the times it lived through. Ditto the textures and rhythms on the likes of the much later *J-Tull Dot Com*.

I've a real soft spot for Ian Anderson's acoustic miniatures such as 'Slipstream', 'Dun Ringill', 'Under Wraps #2', 'Cheap Day Return', 'Salamander', and 'Only Solitaire'. I strongly believe that had he not gone down the band route, he'd have been a successful singer-songwriter who would have been feted in the way the likes of Roy Harper, John Martyn, Richard Thompson and Nick Drake were.

Ian's a one-off in that he excels as a songwriter, lyricist and instrumentalist. He's also an instantly recognisable vocalist, of course. His eye for detail is astonishing. As you can imagine, it was a genuine thrill to get him to guest on some of my solo music.

HEATHER FINDLAY

Whilst recording my solo album, *Wild White Horses*, when a song called 'Winner' was crying out for flute, I decided to contact Ian Anderson and invite him to perform on the track. He kindly accepted and delivered the most wonderful flute solo, along with tasteful ornamentation throughout. He was very thoughtful about how he approached it, offering total respect and consideration for what was already going on in the track. He was so generous with his time and also incredibly supportive with his words about the album once it was released. A true gent indeed.

Ian Anderson and Jethro Tull's music will always have a very special place in my heart. Until writing this down, I don't think I realised just how grateful I am to have been influenced by their music for so many years, and for it to have made such an impact and contribution towards my own journey as an artist. Thank you, Ian, and thank you Jethro Tull!

MIKAEL ÅKERFELDT, OPETH

Let me just start by saying Jethro Tull is one of my favourite bands of all time. I was born in 1974, the same year *War Child* came out, so didn't catch the connecting tour. My parents aren't big music buffs. I remember my mother saying they sometimes argued over who was better, Elvis (Dad) or Tommy Steele (Mum). That's about it really. Jethro Tull were never played at my house as I was growing up. To this day, I doubt my parents ever heard of them. Consequently, I had to discover my musical preferences for myself.

In the late Eighties and early Nineties I was well into metal music. Also, being a slacker meant I had little to no money in my pocket. CDs were costly so I had to resort to second-hand vinyl when it came to purchasing 'new' music. In those days used vinyl was very cheap, so I could afford to take some chances. Glorious times!

I heard that Tony Iommi (Black Sabbath) had a brief stint with this band called Jethro Tull. So one day, flicking through the crates I stumbled upon *Songs from the Wood*. 'Ah, there's that band Iommi was in for a few hours, I'll check it out ...' That's when my Tull journey began. I absolutely loved that album. Not only was the music absolutely fantastic, it was also music I'd never heard before, or since. They are completely unique.

I have since enjoyed their entire catalogue, from *This Was* right up to *The Zealot Gene*. I don't know which one is my favourite, but contenders would be *Stand Up*, *Aqualung*, *Thick as a Brick*, *Minstrel in the Gallery*, *Songs from the Wood*, and *Stormwatch*. I think Ian Anderson is untouchable, really, and admire him no end. He's one of my favourite vocalists of all time, right up there with Macca, Joni Mitchell, Scott Walker, CSN&Y, Ronnie James Dio, Nick Drake, etc.

I absolutely love Jethro Tull in all their incarnations. I've done my research which led me on to more lovely music affiliated with Tull. I have to mention the late great John Glascock (Gods, Chicken Shack, Carmen). Hell, Barriemore Barlow played on the first Yngwie Malmsteen album, even!

On a more sinister note, I have Jethro Tull nightmares. More than once I've dreamt that I'm on stage with Tull and we're about to play *Songs from the Wood* only I don't know the chords, the lyrics, the order of the sections or the vocal harmonies. Luckily, I'm not starting the song, but 30 seconds from 'now' I'm due to do something ... but what exactly? I wake up in a sweat but with a feeling of great relief. They're just out of my league. And it's a humbling experience listening to them, let alone dreaming that I'm actually in the band. I never, ever want to be a member of Jethro Tull. But I will continue to enjoy their music until my dying day. Thank you!

JOHN VIRGO, SNOOKER COMMENTATOR

I have been a Jethro Tull fan for many years. My taste in music has always been determined by music and lyrics, and Tull were perfect for me as I think of Ian Anderson as a great modern-day poet. I have so many favourite songs. The one that resonates with me more than most is 'Up the Pool', about Blackpool. As a child my only holiday was a day-trip to that town, so to hear those lyrics brings back so many memories. Thanks for the great songs. I just know there's lots more to come.

JAKKO JAKSZYK, KING CRIMSON

The radio was permanently on in the house when I was a kid, playing the top hits of the day. It was rare that anything really leapt out as different or unusual. A next-door neighbour, a couple of years my senior, was keeping me updated with what used to be called the underground. But rarely did any of that music pour from our radio in the daytime or appear on *Top of the Pops*. Until ....

Something extraordinary did emerge from the airways, and then pretty frequently. The cool vibe, the halting rhythm, and a flute as a lead instrument! Not to mention the charismatic and unique vocal sound and performance of Ian Anderson. 'Living in the Past' was like nothing in the world of what was deemed to be 'commercial'. I was smitten, and the singles suffused with intrigue and mystery kept coming – 'Sweet Dream', 'The Witch's Promise', 'Teacher' ...

I started learning the flute and poring over the music press for any mention of them, and would buy or borrow the albums. I was ill at home and off school when I pleaded with my mum to buy me *Aqualung* on its release, spending the rest of the week playing it on constant repeat.

Having had the privilege in recent years of remixing live recordings and videos from all eras of Tull, my appreciation and admiration remains undiminished. If anything, that appreciation and admiration is greater. Jethro Tull were - and are - totally unique. There's something instantly recognisable as 'Tull' that just couldn't be anyone else. The combination of folk and rock that's been fused in such an original way, and then some.

With his fantastic acoustic guitar playing, flute playing and amazing writing ability - the argument for Ian being the most multi-talented of all the artists to emerge from that classic era of rock music remains impossible to deny.

JOE BONAMASSA

Jethro Tull are truly their own musical genre. Rising out of the British Blues boom of the Sixties, their unique blend of baroque, classical, folk and heavy rock created a synthesis previously unheard, a fusion of musical styles that makes them one of the most uniquely original bands in the history of rock'n'roll.

The success of many of the more adventurous and progressive bands from the Seventies owes an immeasurable debt to Tull for the fertile ground they provided. The dynamics and subtleties of their compositions would be echoed in the works of bands like King Crimson, Yes, Rush, Gentle Giant, Genesis, and others. Jethro Tull gave their contemporaries permission to experiment and utilise instrumentation not previously embraced by rock musicians. They not only opened those doors for many, they knocked them down and decades later are still inspiring musicians and listeners alike. Lyrically colourful and challenging, each Jethro Tull album took us on another powerful and enchanting journey.

Like everyone, I have had my own personal journey with the music of Jethro Tull. *Thick as a Brick* is a true masterclass of songwriting and arranging. Each movement indelibly linked to the other. That masterpiece, along with *Minstrel in the Gallery*, provided an incredible sonic tutorial of the best guitar tone ever, courtesy of my dear friend, Martin Barre.

As live performers, the spectacle was never absent. The crazed and manic antics of a flute-wielding Ian Anderson was not only entertaining but mesmerising and exciting to watch. Even in their earliest incarnations, Tull and Anderson's command of the stage was remarkable despite the lack of modern staging and pyrotechnics we've all become accustomed to. In the infancy of elaborate lighting and stage shows, Tull entertained like no other. From the clubs to the arenas and even the stadium gigs, they demonstrated the best in musicianship and performance art as every tour took on more elaborate staging and bravado.

And today, that incredible legacy continues.

I learned how to tour from Ian Anderson and the members of Jethro Tull in my formative years on the road. They were kind enough to have me as an opening act following the release of my very first solo album, *A New Day Yesterday*. The title track was a cover of their classic song from the *Stand Up* album. Hell, they even encouraged me to play their own song in front of their own audience! How could any band possibly be more gracious?

I consider Tull part of my family. I have such love and respect for them as musicians and as people and I'm honoured to be a small part of this wonderful project.

DAVE PEGG

It was a most enjoyable period. I learnt a lot about music. Musically it was a lot more complex than the stuff we were playing with Fairport, and organisationally it was amazing because of Ian's ability to put things together. He had an amazing crew who gave him an awful lot of respect, people like Kenny Wylie who did an incredible job as production manager. The gigs all went like clockwork, and it was such a professional organisation. It was on a different level to what I was used to from playing with the Fairports, some of whom also went on to play with Jethro Tull in the course of the next 15 years.

When I joined Jethro Tull, Fairport had split up. Ian and Martin looked after me and I was making serious income. I'd never ever done that with the Fairports. It was always a struggle. We weren't a big band. But Tull was a different league. I lived in Cropredy and was able to build a studio and we were able to start recording our own stuff and stuff for other people, friends of ours. My ex-wife Christine and I started a record label called Woodworm Records, and we started the Cropredy Festival, an annual one-day reunion of the Fairport chums. Fairport never ever fell out. We remained friends all the way through, and still are with our ex-members – at least, the ones who are on the right side of the turf! And the Cropredy Festival grew and grew. In the time off when Tull weren't doing much, and sometimes there was literally six months with no Jethro tull activity, you have to do something, so I was always doing Fairport stuff. And in 1985 the Fairports got back together, because we had the studio and made an album called *Gladys' Leap*.

I learnt a lot from Ian in terms of how you manage the band, and I'd now started to do all Fairport's publicity and organise the festival and do the PR for that and plan tours. We became one of the first cottage industries and it was really successful and really enjoyable. But it got to the point where one year I did about 320 gigs with both bands, and probably an album as well.

When Fairport supported Tull on an American tour, I was doing both gigs. I had to change my outfit in the 20-minute interval. And while I was out playing with Fairport the rest of the Tull boys would be playing table tennis backstage - so I dropped down in the table tennis league!

It just became too much. Ian was having problems with his voice then, and it wasn't as enjoyable as it used to be. He was, and I'm sure he still is, such a great performer in terms of what he would do on stage. It was a very physical show. But having the voice problem, it was sometimes a struggle and the keys of the tunes and the songs would be changed accordingly, and it became a real effort instead of a real pleasure. This is not being disrespectful to Ian. It was just a fact. Every gig was really good before, but now there were gigs that didn't work out as well.

I just thought, 'I'm working too much.' I had enough financial background thanks to Tull that I didn't need to carry on doing both bands. And because we'd got the festival and we'd got the Fairports back together, I thought, 'I'm going to have to ease off and go back to what I did before', which is what I'm still doing. I explained to Ian and Martin how I felt about it, and got a very nice letter from Ian saying, 'Any time you want to come back, you're very welcome - as long as your hair grows back!'

We remain good friends. Ian and Martin came and played at Cropredy. They helped us out. They came and did benefit concerts for Dave Swarbrick, Fairport's fiddle player. I see Martin from time to time and I'll hopefully see Jethro Tull in Paris, the nearest gig to where we live in Brittany. And the band's great. They are great musicians. I hear very good reports. It's an honour to have been involved.

DOANE PERRY

I believe part of the reason the music of Jethro Tull has had such defining characteristics through all the eras, incarnations and evolution of the band is not just because of the extraordinary body of music Ian has written but would also have to be attributable to the talented and disparate musical personalities of the musicians involved at that given time. Like everyone else, I was expected to bring something of myself while historically recognizing and observing the styles of each of the predecessors on my particular instrument. Within the band and across all the instruments there are specific elements which would be considered signature parts. There were certain things which were quite natural and easy to play and other things which were more idiosyncratic and challenging, so I might modify them to fall under my hands more comfortably. However, I wanted to preserve that feeling of what Clive Bunker, Barrie Barlow, Mark Craney or Gerry Conway did, because each were stylistically different but all were exceptionally gifted drummers. I know I learned a lot from each one of them. Ian has always said it was harder for the people who came later on, because they had to assimilate some recognizable semblance of the parts of the musicians who preceded them in that chair, while also bringing their own personality.

Being the drummer in the band it was critical to stay focused and several paces ahead. Even though there's always been an element of spontaneous improvisation within certain parameters, the music is also highly orchestrated, and everyone's parts tend to be compositionally oriented. And of course, you've also got to *project* what you're doing to the audience. I never took that for granted. I tried to play every gig, even if it was the last one on the tour, like it was the first night. I knew some of the audience may never have seen Jethro Tull before. This may be their one and only opportunity, or they may have seen the band a hundred times and had plenty of points of comparison along the way.

Jethro Tull was a singular musical experience and something I could never have anticipated. I was 29 when I joined the band and my career was already going fairly well. I'd been extremely fortunate to have been able to play and record with a variety of gifted artists in a wide range of styles. I was lucky and grateful for that wide musical background which enabled me to call on all those influences during the course of my time with the band, sometimes even in the course of one evening – as well as sketch comedy and bad magic tricks.

But when we picked up our instruments, it was serious business. It was a good counterbalance. The light-hearted, comedic aspects of the band and in-between song patter and sketch comedy offset the more serious nature of the music, creating a comfortable balance of moods. That drew people in, across multiple generations, cultural boundaries and even language barriers.

Tull is one of a very small handful of bands that could be called quintessentially British but musically ecumenical — apart from the fact that they had a tall American in the ranks. In the beginning I was more aware of the cultural differences but over time that just fell away. We were all out there together simply playing music.

There's lots of things that may have gone over the heads of some Americans and those from non-English speaking countries, because they simply weren't exposed to some of those cultural reference points. Of course, certain people picked them up right away, while others probably slapped their forehead later thinking, 'Ahhh ... got it now!' That's part of the subtle beauty of Tull music.

Like any family, musical or otherwise, there are ups and downs, disagreements and arguments, but those inevitable moments have always been outweighed by the positive ones. If you're a musician, the chance of playing in a band like Tull doesn't come along all that often. I feel incredibly fortunate that I found this unique niche in music that fitted my eclectic and fairly broad musical interests within a single band. The overriding feeling and memory I'm left with is one of profound appreciation and gratitude for the experience of playing such challenging, deeply textured and rewarding music night after night, *particularly* on the nights when we got it right. I have a multitude of wonderful memories and the experience has allowed me the freedom to be in this place in my life where I'm composing, recording for myself and other artists, writing prose, studying orchestration intensely and pursuing my expanding interest in astronomy ... all pursuits which have been enormously gratifying. So it's good to be able to explore all these different avenues while I still have the majority of my marbles.

Most importantly, I feel grateful to have had the opportunity to play with every extraordinary and uniquely gifted musician whom I've had the great pleasure, privilege and honour of working alongside in Jethro Tull over those 28 richly-coloured and adventurous years.

CHRIS WRIGHT

Despite my original idea that they would be a seven-piece blues band like Paul Butterfield, they never really did that for very long - even as a four-piece. Ian took them off into a completely different direction which was really at a tangent to what anyone else was doing at the time. Although Martin Barre's a good guitarist, he never became a superstar guitarist. The superstar was always Ian. The flute was not an easy instrument to make popular, especially when we were living in the age of 'the guitar is king'. They've basically done it the hard way with a lot of hard graft, a lot of improvisation and a lot of interesting songs. And Ian's always written songs about what he wants to write about. He hasn't written to a market. He's ploughed his own furrow.

Hats off to Ian.

JERRY EWING, EDITOR, *PROG* MAGAZINE

At *Prog Rock* magazine, we say that in the Seventies you got the Big Six – Yes, Genesis, ELP, King Crimson, Pink Floyd, and Jethro Tull. They were very much the figureheads of the prog scene. Tull always seemed to be the most grounded and the most level-headed of them, with a little more gritty realism to what they did. I don't associate Tull with the musical excess of Emerson, Lake and Palmer. I don't think they've ever been guilty of overdoing it or of showboating.

The album that gets you into a band lives with you, and it often won't be the pinnacle of their recorded output. If I was going to reach for one Tull album it would probably be *The Broadsword and the Beast*, but it depends on my mood. I was a big fan of *Crest of a Knave* and *Rock Island*, because they were more upfront hard rock albums. Then again, I'm a massive fan of *Minstrel in the Gallery*. The album I probably wouldn't reach for is *Aqualung*. I've just heard it so many times.

The other thing I like about *Broadsword* is that it seems to be the perfect transitional album from what they were to what they've become. *Under Wraps* pushed the electronica a lot more but the hard rock side would then come to the fore and they would experiment with slightly more folky forms. All of those musical things you would find on *Broadsword*, and it just seems to be that pivotal moment where they went from being the prog behemoth of the Seventies to a band that would endure throughout the Eighties, Nineties and beyond.

FINAL WORDS

What keeps the show on the road is not me or my willingness or my endeavour or energy. It's the fans who buy tickets. That's what keeps us going. The loyalty and the interest shown by fans across much of the world is always the reason that we continue to sell records and to perform in concerts, and I am always struck by the presence of a willing audience when I walk out onto the stage.

The good times are every night, at the end of a show when everybody gets together and has a glass of wine. Everybody's work is done, the crew are finally packed up and everybody's getting ready to go back to the hotel and get to bed. Thatmagic ten minutes is quite an important part of the day for everybody. You treasure those moments.

You think of the places you've done that – the dressing rooms, the corridors or standing outside under a starlit sky. You think of the amazing theatres and the places rich in history – cathedrals, churches, ancient Roman amphitheatres scattered around the Mediterranean, concrete stadia in the middle of the Bavarian Forest where Hitler held Nazi rallies, or the Ephesus amphitheatre in Turkey.

The fact that you have that little moment of camaraderie and mutual conclusion to the intense experience of doing a concert, those are the things that you really do remember.

And, of course, you never share those with the fans. Because they're trying to catch the last bus home or remember where their car keys are.

IAN ANDERSON

ABOUT THE AUTHOR

Richard Houghton lives in Manchester, UK with his wife Kate. He is the author of 18 music books, many of which are published by This Day in Music Books.

ACKNOWLEDGEMENTS

Richard Houghton would like to thank:

Ian Anderson, James Anderson, Chris Wright, Graham Bonnet, Dee Palmer, Doane Perry, Dave Pegg, Clive Bunker, Mick Abrahams, Ian Burgess, Malcolm Wyatt, Gabriel Smith, Neil Cossar and Liz Sanchez.

And his wife, Kate Sullivan.